W9-BUL-735

LONG GONE

Also by Joanna Schaffhausen

Gone for Good
Last Seen Alive
Every Waking Hour
All the Best Lies
No Mercy
The Vanishing Season

LONG GONE

A Detective Annalisa Vega Novel

Joanna Schaffhausen

MINOTAUR BOOKS
NEW YORK

First published in the United States by Minotaur Books, an imprint of St. Martin's Publishing Group

www.minotaurbooks.com

Designed by Gabriel Guma

Library of Congress Cataloging-in-Publication Data

Names: Schaffhausen, Joanna, author.
Title: Long gone : a novel / Joanna Schaffhausen.
Description: First edition. | New York : Minotaur Books, 2022. | Series: Detective Annalisa Vega ; 2
Identifiers: LCCN 2022005930 | ISBN 9781250264633 (hardcover) | ISBN 9781250264640 (ebook)
Classification: LCC PS3619.C3253 L66 2022 | DDC 813/.6—dc23
LC record available at https://lccn.loc.gov/2022005930

Our books may be purchased in bulk for promotional, educational, or business use. Please contact your local bookseller or the Macmillan Corporate and Premium Sales Department at 1-800-221-7945, extension 5442, or by email at MacmillanSpecialMarkets@macmillan.com.

First Edition: 2022

10 9 8 7 6 5 4 3 2 1

For Elisabeth, Joan, and Mariah, my “sisters” in crime

LONG GONE

PROLOGUE

....

WHEN THE OTHER TWO DIDN'T COME BACK FOR MORE THAN TEN MINUTES, HE WENT TO LOOK FOR THEM. Grown men sometimes broke down and cried for their mommies in the box, and Sandra had priors. She had kids. Paulie felt sure she'd crack easy. But Leo knew her best and he wasn't so sure. His feet dragged, his heart pounding out sweat from every pore because he knew whatever he found down there, it would be bad. These were the last few moments he could make a different choice. He could pretend not to know. The fluorescent lights in the downstairs hallway gave the dark waxy floor an eerie shine. His eyes zeroed in on the restroom, tunnel vision making him stumble around the mop and rolling bucket, past the CLOSED FOR CLEANING sign. He pushed open the wooden swinging door. He saw his palm hit the surface, worn smooth with age, and his mind whispered *fingerprints*. Too late now.

Tom was at the sink, frantically scrubbing his hands under the running water. Paulie wasn't visible except for his boots at the base of the stall.

"What happened? Where is she?"

Tom just kept washing and muttering to himself. The door to the handicapped stall swung open and Paulie emerged, wiping his nose on his sleeve. He had scratches on his hand. "We had no choice. She wasn't cooperating."

"What did you do?" He ran into the stall and found her unmoving on the floor, paper towels clogging her mouth. One shoe had come off in the struggle and her skirt was up around her waist. Flecks of blood dotted the wall and the blue tile floor. "What the hell did you do?" He screamed the words now, but he was screaming them at her because he couldn't look away. Paulie shook him by the shoulders, hissing at him to be quiet.

"We'll fix it."

"Fix it how?" He bent down and yanked the paper towels loose from her mouth but she didn't move. "No one was supposed to get hurt."

"Look, we can—"

"You were just going to talk to her!"

"She wasn't listening. You got me? Nothing we said made a damn bit of difference. It's about damage control now. We've got to put her in the back and get rid of this." Paulie produced something in his hand. A toilet plunger. There was blood on the handle.

He saw the matching red mark across her throat from where they'd choked her with it, and he swallowed back a wave of nausea. "You can't fix this. It's over." His whole life, down the toilet. Fitting that he was crouched next to one. He could just stay here and let them find him.

"It's not over. It's not." Paulie's eyes were wild, feverish. "Find somewhere to ditch this out back. Tom's going to bring in the mop."

He shook his head in denial, reaching out to stroke her wavy hair. Chocolate brown with blond frosted tips. She'd done them herself, he knew. He heard the door open, and someone, presumably Tom, wheel in the mop and bucket. "I'm so sorry," he whispered down to her.

Paulie shook like he had bugs crawling on him. "Come on, man. Think of your kids."

She made a sudden wheezing noise that sounded like a death rattle. It startled him back against the metal door. "She's alive." He looked to Paulie. "We've got to get help."

"Yeah, we will. Just—just get out of here, okay? You can't be anywhere near here right now. Take that thing and go."

"An ambulance," he said, rising to his feet. "We can call 911."

"Yeah, yeah." Paulie propelled him toward the door. "Right after we get this squared away. We'll fix it like I promised. Golden tickets all around."

He let Paulie shove him back into the hallway, dazed and clutching the toilet plunger. He stared at it in his hands. It had her DNA on it. Now his too. Had Paulie been wearing gloves? Had Tom? He couldn't remember. Maybe the girl wouldn't either. Trauma did that to a person, he knew. He'd talked to enough fucked-up people to know that sometimes the damage was bad enough that they stayed fucked, no matter what you tried to do to help them. He glanced back at the door, where he could hear the sounds of them moving around in the room, tidying it up and making it clean. He could take the plunger out front and tell what they did or he could head for the rear exit and the dumpsters in the alley. Trash pickup was tomorrow morning—no, it was today, he realized. It was past one now. Seven hours, give or take, and maybe they would be home free.

A shadow appeared at the end of the hall. Someone was coming his way. He gulped, closed his eyes, and turned for the back exit.

CHAPTER ONE

Icy slush seeped into Annalisa Vega's left boot as she stood over a disappearing crime scene. The snow had picked up intensity, filling in the mugger's footprints by the trees and diluting the victim's bloodstains on the pavement. Annalisa's boots were five years old, the soles worn and separated, but she gave all her extra money to Sassy now, and replacing them never seemed like a priority until she was standing outside in the Chicago deep freeze. Their female mugging victim had been hauled away unconscious in an ambulance, and forensics was busy at another scene. At four-thirty in the afternoon, their perpetrator was already receding into the shadows. "Looks like he waited for her behind those trees over there," she said to her partner, Nick Carelli. "She had a winter hat and scarf on, probably never even saw him before he grabbed her."

Nick's phone flashed as he snapped a few more photos. "A crime of opportunity," he concurred. "He attacked the first vulnerable person to walk by." He craned his neck back to peer up at the nearby apartment building. "The top floors over there facing the park have a pretty good view. Maybe we'll get lucky and someone saw something."

"Sure, maybe." Residents in this area had long ago learned to keep their eyes to themselves. She eyed the hulking brick building with dread at the idea of climbing all those floors for nothing. "What are the odds it has a working elevator?"

"Aw, come on, Vega." Nick gave her one of his easy grins. "I know you like working up a sweat with me."

"You're not allowed to say that stuff anymore," she told him as she started walking toward the building.

"Since when?" He fell into step beside her.

"Since the ink dried on the divorce papers fourteen years ago. Didn't you complete the department's sexual harassment training?"

"Yeah, but turns out there's a loophole."

She stopped walking to look at him. "What loophole?"

"If the two parties have seen each other naked in the past six weeks, then it's flirting, not harassment."

She winced inwardly. New Year's Eve, four weeks ago. A champagne headache that felt like it was still wearing off. "One night in fourteen years does not change the rules," she told him.

"That's why I'm angling for another. Speaking of, what are you doing later?"

"Having dinner with Sassy and the girls. Assuming we're not still canvassing this building by then." Sassy would probably rather she canceled. Just sent the money. Not have to host Annalisa at her dinner table and pretend everything was normal.

"Okay, what about tomorrow night?" They reached the building's entrance and Nick's cell phone rang. He held up a finger to her as he went to answer it. "Hold that thought. Yeah, Carelli here."

Annalisa waited at the door while he finished the call. "Well?" she said at the brightening in his eyes.

"The victim regained consciousness en route to the hospital. Her name is Estelle Roberts. She works at the printing shop two blocks that way and walks through the park to get to the L every afternoon after her shift."

"So maybe it wasn't random after all."

"I'm going to get over there now to interview her."

She widened her eyes at him. "And leave me going door-to-door through the whole building?"

"Hey, at least you're out of the weather, right? And we only need to talk to witnesses on the east side. If I get anything useful from the vic, I'll let you know." He jogged off through the falling flakes and Annalisa suppressed another epithet as she let him go. Her ex-husband was better at talking to people than she was, and she'd been counting on his charm to open doors. But the most important witness right now was the one lying in the hospital, so Annalisa had to agree with his priorities.

The building had eighteen floors and one working elevator car, which moved with the same lurching speed of a downtown bus in rush-hour traffic. Annalisa disembarked, vaguely seasick, on the top floor. No one answered her first two knocks. The third produced a groggy Black male, maybe thirty years of age, wearing pajama pants and a Major Lazer T-shirt. "Sorry, I got off-shift at the hospital at noon, and I've been sleeping since then." He showed her a nurse's badge for Northwestern.

The next tenant at home was an elderly white woman with thick glasses and too many cats. Annalisa glimpsed at least four of them, including a tabby that zipped out the door into the hall. She tracked the feline down and handed her back to the owner. Annalisa tried four more doors with no success, at which point she took the stairs down one flight to do the units on the seventeenth floor that faced the park. The first door, she heard loud music playing on the other side, but no one answered her knock. She banged harder and eventually a white male cracked the door open. She smelled pizza and pot emanating from the other side. "Yeah?" he asked.

She displayed her ID. "I'm Detective Vega, and I'm investigating a mugging that took place about ninety minutes ago in the park outside. Were you home at that time?"

"I been here all afternoon."

"Did you see anything?"

"No."

Annalisa repressed a sigh as she dug out another one of her cards. "Okay, if you think of anything or see anyone suspicious hanging around, call me at that number." He stuck out a hand for the card and she saw he had an intricate tattoo across his hand. "Nice ink," she remarked, holding the card back.

"Thanks. It's a Komodo dragon."

Her phone rang. Nick. "Excuse me one moment." She turned away to take the call. "Yeah, what've you got?"

"Victim says it went down like we thought. He was hiding behind the pine tree and grabbed her when she walked by. He hit her with a rock and took her bag with everything in it."

"Can she ID him?"

"He's a white guy. Pretty big by her account. She says he was wearing a hat pulled down pretty far over his face, so an ID might be difficult. But she does remember he had a lizard tattoo on his hand."

Shit. She turned around to see if the guy had closed the door on her, but he stood there, filling most of the frame, waiting obediently for her card. "I'll call you back," she said to Nick, her gaze on the tattoo on the man's hand. "Sorry about that," she said, forcing a smile, keeping her tone neutral as she stepped toward him. "You were saying how you've been home all afternoon, Mr. . . . ?"

He bolted. Shoved her hard into the wall and ran like hell for the stairs. She cursed and grabbed her radio even as she started in pursuit. "This is Vega," she said as she pounded down the stairs. She could hear him racing ahead of her, several floors below. "I'm in foot pursuit of a suspect in a robbery/assault case, and I need backup at West Granville and North Leavitt. Suspect is a male white, approximately thirty years old, two hundred and fifty pounds, with a Komodo dragon tattoo on his right hand. Dressed in jeans and a black sweatshirt."

He blasted through the emergency exit into the alley with her just seconds behind. "Heading south on Leavitt," she said into her radio as she ran after him. The street had slow-moving pedestrians bundled up against the snow. He grabbed a young woman and threw her backward in Annalisa's direction. The woman screamed as she went down, ass first, in the slush at Annalisa's feet. Annalisa paused to give her a hand up. "Are you all right? You're all right."

The suspect had crossed the street but he was still visible through the snow in the distance. Annalisa took up pursuit again and updated the chase coordinates on her radio. Where the hell was backup? The man turned right into another alley and disappeared from view. Breathing hard, Annalisa rounded the corner to follow him. He hit her with a trash can, sending her careening into a brick wall. Her radio hit the pavement and shattered. "Stop!" she hollered at the guy as she clambered to her feet. "You're under arrest."

He vanished out the other end of the alley. Annalisa followed, ignoring the pain in her flank from where she'd hit the wall. Her feet hit the ground in rhythmic slaps. The cold air burned in her lungs as she ran in the direction she thought he had turned. Yes. There he was. He was bent over one block ahead, winded, and the sight made a laugh escape her. All those years running track in school finally paid off. He looked up and saw her coming, his expression one of disbelief. He took off again but tripped on the slippery curb. She grabbed him as he scrambled to get out of the oncoming traffic.

"I said," she repeated, panting hard, "you're under arrest." The snow melted over her hot neck, sliding down her collar in an icy trickle. The man put up only a token resistance as she applied the handcuffs.

A squad car flashed its lights and pulled to a stop alongside her. The window powered down and the passenger, a lifer beat cop named Harry Finneman, sipped from a paper cup as he looked on with mild interest. "Your pants are wet," he observed to Annalisa.

"Where the hell were you guys? Getting coffee?"

"Hey, we got here as soon as we could."

"Sure, you did." Ever since she'd turned in her ex-cop father last year, the boys in blue seemed slow to answer her calls. "I was bird-dogging this guy for ten straight minutes, and he almost got away. You should've been here backing me up."

Harry raised bushy eyebrows at her. "What are you going to do, report us?"

She bit back a tart reply. "Can you at least take him downtown for booking?"

"Sure thing, Detective Vega, ma'am." Harry looked to his younger partner at the wheel. "Stephens, it's all you."

Stephens took custody and Annalisa half limped her way back to her car, where she used the leftover napkins from her sandwich at lunch to mop up her wet face. Nick met her at the station, where the stale heat made the whole place smell like feet and dried wool. "Are you all right?" he asked with a frown as he rolled his desk chair over to hers.

She flopped down into her seat. "I worked up that sweat you were so concerned about. My cardio is complete for the whole week."

A uniformed officer dropped off paperwork at Annalisa's desk. "Here's the booking report from downstairs," she said.

"Great, thanks." Annalisa looked it over. "Suspect's name is Greg Martinez." She scanned down for additional details and stopped when she noticed the cop's name filled in at the bottom. Arresting officer: Harry Finneman. "That sonofabitch," she murmured.

"Problem?" Nick looked up from where he'd rolled back to his own territory.

"Clerical error," she announced as she stood up. "Nothing some Wite-Out won't fix." She wished she could Wite-Out the whole last year and a half. Or at least dump a bucket of it over Finneman's head.

"About that dinner," Nick said as he rolled to block her path. "I'm buying."

She rolled her eyes. "I told you I can't."

"So, we make it another night," he said, his face open and full of hope. "Name the time."

She hesitated. She'd blown up her whole life last year and Nick was the only one left standing in the ashes. "I'm sorry," she said, not without real regret. "I just can't."

CHAPTER TWO

"Am I imagining things, or does this snowman have fangs?" Annalisa held her wineglass in one hand as she squinted at the child's art tacked up on Sassy's refrigerator. The garish snowman had a misshapen oval head and tiny triangle teeth. Cotton balls had been glued on to form the body.

"Oh yes. If you look closely, she also drew staples on his neck. Mrs. Davis wouldn't let her use the actual stapler." Sassy had her own wineglass, deep into a second pouring of the discount pinot noir Annalisa had brought with her to dinner. Folklore said *in vino veritas*, but Annalisa was finding the opposite, that the rituals of serving and consuming the alcohol gave them something to do in place of real conversation. The trick was getting out of Sassy's place before the third glass.

"Carla made this?"

"Not only did she make it, Carla told the class it's a vampire snowman that goes out at night to consume the carrot noses of the other snowpeople," Sassy said, leaning against the fridge with a sigh. "Her teacher gave her points for imagination but also called to ask me if Carla should be in therapy."

"Should she be?" Of course she should. Carla was six years old and her father was in prison for murder. Annalisa knew this because she had put him there.

Sassy set down her wineglass and began clearing away the dinner dishes. They joined a pile waiting in the sink. "Putting a first grader on the couch? No, thanks. If anyone's going crazy around here, it's me. The new budget at the library is ten percent smaller than last year and my boss said he can't keep justifying my extra shifts at the expense of keeping other people on full-time. Carla's overdue to see the dentist and Gigi needs new shoes. Meanwhile, the place is a wreck."

Annalisa's gaze slid past the dirty dishes to the avalanche of mail, broken crayons, and unopened plastic snack containers, half full of cheesy crackers, that covered the countertop. "It's not that bad."

Sassy gave a dark laugh as she started the faucet. "I give Gigi one cookie and she somehow manages to leave fingerprints over the entire house—all of them tiny and two feet off the ground."

"If you want, I could give you the name of the cleaning service that does my condo. Better yet, let me schedule them—"

"No!" The word came out as a desperate yelp. Sassy squeezed her eyes shut and raised her palms. "No," she repeated more softly. "You've done enough."

Annalisa had brought groceries with her to dinner and a check to help cover the mortgage; it didn't feel like nearly enough. "I love the girls. I love you. I want to help."

"You know what you can do to help."

Annalisa turned away. She knew what her friend wanted from her, but she couldn't make herself say yes. "I can help with the dishes," she said with forced cheer. "I'll wash, you dry. It'll be like the old days when you and me lived in that apartment on Central. The one over the tire store? The whole place reeked like rubber."

"Anna." Sassy's voice was soft as she took up a dishrag to dry.

Annalisa focused on scraping dried oatmeal off the side of a bowl. She shook her head, the barest of gestures. "I can't," she said tightly. "I've thought about it and I just can't."

"He's your brother."

Annalisa dropped the bowl in the sink with a loud clatter. "Yes, and he's also a convicted murderer."

"I know. I was there, remember? I sat behind him the whole trial. I saw the pictures. I heard—" Sassy broke off with a choked sound and paused to steady herself. "—what he did. But it was a long time ago and he was practically a kid at the time. He made a mistake, Anna. A bad one.

Huge. But it was one night out of his whole life. Haven't you ever screwed up? Done something you wanted to take back but you couldn't?"

"Not murder." Annalisa started furiously scrubbing a dinner plate.

"You know him," cajoled Sassy, moving closer. "You love him. I know you do."

"So did you, and yet you divorced him."

"I had no choice! Financially, legally, we had to be separate."

"Yeah? Ma had to put up her house." The home Annalisa loved was still standing, but it was a prison now. For his role in the cover-up, Pops spent his days inside with an ankle monitor, despite being wheelchair-bound from Parkinson's disease. Like he could flee even if he wanted.

"Remember . . . remember when we were kids and Alex helped us build a tree house? Or at the beach, when he used his paper route money to buy us hot dogs and pop? And the talent shows we put on. He was so funny with all the different voices he could do. I knew even then he'd be a great dad. Carla would be screaming with laughter at bedtime. 'Do Papa Bear in the bathroom again, Daddy! "This toilet is too big!"'"

"Stop it. Just stop." Annalisa wouldn't look at her. "None of that matters right now."

"Of course it matters!" Sassy slammed a plate down on the counter, making Annalisa jump. "He's their father, Anna! That's never going to change no matter what. He's part of them, a good part . . . there's good in him, I know it because I see it in their faces and I don't want them thinking they're bad because he was . . . and, oh God." She broke off with a sob, covering her face, and Annalisa moved immediately to embrace her.

Annalisa shushed her, cradling the back of her friend's head with a wet, soapy hand. "The girls are amazing. They are fierce and funny and good to their mama."

Sassy sniffed hard into her shoulder. "So was Alex," she said in a small voice as she pulled away. She wiped her eyes with shaking fingers. The sight of her spiky lashes and the utter despair on her face tore at Annalisa's heart. "I know why you had to turn him in," Sassy murmured. "I—I forgive you for that."

Annalisa stiffened. "I had no choice."

Sassy's face closed off. "It doesn't matter. It's done. He's guilty. But if you spoke at the sentencing, if you asked for leniency, they would listen to you. The courts care what cops think. Our lawyer says it could make the difference between a sentence of ten years or life in prison. Ten years, maybe less with good behavior. Think about that. Think what it would mean for Gigi and Carla. They'd get a chance to have a father again."

Annalisa leaned both hands on the counter, bracing herself. The weight of this case had been with her since her own childhood and it had yet to go away. Some days she felt like it would push her clear into the ground. "Alex took away someone's mother," she said finally, looking sideways at Sassy. "He strangled her to death. Do you know how long that takes? Minutes. It wasn't a mistake, Sass. Alex had to want it."

"He was drunk, a kid. He was angry. He doesn't even remember doing it."

"He remembers." She would never forget the stricken look on his face when he realized she'd uncovered his secret.

"Look, let's not talk about it anymore tonight," Sassy replied, sounding defeated. "Just think about it, okay? If you won't do it for him, do it for me. Do it for Gigi and Carla . . . and for your parents too. Maybe Alex gets out before they die . . . maybe he doesn't."

Annalisa looked away at the mention of her parents. "It's not my decision. It can't be."

"It can be if you want it to." Sassy rubbed the side of her head and checked the clock on the kitchen wall. "Listen, thanks for dinner and your help with the dishes. I've got it from here."

"Kicking me out, are you?" Annalisa kept her tone light, but it was hard to hide the note of hurt. Sassy had been her best friend for so long and now this connection, too, threatened to snap under the weight of Alex's crime. She swallowed and tried to choose her words carefully because Sassy held the real power cards. If she wanted, Sassy could take Alex's kids away and the Vega family could do nothing to stop her. "I should get going," she agreed, even though it was still early. "I'll—I'll call you next week," Annalisa said. "Maybe we can have dinner Saturday. Take the kids somewhere fun."

Sassy gave a halfhearted wave from the sink but didn't look back at her. "Sure, whatever you want."

Annalisa departed into the frigid night air. She sat in the dark in her car across from Sassy's place, something she did a lot of these days when she couldn't bring herself to go home. The confined space felt under her control while the wheels tempted her with escape. *You could turn the engine and go,* whispered the voice in her head. But go where? Annalisa had lived her whole life inside the boundaries of Chicago. Lately, the roots that grounded her had started to curl up and poke through the cement sidewalks. She knew what other cops whispered when she wasn't around to hear. *There goes Vega. She turned in her own family. Imagine what she'd do to you . . .*

She sighed and started the car, preparing to leave, when she saw a black Lexus SUV pull to a stop across the street, right outside Sassy's home. The porch light was still on, Annalisa realized with some surprise. Sassy hadn't turned it off after Anna's exit.

Annalisa watched as a man in a dark coat got out of the SUV. Her detective's brain classified him immediately: male, white, maybe forty years old. He had a large bouquet of flowers in his hand, which he took to Sassy's doorstep. Sassy opened right away and welcomed him inside with a smile. Anna checked the clock on her dash, which read 9:12. Odd time for a date. Sassy hadn't mentioned anything about seeing someone.

Annalisa shifted in her seat, as though her discomfort were physical and not mental. She should leave. Sassy didn't owe her details about her love life. She didn't ask her opinion. Annalisa stared at the house until she saw the porch light go out. Whoever this guy was, he was staying awhile. Annalisa took a deep breath and released the brake. Out of habit, she memorized the Lexus's license plate number as she drove away. Her eyes checked the rearview mirror again. She wondered: What kind of guy drives an expensive car, springs for fancy flowers, and yet picks a prison widow with two small kids for a booty call on Friday night?

Instead of heading straight home, Annalisa drove by her parents' place, which wasn't far from Sassy's. Alex had settled closest out of all four Vega kids. Her oldest brother, Vinnie, had left Chicago completely, opting for Naperville, where he had a family. Tony and his wife lived in a chichi high-rise over in Lakeview. Alex had remained in Norwood Park where they grew up, north and west of downtown, in their own little world that called to mind an idyllic suburb rather than the concrete jungle. The streets there were tree lined and bore names like Myrtle and Rosedale, Oriole and Hyacinth. Annalisa glided to a stop outside her old homestead. It was dark inside except for the blue light that flickered in the window of the den. Pops would be in there, probably watching the Blackhawks game. Ma used to sit with him on the sofa, doing her knitting. Now she slept alone in the bedroom upstairs.

How much did you know? Annalisa had finally asked her mother during the trial. Only Alex went the distance in court. Pops had copped a plea.

None of it, her mother had replied after the barest pause. She had looked out the window as she said it, as though the answers might be out in the street somewhere. Or maybe she had been unable to look her only daughter in the face and lie to her.

Annalisa took out her phone and checked Colin Duffy's photo stream. He hadn't spoken to her since the trial, when her brother was found guilty of murdering Colin's mother. What else was there to say beyond that? Colin's latest snapshot showed an expanse of aquamarine water and pink sandy shoreline tagged as Horseshoe Bay Beach, Bermuda. Geographically, Colin was closer than he'd been all year, but the picture felt a million miles away. Annalisa's finger hovered over the heart-shaped icon a fraction of a second before clicking it. It turned red and she flushed like a teenager at the sight. Sometimes it seemed like this had been their relationship forever: her sending him hearts that were never returned.

Her parents' porch light came on and the door opened. She saw her mother's shape a moment before she heard the call. "Anna?" Annalisa gunned the engine and sped off down the street. She did not go to her condo in Avondale and instead drove to Nick's apartment in Wicker Park. He answered right away.

"Hey," he said, looking pleased to see her. "Change your mind?"

"Turns out Sassy had a date."

"A date? Who's the lucky guy?"

"I don't know," she said as she followed him up the steps. "She didn't exactly introduce me."

He paused to grin back at her. "Oh, that kind of date."

"Yes. Your favorite kind," she answered with a roll of her eyes. "Speaking of, I'm not interrupting . . . ?"

"You? Never." He let her inside the apartment. She saw the dent in the leather couch where he had been sitting, alone, in front of a large-screen TV that was playing *The Godfather,* currently paused on Marlon Brando's face. Nick had an open bottle of Goose Island IPA in one hand. Following her gaze, he said, "I can open the wine if you want."

"No, don't bother. I'm fine."

"Beer? Water? I have a can of ginger ale somewhere if you want it."

"I said I'm fine." She should have just gone home. "What is it with men and this movie?" Her father and brothers could all quote it chapter and verse, but she never saw the appeal.

"Hey, it's a classic." He took one end of the sofa and she sat on the other.

Maybe she just wasn't in the mood for murder and family betrayal. "Guys always watch this movie and imagine they're Vito. More likely, they're Fredo."

"Not me."

She looked sideways at him. He had the dark Italian good looks to pull off any part he wanted. "Oh yeah? Where do you fit in, Carelli?"

"I'm the cannoli."

She laughed, a real one. Her first in a long time. "Maybe I will have one beer," she said as she took off her coat.

"I knew it," he said, rising to fetch her one.

She rubbed her hands together, trying to warm them better before she had to hold a beer. Nick's place looked almost the same as it had when he moved in a couple of years ago—renter's beige walls, mostly empty except for the large handmade quilt tacked on one wall. "You still have it," she said, nodding at his grandmother's quilt when he returned with the beer.

"I always keep what matters."

She looked at her lap. They'd been married less than two years. She was among the things he had not kept, and he swore these days he was sorry. "Remember our first apartment?" she asked. "The water stain in the bathroom looked like the Loch Ness Monster."

"I remember. I remember the first night we spent there. We didn't even have power." A bad rainstorm had knocked out power to the neighborhood and delayed their furniture arrival. They had eaten pizza on the floor by candlelight. "We spent the night there anyway," he said, his voice going soft. "Remember?"

They'd shared a single sleeping bag and that old quilt he had tacked up on the wall. She remembered the wide curtainless windows and how they'd let the lightning flash right inside, making zebra patterns on the bare walls as they'd made love on the floor. The thunder shook them, a prelude to the thousand L trains that would become the bassline to their existence, rumbling by on the track outside. He'd been on top so she hadn't noticed all the cracks in the ceiling, not till morning and by then it was too late.

"I remember my tailbone was sore the next day and we had to move a couch up five flights of stairs."

"We did it, though." He reached over to nudge her. "You were always tougher than you looked."

"Yeah?" She sighed and let her head loll back on the cushion. "Maybe I am tired of being so tough."

"You don't have to be." He cupped the side of her face, his thumb sliding across her cheek, warming her.

She didn't move away, not when his large hand slid down her neck, skimmed the length of her arm, and came to rest over her free hand. He squeezed her. She couldn't go home again but maybe this was the closest thing. "I want . . ."

"What do you want?" he murmured in invitation, and she swallowed. "You came to me, Vega. What do you want?"

She wanted so much that she couldn't have. She set aside the beer and traced a finger down the center of his chest, her fingertip catching the buttons on his shirt, one by one. At his belly, she veered to the side where she knew the scar was. Nick had run around on her while they were married. But last year, he'd nearly died for her. Wasn't that the kind of faithful that mattered? "Does it hurt?" she whispered.

He caught her hand and kissed it. "Not anymore."

She closed her eyes, heard the deepening of his breathing. He was so close she could smell him now, the lavender and oakmoss scent from his shaving cream heady with memory in her nose. He'd shaved after work, she realized. He'd been expecting her. Expecting this.

She let his hand move up her body until it found the bruise where she'd been wounded earlier in the day. "What about you?" he asked. "Does it hurt?"

"Not there."

His breath caught. "Then where?"

She hesitated and then drew his palm across her chest and placed it to the side of her left breast. Her heart. It thrummed under his touch, pathetically excited to be this close to another human being.

"Let me see," he murmured, his face warm against hers. His hand flicked open one button, then two and three. She helped with the rest as he began trailing hot kisses down her neck, the way he knew used to drive her crazy. He felt solid and familiar and she lay back under him and let him take her to the place they'd been before.

....

The insistent buzzing of her cell phone woke her. She twisted around, disoriented and naked in Nick's sheets, and found her phone on his nightstand. The glowing numbers said it was past three in the morning, and her first thought was Pops. A fall, a seizure, something to put him back in the emergency room. Instead, it was their commander, Lynn Zimmer, on the line.

"I'm sorry about the hour, Vega, but I need you right away at a scene on North Nordica Avenue." She gave an address Annalisa did not recognize.

Annalisa clawed the hair from her face as she struggled to sit up. "Commander?" She wasn't on duty that night, and her boss didn't make these kinds of nighttime calls. Not unless it was bad.

"We have shots fired, at least one person dead. I don't know if there are others injured," Zimmer continued. "I tried Carelli as well but got no answer. I'd like you both on the scene as soon as possible."

Annalisa glanced at Nick, who slept open-mouthed on his back beside her. His phone was probably in his pants, which they'd left in the front room. "I'll try Nick. What's the address again?"

Zimmer relayed the number and Annalisa wrote it down on her hand. "Look, I know it's not your turn in the barrel," Zimmer said. "But I need you on this, okay? I'm en route myself."

Annalisa started scrambling out of bed, feeling around with one hand for her clothes as Nick began to stir under the sheets. The commander definitely did not show up at routine middle-of-the-night shootings. "Uh, sounds like something big is brewing."

"The address I gave you is a single-family house." Zimmer paused. "The owner is a cop."

CHAPTER THREE

ANNALISA DROVE. This time of night, it was a straight shot up Milwaukee Avenue back to her old neighborhood. Nick looked pale and disheveled in the yellow light of the passing streetlamps, his dark hair sticking up on one side where he'd been pressed into the pillow only minutes before. Silently, she produced a small comb from the center console and handed it to him. Her hair was neat again, twisted into a knot at her nape, but she wore the same clothes she'd had on yesterday at work and she hoped like hell no one would notice. She made a mental note to keep her jacket on. "This cop, Hammond—have you heard of him?"

Nick paused from fixing his hair. "You mean you haven't? He's part of the Fantastic Four with Vaughn, Monk, and Osborne. They were swinging dicks when I was coming up in Central years ago. Him and his partners had the biggest busts in town and swagger to go with it. They'd roll into division with some big collar and it'd be like Christmas, with Monk handing out cigars. Everyone wanted to be them."

"A real cop's cop," she replied, getting the picture.

"They made lots of gang-related busts, lot of guns, lot of drugs. Once they nailed a bunch of Spanish Cobras with so much cocaine the news cameras showed up to photograph it all laid out end to end on this enormous table. Monk called it 'Operation Mongoose' and the press ate that shit right up. I think the superintendent gave them a Blue Star for it."

"I remember the guys around Pops's table talking about that one. It was a long time ago, though—the late nineties? They're all still on the job?"

"Last I heard. Monk's a lieutenant now."

"And Hammond?"

Her question hung in the air for a beat, and Nick took a breath. "I guess we're about to find out."

Annalisa turned left onto West Devon. She knew where Nordica Avenue was located but had never had cause to be on the street, despite it being only a couple of miles from Ma and Pops's place. It wasn't a main drive. A city as big as Chicago, and still you could spend your life inside a few square blocks. "Maybe Hammond shot an intruder," she suggested, trying to be optimistic. Quick and easy. A clean shoot.

"Yeah, let's hope." Nick's leg had started to bounce, a nervous tic.

"You don't sound that hopeful," she replied with reproach.

He looked over at her. "Zimmer doesn't get our asses out of bed in the middle of the night for a cops-and-robbers shoot. Not if it's clean." He shook his head for emphasis. "Hammond had a wife and kids." He paused and turned his face to the window. "Christ, I hope it's not one of the kids."

Annalisa turned onto Nordica and easily spotted their destination. The large colonial-style home stood out on the otherwise dark street, lit from within like a jack-o'-lantern. A crush of cop cars sat nose-to-tail in the street and on the drive, uniformed officers milling around in the cold night. An ambulance idled with its lights still flashing. Annalisa didn't see a news truck yet and said a silent prayer of gratitude for this small favor. A few heads turned as she got out of the car, uniformed men she did not recognize but who plainly recognized her. Her face had been all over the news last year. She felt their eyes on her neck as she walked by.

"What if Hammond's the shooter and it's his wife who's dead," she muttered to Nick as they reached the cement walkway that led to the house. "And that's why I'm here."

Nick didn't pretend to misunderstand her. She'd turned in a cop already. Zimmer knew she wouldn't flinch. "Then you'll investigate the SOB."

She bit back a groan at the thought. "I'm still hoping for that intruder."

As they entered the home, her first impression was *wow*. It looked like a showplace from a magazine, not a family home. The heavy front door had a panel of leaded glass in the middle with an intricate flower design etched inside. Oak floors gleamed under their feet. The front room had a tailored charcoal-gray sectional sofa, free of stains; a floor-to-ceiling tiled fireplace in coordinating gray and white; dark wood bookshelves displaying hardback titles and selected pieces of art, like a blue vase and a white marble elephant with its trunk raised in greeting.

"I guess Hammond's done okay for himself," Nick said as they took in the room. "You think these floors are original?"

"What are you, into real estate now?"

"I might be looking to buy."

"You're here." Their commander, Zimmer, appeared on the staircase, dressed for work in her gloves and booties. Annalisa spied the open boxes of each sitting on the bottom step and Zimmer gestured for them to help themselves. "You can follow me. The body's upstairs."

Annalisa and Nick exchanged a look at the word *body*. They trailed Zimmer up the hardwood steps without a word. The décor along the walls of the staircase mimicked what Annalisa had seen downstairs, elegant and tasteful, but with no sense that a family lived here. Hammond had kids, according to Nick. Where were their pictures? The family portraits?

She smelled the traces of gunpowder before they hit the bedroom. Multiple shots, she realized, preparing herself for the sight she was likely to see on the other side. The victim was an adult male, white, dressed in only black boxers. He lay unmoving on the far side of the sleigh bed, his naked chest covered in blood. A tube protruded from his mouth and a pair of bloody medic's gloves lay on the white sheets next to him. Annalisa could see one gunshot wound on his shoulder and another in his abdomen. There was also a bullet hole visible in the wall and the bedside lamp had been shattered. A picture frame lay facedown in the ceramic rubble. "Meet Leo Hammond," Zimmer announced grimly. "The homeowner and a detective-sergeant with the Central Division going back twenty-five years."

Both sides of the bed were rumpled. A fine mist of blood had sprayed across the pillows. "Where's his wife? Was she here when this happened?"

"Kayla Hammond," Zimmer replied. "She's being treated downstairs."

"Was she shot?"

Zimmer shook her head. "Bump on the head."

Annalisa moved deeper into the room and noticed a semiautomatic handgun on the floor, a .40-caliber Smith & Wesson from the looks of it, similar to the one she carried herself. "Is that the weapon?"

"It's Hammond's gun," Zimmer replied. "Details are fuzzy at this time, but Mrs. Hammond indicated it was the weapon used in the attack."

"Attack," said Nick. "Someone outside the home did this?"

"That is my understanding. Mrs. Hammond called 911 to say that an intruder entered the home and shot her husband."

Annalisa regarded the lifeless man on the bed. He'd been asleep, she gathered. Did not see it coming. "Entered how?" she asked. "There's an alarm panel by the front door and another in the hall outside. But it doesn't appear that Hammond had any warning."

"We'll have to talk to the security people about that," Zimmer answered. "Responding officers discovered a broken window in the basement, so that may be the point of entry."

Annalisa tried to envision it. The bedroom, absent the macabre death scene, was as tidy as the rest of the place. The dressing table held a hairbrush and some perfume bottles, as well as a jewelry box that appeared untouched. She spied an empty holster on top of the taller dresser. "So someone broke in here, crossed the room unnoticed, and managed to locate Hammond's weapon in the dark?"

"Like I said, details are fuzzy."

"Was anyone else home at the time?"

"Kids are grown and out on their own. Mr. and Mrs. Hammond were apparently alone." Or not, Annalisa thought as she pondered who might have known the habits of the couple well enough to know Hammond's gun would be available for the taking.

"Anything missing from the home?" Nick asked as he peered into the en suite bathroom.

"Too soon to tell. Nothing obvious. Hammond's watch is still on the nightstand. There are a pair of earrings on the vanity in the bathroom that look pricey."

"You said the wife is being treated by the medics," Annalisa said. "What happened to her?"

"Funny thing about that," Zimmer replied archly. "Outside of the bump, there's not a scratch on her."

"Huh."

"Yeah. And the other thing," said Zimmer. "She touched the weapon."

"She what?" Nick poked his head back out of the bathroom.

"According to her, the shooter left it lying on the bed near the body, and she said she picked it up and threw it away from Hammond while she was on the phone with 911. Said she thought it might still be dangerous."

They all looked at the gun in the middle of the floor. A gun without a shooter was no threat at all. How long had this woman been a cop's wife? "So her story is that they were both in bed sleeping when someone broke in, grabbed Hammond's gun, shot him full of holes, and left her unscathed?"

"Oh, it gets weirder than that." Zimmer raised her eyebrows at them.

When she didn't continue, Nick spread his hands. "You want to fill us in?"

"Best you hear it from her."

Nick rolled his neck as if to loosen it. "Okay, then," he said to Annalisa. "Let's go find her."

Zimmer stayed with the body. Annalisa and Nick trooped back down the stairs to the living room, following it past the dining area and into the kitchen beyond. Like the rest of the place, it positively gleamed. "Quartz countertops," Nick muttered as he ran one gloved finger over the closest one. "Nice." Annalisa elbowed him.

"Is that her? I mean, it's got to be, right?" Annalisa wrinkled her brow in confusion at the young blond woman having her blood pressure taken across the room. She sat on a barstool at the end of the island, holding an oxygen mask to her face with her free hand. Zimmer had said the adult children weren't in the home, but this girl looked maybe twenty-two.

"I never met his kids," Nick replied in an equally low voice.

"I think you're going to be okay now," the male medic said as he released the cuff from the young woman's arm. "You can keep the ice pack on that bump so the swelling stays down."

"You think I care about a bump?" she shot back. "Someone just blew my husband's brains out."

Husband. She was definitely the wife. No way she was old enough to be birthing children back when Nick worked out of Central, so this had to be, at a minimum, Mrs. Hammond #2. "Mrs. Hammond?" Annalisa said as the medic began clearing out. "I'm Detective Vega and this is my partner, Detective Carelli. We're very sorry about your husband."

She hugged herself through the silky nightgown. Annalisa saw blood smeared along the hem and another splotch at her thigh. "It was a frogman," the woman said with a shudder. "You should be out there looking for him."

"Excuse me?"

"You know, a frogman. Like the diving people? He had a mask and flippers and everything."

Nick stepped forward with his notebook in hand. "I'm sorry, Mrs. Hammond, are you saying that a man in a diving suit shot your husband?"

"That's right," she replied with a note of challenge in her voice. "Leo and I were in bed sleeping when all of a sudden, the lights came on and there he was. He was covered head to toe in a black wet suit. He even had one of those, what do you call it? Diver's masks. He shot Leo and then went flopping off again like it was no big deal."

"Did he say anything?"

"No." She put her hands over her ears. "The shots were so loud. I thought my head was going to split open. Who would do this? What if he comes back?"

"It sounds like he had the chance to take a shot at you and declined to do so," Annalisa told her. "This . . . frogman . . . are you completely sure it was a man? I mean, if the person was covered head to toe . . . ?"

"I don't know. It happened so fast. He seemed eight feet tall to me, but I guess it could have been a woman."

"And this person had your husband's gun?"

"He must have. I just—I froze, you know? When I could move again,

I ran to Leo and I found the gun lying on the bed. I threw it across the room to get it away from him. That's stupid, I know. Leo would kill me for doing that. He's always saying never to touch his gun." She ran her hands back and forth along her thighs, rocking in her seat. Her pale skin had virtually no color at all. If she was putting on an act, it was a convincing one.

"How long have you and Mr. Hammond been married?" Annalisa asked.

"What does it matter?" The defensive tone was back in her voice.

"We're just trying to get a complete picture of Mr. Hammond's life and habits."

"Two years, okay? It was two years last September." Her chin trembled. "We were trying to have a baby."

"I'm very sorry," Annalisa murmured. "And this house? You bought it together?"

"No, Leo lived here first." She paused and sniffed again. "With his kids. He let me redecorate it, though," she added. "I'm an interior designer."

Annalisa forced a smile. "It shows. The alarm system on the house is functional?"

"What?" She seemed confused. "Oh, yeah, I guess so. Leo takes care of that stuff."

"But it didn't go off tonight," said Nick. He strode to the rear sliding doors and peered out into the black beyond. "You didn't hear or see anything unusual until the shooter appeared in your bedroom?"

"Nothing. Leo sleeps like he's in a coma. We had dinner after work, watched TV, and went to bed around eleven like usual."

Like usual, Annalisa mused. Whoever the shooter was, they obviously had observed the couple enough to know their routine. Or at least to know where Leo Hammond kept his gun. "Okay, thank you, Mrs. Hammond," she said, and the woman made a face, her pink lips drawn together in a sour moue. She grabbed the ice pack from the counter and put it to the side of her head.

"I'm Kayla. Mrs. Hammond is his first wife."

"Okay, Kayla, and you can call me Annalisa."

Recognition dawned across Kayla's delicate features. "Wait, I do know you. You caught that serial killer. The Lovelorn guy. Oh my gosh, Lisa's going to freak when I tell her. Even Leo said you were a badass, and he didn't usually say that about female cops."

"Thanks, I think?"

Kayla put a hand over her chest. "I just feel so much better now, knowing it's you who's going to catch him. The frogman, I mean. It's so terrifying. What if he's out there right now, breaking into someone else's house?"

"We'll do our best, ma'am," Annalisa assured her. "You can help us a lot by pointing us in the right direction. Did your husband have any particular enemies? Someone who might have wanted to hurt him?"

"Oh." She considered for a moment and then sat up straight. "You know, maybe you're right. Maybe it was a woman who did this."

"You have a particular one in mind?"

"You're damn right I do. I call her The Bitch, but you'll probably want to go with Mrs. Hammond."

"You mean Mr. Hammond's ex-wife?"

"Yeah, Maura. She's a real peach. Her and her snake lawyer. She made Leo give her sixty percent of this place to move out, you know. Not half, and he's the one who paid for it to begin with! And we had to use her appraiser's assessment—a million dollars! Can you believe it? They'd have been lucky to get eight hundred thousand before I fixed it up."

In Annalisa's view, this gave Leo motive to murder his ex-wife, not the other way around. "I see. Was there a particular quarrel that they had lately? About the house or something else?"

"Yeah, she found out he had his vasectomy reversed. I guess one of the kids told her, and she flipped her shit."

"Flipped her shit how?" Nick wanted to know.

"Came over here screaming at him, yelling what was he thinking, he's making a fool of himself, embarrassing his grown kids. He's old enough to be a grandpa. But really, she was afraid he'd change the financials. Leave less for his kids and more for me."

"And had he?" Annalisa asked.

"No." She paused. "Not yet."

They left Kayla Hammond in the kitchen and went in search of the broken window in the basement. “Now, this is what I’m talking about,” Nick said when he saw the furnished lair. “Huge TV, a bar, even a full-sized pool table. You don’t find this kind of space downtown.”

“You move out here and it’ll mean a longer commute,” she said.

“Could be worth it. More space means a yard. Great for kids or a dog.”

She turned to stare at him. “You have neither of those.”

He shrugged. “Not now. I meant, you know, maybe someday.”

She watched him a beat longer. He’d better not be signing her up for another round. Nick didn’t seem to feel her gaze on him. He moved to the line of windows on the side wall and took out his pocket flashlight. “This looks like it. There’s broken glass here on the floor.”

She joined him and stood on tiptoe to try to see the outside as well. “It’s big enough for someone to fit through. Maybe the alarm doesn’t cover the basement?”

“We’ll have to check that.” He stuck the penlight in his mouth to get out his notebook and write it down. When he was finished, he felt along the open sash with one hand. “It’s smooth. Nothing to cut open the wet suit, I suppose. What the hell do you make of that, anyway?”

“It’s a wild story.” Annalisa knelt to examine the glass, which was dirty on one side from being exposed to the winter muck on the exterior of the home. It wasn’t that much glass, in her estimation. She rose and looked around the room. Nearby, she saw a sturdy metal frame with shelves that held various items: a coiled garden hose; a high-powered flashlight; empty terra-cotta pots and a half-full bag of soil, neatly tied off. There was also a toolbox. Annalisa found a small saw, a few screwdrivers, a level, a box of nails, and a hammer inside. She withdrew the hammer and examined it.

“What’ve you got there?” Nick asked.

“I don’t know. Maybe nothing.” She replaced the hammer and nodded at the window. “Let’s look at it from outside.”

They trooped around to the side of the house. “Look at all this yard,” Nick said with admiration. “You could get a soccer game going here.” Annalisa had to agree the expanse of rock-hard frozen snow was impressive for the city. Nick stomped at the snow, trying to chip it with his boot, but it didn’t budge. “So much for footprints.”

"Don't you mean flipper prints?"

"Hey, yeah, maybe the guy swam off. How far away is the river?"

"Funny." They had reached the broken window. "Do you have that penlight?"

He produced it and handed it over. Annalisa knelt to inspect the damage from the outside, where she saw a similar amount of broken glass. The more telling clue was the dark line of dirt that had accumulated at the bottom of the window. "Come with me," she said to Nick as she moved one window down. It had a similar buildup of grime, a result of being near the ground and battered by the elements every day. "If you were going to crawl through this window, you'd have to squeeze through either headfirst or feetfirst, on your belly."

"Right," he agreed.

"You'd brush along this outer sash. See?" She brushed her hand over it and the dirt smudged, pieces of it flaking off. The line was no longer straight and complete. "The grime here would be disturbed. But it's not been touched over there on the broken window."

"So you're saying the frogman didn't climb in that way."

Annalisa rose to her feet and dusted off her hands. "If he was ever here at all."

CHAPTER FOUR

THE SOUND OF MEN SHOUTING DREW ANNALISA'S ATTENTION TO THE FRONT OF THE HAMMOND HOUSE. She trekked back over the frozen snow to find Zimmer, palms raised, trying to calm a couple of guys in leather jackets and CPD shields on their belts. "The Division North team has jurisdiction here," she was saying. "You know that."

"Leo's ours," the burlier of the two men replied. "We know him better than you ever will."

"Then help us," Zimmer said. "Help us find who did this."

"Let us inside and then we can help." They tried to push past her again and she scrambled sideways to keep her body between them and the house. A uniformed officer stepped forward from the shadowed porch to back her up, and Annalisa joined him.

"The jurisdiction is clear," Zimmer said calmly.

"You're talking to me about maps?" the man argued, his face flushed. "Fuck the maps. They don't mean shit right now. Leo may have lived here in your territory, but he was our family."

"You know I can't let you into a protected crime scene. I promise I have my best people on it."

The man looked past Zimmer, and his wild eyes found Annalisa. "Her?" he demanded, raising a finger at her. "You can't be serious. She lucked into one big bust, and then what does she do with all that cred? She turns in her own father."

The other cop with him put a hand on his arm. "Frankie, c'mon."

Frankie shook off his buddy. "No. She'll have Leo strung up for his own murder somehow—just watch her."

Nick materialized next to Annalisa. "The forensic team is here," he murmured to her. "You can go inside with them if you want and I'll handle this."

"No. You go with forensics. I'll talk to them." These were Leo's partners. When Nick had been attacked, when he was in the ICU and they didn't know whether he would live or die, Annalisa had felt responsible. She'd wanted to find the person who did it and put him through a wall. She saw those same emotions echoed in the tight set of Frankie's jaw and his companion's wet blue eyes. "Which one of you is Leo Hammond's partner?" she called out as she stepped forward.

Frankie's chin rose. "Twenty-six years," he replied, thumping his heart with a fist. "We were riding together when you were still in grammar school."

Not quite true, but she let the remark slide. "Then I want to start with you."

"For what? So's you can lock me up too?"

"Why? You done something I should know about?" She met his gaze and held it.

A news van rolled up with a satellite attached to the roof, and Zimmer gave an audible sigh. "Film at eleven," she muttered. To Annalisa, she said, "You're okay here?"

"We're fine," Annalisa replied evenly, still watching Frankie and his buddy, daring them to contradict her. Zimmer went to meet the arriving reporters and Annalisa walked forward until she was directly in front of Frankie Vaughn and held up her shield. "It's the same tin you've got, and mine gets me a ticket to this show. You want to know who killed Leo. So do I. We're on the same team here. If you help me, I can help you."

"I don't need your kind of help," Frankie returned.

"Fine." She turned to leave. "Make sure you stand behind the yellow tape, then."

"Wait." The other guy called out to her, and Annalisa turned back. He cast a pleading look at Frankie. "Let's just talk to her, okay? Find out what happened to Leo."

Frankie sucked in his lips, not yielding. The taller, thinner guy took off his black beanie hat and glanced at the house. "We heard he'd been shot. Is that true?"

"Yes." She eyed him. "You are?"

"Paul Monk. I worked with Frankie and Leo."

The Fantastic Four, she recalled. That left one of them unaccounted for. "There's another one of you," she said as her brain tried to find the name. "Osborne?"

Frankie drew up short and looked at her with some surprise that she'd heard of them. "Tom, yeah. He's out on disability right now."

"What happened to him?" she asked.

"He got shot."

"What?" She looked toward the house, imagining another bloody crime scene, and Frankie followed her thoughts.

"Not like that," he said. "Two months ago, Tom was driving home after his shift and he caught some punk kid breaking into a car. The kid ran off, and Tom went after him. But the kid doubled back through an alley and got the jump on him. Shot him in the hip."

"Youch." Annalisa grimaced in sympathetic pain. "Tough break. Did you catch the guy?"

"Not yet. But we will." He eyed her. "Hurts like a sonofabitch, doesn't it? Getting shot." His gaze slid over her body in a probing fashion, like he could see through her to the scar underneath.

Annalisa pushed on without comment. "Look, you can fight me on this case if you want. You can scream and make a scene and call me whatever names you feel like. But my commander over there? She doesn't take shit from anyone. You give her trouble, and she'll have you cuffed and put in the back of a squad car for all those cameras to see. Then she'll freeze you out and you won't hear squat about the case."

Frankie looked to Zimmer as he measured Annalisa's words. The news van had been joined by two others. It was blowing up. "Gonna be a hot one," he noted to no one in particular. "Just the kind of case Leo would've loved."

"I'm sorry about your partner. No one deserves to go out like that."

A tendon in Frankie's neck bulged and his voice got tight. "It's a bad scene, right? Christ, I don't want to think of it."

"He didn't seem to suffer, if that's what you're asking."

Monk scuffed at the snow with the toe of his boot. "We just saw him a few hours ago and everything was fine. It doesn't seem possible he's gone."

"Tell me about today," Annalisa said. "What was he working on? Where did he go? Who did he talk to?"

Frankie took a deep breath. "It was just a normal day, you know? Routine stuff. We got a lead that some jewelry stolen in a burglary before Christmas had surfaced in a pawnshop, so we went there to check it out. The homeowner eventually ID'd the stuff as his, so we started looking for the asswipe who pawned it. Turns out he'd skipped out on his last job as a line cook and disappeared. We looked for him at his girlfriend's place and his mother's but no luck."

"I saw him near the end of shift," Monk added. "We got a coffee and bitched about getting older. The doc says I've got a bad vertebra from too much sitting. Like, how do you even hurt yourself sitting at a desk?" He touched his back for emphasis. "Leo's doc told him to cut out the egg and cheese sandwiches or he'll have to start cholesterol medication. Guess he won't have to worry about that now."

"How was his mood?" Annalisa asked.

Monk shrugged. "It was Friday, near end of shift. He was as happy as it gets."

"Did he mention his plans for tonight?"

"Just said he was going home to the wife." Monk glanced up at the house. "She's okay, right?"

"Seems to be."

"So, what was it, then?" Frankie asked. "Some asshole broke in to rob the place and Leo confronted them?"

"We're not sure yet."

"Come on, you've got to know something. We're cooperating, right? So play ball with us."

"I'm not stonewalling you," she replied. "We can't tell yet if anything's missing from the house. What can you tell me about Kayla Hammond? What was Leo's marriage like?"

"Kayla." Monk grinned once and shook his head. "She won the Miss Teen Illinois pageant, you know."

"Like yesterday," Frankie added drily.

"So she's young," said Annalisa. "What else?"

"What else?" said Frankie. "She's also hot. I mean, you must've talked to her. Everyone loved to watch her run the bases at the annual department family softball game." He pantomimed sliding into home while Monk chuckled.

"I see. And did the boys also line up to watch the first Mrs. Hammond play?"

"Maura was okay, I guess," Frankie said. "She always brought a killer fruit salad. Used to cut out pineapple stars and shit like that. A real Martha Stewart."

Who was also divorced, Annalisa recalled. "Why'd they split?" she asked. "Maura and Leo." Monk and Frankie exchanged a look, not wanting to say. Annalisa blew out a frustrated breath. "I'm going to find out one way or another. You want me to waste time digging around or you want to help me out here?"

"They split when Kayla came into the picture," Frankie said at length.

"And when was that?"

"I dunno. Maybe three years ago?"

"Almost four," Monk broke in. "Kayla was a witness in a murder we were working on. My wife gives me shit about it all the time now. We worked a bank robbery last week and I had to interview the tellers. My wife was all, 'Shopping for a sidepiece, Paulie? Maybe Miss Universe was there depositing her enormous check.'"

"Okay, so they hooked up four years ago. Still going strong?"

"They had their moments," Frankie said. "Kayla liked to go out and party, Leo liked to stay home and watch sports. He was pushing fifty and she must've known what she was getting when she said I do. But no one was filing for divorce, if that's what you mean. After what he went through with Maura, Leo wanted this relationship to stick." He blanched and looked at Monk. "Hey, you remember what he always said? He joked that the only way anyone was leaving this marriage was in a body bag." He started tearing up again and muttered another curse. Monk put a hand on his shoulder.

Annalisa cleared her throat. "Anything else? Anyone at all you can think of who might have wanted to get to Leo?"

Frankie pursed his lips in thought. Monk shifted his feet, plainly feeling the cold. "We've busted over three hundred murderers," Frankie said, squinting at her. "Twice that many dealers, hookers, pimps, con men, and bangers. You could make a line of folks from here to Topeka who might have wanted to take a shot at Leo or any one of us."

"I'm thinking Leo specifically."

Monk nudged him. "There was that guy."

"What guy?" Annalisa perked up.

"The one from the tiki bar," Monk said. "Remember?"

"Oh yeah," Frankie said, frowning as he remembered. "Him. Moe Bocks."

"Wait," said Annalisa. "The car guy?" She'd grown up listening to the jingles for the used car lots. *Save more bucks with Moe Bocks.*

"That's the one. Or more to the point, his son. Moe Bocks, Jr. Leo had a run-in with him about a month ago. He and the missus were out at the bar, enjoying their evening, when Leo spotted Moe across the room with his own lady friend. I guess they were looking pretty cozy, and so Leo went over there to warn her."

"Warn her of what?"

"That she's dating a murderer."

"It was before your time," Monk told her. "About twenty years ago now. Leo took a call one night, a welfare check from some hysterical woman who couldn't raise her friend. Turns out she was right to be worried because the friend was dead inside her apartment, garroted and left on her bedroom floor. No sign of forced entry, so we figured she knew the guy."

"And Moe did it?"

"Moe Junior. Leo thought so, yeah. Moe had been dating the girl and she broke it off with him. I guess he wasn't too happy about it. But there was nothing anyone could ever prove. No DNA, no prints. Someone at the scene reported seeing a white van on the street outside her apartment the night she got killed, but Moe drove a Jetta."

"His father's car lot might have a van, though," Annalisa said, thinking of the rows of vehicles.

Frankie looked disgusted. "You think Leo didn't think of that? He searched the lots himself—no van. Also, the kid's mom alibied him. Said he was home all night with her. Between that and the generous checks that Moe Senior wrote every year to the policemen's association fund . . ."

"The case got dropped."

"You're quicker than you look," said Frankie wryly. "Anyway, I guess Leo ran into the guy at the tiki bar a couple of weeks ago. He started snapping pictures of Moe and his date with his phone, saying they would be evidence for when he decided to strangle this new girl, and Moe got furious. He took a swing at Leo and Leo put him on the floor."

"I'll look into it," Annalisa said. "Thanks."

Frankie answered with a short nod and he looked at Leo's house. "When you find the guy who did this, I want five minutes alone with him. Five little minutes. I'll even leave my piece at home."

"You know I can't do that."

Frankie stared at her. "Then I suggest you find him before I do."

"Vega!" Nick called to her from the front steps. "I need to talk to you." Annalisa nodded her goodbye to Frankie Vaughn and Paul Monk before making her way back up to the house.

"What's up?"

"Come with me."

She paused to put on fresh gloves and booties. Nick led her back upstairs to the bedroom where Leo Hammond still lay, mostly nude and festering on the bed. She averted her eyes. "What is it?"

"See the pillows? Look closer at the high-velocity spatter." He indicated the fine mist of tiny blood drops that emanated from the body. Annalisa stepped to the bed and leaned down for a better look. The blood droplets landed not only on Leo's side but on Kayla's as well. There weren't as many of them, but the visible ones fell in an even pattern across her white pillowcase.

"She wasn't in the bed," Annalisa said as she straightened. If Kayla had been sleeping next to her husband as described, the blood droplets would have hit her instead.

"There's more." Nick beckoned her into the bathroom. "See the baseboard down near the vanity? More blood."

Annalisa crouched and saw a small smear. "Whose?"

"Don't know yet. The techs are going to run the sample. But I have a theory."

She stood up and put a hand on her hip. "Go ahead, then. Impress me."

"I was thinking about that ice pack Kayla had with her in the kitchen. When we walked in, she had it on her head. But why? What did she need it for?" He crossed back into the bedroom as he spoke. "Look at this." He took Leo's limp arm and raised it up so she could see the hand.

"Bruised knuckles." Heat prickled over her neck. If Leo had been beating Kayla, the murder took on a whole new ugly dimension.

"I have a possible inkling of what they could have been fighting about." He reached over to the women's suit jacket that hung over the back of the vanity chair. With one gloved hand, he plucked a rectangular piece of plastic out of the right-side pocket.

"Hotel key."

"Look at the name. Pendry Chicago."

"What's a married lady with a huge house like this need a hotel room in town for?" Annalisa nodded as she caught on to what he was suggesting. "Bag it as evidence."

....

She left the bathroom and her gaze fell on the cell phone sitting on Leo's side of the bed. It was covered in glass from the broken photograph frame and plugged into a wall charger. ***He snapped photos of the guy,*** Frankie had said. Annalisa turned to Nick and indicated the phone. "Has this side of the room been documented yet?"

"Yeah, they did the whole thing. Why?"

Annalisa extracted the phone and examined it. An older model, the phone required Leo's fingerprint to activate it. She hesitated only a moment before taking the dead man's hand and using it to unlock his phone. She found the photos and swiped past pictures of Kayla, a young man who resembled Leo and might be his son, a random bulldog, a pitcher of beer, a set of bowling scores, and a bunch of pictures from Christmas.

"What are you looking for?" Nick asked.

She found one that looked like what Frankie had described. A low-lit bar with dried grass fringe for décor, and a couple sitting together in a booth. She opened the picture and zoomed in on the faces. The man was angry, his mouth twisted in fury. The woman looked shocked. Annalisa gasped and fumbled the phone, which clattered onto the beautiful, refinished hardwood floor.

The woman in the photo was Sassy. The man was the guy with the flowers she'd seen going into Sassy's house.

CHAPTER FIVE

THE DASHBOARD THERMOMETER READ SEVENTEEN DEGREES WHEN ANNALISA PULLED TO A STOP OUTSIDE SASSY'S HOUSE. The rising sun was a mere hint of light on the horizon, a distant glow that suggested the winter temperatures weren't likely to improve much over the course of the day. She pulled out her lip balm and applied it to her perpetually chapped lips, stalling for time. It felt more like zero as she opened the door into the bitter wind. She took two steps before her boot grazed a dead rat on the sidewalk. The creature lay paws up, frozen stiff, a look of surprise on its pointy rodent face. Rats didn't usually come out in January, but maybe this one had been trapped in the elements, confused and unable to find its way home. ***Should've stayed underground,*** she thought as she stepped around it.

She pressed the doorbell and looked around as she waited for Sassy to appear. No sign of the Lexus, so either Moe Bocks, Jr. hadn't stayed the night or he was already gone. Through the door, she heard a child screeching and Sassy's voice, already shrill at 7 a.m. "I said go find your bathing suit!" Sassy yanked open the door and regarded Annalisa with surprise. "Anna, what's up?"

Annalisa spoke instead to her two-year-old niece, who was clutching Sassy's leg and whimpering. The girl had on a Cinderella T-shirt, a diaper, and no pants. "Hey there, Gigi. Love your princess shirt."

Gigi, normally delighted to see her, buried her face in Sassy's leg. "Want more O's."

"You've had two bowls of Cheerios already. Come on, let's get dressed." Sassy backed up so she could widen the door to admit Annalisa, dragging the child with her. "Did you leave something here last night?"

"Not exactly."

"Then what?"

Alex and Sassy's older daughter, Carla, came charging into the kitchen at full speed and launched herself at Annalisa. "Auntie Anna! I have a swimming lesson. Are you going to come watch?"

"Don't you need a suit for swimming?" Annalisa asked her as she tickled her belly. Carla wore a child-sized feathered boa, a black T-shirt on inside out, and a pink tutu. She was also wearing makeup—a thick smear of lipstick around her mouth and enough purple eye shadow to make her look like a cartoon raccoon.

Sassy noticed the same time Annalisa did. "Carla Marie Vega. Did you get into my makeup again?"

"No." Carla batted her thick charcoal-gray lashes, Alex's greatest beauty, and lied through her pearly little teeth.

Annalisa swiped one finger over the purple streak running down on Carla's cheek and showed her niece the result. "You've been busted, kid."

Carla placed two soft hands on Annalisa's face and looked deep into her eyes. "Auntie Anna, you're my best friend, right?"

"For always." Annalisa rubbed noses with her, not caring about the purple that might get transferred in the process.

"So then you know. Aren't I old enough to have my own makeup?"

"No. Sorry."

Carla scowled and wriggled out of her arms down onto the floor. "You're no fair at all." She stomped out of the room as Sassy yelled after her to wash her face, and for Pete's sake, put on the bathing suit.

"Want! More! O's!" Gigi started stamping her feet, her small face turning pink then red as she worked herself into a tsunami of toddler rage.

"You can have apple slices if you want," Sassy offered as she started throwing things in a backpack: packets of cheddar crackers, wet wipes, fresh diapers. "Hand me that water bottle, would you?" she asked Annalisa.

"Don't wanna apples." Gigi fell into a puddle of sorrow on the floor, sobbing as though her heart were broken. Annalisa glanced at her harried friend. Would it kill her to give the kid a few more Cheerios? She'd already lost her father. Annalisa scooped up Gigi and patted her back. Gigi's sobs grew muffled as she clutched Annalisa for dear life, quieting under her soothing touch.

"I'm sorry," Sassy said, still assessing the kitchen for anything that belonged in her to-go bag. "What is it you need? As you can see, we're in pandemonium around here right now."

"I need to talk to you." Annalisa paused to gather herself. "About Moe Bocks."

Sassy froze but didn't turn around. "What about him?"

"Are you seeing him?"

Sassy did face her then, arms folded over her chest in defensive fashion. "So what if I am? I'm single now. I can see who I want."

"You didn't tell me."

Sassy shrugged and looked at the floor. "Yeah, well, there's not a lot to tell. He came into the library a few months ago with a research question and we got to talking. He asked me out for coffee and Maria said she'd watch the girls . . ."

"My mother's involved with this?"

Sassy's head snapped up. "Involved? She did a couple hours of babysitting while I had a cup of coffee. You make it seem like some big thing."

"It is big. You're serving him coffee here at home. With the girls around."

Sassy's mouth fell open. "How—are you spying on me?"

"I saw him come in last night after I left."

"And then what? You immediately ran down to the station to do a background check on him? God, Annalisa." She extended her arms, trying to take Gigi back, but the toddler, sensing a shift in power, shrieked and tightened her hold on Annalisa's neck.

Annalisa swayed with the little girl, keeping her tone as neutral as she could. "He's bad news, Sassy. The man is a murder suspect."

"Was a murder suspect."

"Is. The case is still open."

Sassy grabbed a dish towel and started wiping down the counter. "He was questioned and cleared. He had an alibi."

"Yeah, his mother," Annalisa said with a snort.

Sassy halted her cleaning and widened her eyes at Annalisa. "You really did run him through the computers. You're a piece of work, you know that? Is that why you still have yesterday's clothes on? You spent all night investigating my date."

Annalisa looked down at the red blouse and black trousers visible behind the armful of toddler. She hadn't been home yet and wouldn't be for at least a few more hours. She was due to meet Nick at Maura Hammond's home at nine. "This isn't about me. It's about Moe Bocks and Josie Blanchard. That was her name, by the way—the girl Moe strangled to death after she told him she wanted to stop seeing him."

"Watch it. Do you have to talk like that in front of my kids?" Sassy did grab Gigi back this time.

"O's?" Gigi said, her small voice full of hope.

"Sure, fine," Sassy replied, defeated. She set her daughter down and got her a cup full of Cheerios, after which Gigi ran giddily from the room, tiny bare feet slapping in victory on the hardwood. Sassy watched her go, shaking her head sadly. "I feel sad for you," she said to Annalisa without looking at her. "You used to be kind and open. Now you distrust everyone. And for what? What does it get you? More 'atta-girls' from your boss? Another pin for your uniform? You know, when I go to your parents' place for Sunday dinner, they always set a plate for you at the table. No one talks about it. It just sits there empty. But you should see the way your mom watches the door with the hope you might be walking through it."

Annalisa squeezed her eyes shut. She'd grown up around that table, eating Ma's pork roast, potatoes, and Jell-O salads, with the ever-present pot of meatballs bubbling on the stove, no matter what else was on the menu. Vinnie and Tony arguing over who got to eat the last roll. Pops leaning back in his chair, trying to see the football scores in the den, and Ma slapping him with her napkin. Alex telling jokes a mile a minute until Pops hollered at him to shut up and eat already. They'd had those dinners every week without fail, both before and after Katie Duffy died, eating the same huge plates of food and squabbling over whose turn it was to do the dishes. At some point, it had become a lie. Or maybe it always was. "I don't think it matters much," she told Sassy, "whether I'm there or not."

"Suit yourself. You always do."

"And you be careful," Anna said, deliberately keeping her voice down so the girls wouldn't hear. "Please think about this thing with Bocks. There are a million guys in the city. Surely you can find one who hasn't been accused of murder."

"You're the only one accusing him!"

"He was a suspect. A strong suspect. Josie knew the guy who killed her."

"Enough. I don't want to hear it anymore. You've said your piece, okay? You think I'm stupid enough to divorce one guy in jail for murder and then take up with another killer. That's what you think. I'm just a sucker for a man with murder in his heart."

"No." Annalisa looked her over with sympathy. "I think you see the good in people, always. I love that about you." She paused, hesitating before the next part. "And maybe you see the broken parts too. Maybe you think you can fix them."

"Maybe." Sassy gave her a hard stare. "It would explain some things about us."

Annalisa felt herself go hot under Sassy's rebuke. "It's not just about the old murder. Bocks attacked a cop, and you know it's true because you saw it happen. You were there."

"Are you talking about that jackass from the tiki bar? He was drunk. He kept harassing us, snapping pictures and calling Moe names. Moe asked him several times to leave us alone but he wouldn't. When he tried to drag me out of the booth, then yeah, Moe got up and defended me. I was scared out of my mind, all right—by the guy with the badge. Don't believe me? Ask the waiter. He gave a statement for the complaint Moe filed against that cop."

"He filed a complaint against Leo Hammond?"

"Hammond, yeah. That was his name." Sassy seemed mollified now that the blame had shifted. "You want to talk dangerous? Go look at him. I can't believe that man is allowed to carry a gun."

"Not anymore."

"What do you mean?"

"Leo Hammond was murdered last night."

Sassy blinked rapidly in surprise. "What? Where?"

"Never mind that," Annalisa said. "What time did Moe leave here?"

"Oh, I get it now." Sassy's face grew hard again. "That's why you're here. Of course. It's not about me or the girls. It's about getting your man. Always on duty, right, Anna?"

"Just answer my question. When did he leave?"

Carla reappeared in the doorway wearing a pink-and-white-striped bathing suit, her black patent leather church shoes, and her mother's sunglasses. "I'm ready for my lesson," she said, striking a pose. "But I won't put my face underwater."

The fight drained out of Sassy as she looked at her daughter. "He left around midnight," she said quietly. "Why? When was . . . when was the thing that happened to Leo Hammond?"

Annalisa wished she didn't have to answer, wished she had another answer to give. She looked at Sassy with enormous sympathy. "Not till three."

CHAPTER SIX

Annalisa arrived early to meet Nick at Maura Hammond's home in Jefferson Park. The first Mrs. Hammond hadn't landed too far away when she'd left the family homestead, opting for a brick bungalow inside one of Chicago's havens for county workers like cops, firefighters, teachers, and other municipal staff. Indeed, Maura Hammond herself worked in the Loop downtown in the Cook County Clerk's office. The cozy row of homes, tucked under a blanket of snow, reminded Annalisa of her neighborhood. A pair of pink-cheeked boys in bulky snowsuits staggered around a nearby yard, trying to form a snowman. A guy jogged by in the street with a thick-coated Siberian husky trotting at his heels. The animal's tongue lagged out sideways through his grinning mouth—finally someone happy about the frigid winter weather.

Annalisa startled when her car door opened and a burst of cold air rushed in. Nick took over her passenger seat without asking, but he handed her a steaming paper cup of coffee. "Thought you might need this."

"Thanks," she said, meaning it. Her stomach gave a feeble rumble as the rich toasted scent of dark roast coffee hit her nose.

"These too."

"Oh God," she said when she saw him produce a bag from Stan's Donuts. She grabbed it and peered inside. "If there's a peanut butter pocket one in here, it might be love."

"Jelly," he replied, sounding dismayed. "I thought you liked them."

"I do." She took one out and bit off nearly half of it in a single famished chomp. Her eyes rolled back in her head as the sweet strawberry spread across her tongue. Nick took the bag from her lap and fished out the matching donut.

"How did it go with Sassy?" he asked.

"I don't want to talk about it." She licked a bit of jelly from her thumb.

"That good, eh?"

"Apparently I see murderers everywhere I go."

He considered a moment. "I guess that comes with the job."

"The job," Annalisa repeated darkly. "She didn't have a lot of kind words for it either."

"Well, try to see things from her perspective."

"What makes you think I haven't? I go over there every chance I've got. I've given her money, groceries . . . I watch the girls so she can get her hair done. Nothing I do is ever enough."

"To make it up to her, you mean." He sipped his coffee.

"I didn't murder anyone. I don't have anything to apologize for."

"Hey, you don't have to convince me."

She glanced at him. "What would you have done? If it was your family, I mean."

"Your family was my family."

"Yeah, for about twenty minutes." She made an annoyed face at him. "I'm just saying, if you were in my position, would you have turned them in?"

"Yes." He didn't have to think about it. He shifted in his seat so he could look her right in the eyes. "After my dad killed my mom, I got sent to live with my grandma. Her place was quiet and she liked it that way, so I made myself quiet too. If she kicked me out, there was nowhere else for me to go. So I did everything I could to follow her rules, and then the second I turned eighteen, I got the hell out of there. I came up here, and a few years down the line, I met you." He stopped to smile at her. "I met you and your crazy, loud family—always yelling over one another, joking around. I remember that Christmas, it was like twenty degrees outside, but the door was always open, people coming in and out, music blaring, tissue paper and bows everywhere like some gift shop exploded in the living room. I loved it. We stayed till way past midnight because I didn't want to leave."

"I remember." They'd crawled into bed at their apartment in the matching pj's Ma gave them and slept like spoons.

"What I'm saying is . . . I know what you gave up." He grabbed her hand and squeezed it. "I know better than anyone. Still, you made the right call."

She blinked back sudden tears. "Thanks," she replied with effort, sniffing back emotion. When she tried to break contact, he held fast.

"About last night," he began, and she pulled back sharply.

"Don't."

"Don't what? Admit it happened? Because it did and it was pretty great."

That part of their relationship always was. She shook her head, denying it anyway. "Not now."

"We have to talk about it sometime, Vega."

"Not while we're on a case." The clock on her dash said it was five till nine, and they were due inside with Maura Hammond soon.

"We're always on a case," he said with affectionate exasperation. "We finish one and Zimmer immediately gives us another. But okay. I'll back your play . . . for now."

She took a final swallow of coffee and wiped her hands and mouth with a paper napkin. "Do you see what I see?" she asked as they got out of the car.

"Yep. Three cars in the driveway. Maura's brought in reinforcements."

Nick proved prescient when the door opened and Maura Hammond did not appear on the other side. They were greeted by a young man, maybe in his early twenties, tall with broad shoulders and Leo Hammond's big hands. This had to be his son. "I'm Brian," he said as they showed off their identification and he let them inside. "My mom is expecting you."

They found Maura in the den, looking for all the world like she was the rightful widow. She was dressed in black and her face looked haggard, like she hadn't slept in days. A young woman sat with her on the sofa, holding her hand and patting it. They had a box of tissues between them. Brian reappeared with a cup of tea and placed it on the table to Maura's right. Maura raised a watery blue gaze to Annalisa and

Nick. "So, you're the cops," she said as she looked them over critically. "Funny, I don't recognize you."

"We didn't work with your husband, ma'am," Annalisa said. She introduced herself and Nick. "We're very sorry about your loss."

"Yeah?" Maura replied with a weary sigh. "I've been sorry about him for years." She nodded at the young woman to her left. "This is Nicole, our daughter. You met Brian already. That handsome devil over there is Luke, Nicole's husband—he's in law school, by the way, in case you're thinking of trying any funny business."

From the armchair by the windows, Luke gave an uncomfortable grimace. "I still think you should have an actual attorney here with you, Maura."

She waved him off. "So I can get hit with another two-hundred-dollar-an-hour bill? And for what, telling me to keep my mouth shut? I already know everything about cops and how they operate. Leo was good for that, at least." She looked from Annalisa to Nick and back again. "Besides, I've got nothing to hide."

A sheepish, sandy-haired guy in a rugby shirt waved from the doorway. "Do you want any tea, Detectives?" he asked them. "There's water on."

"That's Caleb, Brian's roommate," Maura informed them. "Good kid. Makes a strong pot of tea if you want some."

"No, thank you." Annalisa remained bemused by the crowd who had gathered to prop up Maura. Brian and Nicole had lost a father, but their energy seemed to be directed at soothing their mother. No wonder each of them had brought along their own support person. Nicole grabbed a tissue and dabbed at her eyes surreptitiously before balling the tissue into her fist away from Maura. "I can't believe Daddy's gone," she said to no one in particular. "And murdered in his own bed? How does that even happen?"

"It's awful," Maura agreed, but Annalisa noticed her eyes were dry. She also noted the family seemed to have details of the crime. They must not be entirely cut off from the police grapevine.

"When was the last time you saw Leo?" Annalisa asked Maura.

Maura squinted at the ceiling, making a show of remembering. "I glimpsed him in the car when he dropped Brian off here at Christmas. We didn't wave."

"I see. And when did you last speak to him?"

"Not in months. Once he took up with that floozy, the lawyers did most of the talking."

"What about screaming?" Annalisa asked, and Maura's eyebrows rose up to disappear beneath her chestnut-brown bangs. "I understand you visited his house a few months ago and the conversation got loud."

"Oh, I know exactly who told you that little story. Yeah, I had some words with him. And some words for her too. She wants a baby with him, did you know that? A baby! He was pushing fifty years old and he's got two grown kids already. What does he need with a baby? But then one day, Brian tells me Leo's planning on having his vasectomy reversed so he can give her what she wants. Like my house—my life—wasn't enough for her!"

"Mom," Nicole said, "maybe take a deep breath. Have some tea. You're getting worked up again."

"Shh, honey, I know it was embarrassing for you, but you don't have to cover for him anymore. He was screwing someone your age and then he wants to procreate with her too?"

"Mom," Nicole repeated in a voice that said *you're the one embarrassing me*. "Stop it." To Annalisa, she gave a small shrug of apology. "My dad made her crazy, but there's no way she'd kill him."

"I didn't ask if she did," Annalisa pointed out.

"No, but that's why you're here, isn't it?" Brian, the son, stepped forward with a challenging stance. "I bet Kayla sent you."

"She's still breathing," Maura interjected. "That's how you know it wasn't me."

"Mom!" Nicole stood up and put her hands on her hips. "Do you want them to arrest you?"

"They can't! There's no evidence I did anything. You know why? Because I didn't." She peered around her daughter to look at Annalisa. "Look, I murdered that bastard a hundred times in my sleep, but I never would have laid a finger on him in real life. I'm a vegetarian."

Annalisa looked to Nick, nonplussed. "Do you own a gun?" Nick asked Maura casually.

Maura hesitated for the first time. "For protection, yeah. It's registered and legal and I have my FOID card. I didn't use it to shoot my ex-husband, if that's what you're asking."

"Can we see it?" asked Annalisa. Leo Hammond's gun was the presumed murder weapon at this point but Annalisa was curious if Maura's gun was a similar model, and if so, did she know how to use it?

Maura didn't reply right away. She reached over and picked up her teacup, sipping and thinking. "Two weeks after I left Leo, I was driving home from the grocery store when a cruiser pulled me over. The officer says I ran the light a few blocks back and he's going to have to write me a ticket. I said no way I ran the light. It was yellow when I went through it. He says he saw me plain as day, and he wrote me up."

"And?"

Her mouth thinned into a grim line. "Not too long after that, I was driving home late from my mother's place. The roads were pretty empty that time of night. All of a sudden, someone's right on my tailpipe, flashing his high beams in my mirrors. He's riding me, practically running me off the road. I'm digging around in my purse with one hand, trying to get my cell phone to call 911 while still keeping ahead of this A-hole. I just get my fingers around the phone when the blue lights come on. It's a cop. He pulls me over and I recognize it's one of the guys from Leo's division. I ask him what's the problem and he says my taillight is out. I know it's not, because I was running the car to warm it up before leaving my mom's place. I could see the taillights from the house. The cop insists I'm wrong, but he's creeping me out and we're pulled over outside this abandoned building, right? No witnesses. I'm not about to get out of the car to check. So I say sure, write me up. I figure I'll fight it later in court. He hands me the citation and as he's leaving, I hear a crack and a smashing sound at the back of my car. He broke the light."

"Did you get his name?" Annalisa asked.

"Yeah, Sergeant Dickhead," Maura replied. "No, I didn't get his name, because he wasn't wearing a tag. Funny how that works, huh? Must've left it in his car."

"But did you report it?" Nick wanted to know.

Maura pinned him with a look. "Report it to who, exactly? Leo? Leo's boss?"

"You could have made a complaint to COPA," Annalisa said, naming the civilian agency tasked with investigating complaints against the Chicago PD.

"Sure," Maura said bitterly. "Then maybe it's not just my taillight. Maybe it's my whole car that ends up broken. Or maybe worse. Maybe I have an accident myself."

Nicole moved back to her mother's side, putting an arm around her. "Dad wouldn't have let them hurt you, Mom. I know it."

"You're saying you believe your ex-husband used his fellow officers in a campaign of harassment?" Annalisa asked Maura. "That's a serious charge."

"The thin blue line," Maura replied. "It cuts pretty deep when you're on the other side. Leo wanted me to let him keep the house. He wasn't taking no for an answer, if you get my meaning. Little Miss Perky Tits wanted it, and he was willing to do whatever it took to make her happy."

"You gave in," Annalisa surmised.

"We signed the papers and suddenly I could drive through town without being stopped again." She looked to Brian. "Show her the gun. She'll see I haven't touched the thing in years."

Brian escorted Annalisa to the back bedroom where his mother slept and opened her closet door. On the top shelf he located a storage box and handed it to Annalisa. "It should be in there."

She removed the lid to find a Taurus snub-nosed revolver. As Maura had said, it appeared untouched for some time. "Your parents' breakup sounds kind of stormy," she said to Brian as she examined the weapon.

He gave a dark chuckle. "That's one way of putting it."

"What about while they were married?" She wondered about the bruises on Leo's knuckles and whether he got them knocking Kayla around. Chances were good he hadn't started with her, if it were true.

Brian shrugged, looking uncomfortable. "It was okay most of the time. Dad worked a lot. Mom was our constant. But he was good to us when he was here—barbecues on the weekend, trips down to the lake. Mom never let us have the extras, you know? When we went with her, it was sandwiches from home and thermoses of water. Dad bought us hot dogs, cans of pop, balloons, and ice cream. He took us on some really rad vacations like Disney World and Hawaii. Made my friends pretty jealous. Like in high school, sometimes he'd come down to the basement when I had the guys over and he'd slip us a six-pack. 'Don't tell your mom,' he'd say. My buddies would try to get him to stay with us and tell cop stories." Brian smiled sadly. "I think that's why he did it. Brought the beer, I mean. He loved to be the life of the party."

"Until he took the party somewhere else."

"Yeah." Brian averted his gaze.

"Must've been hard on you and your sister when he left."

Brian gave a noncommittal shrug. "Nicole and I were already out of the house when Dad met Kayla. The worst was right before the split when Mom was calling up, crying about what piece of evidence she'd found this time. But Nicole got more of that than me."

"What about when the fights got ugly?"

"Like I said, I wasn't really here." He leaned against the closet door, feigning disinterest.

"I see. But they exchanged nasty words. Did it ever get worse than that?"

"I don't know what you mean."

"Did anyone get hurt? Physically."

Brian paled and started squirming. "I think I should be getting back to my mom. You've seen the gun now."

"Brian, I'm not trying to pry, but—"

"What do you care?" He cut her off with sudden vehemence. "We know how it works because Dad told us over and over. Cops on one side, everyone else on the other, right? He was one of you."

"Are you saying your father hurt your mother? Hurt you?" She ducked her head to try to meet his gaze but he turned away, refusing her. "Brian, talk to me."

Tears leaked out and down one side of his face, and he swiped them away with an angry jab. "I was ten. Nicole was fourteen. Dad came home drunk and angry, and my mom laid into him about spending his paycheck at the bar with his friends. He'd bought a big-screen TV and it wasn't even paid off yet, so she was on him about that. It wasn't that weird to have them shouting at each other. We usually just put on earphones or went down to the basement where we couldn't hear them. But this time, there was a crash and then . . ."

"And then?"

"A gunshot." His throat bobbed as he swallowed. "I swear to God, we thought he'd killed her."

"What did you do?"

"Nicole called 911 and they said help would be coming. Downstairs, we heard yelling again so we knew then she was alive. But we were still scared because what if she was hurt? We were too terrified to go down and check." He looked at her. "Some kids, right? We didn't even try to defend our mom."

"You called for help."

He chuffed. "Help. Right. Yeah, about ten minutes later, a car rolled up and guess who was on the scene? Some of Dad's best buddies—Vaughn and Osborne. They calmed Mom down by telling her they would pay to have the TV replaced. They told me and Nic that it was just a big misunderstanding. They said sometimes passionate adult relationships like my parents' got a little out of control and that we would learn this when we were older. I'll tell you what we learned: not to bother calling the cops for help."

Caleb appeared behind them, clearing his throat to get their attention. "Brian, your mom wants to see you. Something about a class ring that your dad would've wanted you to have."

Brian left and Annalisa replaced the gun on the closet shelf in its spot between a folded blanket and two chunky photo albums. After a pause to consider, she pulled down the top album. She was flipping through the pages when Nick appeared. "What have you got?"

"The gun wasn't touched—but then again, Leo's service revolver is apparently the weapon. Maura likely would have known his habits and where he kept it. Brian confirmed Leo had been violent with the family in the past. What about you?"

"Not much. Maura has no alibi for last night. She says she was home sleeping in that bed right there all night, alone. Like she's been alone ever since Leo walked out on her."

Annalisa regarded the photos that backed up Brian's story about happier times. Leo and the kids at the beach with crazy balloon hats.

Nicole and Brian posed with Mickey Mouse. Nicole and Maura wearing leis and learning to hula in what was presumably Hawaii. "Wait a minute," she said as Nick turned to leave. "Look at this."

It was a picture from Hawaii of all four Hammonds on a boat—in diving gear.

CHAPTER SEVEN

FRANKIE PAUSED IN THE PROCESS OF PUTTING ON HIS CLEAN WHITE SHIRT. Maggie May had ironed it for him, bless her heart, even though he told her the boys were just meeting at Sully's for a pint. A drink in Leo's honor. "It's a wake, what you're describing," Maggie had said to him as she'd plucked the shirt from his hands. "You want to look your best. What if Leo himself is looking down on you?"

"Leo would want me to wear number twenty-three," Frankie had grumped in reply. Leo Hammond had come of age worshipping Michael Jordan, even took his kids to Bulls games when they were small to try to convert them, but by then MJ was a Wizard and the magic was gone.

Frankie went to the full-length mirror that Maggie kept in the corner of their bedroom and studied himself in his sleeveless undershirt. Normally he didn't use the mirror. The small rectangle in the bathroom worked fine for him; just enough to make sure he got a clean shave. Now he brought his shoulder in close to the glass and frowned at the small indentation in his flesh, his own personal crater. He remembered his surprise as the bullet hit him. No pain at first, only shock. Nobody was supposed to get hurt. He touched the old wound and wondered about Leo and whether he'd seen it coming, if he'd known this was the end. The thought of his buddy lying there bleeding out made Frankie's eyes well up and he muttered a curse as he furiously blinked back tears.

Don't be a pussy, he ordered himself. *Pull it together and get down to Sully's. You've got to warn the others about Vega.* He'd made some calls today to try to ascertain what he could about the direction of Leo's case, and the news that came back wasn't good.

He eased his dress shirt over his shoulder and buttoned up with nimble fingers. Maggie appeared in the bedroom with his red silk tie. "Mags, no. This ain't a funeral." That would be coming soon enough, he knew. For a decorated officer like Leo, the department better pull out the full twenty-one guns. Everyone in dress uniform, ready to salute. He and Paulie and Tom could carry Leo with them one last time. He hoped like hell Vega or whoever caught the shooter before then, because otherwise talk of the killer would overshadow everything.

Maggie made a fretful noise as she set the tie down on the bed. "I wish you didn't have to go out. It gets dark so early these days."

"I'm just going down to Sully's like usual. No trouble." He took her in his arms and kissed her forehead. She smelled like Ivory soap and cotton, clean and fresh as the day he'd married her. Only when he pulled back could he see signs of age: the fine lines around her blue eyes, the softening of her cheeks, her thinning lips, and the guarded, worried expression she trained on him. Maggie May was no innocent girl anymore.

"This thing with Leo has me rattled," she admitted, and he hugged her closer.

"I know. It's terrible."

"You think you'd be safe in your own home."

He kissed her again and smiled the reassuring way that crinkled his eyes. "You are. I promise. You have Pepper to keep you safe." At the sound of her name, their eight-year-old corgi zipped into the room with her ears up and rear end waggling, ready for adventure.

"Ha," Maggie said as she pushed him away with a playful shove. "We both know she only has eyes for you. I feed her, brush her, walk her—and she lives for the minute when you walk through that door. It's like the kids all over again."

Frankie grinned and reached down to scratch Pepper under her furry chin. "She knows I love my girls."

"And the biscuits you keep in your pockets."

He pulled one out and waved it at Maggie. "It's yours if you want it, dear." She made a face and snatched it from his hand so she could be the one to give the treat to the dog. Pepper gobbled it up and pivoted once more to Frankie, eyes shining. "Not this time, baby," he told her. "I'll be back before bedtime."

"You better," Maggie said. "You know we don't sleep well when you're gone. Tell the boys hi from me."

"I will." He went out the back door to the alley behind the house where the detached garage held his Land Rover. As he pulled around he could see Maggie's silhouette in the window, watching for him. Like she had some power to keep him safe by maintaining her vigilance. He put the radio on and cranked the first grunge tune he could find. When did Nirvana start playing on the classics station? He mentally rehearsed what he would say to Paulie and Tom. ***Don't freak out but . . .***

Despite the cold air, he started sweating on his way into Sully's. The bar itself was packed and jumping, teeming with guys from Central Division. Tom and Paulie already had a booth in the rear, but it took Frankie more than fifteen minutes to get there, what with everyone slapping him on the back and offering sympathy about Leo. Tough break. What a way to go. Thought he was gonna outlive us all. Frankie made small talk and accepted the pint of beer someone pressed into his hand. When at last he reached the booth, he sank down like he'd just run the Chicago marathon. "Jesus, the whole precinct's out tonight. Who's minding the station?"

"People are wigged," Paulie said. "Can you blame 'em?"

"He didn't get shot on the job. Not like Mr. Disability over there," Frankie said, nodding at Tom. "Thinks he's still twenty-five. Thinks he's Usain Bolt, trying to run down a punk car thief all on his own."

"Hey, watch yourself. I'm coming back soon. Doc says my leg healed up like new."

"Yeah?" Frankie was skeptical.

"Yeah, and he also said it could kick your ass any day of the week." He blew a kiss in Frankie's direction and cracked up at his own humor. Frankie rewarded him with a smile but he felt cold on the inside.

"Glad you can make jokes." Paulie was shredding brown paper

napkins into a pile in front of him. "Someone pumped Leo full of lead last night and we're not allowed anywhere near the case."

"If Leo were here, he'd be busting on us, same as usual," Tom said, and Frankie knew it to be true. He raised his glass.

"To Leo," he said, and the other two scrambled for their half-drunk beers.

"To Leo," they echoed.

Frankie waited while everyone took a drink. Then he drew in a long breath. "Listen, I've got to tell you guys something. It's nothing to worry about . . . yet. But you should be aware in case someone comes around asking."

"What is it?" Paulie asked, his shaggy brows drooping in concern.

"I talked to my friend over at COPA. He tells me that the chick they have working Leo's case, Annalisa Vega, she's pulled Leo's records."

"You mean about the complaint that car guy filed? Moe Bocks."

"No, I mean she asked for all of it." He paused meaningfully. "Every complaint in his file since the dawn of time."

Paulie froze for a moment and then licked his lips. "Do they even keep records back that far? COPA didn't even exist until a few years ago."

"Hey, maybe we get lucky and they don't have much to show her. All's I know is that she asked for everything, not just the thing with Bocks. I told Paulie she was bad news."

"But Leo was killed in his own bed," Tom said. "We all know who did it." Frankie and Paulie looked to him and he held out his palms. "Kayla, right? If I'm working this case, she's got my bet. For one thing, she was actually there when it happened. For another, what about the money?"

"What money?" Paulie asked, confused.

"You didn't know?" He gestured down to his leg. "After my little incident, Kayla had Leo increase his life insurance. Now she gets at least a million bucks."

Frankie leaned over the table. "Yeah, yeah. That's good. We have to make sure Vega knows about that. Make sure her attention stays focused where it belongs."

"Sure. Between Kayla and that sicko pervert Moe Bocks, they've got plenty to keep Vega busy." Tom nodded at him. "What are you so worried about, anyway?"

"Christ, Tommy, do you not read the papers? Do you not follow the news? This chick turned in her own damn father and brother for something that happened more than twenty years ago. If she gets ahold of something, she's not letting go. We don't need her digging around in our business."

Tom took up his beer and swallowed a long sip. He looked at Frankie coolly. "No, I mean why are you so worried? You weren't even there."

Frankie felt the bullet hole in his shoulder start to burn. "What the fuck are you talking about?"

"I mean you weren't there in the restroom when she died!" Tom banged the table and Paulie jumped.

"Keep it down, will ya?" Frankie forced his face into a broad smile like Tom had said something funny. "I'm in this deep as you, deep as ever. We rise and fall together just like always."

Tom turned his head toward the wall. Paulie drained his beer and let out an involuntary belch. Shit, thought Frankie. The nerves were already starting. Leo wasn't here anymore to rally the crew, so it fell on Frankie to do it. He adopted a more relaxed posture, modeling for the others.

"Listen, we've just got to keep cool about this, okay? Stick to the narrative we gave back when it happened. Don't give Vega any loose threads to yank on, and we'll all be fine. How about I buy the next round? Order whatever you want because after this, I'm out. This thing with Leo has Maggie spooked and she wants me back home early."

Paulie grinned and nudged him under the table. "Gonna role-play the big brave policeman for her?"

"Hey, who's playing?" Frankie looked around for the waitress.

"What about Leo's wife?" Tom had not relaxed one bit. If anything, he looked wound tighter than ever, his face flushed like the top of his head might pop off. "What if she's not playing?"

"You mean what if she offed him," Paulie supplied.

"No, I mean what if she knows? Maura did."

Frankie's spine stiffened like a rod. "Maura knew what?"

"She knew where the money came from. Why do you think she got so much in the divorce?"

Frankie considered this, shifted uncomfortably in the booth. The hardwood bench felt like a raw plank all of a sudden. "Maura doesn't know anything that matters," he reasoned. "If she had, she'd have put the screws to Leo a long time ago."

"He was her kids' dad," Tom argued. "She was happy to take him to the cleaners financially, but she's not out to destroy him. But Kayla . . ." He sat back and gave an exaggerated shrug. "She's a wild card. Especially now. If she actually killed Leo and Vega can prove it, Kayla's going to be looking to make a deal. Who knows what she'll say?"

Frankie scowled, angry at Tom for arguing and at himself for not seeing this possible wrinkle. "Kayla doesn't know anything. She was a toddler back then."

"She still is," Paulie quipped, making fun, but Frankie saw the sweat coating his upper lip.

"Okay, so we find out what Kayla knows," Frankie said. "I'm sure it's nothing."

"And if it's not?" Tom pressed. "This thing with Vega could become a real problem."

Frankie caught the waitress's eye and raised his hand to signal her. "Then we take care of it. Same as always."

CHAPTER EIGHT

....

THE STATION AROUND HER HAD GROWN QUIETER AND DARKER AS ANNALISA'S COLLEAGUES FILTERED OUT. The graveyard shift would be coming on at midnight, which was only twenty-five minutes away. Nick had left hours ago with copies of the reports on Leo Hammond and his Fantastic Four buddies tucked under his arm. He'd asked her if she wanted to grab dinner, and she hadn't even glanced up as she declined.

He'd lingered for a moment, like a teenage boy at her locker, before loping off into the night with a shake of his head. He didn't understand what it was like to be a woman on this job. If word got out they'd slept together, he'd get congratulatory high fives and she'd get leering invitations. The boys in blue would literally hang a sign on her that said OPEN FOR BUSINESS. The only way to combat this was to do business—to be business—all the time.

She rooted around in her desk drawer until she found a small bottle of ibuprofen, which she washed down with the cold coffee sitting at her elbow, and then she reapplied her lip balm. She made a disgusted face as the mint flavor mingled with the coffee aftertaste. The precinct heating system had just two settings, off and Sahara Desert, so she had to continually moisturize inside and out or risk turning into a raisin at her desk. On her screen was every bit of information she could find about the murder of Josephine "Josie" Blanchard back in 1998. Because Josie's death occurred outside her jurisdiction, Annalisa did not have direct access to the case file or its investigators. The case was listed as open and the current assigned investigator was Tom Osborne, the one Fantastic Four member whom she had yet to meet. Since the murder took place before everything news-related went online, a regular internet search turned up relatively little information. However, she did have access to a database of the print stories that ran at the time, and she discovered why the murder had received less attention than it might otherwise have. For one thing, Josie Blanchard was not a US citizen. She was from France and staying in the States on a student visa to study pharmacy at the University of Chicago. This meant there was no family present to advocate for Josie's case, no one to keep it in the headlines. Furthermore, Josie died the same week that two little boys, ages seven and eight, were charged with the murder of a fifth-grade girl. The boys had beaten her to death with rocks in order to steal her bicycle. By contrast, a woman strangled to death in her apartment was a pedestrian crime.

"Working hard," a voice behind her said.

Annalisa turned in her chair to see Frankie Vaughn standing there, still dressed for the outdoors. "Detective Vaughn," she said, leaning back. "Can I help you?"

"I came to help you." He grabbed the rolling chair from Kolcheck's desk and took a seat next to her, frowning when he saw her screen. "What're you digging around in the Blanchard case for? I thought you were working Leo's murder."

"I am." She clicked off the screen. "You were the one who said Leo had a beef with Moe Bocks."

"Moe, yeah. Right. Definitely." His leather jacket squeaked as he leaned forward. "Confidentially, what do you think of Kayla for the crime?"

"She was there when it happened. She's automatically a person of interest. Why?"

"Well, I was just remembering how Leo said he'd increased his life insurance recently."

"How recently?"

"Like in the past few weeks, after Tom got hurt. Leo said it was Kayla's idea to up his life insurance on account of his job was so dangerous. She's due to collect a million bucks now."

"I see," Annalisa said, making a note of it. "Thanks for the tip."

Vaughn made no move to leave. "Like I said, I'm trying to be helpful."

He'd mentioned this virtuous intention twice now, when in fact his presence already said as much, meaning he was giving her a line for some reason. But why? He should want his buddy's murderer caught even more than she did. Maybe he was like the others, out to yank her chain. Steer her in the wrong direction and then watch her fall flat on her face. "Anything else?" she asked him.

"What else should there be?"

"Anyone else who might've had it in for Leo." She paused. "I checked his file and he was hardly Mr. Popularity out there. He's got twice the usual number of civilian complaints—excessive force, bribery, abuse of authority."

"He's got twice the commendations too. You can't believe that COPA bullshit. Come on, you know none of these assholes enjoys getting busted. Of course, they're going to whine about 'unfair treatment' to anyone who'll listen. Anything to get the charges dropped. None of those complaints against Leo was ever substantiated, so if you're thinking of starting some smear campaign—"

"I'm not starting anything. I'm investigating, and I'll follow wherever the leads take me."

He stood up so he loomed over her, his shadow on her desk. "Leo was a good cop. He was my brother. I would've died for him, and him for me. Maybe you don't have a partner like that. Maybe you don't know how it is. But I'm going to make sure his killer gets what's coming to them because Leo would've done the same if it was him standing here."

"You said you wanted to help me. You can help by staying out of my way."

"Yeah, I'll do that." He chuckled without humor and rapped his knuckles on her computer monitor. "And darlin', you be sure to stay out of mine."

When he'd gone, Annalisa switched the screen back on and began reading more on the Blanchard case, taking note of everyone quoted in the stories. Josie was well liked. Her advisor at the university, Tobias Flanders, said she was a top student with a bright future. "Josie performed well on exams and papers, but that's expected at the graduate level. What set her apart was her curiosity and empathy. She went into pharmacy to help people, not dispense pills. For example, the study we're running on simplifying cardiac regimens among elderly patients involves taking interviews with them, visiting their homes, and learning their routines. They don't get many visitors and some would keep her there for hours talking, but Josie didn't mind. Last week, I found her writing out a sympathy card because one of our patients lost their pet cat to cancer. I don't remember the animal's name, but Josie would. That connection, that humanity . . . these are qualities you can't teach."

A married couple living in the apartment downstairs from Josie, Stephanie and Alvin Cooper, had not been home at the time of the attack, but they reported Josie had a lot of male visitors, including Moe Bocks. They had seen his Jetta parked on the street outside a bunch of times, although not recently in the days before the murder. In fact, Josie hadn't seemed to be home much at all.

A comment from Daisy Chavez, Josie's friend in the pharmacy program, suggested why: "Josie was being harassed. Stalked, I mean. She was getting lots of hang-ups at her place and she said she felt like someone was following her a few times. I asked her who it was and she said it was probably her ex-boyfriend. She asked to stay at my place one night just to get a break."

The most recent ex was Moe Bocks, who had an alibi: his mother. He was living at home with his parents in Winnetka at the time of Josie's murder. Annalisa performed a records check and found Linda Bocks was apparently still alive and living in the same house. She also checked on the availability of the one witness who did see a van on the street the night of Josie's murder. Vivian Catalano had no current address listed. She was a long shot to add any new evidence at this late date, but Annalisa wrote her name down too.

Annalisa found articles praising Moe Bocks for keeping his father's free "Bocks Lunch" program for needy schoolchildren. She unearthed a photo of him with a glitzy-looking date from the mayor's ball three years ago. Moe had waxed his bald head and smiled big for the camera, a sequined red bow tie around his thick neck. More troubling, Annalisa's image search had turned up Moe's profile on a dating site, and it was listed as active. So much for his big romance with Sassy.

"That's not Leo Hammond," said Zimmer's voice from behind Annalisa, making her jump. Her commander appeared dressed in jeans, boots, and a red pullover sweater. "And you're not supposed to be here," Zimmer added, checking her watch. Normally, Annalisa found it amusing and adorable that her boss still wore a watch—analog, no less—but not when she'd been caught working unapproved overtime.

"You work graveyard?" Annalisa answered, ignoring the larger point. "Since when?"

"Since the hot flashes are keeping me up at night," Zimmer said drily as she dragged the rolling chair from Nick's empty desk and took a seat next to Annalisa. "I'll tell you what else has got me up nights—the deputy chief riding my ass about the Hammond case. Where are we and what can I tell him to keep him happy for at least six hours?"

"No arrest is imminent, if that's what you're asking. Kayla Hammond is our best lead, and she's lawyered up."

"Not such a dumb blonde, that one." Zimmer nodded at the screen. "So who's he?"

Annalisa explained about Moe Bocks and his run-in with Leo Hammond at the tiki bar. "Bocks did file a complaint against Hammond for harassment and assault," Annalisa reported. "COPA was investigating. Get this: they have a bunch of files on Hammond and his buddies. I had them pull the whole lot going back twenty years." She indicated the thick stack of folders on her desk.

Zimmer let out a low whistle. "There used to be a saying: you've got to break heads to break cases, and some cops lived it like a personal creed. These days with cell phones and cameras everywhere, you're more likely to end up on the wrong end of a lawsuit."

"Funny you should mention that. There was a lawsuit about twenty years ago. Leo Hammond, Tom Osborne, Paul Monk, and Frankie Vaughn responded to a robbery in progress at a nightclub called the Bass Lounge. Only they shot the owner, Cecil Barry. I gather they confused him with the robbers, who had already fled the scene. Barry was armed and returned fire when the cops started shooting at him. Frankie Vaughn was injured in the exchange, Barry was DOA when the medics showed up."

"Wait, so who sued?" Zimmer asked.

"Cecil Barry's wife, Roxanne. She was at the club when it went down, hiding in the back with one of the other managers. The city eventually settled with her for a half million dollars."

Zimmer shook her head and sat back in her chair. "That's the kind of mistake that eats at you, shooting the wrong man like that. I'm surprised Hammond and the rest of them stayed on."

"Yeah, well, like you said: some people have a taste for breaking heads."

"And we're thinking what? One of those heads might be Kayla Hammond's? And she shot him because he beat her?"

Annalisa shrugged one shoulder. "Wouldn't be the first time."

"Okay, so we sweat Kayla, then," Zimmer said. "What've we got on her?"

Annalisa ticked off the facts on her fingers. "She was there when it happened. Her prints are on the weapon. Leo got violent with the first Mrs. Hammond so it's probable he did the same to Kayla. The paramedics treated her for a head injury at the scene but she won't say what it's from, and forensics found a smear of her blood in the bathroom. Not to mention, there's no sign anyone actually crawled into the open window in the Hammonds' basement."

Zimmer snorted. "And she's got that horseshit story about the diving suit."

"Right." Annalisa hesitated a beat, glancing away, and Zimmer caught it.

"What?"

"It's just such a crazy thing to make up. Why a diving suit?"

Zimmer rocked in her chair as she considered a moment. "Hypothetically? It would be a great way to keep your DNA from the scene. No hair, no fibers, no skin cells. But you just got done saying no one broke into the Hammond place."

"Not through that basement window. Maybe there's another way in."

"That would mean the killer took the time to make us think he came through the basement window, at a crime scene with a living witness and a rapidly cooling corpse. Why?"

"I can't answer that yet."

"Maybe that's your answer. It doesn't make sense, so it didn't happen."

"Maybe." Annalisa's gaze returned to her screen and Moe Bocks's smiling face. They hadn't been able to determine how the killer got into Josie Blanchard's place either. The police found it locked and decided she must have let the guy in.

Zimmer looked to Nick's empty desk. "You're burning the midnight oil all by your lonesome, I see."

"Nick took files home to read."

"And what? You just love these cheap-ass plastic chairs?" Zimmer grabbed the armrests for emphasis.

"I've just been busy working. Lost track of time."

Zimmer watched her for a moment and then scooted her chair closer. "Look, I understand why this old murder might be getting to you. A young woman strangled to death in her own home, the murder unsolved more than twenty years later. There's more than a passing similarity to the Duffy case here, and I can see you getting that old itch."

"That's not what this is about."

"No, it's about Leo Hammond and who killed him. I know you feel for this girl—what's her name, Josie? But she's not your case. Kayla Hammond is your best suspect right now, so that's where your attention should be."

"It is," Annalisa assured her.

Zimmer waited a beat, holding Annalisa's gaze like she was trying to be convinced. "Good," she said eventually. "Listen, while I have you, I wanted to ask you about that post that is opening up in the new Area Four. They are looking for a seasoned squad, and word on the street is that they would be especially receptive to female candidates. You, ah, might enjoy a change of venue."

Vaguely, Annalisa recalled Zimmer mentioning the reorganization that would result in the creation of two new districts from the existing three. More investigators and less drive time to the scenes. "Not interested," she said, weary at the thought of starting all over somewhere new, especially when her reputation preceded her. At least here, she could find the coffee machine. She forced a smile for her boss. "I hate change."

"Well, change may be coming for you whether you like it or not," Zimmer replied as she hoisted herself out of the chair. "Carelli already put his name in the hat."

"Is that right?" Annalisa glanced at Nick's shadowed desk, suddenly feeling the lack of his presence. He hadn't said a word to her about a transfer. Zimmer was still watching her so Annalisa shook herself loose from her thoughts. "Good for him, I guess. He'd be great at it."

"Yes, he would. Now, you go home and get some sleep. That's an order."

"Yes, ma'am." Annalisa made a show of turning off her monitor. She put on her coat and watched Zimmer out of the corner of her eye, waiting until the commander disappeared into her own office. When she was out of Zimmer's sight, Annalisa powered on her monitor and scrolled down to double-check that she'd seen what she thought she'd glimpsed on Moe's dating profile. Yes, there it was. Hobbies include cooking, watching 1950s screwball comedies, running 5Ks, and deep-sea diving.

....

Annalisa did not follow Zimmer's orders to go home. Instead she drove to Logan Square, where Josie Blanchard had lived at the time of her murder. Annalisa located the old house on North Sawyer Avenue. It had been converted into upstairs/downstairs units some time ago, and Josie had lived in the upstairs flat. Annalisa found an open spot among the line of cars parked along the street and got out to walk down the block to Josie's former place. It sat in total darkness. The whole street was black and quiet.

Annalisa assessed the scene. The front doors looked original to the house, strong and sturdy. The windows appeared modern and might have been replaced more recently. She noted that Josie's upstairs unit came with a small balcony at the front. It was too high to reach from the ground without a ladder, but . . . Annalisa turned on the sidewalk and regarded the large oak tree behind her. Its sturdy branches stretched out over the small front yard in what probably offered lovely shade in the hot summer. Presently, the naked branches created creepy bobbing shadows over the pale front of the white house. She wondered if it would be possible to shimmy up the tree and use the largest branch to drop down onto the balcony.

She found a slight bulge in the trunk, just big enough to act as a foothold, and started to climb. She made it up past the first story with no problem and paused in the main Y of the branches to test their weight. The big one didn't budge, no matter how hard she shook it. When she inched outward, it easily held her weight. She didn't dare go all the way out to the edge and lower herself onto the balcony—there would be no way to get down and she'd be arrested for trespassing—but it seemed feasible. Sitting there above everything, she noticed another curious fact: her silver car looked white under the streetlamps. Maybe Vivian Catalano had been wrong about the color of the van she saw outside the apartment that night. It might have been silver rather than white.

Annalisa eased backward in the tree, preparing to dismount, when a flash of movement caught her eye. There was someone sitting in one of the parked cars approximately twenty yards away. She saw a shadowy figure in the driver's seat but couldn't make out a face. Then again, she didn't have to see him, because she recognized the plate number on the black Lexus. It was Moe Bocks.

CHAPTER NINE

ANNALISA LEAPT FROM THE TREE, HER ANKLES CRACKING AS HER BOOTS HIT THE CEMENT SIDEWALK. She approached his car with her hand at her holster and used the other to hold her shield up to the driver's-side window. "Get out," she ordered. "Now."

Bocks held up his palms and tried to maneuver the door open with his knee. When this failed to work, he used one hand to ease open the door, forcing her to back up. "Detective Vega, I presume," he said in a friendly tone as he got out of the car. "I'm Morris Bocks, but I'm guessing you already knew that. Most people call me Moe. I'm betting you know that too, seeing how you're a famous detective and all."

"What are you doing here? Are you following me?" She kept her hand by her gun, scrutinizing him for any sign of a weapon. He didn't appear to be carrying, but the leather jacket he wore made it difficult to be certain.

"I was here first," he said reasonably, his breath fogging in the chilly winter air. "Perhaps you're following me."

"Why would I be following you?"

He gave an expansive shrug. "Cecilia mentioned you'd taken an issue with the pair of us seeing each other. You're a cop. Cops sometimes follow me around."

Annalisa's irritation flared at the use of Sassy's given name, Cecilia. No one who loved her called her that. "Why are you loitering out here past midnight?"

He looked around at the trees and closely set houses. "Loitering? I was just sitting in my car, which is legally parked. As is yours, I see. A 2016 Camry SE with the V6 engine, which is more horsepower than standard and capable of doing zero to sixty in six seconds." He tilted his head at her. "You like to get places fast, Detective."

"You never know when you might need to catch a bad guy," she replied evenly. "I'll ask you again: What are you doing here outside Josie Blanchard's old place?"

He looked past her to the house itself, his expression turning pensive. "The same thing you are, I suppose—looking for answers. I come here sometimes to do that. It's the last place I saw her. We spent so many days and nights here, she and I. We fixed clams casino together in the galley kitchen. We made love by the fire. She taught me how to make crepes and I showed her how to change a tire." He paused and looked Annalisa in the eyes. "Josie kept insisting it wasn't necessary, because she didn't own a car. I told her, 'Someday, you will.'"

"She broke up with you."

"Yes, I think I remember."

"Must have been hard to take, after you'd invested so much in the relationship. I heard you'd wanted to marry her."

He inclined his head slightly in acknowledgment. "I was twenty-five. I wanted many foolish things back then. Josie and I weren't meant to be, and she saw that sooner than I did. She was smart—two years older than me and a world traveler. I could tell she was going places and I wanted her to take me along."

"You were living with your parents," Annalisa recalled.

He gave a wry grin. "Literally in their basement, if you can believe it. My father somehow convinced me it was a cool bachelor pad because it had its own separate entrance. Josie was the one who made me see the truth when I took her home to meet the folks. I can still remember her picking up the afghan from my bed and asking if my mommy made it for me. She hadn't, but it didn't matter. My parents had bought the furniture, the bedding, the rug on the floor, and the paint on the walls."

"Josie was your ticket out." Annalisa glanced at the house. "She had her own place."

"Filled with secondhand chairs and recycled rugs from tag sales and the like. Bohemian, my mother called it. She meant it as an insult, but when I told Josie what she'd said, Josie laughed and clapped. She said a bohemian lives a life of art and adventure and that's not something you can buy from a store." His expression turned dreamy, lost in memory. "She was so alive she made me come alive just being around her. I felt like I'd been sleepwalking until then, going to the same restaurants, wearing the same clothes, doing everything that was expected of me because that's what I'd always done. Of course, I'd been to the Art Institute a bunch of times. It's amazing. But Josie took me around to look at murals on the buildings, stuff I'd walked past but never really seen before. A bird two stories tall. Butterflies and sea monsters and faces from Chicago's past. I don't know if you've ever had that . . . that kind of awakening. And then to be so suddenly cut off."

Annalisa shifted as a cold wind blew past them. After Katie Duffy got killed, her son Colin had left to live with relatives. *I'll write to you every day,* he'd insisted as Annalisa clung to him, both of them crying outside her house while the taxi waited to take him away. *I love you, Mona Lisa.* He hadn't written once. Answered none of her letters. It had felt like someone dropped her in the middle of a concrete maze with ten-foot walls. "You got dumped," she told Bocks. "It happens to pretty much everyone."

"Not to me," he said, and the abrupt edge in his voice sent a chill through her. He must have noticed her stiffen because he softened his posture. "Not until then. Yes, I was angry. I said things to her I regret. Things I can never take back . . ." He turned a searching gaze to the house and its environs. "I come here sometimes because it's the only place I can think to go. This is the last place Josie existed. The answers to what happened to her, they must be here."

"Leo Hammond thought he knew the answer," she said, and his mouth tightened at the sound of Leo's name.

"He was wrong."

"I saw the case file," she lied. "You were the number one suspect in Josie's murder. You still are."

"Then you cops are never going to solve it. Because it wasn't me."

"You were furious at her. You were stalking her."

"No," he insisted with a vehement shake of his head. "Not stalking. I never stalked her. I called, maybe too many times, trying to get her to talk to me, and I drove by sometimes to see if her light was on, but I didn't follow her and I didn't stalk her."

She remembered after Colin left, finding reasons to walk past his house. Even before that, when she'd felt him pulling away, she watched his place from her bedroom window to see who was going inside. Colin had always attracted female attention but never more so than in the weeks after his mother's murder. Cindy McPherson had baked him an apple pie all by herself. "You wanted to see what Josie was up to—who she was spending time with and where she went. Maybe you parked on the street like you are now, watching the house."

"No, I—" He regarded her warily. "I didn't do anything wrong."

"You saw she wasn't home. She didn't come home all night." The news reports indicated Josie had been staying with various people before her murder. One of them, a bartender named David Barker, admitted he'd been sleeping with her. It was casual, he'd said. The police cleared him when he had proof he'd been working the night Josie was murdered. "She'd dumped you and moved on immediately to someone else. You wanted to marry her and she wanted nothing to do with you."

"That's not how it was."

"The person who killed her meant to do it," Annalisa said steadily. "It wasn't some accident in the heat of the moment. The garrote around her neck was homemade and the killer brought it with them."

He shoved his hands in his pockets. "You think I don't know that? The police tore my basement apart looking for proof I made it. If you've read the reports, you know what they found: nothing."

"Do you own a wet suit?" she asked, changing tactics.

His face contorted in confusion. "What's that got to do with anything?"

"Humor me."

"Yes, I own diving gear, but it's been ages now since I've used it. Why?"

"Where were you on Friday night?"

"Ah," he said, his dark eyes glinting as he caught her logic. "This is about that cop. Leo Hammond. I saw on the news that someone killed him."

"That's not an answer."

"I was at work at our main dealership until closing, and then I went to Cecilia's. I believe you saw me there." He paused but she did not confirm or deny. "I left her house sometime after midnight, and from there, I went home."

"Alone."

"Well, I have an orange tabby cat, Buffy, but I doubt she'll vouch for me." He eyed her. "Mother always told me dogs were more loyal." When she didn't smile or otherwise react, he exhaled with a huff. "I'm not a killer, Detective Vega. Not then and not now."

"You hanging around an old crime scene isn't exactly convincing me."

He held up his hands. "You got me! I'm guilty—of nostalgia."

The wind picked up again, stirring her hair. She clawed it back from her face. "I want you to stay away from Sassy."

"I like Cecilia and she likes me. I believe she's able to make her own decisions."

"Her name is Sassy."

"Really? That's not what it says on her name tag at work. It's not how she introduces herself either." He squinted at her. "Maybe you don't know her as well as you thought."

"I'm warning you to back off. Sassy doesn't need any more problems right now."

"Then I suggest you don't create any." The edge was back in his voice. By the time she had a chance to register his words as a threat, he'd already relaxed back into a broad smile. "We can be friends, Annalisa, if you'll just let it happen."

"I have enough friends."

"Oh? I don't see anyone around." He stared straight at her for a long moment and she felt how alone they were on the dark street, not thirty yards from where another woman had died.

"Yes, well, it's late, and I think you should be moving on now," she said, her tone one of warning. "Consider it a message from a friend."

He held up his palms in surrender. "I'm going. Oh, but before I do, maybe you'd like to know I wasn't the only one sitting parked out here back then, before Josie died."

"What do you mean?"

"I drove by here one night to check on her and found she was at home and entertaining. The car parked outside on the street belonged to her academic supervisor, Toby Flanders."

"How do you know that?"

He grinned. "The vanity plate. It read PHARMD, as in doctor of pharmacy. Toby was newly separated from his wife at the time and he definitely had a thing for Josie."

"He told you this?" Annalisa was skeptical.

"No, she did at one point. I thought she didn't return his interest but maybe I was wrong. Like I said, I believed a lot of foolish things back then."

There had been nothing in any of the reports to suggest an improper relationship between Josie and her advisor. "You should have told Leo Hammond or the other investigators this information at the time."

"I did. No one seemed to find it interesting. Not even when I said someone had slashed up my tires when I was visiting Josie on the university campus. No, Leo Hammond and his friends remained quite focused on me to the detriment of any other avenue of pursuit. But I hear you like cold cases." A beat, while he let the barb sink in. "Maybe you can run with it."

"Sure," she said. "I'll look into it—as long as you agree to stay away from Sassy."

His forehead wrinkled in reply. He took a long time with his answer. "I'm not twenty-five anymore. I know what I want, and I don't let anyone stand in my way. Especially not emotionally unbalanced cops. I've had enough of them to last a lifetime."

"That sounds like it might be a threat."

He laughed lightly as he moved to get back in his car. "I don't make threats. I have my lawyers do it for me. You can ask Leo Hammond about that." He halted and snapped his fingers as if remembering. "Oh, wait. You can't. More's the pity."

"Listen," she began, but he cut her off with a sudden lunge in her direction.

"No, you listen. The cops tried to wreck my life once over this. I'll be damned if I let you mouth-breathers with a badge railroad me a second time. You back off and leave me alone or I will make you regret it."

She held his stare. "So much for being friends."

He pulled back, amused again. "Ah well. I have others. You? Maybe not so much. Good night, Detective Vega."

CHAPTER TEN

Annalisa jerked awake to the sound of her cell phone, which was lying next to her on the sofa. Bright sunshine streamed in through her windows, alerting her to the fact that she'd overslept. Suppressing a curse, she answered Nick's call. "You ready?" he said. "I'm outside and I've got coffee."

They were supposed to go interview Tom Osborne today. "Uh, yeah. I'll be right out." She stumbled into the hall, trying to shuck her pants and walk at the same time. In the bedroom, she grabbed the first clean suit she laid hands on and struggled into it while using one hand to comb her hair. She paused in the bathroom to brush her teeth, holding the brush in her mouth as she twisted her hair into its usual knot. Sloppy, but it would have to do. She snapped on her holster and gun, grabbed her phone, and ran for the front door.

Nick chuckled when he saw her emerge. "Running a little late this morning, are we?" He was leaning against his car, some kind of flower in his hand.

Her heart pounded crazily in her chest from her mad dash to get ready. "Hmm?"

He touched his mouth to signal her and she realized she still had the toothbrush sticking out of it. She rolled her eyes and ducked back into her condo. When she returned, Nick stood on her stoop with a paper napkin, which he offered to her. "Figured you might need this."

"Thanks," she said before wiping her mouth. She nodded at the single red rose in his hand. "What's that?"

"This? It's for you." He handed it to her.

"Nick—"

"I found it here half-frozen. See?"

She noticed ice crystals on the petals.

"You got some action going I should know about, Vega?"

"No. It's not for me. Someone must have the wrong house or just tossed it when they didn't want it anymore." She did the same, finding the nearest public trash bin and sending the rose inside.

"That's cold," he told her as he returned to the driver's side of his car. "Where's your sense of romance?"

"You just saw it in action. Now, where's the coffee?"

"I got them in the car fully loaded. We'll need it for our trip to Chicagoland. How did Osborne score a place out in Winnetka, anyway? You're supposed to live in the city limits."

Growing up, Annalisa had imagined Chicagoland to be like Disneyland, a magical place with rides and candy, only closer to home and therefore more attainable. Someplace Ma and Pops might actually take her. Tony, her second-oldest brother, had set her straight with a sneer when she'd dared mention her dream out loud. ***Chicagoland is where you live, doofus. You're already there.*** She'd learned as she'd grown that Tony was right and not quite right at the same time. Chicagoland didn't have a specific border but was generally accepted to encompass both the city and its surrounding suburbs, including those in Wisconsin and Indiana. But inside Chicago was where it was at, with the rest of the pretenders hanging on. No one called it ***Winnetkaland.***

"Listen, do you mind if we take a detour first?"

He looked sideways at her as he started the engine. "You want to pick up breakfast or something?"

"I want to talk to Toby Flanders."

"Who?"

"He was Josie Blanchard's academic advisor at the time of her death. He lives in Rogers Park so it's not that far out of our way."

Nick said nothing, nor did he change course.

"It would only take a half hour," she said, cajoling. "Plus we could grab a sausage and egg sandwich from that café you like."

"It's not the timing I'm worried about." He glanced at her. "It's you. Josie Blanchard isn't your case."

"It isn't anyone's case. You think Tom Osborne is working it? You think Leo was? She was murdered, Nick. He strangled her to death and left her decaying like a piece of trash on the floor. She let him inside, probably thinking he was a nuisance, thinking she could find the right words to make him go away, and instead, he attacked her the moment her back was turned. She never saw it coming. She never had a chance. He just took the scarf and choked her and choked her until she stopped moving."

"Took the wire, you mean."

"What?"

"You said scarf. Josie Blanchard was strangled with a wire."

"Right, wire. Of course." She grimaced at her mistake, her face flaming. It was Katie who'd been strangled with a scarf. She looked away from him, out the window at the passing scenery. They drove in silence for a few miles, but she glanced over in surprise when he signaled to exit at Touhy Ave. "You agree? We're going to see Flanders?"

"I didn't say I agreed. But I figure you're pursuing this with or without me."

Satisfied now, Annalisa gave him the address and checked her phone to review what she knew about Toby Flanders. His driver's license photo showed a pale, pudgy man in a gray sweater vest. He was listed at five foot seven, sixty-eight years old, and he had a fluffy ring of gray curls around the top of his otherwise bald head. He'd smiled for the picture even though the DMV always told you not to and the twinkle in his eye said he knew he'd get away with it. Unlike Moe Bocks, who was born into an auto empire, Flanders was a blue-collar baby who'd played the long game, working his way through school, up and up, until he never had to leave the ivory tower. He was a tenured professor, now a dean, and the head of the most successful pharmaceutical research group on campus. Annalisa tried to imagine Flanders as Josie would have seen him: a mentor, a boss, someone with the power to shape her career. You had to be nice to these men, Annalisa knew, whether you liked them or not.

"He looks kind of like my uncle Stuart," Nick said, leaning over to peer at the picture. "Remember him? He came to the wedding."

"The one who gave us the matching plaid house slippers?"

"'Happy feet, happy life,'" Nick quoted from the card. He looked sideways at her. "Did you ever wear them?"

"No. You?"

He shook his head as he rolled the car to a stop. "This is the place." The trilevel house was made of brick and limestone, with massive floor-to-ceiling windows across the front of every story. The price tag probably started at two million. They got out and Nick stomped his boot on one of the large pavers in front of the garage. "I think this thing is heated. He's got a heated driveway. Can you imagine?"

"He's in pharma, and drugs pay," she replied as she headed for the door. "Doesn't matter whether it's South Side or North Side."

Toby Flanders himself greeted them at the door with a blank but pleasant expression. He wore a pristine white apron and house slippers on his feet. Uncle Stuart would have been ecstatic. "Yes?" he said.

Annalisa displayed her ID. "I'm Detective Vega, and this is Detective Carelli. Do you mind if we come in to chat with you for a few minutes? It won't take much time."

"Chat about what?"

"Josie Blanchard," Annalisa said, and his face instantly turned contrite.

"Of course," he said without hesitation as he widened the enormous door. "Please come in. I've got beef vegetable soup on if you're hungry."

It smelled amazing and she inhaled deeply, feeling the absence of her mother's cooking. Annalisa looked at her gritty boots on the clean white marble tile. "Should we remove our shoes?"

"Don't worry about it," he said breezily. "Come this way to the kitchen." They followed him to a gourmet kitchen with sleek black cabinets and brilliant white countertops. A large pot bubbled on the six-burner stove and Flanders paused to stir it with a wooden spoon. "Nothing like hot soup on a cold day," he observed with a smile. "Please, take a seat and make yourselves comfortable. Can I get you any coffee? Water? Scotch on the rocks?"

"We're fine, thanks," Nick said as he pulled out a chrome-and-leather stool. Annalisa took off her coat and did the same.

Toby looked into the pot again. “It’s been years since anyone came to see me about Josie. They say on TV that murder cases are never closed until they’re solved, but it’s been so long that I didn’t think anyone was actually pursuing it anymore. Does this mean you have a new lead?” He turned to give them a hopeful look.

“Just lots of old ones,” Annalisa replied.

His scruffy gray eyebrows knit together in concern. “Then you should be talking to Moe Bocks.”

“We have,” she assured him. “Did you know Moe at all?”

“Josie brought him around a bunch at first, so I knew him some. He struck me as gregarious and charming but a bit aimless. He had a degree in business but he wasn’t using it. Once, Josie had to give an interdepartmental research presentation that was well received, so the lab went out as a group to celebrate her success and she asked Moe along. He sat so close in the booth he was practically in her lap. But he was funny—almost like a clown. He told us this story about a woman who bought a car from their family and then called up to complain that it wouldn’t run at night, only during the day. This made no mechanical sense, so his father actually went to her house to find out what was going on, and it turns out she put the car in *D* during the day and *N* at night.”

“No way,” Nick said, grinning broadly.

Flanders made a “there you go” gesture at him. “Funny, right? He had a dozen stories like that, so he was amusing to have around. But he also made a show of telling everyone he would pick up the tab for the drinks, and we knew his family background. Crazy wealthy. He was obviously good for it.”

“And?” Nick prompted when Flanders didn’t continue the story.

“And when the end of the evening came, Josie said she was tired and wanted to go home, so Moe leapt up at the chance to take her. He took out his wallet and said he’d leave money for the booze, but when I checked later, he’d put down just forty dollars. There were a dozen of us at the bar, and the costs ran more than three hundred for the alcohol alone.”

“It seems like you probably could cover that,” Annalisa said, looking around.

“Of course, but that’s not the point. Moe said he would do it and then he didn’t.”

"You thought Josie could do better," Annalisa concluded.

"She was beautiful. She was whip smart. She was kind. Josie Blanchard could have had any man she wanted."

"Even you?" Annalisa asked.

He hesitated and moved closer, until the hard edge of the marble countertop dug into his squishy middle. "Are you married, Detective?"

"Divorced," she answered. Nick said nothing.

Flanders nodded sagely. "Then you might understand. My wife and I got together in college. She was brilliant and funny and the first woman who wanted to take this schlubby guy into bed. When I asked her to marry me and she said yes, I felt ten miles high. I saw our whole future together—a couple of kids, a nice big house, then eventually double rockers on the porch when we got old. But it turns out we couldn't have kids. Somehow, we got an even bigger house to make up for it." He spread his hands to show the expanse of the room. "We could go days and not even pass each other. Oh, it was my fault, most of it. I own that. If you want tenure you've got to work your ass off, joining committees, bringing in grants, schmoozing the right people so they remember your face come promotion time. I was at work more than I was here."

"And that's where you met Josie," Nick said.

"You'd understand about Josie if you'd met her. Blond ponytail that swished when she walked, always smiling, always happy to see you. She had a voice that you'd follow into a forest. And that accent!" He broke off, clutching his chest. "She charmed everyone. Most of the young women in the lab dressed for Chicago winters, bulky sweatshirts and jeans. Josie wore skirts and tight, fuzzy sweaters. One day, she brought me a leather jacket. It was vintage and she said she'd picked it up cheap in some consignment store. We'd had this talk about how I'd been dressing like an old man since I was twenty-five, and she said I was too young to look like a grandpa. I was pushing fifty at that point. No one had called me young in years."

"Did you ask her out?" Nick inquired.

"I was married." Flanders frowned at him. "Also, it was against the rules, even then. I was her advisor."

"Yeah, but that didn't stop it from happening, right?" Nick said. "You had tenure by then. What could they do to you? I see plenty of academics with a young woman on their arm. You work all those hours together and nature takes its course."

Flanders stirred his soup and seemed to be weighing how much to say. "You're young yet, the pair of you. Wait until you hit fifty-something and realize you're on a raft heading for the final horizon. You can't stop the current. It's slow but inexorable. Then, maybe, you meet someone who creates a ripple big enough to bobble you on the sea. My ripple was Josie. I admit my head was turned. I told myself it was a crush and would pass."

"But it didn't," Annalisa said.

"One night my wife was out of town visiting her mother, and I asked Josie to dinner. I made it sound like a group thing but it wasn't. She didn't seem to mind when the rest of the crew didn't show up and I told myself she'd wanted it this way. She was laughing, playing with her hair, asking me questions about my work. You see, I'd done my postdoc overseas with James Black—he won the Nobel Prize for Medicine in 1988—and she acted like I'd toured with Mick Jagger. I felt like the most interesting man in the world." He smiled a little sadly. "I know it sounds foolish, so cliché, the middle-aged man falling for his pretty young student. All I can tell you is that it feels incredibly powerful in the moment, like you've invented fire. I burned for her."

"What did you do about it?" Annalisa asked.

"When I took her home after that dinner, we sat talking in the car outside her apartment, and I made my move. I kissed her and she kissed me back. I swear she was into it. But when I tried to get her blouse off, she pulled away. She said she really liked me but we couldn't do this. Our work was too important." He shook his head.

"What did you say?" Nick asked.

"I told her that her project was just about getting old people to take their medication properly. No one would care if the whole thing got canceled tomorrow."

"Ouch," said Annalisa.

"Big mistake," Flanders agreed. "She got out of the car and wouldn't answer the phone when I tried to call and apologize. She started dodging me at the lab—leaving the room when I entered it, locking herself in the library. But the more she avoided me, the more I wanted her. I sent flowers. I went to her place. Even when my wife left, I couldn't stop. It was like I had a fever that wouldn't break. I designed assignments for Josie that put her in contact with me. When she resisted, I resorted to bribes, like promising to take her to conferences, to faculty events where I could introduce her around."

"That sounds like the same thing Moe Bocks was doing to her," said Nick.

"Oh yes. I recognized the sickness when it started in him. He called the lab looking for her so many times that we stopped answering the phone. We just took it off the hook. At first, when she broke it off with him, I was hopeful. I thought she'd seen the light and would want to be with me. Instead I followed her to a bar one night where she picked up some undergraduate with a flattop and a motorcycle." He shrugged. "That did it. I realized if she wanted that guy, she'd never really wanted me. It was like I woke up and could breathe again. I apologized to Josie for my behavior and she accepted. Three weeks later, she was murdered."

"Where were you that night?" Annalisa asked, although she knew the answer. He had no alibi.

"I was here. Alone, of course, since my wife had moved out. I drank a bottle of Malbec in my underwear, feeling very sorry for myself because of the way I'd wrecked my life."

"Maybe you blamed Josie," Annalisa suggested. "She led you on."

"No, I knew I'd made an ass of myself. Seeing Moe's behavior helped cement that for me. The more he badgered her, the more Josie retreated. I realized I'd tried the same tactics and received the same dismal results. All I can tell you is that my actions felt justified at the time—like if I could just find the magic words to explain myself, Josie would understand and want me again. That cop who came around after she was killed, he understood. I got the feeling he'd been there too."

"Leo Hammond?"

"That's the one. He said he'd known a few Josies in his day."

"I'm sure he had," Annalisa remarked drily. "And they're all asking for it, right?"

"Oh, no. I didn't mean it that way." Flanders looked horrified. "What happened to Josie was awful and in no way justified. I only meant that love makes fools of us all."

"The person who killed her didn't love her," said Annalisa. "They strangled her with a wire so tightly it almost severed her head."

"Yes, well, I again suggest you talk to Moe Bocks. The fever had broken for me but he was still very much in its grip."

"How do you know?"

"Well, it's like I told Hammond. Bocks had been skulking around the university after her. I called campus security once when he followed a student researcher through the security doors and inside the restricted lab area. Josie wasn't even there, but he wouldn't believe me. He said, 'I know you're hiding her! Josie, you have to talk to me!' I held him back when he started going through the rooms looking for her, and he took a swing at me. Bloodied my nose. That was about a week before she got killed."

"Did you press charges?"

"No." He looked sheepish. "I didn't want the cops asking Josie questions, because I was worried she'd mention me and how I'd been hanging around after her the same as Bocks. After he hit me, Bocks took off. When security finally showed up, we told them everything was fine. Maybe if I had made a bigger fuss . . ."

"Moe says someone on campus slashed his tires," Annalisa said, and Flanders looked surprised. "He thinks it was you."

"I didn't know anything about that," he replied. "I never touched his tires. I never saw him again after he hit me, not until his face turned up on the news when Josie died. We all knew he'd done it. It seemed like an arrest was imminent, but somehow it never came." He looked at Annalisa, not with accusation but like she was one of his students and was expected to have an answer.

"No one has forgotten Josie," she said.

He smiled faintly. "No one who met her ever would. It's a shame what the world missed out on." He checked his watch. "Listen, I don't want to rush you out but my wife will be back from shopping any minute now, and I'd prefer not to talk about any of this in front of her. As you might imagine, she finds the whole story upsetting."

"Your wife? You remarried?"

"Reconciled," he said, obviously pleased and maybe even relieved. "It took time and a lot of groveling, but she finally forgave me. Sometimes I still wake up in the night and can't believe how close I came to losing it all over a brief midlife crisis. What I would have missed. The fever broke just in time. That brilliant young painter I married back in college—somehow, she still loves me, and I'm still ten miles high. So you can understand that I don't want to go dragging up the ugly past and hurting her all over again."

"There's hope for the double rockers on the porch," Annalisa said.

"You bet." He smiled but gestured in the direction of the door, indicating they should leave. Nick rose to his feet but Annalisa didn't budge just yet.

"It probably helped that Josie was dead, right?" She kept her tone upbeat and Flanders's own smile froze in return.

"I'm sorry?"

"Josie was gone, never to return. Like you said—the fever was cured."

"It was gone before, like I said. Watching Moe Bocks pull escalating antics made me realize where I was headed and how foolish it would be. He was single, a decade younger, with a wealthy family ready to pull his fat from the flame if it came to that. I had a wife and my research. The grants go to me, not the lab. If I faltered in some way, the whole enterprise would have come tumbling down."

"Good thing you got that wake-up call." She slid off her stool and Flanders seemed to relax again now that she was moving for the exit.

They weren't quick enough, though, as a woman with silver hair breezed in through the kitchen from the garage entrance. She held two canvas totes filled with groceries, which she set down when she realized her husband wasn't alone and the energy in the room wasn't quite friendly. "Hello," she said with an undertone of caution.

"This is my wife, Tabitha," Flanders said, moving to her side. "Tabitha, this is Annalisa Vega and Nick Carelli." He paused slightly. "They're detectives from the Chicago Police."

"Police? What happened?"

"Nothing, dear," he murmured as he hugged her around the shoulders and kissed the side of her head. "They were just leaving."

"We're here about Josie Blanchard," Annalisa said, watching the pair carefully. Mentioning Josie like this was a gamble. Flanders had let them into his home and answered their questions willingly, and provoking his wife risked making him uncooperative in the future.

Tabitha Flanders's blue eyes widened and then darkened like a bruise. "Have you finally caught someone? Is that why you're here?"

"No, dear. The case is still open so they reinvestigate periodically." He looked from Annalisa to Nick. "Isn't that right?"

"I thought that other detective had the case," Tabitha said. "Leo something. Toby talked to him several times."

"Leo Hammond was killed a few nights ago," Annalisa said.

"I see. That's terrible. And it's your case now?"

Annalisa felt Nick's eyes on her. "We're looking into Josie's death, yes. Did you know her?"

Toby looked at the floor as Tabitha studied him and considered her answer. "No, I didn't. She was only in his lab about eighteen months, and during that time, my husband was careful to keep us apart. I think I sensed something was different when he stopped talking about her. I would hear the names of the other students, of his colleagues, but nothing about Josie. Then he got a new haircut and started going to the gym three times a week. Who was he trying to impress? Certainly not me."

"Tabby, I—"

She held up a hand, forestalling him. "Then one day he showed up wearing a leather jacket that I hadn't bought for him. That's when I knew."

Annalisa thought about her father carrying on with Katie Duffy. It was the same story, more or less; as Flanders had noted, a cliché. She wondered again what her mother had known and when. Had she realized Pops was stepping out on her and that his partner was her neighbor and best friend? The hot flash of anger that went through Annalisa on her mother's behalf, even now, decades later, made her sick. He had shamed the whole family. Ma took him back, though. Maybe she saw it as victory. Annalisa noted the same determination on Tabitha's face as she looked at her disgraced husband. Tabitha had forgiven; she did not forget.

"I hope you're also talking to Moe Bocks," Tabitha said stiffly as she linked her arm through Toby's.

"We're talking to everyone," Annalisa assured her.

She seemed surprised. "Everyone? After all this time? Can't you just go and arrest him?"

"No, ma'am," Nick said. "Not without evidence."

"I assumed there was some new evidence found," she replied.

"No," Annalisa said lightly. "Not yet."

They left the Flanders couple alone together in their massive house. As they paused on the stoop outside, Annalisa noticed that as impressive as the place was, it did not have a porch for rocking chairs. "What did you think?" she asked Nick.

He'd put on his shades to block out the bright winter sun. "I know only one thing for sure," he said. "Somewhere, somehow, he's still got that leather jacket."

CHAPTER ELEVEN

....

Tom Osborne leaned on his cane and peered out from his large front windows, carefully concealed behind the heavy damask curtain that Jane had picked out years ago, so that he could watch the detectives pull up in the driveway. His great stone house resembled a fortress from the outside, but he felt it under attack when he saw Nick Carelli and Annalisa Vega get out of the red coupe and start walking for the front door. His anxiety only intensified when Carelli stopped by Tom's Tesla to look inside the driver's window. The car was no longer that unusual. It shouldn't attract attention. Tom watched as Carelli signaled Vega to look too. What the hell could they be looking at? Okay, so he was a bit of a slob. The car had piled up receipts, gum wrappers, old coffee cups stacked in the holders. His gym bag sat on the passenger seat along with assorted articles of clothing. So what? The housekeeper didn't clean the cars and Jane never set foot in his. He could do what he wanted there.

Carelli and Vega tore themselves away from his vehicle and resumed walking toward the house. He limped as fast as he could to the door, pulling it open just as Vega's hand was raised to ring the bell. "Hi," he said, a little breathless from his exertion. "I saw you pull up."

"Thanks for seeing us," Vega said as he let them inside. "I know Sunday is family time."

"No worries. My kids are on their own and my wife is at church. She's a true believer—does the whole three hours."

"You don't attend?" Vega asked.

"I find God in other places. Come sit down, won't you? I could use the break."

He led them to the great room, the one with the grand piano at one end and the grandfather clock at the other. He collapsed into his high-backed chair by the fireplace, which gave him a perfect view of the framed family portrait, taken eleven years ago, that hung above the upright piano. It had been printed on canvas, almost like a painting, with Jane in the pearls he'd given her for their fifteenth anniversary and the kids coming out of their most awkward young teenage years—braces gone, acne cleared. A perfect moment in time, frozen forever. Jane was going to kill him if it all came out. "So," he said, forcing a bright tone as he sat forward toward his guests. "How can I help you? I'm afraid I don't know much about Leo's recent caseload. I've been on disability for a few months now."

Vega had her notebook out already, which made him nervous. Her gaze went to his bum leg. "Yeah, sorry to hear about your injury. What happened?"

"Chased the wrong car thief down an alley. This one had a gun."

Jane's was the first face he saw when he woke up in the hospital and realized he wasn't dead. The worry lines around her eyes and mouth told him she still cared enough to want to keep him that way. She'd held his hand and wiped his brow with more feeling than they'd shared in years. God help him, lying there on what should've been his deathbed, he almost confessed. Told her everything and lived with the consequences. But then the kids showed up and he was reminded of the stakes and everything he could lose if the truth came out. It wasn't just his life he was protecting.

"They didn't catch the guy?" Carelli asked.

Tom's mouth twitched. "No, as I'm sure you're aware, sometimes they just get away with it."

"Not on your watch, though." Vega consulted her notes. "You and Hammond, Vaughn, and Monk have racked up more than a thousand homicide busts."

"Thank the bangers for keeping us in business."

"And the city for bailing you out," she replied, deadpan.

"I'm sorry?"

"I looked up the numbers, and you and your buddies have cost the city almost four million bucks in settlements. Just last year, you and Vaughn answered a report of a robbery at a corner store, and you responded by shooting up the place to the tune of twenty thousand dollars in damages."

Tom held up a finger. "Yeah, but we got the guy."

"Yeah, him and the hundred and forty bucks he stole from the till. That's some funky math. But the biggest cost was that half million paid out to Cecil Barry's widow."

He pointed at her. "Now, that was an accident. Barry shot first, remember. He hit Frankie in the shoulder as we were coming through the door. We were responding to a 911 call of a holdup in the club. How were we supposed to know it was the owner shooting at us?"

"So Barry calls 911 because his place is being robbed, and you guys show up to kill him?" Nick asked, incredulous.

"I said it was an accident," Tom snapped. "And look, the city paid her five times what that club was worth. It was a dive back then. 'Debase Lounge,' we all called it. Cecil Barry was a lowlife, always trying to be bigger than he was, always looking for a score. Well, somewhere along the line, he crossed the wrong guys. I'm sorry for what happened to him, but if you ask me, his widow is better off." He took a breath, calming himself with this truth. "I don't know why you're asking about Barry, anyway. I thought you wanted to talk to me about Leo."

"You rode with him a long time," Vega observed. "You must've been pretty tight."

"Sure. We came up together at the academy. I still can't believe he's gone."

"What about Kayla Hammond? Are you friendly with her too?"

He eyed her. "I knew her, sure. Are you thinking she could be the shooter?"

Vega tilted her head like the damn shrink they made him see after the shooting. "What do you think?"

"It ain't my case, so it ain't my call." He scowled and lurched to his feet. "Can I get you a drink? I'm going to have a little one myself."

Carelli shook his head. Vega jotted something down in her damn notebook. "No, thanks," she said as she wrote.

Tom somehow kept his hands from shaking as he fixed his bourbon and water at the wet bar. Michter's limited edition crafted in aged Kentucky barrels. He raised the amber liquid high in a toast to his guests. "Now, that's God," he told them before he took a swallow.

"Tell us more about Kayla and Leo," Vega said. "What was their marriage like?"

"How's anyone's?" he replied with a shrug. He limped back to his chair and sat down with his drink. "Did they fight sometimes? Sure. Kayla's grandparents came from Sicily. She has a temper on her like TNT. When the sparks start, you'd better run for cover because there ain't much time before the boom. I remember one night, Leo stayed out with us after shift, hitting a couple of different bars, and we didn't get home till almost morning. Kayla was so pissed when he turned up that she bounced a coffee mug off his head. He got a nice goose egg right here." He tapped his right temple. "She wasn't serious, though."

"How do you know that?" Annalisa asked.

He grinned. "'Cause there wasn't any coffee in it at the time."

"What else did they fight about?"

Tom sobered, looked at his family portrait. He swore he felt Jane's eyes on him. "I don't know. The usual stuff, I suppose. Money. His kids."

"Maura Hammond told us Leo had a wandering eye."

Tom's hip throbbed and he shifted to try to alleviate the pain. "Well, sure. It wandered over to Kayla."

"Anywhere else?" Nick asked.

"I didn't keep track of what Leo was doing or who he was doing it with."

"What about Kayla?" Vega asked.

"What about her?"

"Was she seeing anyone on the side?"

"If she was, I don't know about it."

Vega made another scribble on her notepad. "Have you ever been to the Pendry hotel?" she asked, not looking at him.

The liquor in his belly did the wave. "What's that?"

"The Pendry hotel downtown. Have you been there?"

"What's that got to do with anything?"

Vega jerked her thumb toward the outside. "There's a key card from the Pendry sitting in your car. Have you been there recently?" He said nothing and she just stared at him. "We can check."

"Check for what?"

Carelli got up and went to the decorative table where they kept the more casual photos. "How's your marriage, Tom?"

"None of your goddamn business." He got up and hobbled over to yank away the picture of his kids that Carelli held in his hands. Carelli picked up another one—a shot of Jane on their boat ten years ago, her brown hair windswept. She looked like a movie star in her red top and dark glasses. Jane had been against it at the start, but her brother Pete had been plenty happy to run the money through his dry cleaning business, taking a cut in between. Tom looked around at the sturdy Ethan Allen furniture, the paisley drapes, and curio cabinet filled with glass horses or whatever knickknacks caught Jane's eye. Jane didn't love where the money came from, but she sure did love the money.

"See, the thing is," Nick said as he replaced the picture, "Kayla had been to the Pendry hotel recently as well. We're thinking maybe you met her there."

"Then you can think again." He glared from one to the other. "And I think it's time you both were leaving."

"One more thing," Vega said, not moving from his couch. "You've got the Josie Blanchard case now, is that right?"

He looked at her, befuddled. "Yeah, my number came up when Bob Dickey retired last year." The case had been passed around like a hot potato. At first, everyone wanted it. After the years piled up with no new leads, no one did. "Why?"

"We heard Leo and Moe Bocks had a run-in over it recently."

"That's right," he said, relieved to have the conversation moving off of him for a moment. "Moe tried to fight him in a restaurant in front of his own date. That guy is a psychopath."

"But the case was dead. You weren't working it."

"It was never dead. Leo was there the night they found that girl with her head nearly cut off. You don't forget something like that, no matter how many years go by. We all wanted Moe Bocks locked up for what he did."

"And you're sure he did it," Vega said.

"He was obsessed. He called her place something like fifty-seven times in the two weeks before the murder. She'd started crashing with friends, staying late at work, just to avoid him."

"There was a witness who saw a van on the street outside Josie's place that night."

"Yeah, Leo figured it came from Moe's daddy's car lot. The witness was a neighbor from across the street. She said she saw some writing on the side of the van and she thought she remembered an eagle. The Bocks logo at the time had a bald eagle and an American flag. But we went through their entire inventory on both lots—no white vans. Bocks must've ditched it somewhere after the murder. Either that, or Daddy helped him repaint it."

"Moe was pissed that Leo was still on him about the murder," Carelli said. "You think he might have been mad enough to shoot him?"

"Like I said, he's a psychopath."

Vega finally took her ass off of Jane's floral couch. "We'd have to figure out how he broke into Leo's home, though."

"I thought there was a busted window."

"Yeah, but no one went through it." She paused meaningfully. "We think someone came through the front door. Someone who knew the alarm code."

Carelli gave him a guileless look. "You wouldn't happen to know that code. Would you, Tom?"

"I'm tired," Tom said. "You need to go so I can rest."

"Sure, we can go," Vega said. She started for the door and then halted. "Just one last question before we leave. Do you own a wet suit?"

Every hair on his body stood up. "What did you say?"

"You know, a rubber suit for diving. Do you have one?"

"Why the hell are you asking?"

She waited without answering, and he snarled his reply.

"No. I look like I'm going scuba diving to you? Get on out of here now." He hoped they couldn't see his rising panic. He chased them toward the door, hobbling with his cane, and when it closed, he leaned against it. His heart pounded out of rhythm, like it had the night he'd lain there bleeding in the street, so scared he thought he might piss himself. He waded across the floor to the couch where Vega had sat. With trembling fingers, he pulled out his phone.

"It's me," he said when Frankie answered. "We've got to meet."

"Fuck that. The Bears are on at noon."

"Vega and Carelli were here. They asked about Cecil Barry."

This got Frankie's attention. "What do they know?"

"Nothing."

"Then we're golden," Frankie said, his voice relaxing again. "You want to come watch the game? I got beer and Maggie put a pot of chili on."

"I'm telling you we're in trouble. It's bigger than Vega."

"What do you mean?"

Tom gripped the phone with one sweaty hand. He hadn't told the whole story of the night he got shot, not to anyone. Not Jane, not the doctors or nurses at the hospital, and definitely not Leo, Frankie, or Paulie. He'd thought it was a hallucination as he'd lain there dying. The bullets had ripped through him and put him down on the cold, gritty pavement, alone in that alley—or so he'd thought. It had been dark on the street and darker still around the corner where he'd chased the punk kid. He'd tried to crawl for help but made it only a few feet before unconsciousness started to overtake him. He'd heard footsteps and thought he was saved. He'd rolled up to face the night sky and forced out one raspy word: *Help.* But the alien-like face that had appeared over him did not help. It stared down, almost curious, watching him struggle to breathe. The figure vanished like a ghost, and later Tom figured his dying brain, deprived of oxygen, had invented him. A crazy, fevered dream. Because who the hell wore diving gear at night on the backstreets of Chicago?

CHAPTER TWELVE

....

"So I have a question," Nick said as they drove back across city lines. "How did you hear about that story of Moe Bocks's tires getting slashed? And he thinks Flanders did it?"

"Oh. Well, Bocks told me."

"You went to see him?"

"No, we ran into each other."

Nick looked sideways at her. "Oh yeah? Where was that? The frozen food section?"

"Josie Blanchard's old place—the murder scene."

He sat up straighter behind the wheel. "And you didn't think to mention this?"

She shrugged, her attention on the scenery outside. "You didn't mention you put in for a transfer to Area Four."

He said nothing for a beat. "I was going to tell you."

"Oh yeah? When? After you were done screwing me?"

"Hey, you're the one who showed up at my place, remember? I didn't exactly have to convince you to—" He stopped and blew out a frustrated breath. "Look, nothing's been finalized. They might not pick me." She replied with stony silence, and he gave a deep sigh. "I haven't made a secret about what I want, Anna. I want to settle down, have a family. Taking a job with more control over my caseload is one way to get that."

"Sure, fine. Whatever." She folded her arms and slouched in her seat.

"Or maybe I'll just quit."

"Quit?" She rose up, intrigued. "You wouldn't."

"Why not? I've done my twenty. Maybe I'll go open a fishing boat rental place and live out my days on the beach."

"Not much beach around here," she pointed out.

"It's not a firm plan." He drove without speaking for several miles. "But think about it. People dying every day, but for once, it wouldn't be your problem."

Annalisa had worked a couple dozen homicides as a detective and been at the scene of at least two dozen more. Some murders felt plain senseless, like the taxi driver shot in the head for fifteen bucks. Others felt almost inevitable. Annalisa's first day on the job, her partner Novak answered a radio call that put them on the South Side on a day registering triple digits on the thermometer. Six floors up, no elevator, and Novak was huffing pretty good by the time they found the apartment with the woman, high as a kite with blood in her eyes and a knife in her hands. The man had broken knuckles from hitting her and a slice down the side of his arm from where she hit back. Each one swore the other one started it. Annalisa took their statements for her reports, but there weren't enough lines on the page to get to the bottom of who did what to whom. The couple had scars going back ten years. When they finally got the call three months later about the woman's murder, no one was surprised.

"Someone has to be responsible," she said to Nick. "Turn right up here."

"Where are we going?" he asked as he complied with her direction.

"It's Sunday dinner."

He regarded her with curiosity. "Not that I don't love your mom's pot roast, but—"

"Bob Dickey and my father were on the same bowling team in the eighties, and they kept in touch," she replied. "He might be able to facilitate a connection there so we can find out more about the Josie Blanchard case."

Nick didn't reply for a long moment. "The Blanchard case isn't ours," he said finally. "It's not even our jurisdiction."

"No, it's Tom Osborne's, and you heard him—he's not actually working it. He thinks it's a dead end. Bocks gets away with it."

"I don't like it any more than you do, but legally, you've got no cause to go after this guy."

"I'm not going after him. I'm investigating him as a suspect—"

"Annalisa . . ."

"In the murder of Leo Hammond," she said, her voice rising. "If Moe Bocks killed Josie Blanchard in 2002 and Leo Hammond was determined to make trouble for him now, then that gives him plenty of motive for wanting Hammond gone."

Nick shut his mouth on whatever counterargument he was about to make but the set of his jaw said he did not agree with her. She turned her face to the window. Nick's father had murdered his mother and then killed himself when Nick was eight years old. This heartrending narrative explained both his desire for justice and his equanimity when it came in imperfect form. Sometimes no one went to jail. There was no trial or chance to lay out all the evidence. No explanation, no accountability. Sometimes the end was all you got.

He pulled up outside her parents' house and stopped the car, shifting into park with an emphatic jerk. She looked at him. "You're coming?"

"Someone has to protect you."

She cast her gaze to the familiar windows with Ma's lace curtains hanging in them. "They won't hurt me."

"I meant protect you from yourself," he said as he climbed out of the car. Annalisa considered her approach. In the old days, she'd go around back and enter through the kitchen, which would be crowded with people and humid from all the pots simmering on the stove. Only strangers and package deliveries came to the front door. Nick looked to her, uncertain when she just stood there on the sidewalk. "Well?"

She squared her shoulders and walked determinedly around back, only to stop short when she saw the cars parked by Ma and Pops's garage. Vinnie's Subaru and Tony's silver preowned BMW were joined by a familiar black Lexus. "He's here," she said to Nick. "Moe Bocks."

"Here?" He looked incredulous. "Why?"

There was only one answer to this, and she was the mother of Ma and Pops's youngest grandchildren. "Sassy." She climbed the weatherbeaten wood steps and leaned her shoulder into the door like usual.

It had apparently been fixed because it didn't stick and she ended up stumbling across the threshold into the kitchen.

"Annalisa." Her mother, dressed in an apron over her navy wool church dress, looked at her with shock. She stood at the stove with a wooden spoon in her hand, and the sight and smell were so familiar it made a hunger well up in Annalisa that had nothing to do with food.

"Ma," she whispered.

Her mother's chin trembled and she dropped the spoon into the pot so she could extend her arms to Annalisa. "Come here. Let me look at you." She grabbed Annalisa and held her close.

Annalisa welcomed her mother's embrace, laying her cheek on Ma's shoulder as she did as a child. She heard loud voices coming from the next room where the others were eating. "Chad is a perfectly nice name," Vinnie's teenage daughter Quinn was saying. "Daddy doesn't like him because he does theater and not basketball."

The men laughed and started jockeying each other for the best retort:

Ooh, a regular Romeo.

Quinn's gone Hollywood.

So long as he's not doing my daughter I don't care what else he's into.

Annalisa squeezed her mother with pent-up longing. She should be at that table defending her niece and taking up for her against the guys. "I've missed you so much," she said to Ma.

"I missed you." Ma gripped the back of her head. "You are always welcome here. You know that, right? Always. I don't care what he says."

Annalisa stiffened and pulled away at the mention of her father. "Is he in there?"

Ma looked back over her shoulder with a guilty glance. "He is there, but he's not eating like he should." She hesitated. "Maybe if you talk to him."

"Ma, I'm the last one he wants to see."

"Not wants. Needs." Her mother gave her a shove. "You go in there. I'll make you a plate." Then, noticing Nick for the first time, she straightened to a more formal posture. "You didn't tell me you brought company."

"It's just Nick, Ma."

"I can see that," her mother replied, annoyed. "My eyes aren't so bad I don't know my own son-in-law."

"Ex-son-in-law," Annalisa corrected.

"Maria, it's good to see you again," Nick said with genuine warmth. "This spread looks amazing as usual. Did you know your meatballs remain one of my all-time favorite smells? Heaven in a Crock-Pot, right there."

He coaxed a grudging smile from her mother. "Oh, go on with you. I'll fix you a plate too . . . extra meatballs. You two find a seat at the table. There's folding chairs in the den if you need them."

Annalisa crept toward the doorway and froze on the threshold. The packed dining room ceased all conversation the moment she appeared. Her father glowered. Her brothers stared in stunned silence. Finally, the baby, Gigi, screeched with delight from her toddler seat. "Auntie!" She waved a plastic spoon and grinned a sauce-covered smile at Annalisa.

"Yes, baby, what a surprise, huh?" Sassy held Annalisa's gaze as she wiped her daughter's dribbly chin. Moe Bocks sat on the other side of Sassy, in Annalisa's usual seat. The one she'd owned through all her growing-up years and into adulthood. She felt steam rising in her like from Ma's teakettle as she looked at him.

"That's where I sit."

"Beg your pardon," he said agreeably, moving to yield, but Sassy stopped him with a hand on his arm.

"She can find another spot. There's room down on the end."

There wasn't room. Pop's wheelchair took up the whole head of the table, and his expression made clear he wouldn't be moving aside for her. "You can squeeze in here," Vinnie told her, rising so he could give her a hug.

"Yeah, everyone, move down to make some space," Tony said as he tried to shuffle the plates to make room for Annalisa and Nick.

"It's fine," Annalisa said. "We can eat in the kitchen."

"No, we'll make room." Tony tried his best, but the table already had seven adults and four kids around it. Shifting the chairs a few inches here or there did not make a difference. Quinn looked at her plate, her cheeks red from the tension in the room. Carla whined that she wanted Annalisa to sit next to her, and Sassy shushed her.

"Auntie Annalisa isn't staying long."

"Oh yeah? Who says?" Annalisa challenged her.

Sassy's reply was mild as she poured milk for Gigi. "You never do. There's always work."

"Sh-sh-she can have my place," Pops stammered from the far end of the table. The head, where he always sat, even if his sturdy oak throne had been replaced by a wheelchair. He wheeled awkwardly out the back, disappearing toward the den.

Ma materialized behind them with two heaping plates of food. She made a dismayed clucking noise. "I'll talk to him."

"No, I will," said Annalisa. She squeezed Nick's hand briefly. "You stay and eat."

She followed Pops into the den, where she found him looking at the wall of family photos that had been there since the 1980s, their thin gold frames now out of fashion. His gaze settled on a rectangular shot from their last big camping trip as a family. Annalisa was eight, her thick brown hair in a messy ponytail, while her oldest brother, Vinnie, was seventeen and about to leave for college, as tall and strong as Pops in the picture. Tony was a scrawny awkward fifteen, his brown locks in a spiked hairdo that had required daily application of three different hair products and generated much mocking from his father. He stood farthest away in the shot, like he couldn't stand to be associated with the rest of them. Alex and Annalisa knelt in front of their parents, arms around each other. He was ten and still a kid like her, her closest confidant. Alex made a goofy face the way he always did and Annalisa was looking at him and not at the camera. What most surprised her was how young Ma and Pops had looked. They were just barely older than her in the picture.

"I don't remember who took it," Annalisa said as she stepped forward to stand next to Pop's wheelchair.

"A stranger. Just a hiker going past." His watery gaze slid from one photo to the next, probing for something he couldn't seem to find. "I s-s-saw you on TV," he said without looking at her. "You were at the Hammond m-murder."

"It's my case," she agreed. "Mine and Nick's."

His head shook and she couldn't tell if it was deliberate or one of his tremors. "You spend every day thinking the streets are gonna get you. Then something like that ha-happens."

"Did you know him? Leo Hammond?" She tried to keep the conversation going.

"Reputation only. He—he got a lot of drugs off the street. Lotta pictures in the papers. You know the kind. Him and his buddies standing behind a table full of coke."

"That's good, right? He took it out of circulation."

"Good, yeah." His thin shoulders rose and fell. She could see the ridge of his collarbone and the grizzle on his neck. "Somehow, though, the streets always found a way to get more." He shifted to look up at her, the effort generating a tremor that caused his head to bob. "You're breaking your mother's heart, you know. Staying away on Sunday. Every week, she makes a Jell-O mold with those little oranges in it, even though no one wants to eat it but you."

"She brought me some at Christmas."

"I remember. I heard her c-car leave to go visit you." He paused. "When she goes out the door, I always wonder if this is the time she won't come back."

"Ma's not leaving you. Not at this late date." They had talked about it one time, not long after the arrests, waiting outside a lawyer's office in hard leather chairs while Pops heard about his options. *You don't have to be here,* Annalisa had told her mother. *I don't care what the lawyer says about appearances. You don't owe him anything.*

Ma gave her the look, the one she used to nail Annalisa with in church when Annalisa scuffed the pew in front of them with her patent leather shoes. *We've been together since I was seventeen. I'm almost seventy now. You say I should leave him, but where would I go?*

You can come live with me. I have the space.

Space? What do I need space for? I raised four kids in a three-bedroom house and did just fine. Then you all grew up and away and I've got plenty of space right now, thank you.

A laugh went up from the next room where the others were eating. Nick was telling one of his greatest hits, the one about the house party he busted up because they'd gotten a tip that drugs were present. People scattered, crawling out second-story windows, and Nick chased down one guy three blocks away. Sure enough, he had a bag of heroin in his pocket. Nick's voice grew deeper as he imitated the perp. "*'Officer,' he says, 'these aren't my pants.'*" Everyone howled.

Pops looked at Annalisa. "Nicky's stuck by you. That's good. I—I was wrong about him back in the day. He's a good guy. Loyal."

Annalisa didn't tell him about the possible transfer. "He wasn't so loyal when we were married," she reminded her father.

"You think he ain't sorry about that?" Pops huffed and a roar went up from the family as Nick landed his punch line. *"So the other guy goes, 'Hey, where'd you get my pants?'"*

Pops smiled faintly to himself. "But I forgot. Sorry don't make much difference to you."

"Are you?" She fixed him with a hard look. "Sorry? All I've heard from you is righteous justification."

"You don't have kids. You don't understand. I would've done the same for you."

Annalisa sank down on the nearby sofa and put her head in her hands. "Oh, you did me, all right. You did me right good."

"Me?" He scoffed. "What did I do to you? Look at me." He stuck out one foot to show off the ankle monitor.

"No, that's on you! I still don't get it, Pops. Of all the people to pull something like this . . . I thought you were the most honest cop on the beat. George Vega—he won't even accept a free cup of coffee at the diner. What'd you tell me when I joined up? 'The badge is shiny so you can see yourself in it. Make sure you like the reflection.' Tell me, how are you liking it now?"

"How are you?" He stuck out his chin but it wobbled, whether from uncertainty or his illness, she could not say. He'd shrunk since she'd seen him last, disappearing into his bones, but in her head, he remained the Popeye figure from her childhood.

She took a deep breath, trying for calm. "I didn't come here to fight with you, Pops."

"Yeah, why did you come?"

She jerked her head at the dining room. "Moe Bocks. What do you know about him?"

"Not much. Seems like a good kid."

"Kid?" Moe was pushing fifty.

"He got Carrie a good deal on a used Camry," Pops replied, naming Vinnie's wife. "And he said he knew someone who could help us put in a ramp to the house." This last bit was important, Annalisa knew, because it said Moe foresaw a time when Pops would be free to come and go. *You don't deserve this. I'll help you fix it.* Moe had maneuvered his way into her family like someone gave him the key to the back door.

"He's a suspect in the death of Leo Hammond," said Annalisa in a hard voice.

Pops came to attention, a flash of his old self. "What's that you say?"

Annalisa laid out how Hammond had confronted Moe about the murder of Josie Blanchard, coming to blows inside the tiki bar. "And that's the thing," she told Pops, "Hammond has a point. Moe also remains the best suspect in Josie's murder in 2002. That's two dead bodies in his orbit. You're telling me you want this guy at your dinner table?"

Pops looked to the dining room with uncertain eyes. "I asked him about the Blanchard thing. He said the cops cleared him when his alibi checked out."

"It didn't check out. They just couldn't break it. Your old buddy Bob Dickey worked the case at the time."

"Bob, yeah. He and Helen sent us a Christmas card with Yorkies on it. Your ma still has it up on the fridge."

Annalisa felt a pang. At one point, her mother had needed string along the whole staircase to hold the Christmas cards. The fridge wouldn't have held half of them. "I was thinking maybe you could get in touch with him to see if he has any records of the Blanchard case."

Pops looked surprised. "You're working that one too?"

"Nobody's working it," she replied impatiently. "Meanwhile, the main suspect in a brutal homicide is in there, romancing Sassy, spending time with her and the girls. Your granddaughters, Pops. You really want to take chances with them?"

He wavered, rubbing his chin with one shaky hand. "I don't know."

She stood up so she loomed over him. "Josie's head was almost severed. Leo Hammond was shot full of holes. Who's next, Pops?"

"You don't know he did it," he replied with a scowl. "If they'd had the proof, they would've arrested him. This hobby of yours, mucking around in the past, looking where you don't belong . . . it's going to get you burned one day."

"Yeah? It already has."

He deflated under the force of her fire. "Everything I did, it was for you. You and Alex, Vinnie and Tony. I was protecting the family."

"Sassy's family too," she reminded him in a low, urgent voice. "Her and the girls."

He shook his head vaguely, like a movie had just finished and he couldn't believe it was over. When he spoke, his voice was a crack of ice on a frozen puddle. "He's a young man still. Successful. S-Sassy is smiling for the first time in two years. What if you're wrong?"

He raised his head to look at her. She folded her arms, resolute. He'd calculated the stakes backward; he always had. "What if I'm not?"

CHAPTER THIRTEEN

....

BACK IN NICK'S CAR, ANNALISA PRESSED HER FINGERS TO HER TEMPLES AND SLUMPED IN THE SEAT, EMOTIONALLY EXHAUSTED. "How did it go with your pops?" he asked as he started the engine. "Must've been okay since I didn't hear any shots exchanged."

She snorted a reply. "Don't kid yourself. He's still pissed at me for squealing, like it's my fault he's got to wear the ankle monitor."

"He's not mad at you for that."

"Like you'd know. You were in the other room doing your greatest hits reel. I think the family's ready to junk me and keep you."

"Not in a million years. Tony would still break my face if he got the chance."

"You don't know that."

"I do. He told me so right after I passed him the potatoes."

She gave a tight smile. "That's almost sweet, considering."

"Pops thought he was doing the right thing, protecting his family, and then you came along and showed him the truth of what he'd done. Now he's got no excuse. He's alone in the mirror." He glanced at her. "I know how that feels."

"You didn't cover up a murder, Nick."

"No. But when you realize all the lies you're telling weren't for the reasons you thought, you feel like a fool for believing your own bullshit."

"Oh yeah? Tell me, then. What was your lie?"

His brow wrinkled. "You know already. It's the same as yours."

"I never lied to you."

"Not to me," he said as he pulled up in front of her condo. He grazed her cheek with the backs of his fingers. "To yourself."

"Nick." She looked at her lap. "We can't do this."

"It's too late," he said with a smile. "We already have."

"Wait. The other night . . . I don't mean . . ." She broke off and started over. "We tried the romance angle once and it didn't work out. I won't do this again. I'm not going on a date with you."

"I know," he replied as he unbuckled her belt.

"You do?"

"Sure," he said with a grin. "I haven't asked you." She gave him a shove in reply. He might have retaliated, but his phone buzzed in his pants. "Forensics," he said to her as he accepted the call. "Yeah, Evan, hit me. What've you got?"

Annalisa watched his face as he digested the information. "Well?" she said when he hung up.

"There were two male hairs in the Hammond bed that match neither Kayla nor Leo. The blood in the bathroom is Kayla's, like we expected. But there is one wrinkle: it came back positive for cocaine."

"So she was in there using when the shooting went down?"

"Could explain why she lied about being in the bed. Also why the shooter didn't take her out. He didn't know she was there."

"So who do the hairs in the bed belong to?"

"Maybe a friend or relative. Maybe random. Or maybe Kayla and Tom Osborne had a date that wasn't at the Pendry hotel. I'm thinking of running over there to see if I can find any direct link that they stayed at the same time. You want to come with?"

"You think he's our shooter?"

"I think if they were having an affair, it could've been a joint thing. She gives him the code to the front door. He does the actual murder."

"Check it out and let me know what you find."

"What are you going to do?"

She opened the car door and looked back at him over her shoulder. "I'm just going to crash. The thing with Pops wore me out." She felt bad lying to him but there was no way he'd sign off on her current plan and she didn't want him to face any consequences if it went bad. Her family was her problem.

Nick looked her over like he maybe sensed the truth, but he didn't question her. "Okay. Call me if anything shakes loose."

She stood on the stoop and waved as he drove away. She waited three seconds after his taillights went around the corner before she took out her own keys and went for her car. Moe Bocks showing up at her parents' place like some parasitic cuckoo bird in the wrong nest did have one advantage: it meant his mother was home alone.

....

Her thought as she pulled into the long driveway outside the Bocks family home was that it had been more than twenty years since Linda Bocks provided Moe an alibi for Josie's murder. Maybe she'd let something slip. Sometimes all you needed with a cold case was to reinterview the right witness. Annalisa parked and walked up the wide concrete steps to the ornate front door, with its double panels and heavy brass hardware. She rang the bell, which created a resounding *bong* on the other side, to the point where Annalisa feared someone named Jeeves might appear dressed in a suit and tie. Instead, Linda Bocks herself answered the door. "Yes?" she said, her features arranged in a bright, fixed smile.

She'd had work done, Annalisa noted. The expensive kind. Linda was over seventy but there was barely a wrinkle on her. She wore a burgundy-colored velour tracksuit and about ten thousand dollars' worth of diamonds. Annalisa showed off her shield. "Detective Annalisa Vega, ma'am. I was hoping I could ask you a few questions."

"About?" The slight twitch in her face suggested she tried to arch an eyebrow but the plastic surgery had rendered it near impossible.

"About the death of Josephine Blanchard."

Linda put a jewel-encrusted hand to her chest. "Good heavens, now? That poor child's been gone for ages, may she rest in peace."

"The case is still open." Annalisa didn't mention she wasn't assigned to it. She nodded past Linda to the inside of the house. "So do you mind if I come in? I promise I won't take up much of your time."

"I guess it's all right," Linda said uncertainly. "You'll need to remove your shoes. Luisa!" She clapped and a slim woman with dark hair appeared wearing an apron. "We have a guest," Linda explained. "Please find her some house slippers."

"That isn't necessary." Annalisa glanced at her feet and discovered that, in her hurry to get out the door that morning, she'd put on one dark red sock and one brown one.

"I insist," Linda said as Luisa returned with a pair of basic slippers—still wrapped in plastic, like you might see at a fancy hotel. Linda handed them to Annalisa and turned to her maid/assistant. "I'll take my tea in the parlor now, please. Some for Detective Vega as well."

"No, really—"

"This way," Linda said briskly as she directed Annalisa to the large sitting room. It contained floor-to-ceiling bookshelves and a baby grand piano.

"Do you play?" Annalisa asked, making conversation as she perched on the overstuffed floral sofa.

"No."

"Your son?"

"Moe took lessons for years." A pause. "The lessons didn't take to him." She smiled as Luisa appeared with a tray. "Ah, here's our tea. You don't put milk in yours, do you? The British do and I always found it so strange."

"No milk, thank you."

"Have you been to England? So much history there—everywhere you look, another castle."

"No, I haven't made it there yet." Annalisa and Colin had been set to travel the world together. Now she lived through his photo stream. "I understand Josie Blanchard was from France."

"I didn't like France." Linda pursed her lips. "The women don't shave their armpits, you know."

"Josie?"

"I can't say about her. I only met her once and she was wearing sleeves at the time. But it wouldn't surprise me. Josie was a . . . free spirit."

"Moe was very taken with her. He wanted to marry Josie?"

"He was infatuated, yes. She turned his head completely around. For a while there, he was talking about moving to France and raising goats with her. Goats! What are they even good for?" She took a slurp of tea. "Thankfully, the girl had more sense than Moe did and she turned him down."

"He took it hard."

"He got over it." She put down her cup and gave Annalisa a cool look. "You're not fooling me with this little visit. I know you think he killed her because that's what all the police think. The first one decided it straightaway and then the rest of you have been following his notes ever since. But my son is innocent."

"What do you remember about the night Josie died?"

"It was a Friday. Big Moe and I went out to Morton's for supper, and then he went to the dealership downtown—it's open till eleven on Fridays. I watched my usual programs, which are nothing like the trash you get on the networks right now. I miss the days of Barbara Walters on *20/20*, doing those interviews that made everyone cry."

"Mm-hmm. What about Moe Junior?"

"I'm getting to that part," Linda said, annoyed. "I saw him in the kitchen when I got a late-night snack. Apple slices with peanut butter. I gave Little Moe—that's what I call him, Little Moe—I gave him half the apple and he went down to his little apartment in the basement."

"It has a separate entrance, right?"

"Yes, but the garage is right under the master bedroom. I hear all the cars going in or out."

"Even at three in the morning?"

Linda gave her a skeptical look. "Do you have children, Detective Vega?"

"No, ma'am."

"I didn't think so. Once you have a baby, you never sleep right again. You'll hear every little noise, no matter what the hour." She smoothed her hands over her legs. "If Little Moe had left that night, I would have known about it."

Maybe it was the fidgeting or the way Linda couldn't quite look her in the eyes as she repeated the alibi, but Annalisa did not believe her. She decided to press her with a white lie of her own. "What would you say if I told you we'd turned up a witness who could place Moe's Jetta outside Josie's house the night of the murder?"

Linda did meet her gaze then. Her blue eyes widened with surprise. "Then I'd say your witness is lying."

"You sound very sure of that."

"Little Moe wasn't driving the Jetta that night," Linda said with a note of triumph.

"Oh no?" Annalisa leaned in, trying not to look eager. The neighbor witness said she'd seen a white van. If Linda put Moe in a van the night of Josie's death, they'd be one step closer to nailing him. "What was he driving?"

"Big Moe loaned him a red Pontiac Grand Prix on account of the Jetta was in the shop."

"In the shop for what?"

"Well, someone slashed all four tires. Busted one of the rims too."

"Someone?"

"Oh, Little Moe knew who did it. It was that boss of Josie's over at the university. Moe went over there to see Josie and that's when his car got damaged."

"Did he report it?"

"And pay the insurance fees? No. He couldn't prove it was that boss, because there weren't any witnesses. But Moe knew it was him. His name was Tony, I think?"

"Toby," Annalisa supplied. "Toby Flanders."

"That's the guy. It's terrible what you all have done to Little Moe. Look at him now, coming up on fifty, and he's got no wife, no kids. He's got the family business to keep him occupied, but I know he wanted more. People always look at him with suspicion, no matter how many years go by. Funny how you cops can ruin someone's life without any proof. It was worse right after it happened—no one would even sit with us in church. In church! God forgives, but Doris McGillicuddy does not, let me tell you."

"Your son was stalking Josie Blanchard."

"Nonsense." She waved her hand. "Girls like it when a man is persistent. They appreciate a grand gesture."

"What kind of grand gesture did Little Moe do for Josie?"

"He bought her a fancy necklace made one of a kind, special for her. It had a solid gold elephant pendant with emerald eyes. She might've said she didn't want to be together with Little Moe anymore, but she didn't give that necklace back. That's how he knew."

"Knew what?" Annalisa asked, confused.

Linda looked over the rim of her teacup with mild surprise. "She didn't really mean it."

CHAPTER FOURTEEN

Kayla Noelle Kaminski had always picked the wrong man. She certainly always did have her pick. From the time she was thirteen and her boobs came in, boys lined up from far and wide for the chance to ask her out. It had started with Mickey Hill back in the eighth grade, when she thought he took her to the spring dance because he liked her and they were going to go steady, when in reality, he'd just wanted to grab her butt in front of Holly Parker to make her jealous. Since then, there had been a dozen different Mickeys; the last one before Leo was a blue-eyed charmer who'd tucked her under his arm and sworn he'd take care of her. He'd taken care of her bank account instead, using her own money to buy her presents at first, and then later bags of weed and a seven-hundred-dollar leather jacket for himself.

Kayla had kicked him to the curb one week before the lady in apartment 12B turned up dead. As the occupant of 12A, Kayla had to be interviewed and that's how she met Leo Hammond, a cop. His profession was exciting to her at first. He had a real job with real money. He had a real family too, but Kayla hadn't known about them until it was too late. Then again, back then, there were lots of things she hadn't known.

She parked her Jag in the driveway like always and walked up the front walk, careful to avoid the new icy patches that had formed by the melting and refreezing snow. Leo usually took care of the outside, salting and sanding. She hadn't realized it would get bad this fast. She looked around to see if anyone was watching, but the street was quiet and dark. There was no one present to see her sneaking back into her own house like a criminal. She blinked rapidly and saw a notice tacked to the door. Upon closer inspection, it read: CRIME SCENE DO NOT ENTER.

"Screw that," Kayla said, yanking down the notice. The cops said the place was still a crime scene, but near as she could see, they'd driven off two days ago and hadn't been back since. They'd left it looking like something from Halloween or fucking *CSI*. Her hand shook as she cut the tape loose with her key. What were the cops going to do, throw her in prison? It was her fucking house. At least she was pretty sure it was. Leo had said he'd put her name on the deed. This was part of why she was there, to find it. She'd find the deed and whatever else he kept from her in the safe in his office, the one he hid behind that awful dog picture. The banks had already frozen the accounts due to the murder investigation. They were all in Leo's name and he was dead now. Her card with the PIN did absolutely zippo, as did screaming at the teller to *give her the money fucking now*. Security had escorted her out after the frigid bitch in the navy suit informed her frostily that she had better talk to an attorney about her "options."

She would have about a million "options" coming to her once the insurance policies cleared, but for that to work, someone had to be arrested for Leo's murder. Someone who was not her, according to her attorney—who, come to think of it, was really Leo's attorney. She should probably fix that too. But a new lawyer cost money, and that was what she didn't have. "Is there anything on this whole planet that's fucking mine?" she muttered as the front door finally came free. She flicked on the recessed lights and saw her year of hard work reflected on every surface. Soothing gray walls, bright ecru white on the bookshelves. A white shag rug in front of the fireplace, anchoring a conversation space that included a scrumptious peacock-blue sofa with classic English arms, a sweetheart back, T-cushions on the seat, and turned front legs. Each detail enhanced the function and aesthetics of the home, working seamlessly to create an atmosphere that was modern but welcoming. Leo's lone contribution was the black leather armchair and the giant TV above the gas fireplace—the only two pieces in the room he ever touched, and that included Kayla when she was in it.

The slate tiles of the entryway made her heels *click, click* as she marched through the front room and toward Leo's office. She tried not to think about him dead upstairs in their bed. The coroner had taken him away, of course, but every time she closed her eyes she was back in that bathroom, cracking her head on the wall when the gunfire started. That's why she needed something—to help her nerves. The medics had given her five Xanax but she'd used them all up within a few hours. Tom was no help at all. She'd texted him and even called him when he was home, despite his repeated warnings not to. Ever since he'd gotten shot, he'd acted all paranoid.

I can't do this anymore, he'd said when she finally managed to lure him over. Leo had been working the late shift.

Baby, relax. No acrobatics, okay? I can just give you a BJ. Think of it like therapy.

This had worked for a while but since Leo's death, he'd cut off contact completely. Didn't answer her calls; her texts went unread. She'd been scared shitless Leo would find out about them. But to notice her cheating, he'd have to notice her at all. Every night, he took his Coors Light straight to the chair like usual, barely looking at her as he passed. Maybe one of his kids could've squealed. Nicole was all right, but uptight Brian always looked at her with the same expression—thin lips and his nose in the air like he was too good to be in her company.

In Leo's office, Kayla took down the frightful painting—a bulldog dressed as a mermaid, complete with a seashell brassiere—and revealed the safe. It had a keypad to enter the combination, which she did not know. She tried the alarm code he'd set up for the house. No dice. Leo's birthday. Her birthday. Fuck, when were his kids born again? She had no clue. She started sifting through the papers on his desk. The man kept a shocking amount of junk mail. Old bills. Sticky notes with his illegible handwriting on them. He had a birthday card from Nicole last year still open and propped up where he could see it. Kayla doubted that prig Brian had sent his father anything, not even after Leo took him and his "roommate" Caleb to the Blackhawks playoff game.

Kayla opened the drawer and felt around under it. "Aha," she exclaimed when her fingers made contact with an index card taped to the underside of the drawer. She yanked it out and saw it had a bunch of accounts and passwords written on it. One by one, she tried them on the safe but she got nowhere. She cursed again and threw the card back on the desk. She needed a hit so bad. Screw Tom for screwing her, and an extra fuck-you to Leo for landing them all in this mess. She'd about peed herself when she'd cracked open the bathroom door and seen the frogman standing there.

He'd turned at the noise, the gun still in his hands.

She'd yelped and thrown her arms in the air. *I'm sorry, don't shoot!*

She didn't know what she'd been apologizing for. The only one she should be sorry to was Leo for cheating on him, and he was already dead. Sweat had started pooling under her arms. Her heart turned to liquid in her chest and she'd been sure she was about to die.

The frogman had looked her over for a long, agonizing minute. Tossed the gun on the bed. Then he'd *flop-flopped* his flippers out of her bedroom and out of the house. She'd been too terrified to move, so relieved to be spared that she hadn't budged for several minutes. When she finally did move, her first thought was to grab the gun in case he came back. Well, the police took that too, so now she had her friend Suzy's little snub nose on loan. Kayla sat in the chair behind the desk, clutching her purse with the gun in it. She'd loved this old house once and couldn't wait to make it hers. Now every creak felt like someone coming through the door.

No one came in through the basement window, that female detective had told her. That meant they couldn't explain how he got in. They asked Kayla for her ideas, plainly expecting her to admit to shooting Leo herself. As if she'd ruin the Sferra sheets like that! Put a bullet hole in her wall? No fucking way.

Kayla took a deep breath, trying to think. She studied the picture of Leo and his kids that he kept on his desk, taken when they were all young. They hung on him like baby chimps. Maybe she could call up Nicole and ask her birthday. Try to make it sound casual. The poor girl was probably home crying her eyes out. Nicole was always her go-to source for information in this family. Like when Kayla discovered her new husband was a sleepwalker. She'd touched Leo that first time and he'd shoved her so hard she'd landed on her ass. He'd screamed loud enough to rattle the chandelier. *It wasn't my fault!*

What's that about? Kayla had asked Nicole when they'd had her and her hubby over for dinner the week after that. The men were in the other room catching the last quarter of the football game.

Nicole had turned beet red. *I don't know.*

The red color said she did know something. Kayla had to get it out of her, if only for self-preservation the next time Leo started wandering the house. She'd made her eyes big and wet—a trick that worked as well on women as it did on men. *Please. I want to help him.*

Nicole had appeared stricken. *I'm not positive,* she'd whispered. *But you know they killed a guy by accident, Dad and his partners? It was a long time ago, but I'm sure he still feels guilty about it. I mean, wouldn't you be?*

What Kayla wanted to be was out of here. Away from the house. Maybe she'd even get out of town completely—go visit her aunt in Seattle. She could almost hear Leo's lawyer frowning. Don't leave town. Sure, they'd all love it if she stayed put waiting for the frogman to come back. Because despite all the questions she'd answered, Kayla still hadn't voiced her true fear about that night. She couldn't put it into words. There was something in the way the frogman stood, something in his posture that was familiar. She couldn't explain what it was, whether it was the set of his shoulders or the curve of his face under all that rubber. She'd been too far away to see the color of his eyes, but close enough that she'd seen the recognition in them. He knew her. Which meant she probably knew him too. She'd be damned if she was going to hang around long enough to be reintroduced.

"Dammit, where the hell are you?" She rattled the desk drawer as though she could literally shake loose the combination to the safe. The tremor caused the picture frames to pitch face-forward onto the desk. She righted them, first the one of his kids and then the second one, Leo as a boy with his beloved bulldog, Stan. No, not Stan. Steve? She picked up the picture and squinted at it. There was a name in silver letters on the collar. Samson. On a whim, she turned Samson into numerals—726766—and punched them into the keypad. The safe unlocked.

Kayla let out a tiny squeal and bounced with happiness. Inside, she found some papers, including the deed—no, her name wasn't on it—as well as several thousand dollars' worth of treasury bonds. The biggest item was a canvas duffel bag that had been crammed inside the metal safe. She hauled it out and unzipped it to reveal an enormous pile of cash. Hundred-dollar bills, banded together in stacks of twenty each, and there must have been at least a hundred of those. "Holy shit," she said, laughing as she pawed through the money. She wanted to dump it on the floor and roll around in it.

Her fingers brushed something that wasn't cash. She pulled it out and discovered it was an envelope. Inside was a folded piece of paper and the handwriting was Leo's. *Make sure this gets to Eddie,* he wrote.

Kayla's shoulders sagged. Her mind whirled as she searched her memory banks for anyone named Eddie or Edward. There was a guy at Leo's precinct named Ted, but Leo couldn't stand the man. Said he had a stick up his ass about some procedural form Leo didn't think was necessary. Kayla doubted this could be the man Leo intended the money for. But maybe it didn't matter what Leo wanted, she reasoned as she started stuffing the money back in the bag. Leo was dead.

The house creaked like someone walked across the upstairs. *The wind,* Kayla told herself. *It's the wind.* She started shoving the money in faster. She had a flash of the frogman standing there with the gun, deciding whether she lived or died. He'd spared her life once but no telling what he might do next. Was this man Eddie, come to collect his money?

Leo had secrets. They seemed sexy at first. Dangerous and fun. Her friend Suzy had married a urologist with a fancy practice off of Michigan Avenue. Suzy said he was nice and the money was outrageous. It was also boring, which is why Suzy didn't need her gun. Kayla married Leo thinking he was mysterious, the way he came and went in the night, prowling the city streets for the monsters that had come out from under their beds. She hadn't realized the streets didn't stay outside at the end of shift. That in the dark the cops and monsters sometimes looked alike.

Kayla cleaned out the safe and replaced the ugly picture in front of it. She slung the bag over her shoulder and as she headed out the door, she grabbed her phone. She wasn't going to let Tom ignore her this time, not when one of Leo's secrets could come out of his grave and track her down. She had just one important question:

Who the hell is Eddie?

CHAPTER FIFTEEN

....

Annalisa lay curled with her phone under the weight and warmth of the down comforter, not ready to face her day. The bedroom was spacious enough to accommodate a king, the Realtor had told her with a bright smile, so Annalisa had purchased one even though she, at five foot eight, would have fit comfortably in a double. Now she rolled around in an ocean of space, alone under a white ceiling sky. She checked her email and found a note from Sassy. *Good to see you at dinner yesterday. I hope this means you've changed your mind about testifying at Alex's sentencing. The lawyer needs a decision soon.* Annalisa deleted it without replying and tossed the phone across the bed. It chimed as if in protest.

Annalisa raised her head from the pillow so she could see the screen and found an alert that Colin had updated his photo stream. Eager to imagine herself somewhere else, she flopped across the bed on her belly and grabbed up the phone to check it. She found a half dozen photos of old cars and the old men who owned them, standing next to their shining chrome babies like proud papas at a hospital nursery. Annalisa admired the way Colin shot the Chevy Bel Air straight-on so its headlights became eyes and the grille gleamed like a metal shark's mouth. She tapped "like" on the newest photos and took the phone with her to the bathroom just in case he saw her activity and replied. He hadn't spoken to her since he'd left. No texts or calls. Most days, she understood why, but sometimes she wanted to scream at him. *I burned down my whole life to make them pay. Why can't you forgive me?*

She spat her toothpaste into the right-side sink. The left one went untouched, despite the Realtor's fawning over what a selling point it was. Annalisa was buying on her own at the time. How many bathroom sinks did the real estate lady think she needed? Maybe she'd been looking down the line. Room to grow, the Realtor said when she'd pointed out the second bedroom. But five years later, Annalisa was exactly the same size.

She wiped her mouth and checked her phone again. No message from Colin. She looked at his pictures once more, tracing the outline of a wheel with the gentleness she might have used to touch his face. She imagined him crouching down with his camera to get the best shot and the visual caused an idea to spark in her brain. *Car cameras. Of course.* She raced through the rest of her morning routine and ran out the door to her car. The extra kick in the engine that Moe Bocks had admired did her no good as she had to fight her way through Monday-morning traffic. When she finally arrived at division headquarters, Nick was already at his desk.

"We need to check traffic tickets from the night Josie Blanchard was murdered," she said, breathless from her sprint into the station. She hadn't even unwound her scarf. "Moe wasn't driving the Jetta or a van."

Nick shifted uncomfortably. "Listen, you have to—"

"No, wait," she said, cutting him off excitedly. "His father lent him a red Pontiac Grand Prix, maybe with dealer plates, maybe registered to himself or the business. Why wouldn't Moe have said this at the time? Because he was fleeing the scene of the crime."

"Annalisa . . ."

"He was there the night of the murder. He was there and he knows we can prove it. He didn't want the truth coming out about his car so he didn't mention the swap."

"Vega!" Zimmer's voice rang out from across the floor. "My office, now, please."

Annalisa looked in her direction and the commander did not appear happy. "What's going on?" Annalisa asked Nick under her breath. "Did the commander get decaf by mistake this morning?"

"I was trying to tell you. Bocks is here . . . with his lawyer."

Great. Annalisa closed her eyes and shook her head. "Check the traffic tickets," she told Nick as she started a slow walk to her doom. "You'll see I'm right."

"Yeah, right out of a job," he replied as he pulled over his keyboard and began tapping on it. "I told you not to mess with Bocks."

Annalisa straightened her spine and walked into Zimmer's office with her head held high. If Bocks was here with a lawyer, it meant he was scared. "—won't stand for this campaign of harassment," the lawyer was saying as Annalisa entered the room. Zimmer's expression was sullen, her arms folded in a defensive posture.

"Detective Vega," she said. "I believe you know Morris Bocks. This is his attorney, Bradley Sheffield. They have concerns about your visit to Mr. Bocks's mother's house yesterday."

Bocks pointed at Annalisa. "You have no right questioning my mother, intruding in her space like that."

Zimmer cast a beleaguered look at Annalisa. "Is this true? Did you question his mother?"

"We had a friendly conversation. She invited me in," Annalisa said in protest. She spread her hands. "We even had tea."

"You talked to her about Josie Blanchard," Sheffield said. "It was a police visit, not a social call." He appealed to Zimmer once more. "She has no jurisdiction. It's not her case. She's just targeting my client because she doesn't want him dating her brother's ex-wife."

Zimmer's eyes widened. "He's dating your brother's wife?"

"Ex-wife," Annalisa mumbled.

"We had a family dinner yesterday," Bocks said heatedly, "and she didn't like me being there. So in revenge she drove to my mother's house and harassed her with a bunch of pointless questions."

"They aren't pointless," Annalisa shot back. "Josie was murdered and no one has paid for it."

"You see?" Sheffield said to Zimmer. "She's decided he's guilty, and she's just running around town, smearing his name and interfering with his family. She has no cause, no evidence, and no standing. She's basically a stalker with a badge."

"Now, hold on one minute," Zimmer said, "a single conversation with a witness does not equal stalking."

"She followed him the other night."

"I didn't follow him." At Zimmer's pointed look, Annalisa sighed in frustration. "We ended up in the same place." She glared at Bocks. "Maybe he was following me."

Zimmer held up her hands. "Enough. Let's put an end to this right now. Vega, you will stop all investigation of Mr. Bocks. Central Division has the Blanchard case and it's theirs to reckon with."

"I want an official reprimand," Sheffield huffed. "I want something on the record."

"And I want a pony," Zimmer replied drily.

"Commander, listen," said Annalisa, leaning over Zimmer's desk. "Don't you want to know what his mother said?"

"Did she take back his alibi?" Zimmer replied.

"Well, no, but—"

"Then we're done here. Get back to work on the Hammond case. Steer clear of Mr. Bocks. Am I understood?"

"What if he shows up at Sunday dinner?" Annalisa said petulantly. "Am I supposed to let him have custody of my family too?"

"I wasn't aware you wanted anything to do with them. Nor they with you," Sheffield added in an icy tone. Annalisa felt the rebuke and it stung, having her personal business dragged out in front of her boss like this. "We find it highly suspicious that Detective Vega decided to drop by her parents' place at the precise moment my client was visiting."

"It was family dinner," she said, throwing up her hands. "And it was my family."

"I've made my decision clear," Zimmer said with a note of finality. "If Mr. Bocks wishes to object further, he can file a complaint with the Civilian Office of Police Accountability." She gave a meaningful pause. "We know he knows the way."

Bocks rose to his feet. When he spoke, his voice was low and threatening. "If you Neanderthal cops would get it through your tiny pinhead brains that I did not kill Josie, then I wouldn't need to file so many complaints."

"Thank you," Zimmer said with no trace of gratitude. She made a sweeping gesture at the door. "I'll take that under advisement. Good day, gentlemen."

Bocks locked his gaze with Annalisa's as Sheffield gathered his briefcase and overcoat. The lawyer moved to the door and opened it, looking back expectantly for his client. Bocks took two slow steps and stopped right in front of Annalisa. "You won't beat me," he told her softly. "So don't try."

"Your mom says you suck at the piano," she told him.

"Moe," Sheffield said in warning from the doorway. "Let's go."

Bocks's nostrils flared and it looked like he wanted to say something more, but he eventually followed his attorney out the door. Annalisa's shoulders sagged in relief as they left, but when she turned, Zimmer was glowering at her. "I mean it," she said. "I don't want a repeat of that. You keep out of the Blanchard case. Central is working it."

"They're not," she said. "They're not even trying."

"I don't care. It's not our problem."

Annalisa felt stunned. She watched as Zimmer pulled out a folder and began reading the top printed page, essentially dismissing her. "So that's it? We just let him get away with it?"

"You're not getting me here," Zimmer said impatiently. "We signed up to obey all the laws, not just some of them. These include laws about jurisdiction and harassment of public citizens."

"I wasn't harassing him!"

"I can't protect you. Do you understand that? You are not operating within legal bounds, Detective. I don't care how righteous your cause. Sure, you believe you're on the side of the angels and that the circumstances demand your action, but you're over the line here. What's more, you don't seem to see it. That's what concerns me . . . because it's exactly what happened to your father."

Annalisa felt her blood leave her body. Her heart actually stopped. "Wh-what did you say?" she murmured when she could breathe again.

"He had his reasons. You have yours. The law disagrees with both of you. Maybe you're right that Moe Bocks murdered that girl, but if you go outside the law, you'll destroy any chance she has for justice. And you'll ruin your career in the process. Now, please go work on the case that is actually assigned to you. I hear Leo Hammond needs justice of his own."

Annalisa walked in a trance back to her desk, her feet carrying her out of habit. She sank down in her chair and stared blankly at her computer monitor. She felt like she'd just gone nine rounds with a heavyweight and lost. Gradually, she became aware that Nick was waving at her from across their desks. "Earth to Vega . . ."

She jerked to attention and smoothed her hair behind her ears. "Yes, what?"

He held up a slip of paper. "You were right. A Pontiac Grand Prix registered to Moe Bocks Senior was flagged by the traffic camera at Kedzie and Belmont the night Josie Blanchard died. Bocks paid the ticket straightaway. Obviously there's no record of who was driving."

"What was the time?"

"Two thirty-three a.m."

"So he was there," she said, smacking her hand on the desk.

"Well, he was six blocks away. That's all we can prove." He scooted around on his chair until it rolled up alongside her. "What did Zimmer have to say?" he asked her in a low voice.

"To leave Bocks alone," Annalisa replied, disgusted. "She says I could ruin my career."

Nick looked concerned. "And?"

Annalisa grabbed the piece of paper from him that contained the traffic ticket information. "And it might be worth it."

CHAPTER SIXTEEN

"I THINK WE NEED TO TRACK DOWN VIVIAN CATALANO," ANNALISA SAID. Across the desk, Nick took a crunchy bite of apple and fixed her with a puzzled look.

"Who?" he asked with his mouth full.

"She's the witness from the night Josie Blanchard died, the one who saw the white van with the eagle. No one asked her about a Pontiac Grand Prix, because they didn't know that's what Bocks was driving at the time. I figure it's worth asking her to see if we can put him on Josie's street that night."

Nick scooted his chair closer. "Bocks left with his lawyer not twenty minutes ago," he said. "You really like living dangerously, don't you?"

"They told me to stay away from Bocks. No one said anything about Vivian Catalano."

"What about the Hammond case?"

"What about it?" She fished around in her desk drawer for her lip balm but came up empty. Maybe she'd left it in the car.

"We're supposed to be working it."

"We are. We don't know for sure Moe Bocks isn't involved in Hammond's death too. Anyone sick enough to design his own garrote might also dress up in a diving suit to commit murder. In fact, it might be a stroke of genius. If they ran his DNA against the garrote at the time, then he's already in the system. A single hair at the Hammond home would give him away. So instead he covers himself head to toe in rubber, ensuring no skin cells, hairs, or sweat stains are left behind. It's brilliant when you think about it."

"There's just one problem with that." Nick crunched some more apple. "The killer definitely used the family's alarm code to get in."

"What? You didn't tell me that."

"The alarm company just provided the info this morning. The security system at the Hammond house was armed at 11:11 p.m. and then the family code was used to disarm it at the front door at 2:47 a.m. So unless Moe Bocks somehow had access to that code, he's not our killer."

"I think we need to go back to the house again." She wanted to see it with this new information in mind.

"Okay," he agreed as he rolled back to his desk and grabbed his coat. "Then we should talk to Tom Osborne and Kayla Hammond again. I found a reception desk clerk who remembers seeing them together a few weeks ago. She said Kayla wore dark glasses and a hat, like she was trying not to be recognized, and the clerk thought she might be someone famous. But when she saw Tom and his cane, she figured not so much."

"Let's start with Kayla." Tom was on the job. He'd know all their tricks.

She headed for the door, and Nick followed, holding the apple with his teeth as he shrugged into his jacket. "Are we taking my car or yours?" he asked when he could talk again.

Annalisa already had her key fob ready. "I thought you might want to take separate cars. Seeing as how you want to go your own way."

"I haven't gone anywhere."

"Yet." The car chirped and she climbed in the driver's seat. Nick ditched the remainder of his apple and got in the other side.

"You're one to talk, you know. You're the one who doesn't want a partner."

She gunned the engine. "That's crap."

"Is it? You run off to the Blanchard murder scene and don't say anything to me about it. Then you ditch me yesterday to go interview Bocks's mother without a word about where you were going. Zimmer asked me this morning about it and I had to say I had no idea."

"Sassy's my family. It's my problem."

"Right," he said, backing away from her. "Your problem all by yourself. The way the Lovelorn Killer was also your problem alone. Your rules, your way, always and forever, amen."

"Now who's not being fair? Partners are supposed to back each other's play."

"Yes," he agreed. "And you don't even let me in the game."

She gripped the wheel in frustration. "Do you want to go after Bocks with me or not?"

"It's not about Bocks. It never was."

She simmered at a red light, ignoring him. *You didn't do this,* she told herself. It was everyone else who screwed up, disappeared, or walked out and left her to do the cleaning up. Nick had tomcatted his way around town but she'd had to do the legal work to end their marriage. All he had to do was sign the papers—which, she supposed, was all he'd done to marry her in the first place. He was quiet on the drive but his leg took on a nervous bounce. Nick was the rare cop who didn't enjoy conflict; he'd give you anything you wanted in the moment just to make it stop. "Relax," she said as she reached the Hammond house. "I'm not going to fight you. If you want to move divisions, go."

He looked her over cautiously. "What is it you want, Vega? You've never said."

"What I want, I can't have." She turned on her heel and walked up the path to the Hammond house, where she stopped short at the broken seal on the front door. "Someone has been here."

Nick jogged up the steps next to her and crowded in for a closer look. "The lock is intact, so they used a key."

She brandished their copy and opened the door. The downstairs looked as pristine as when they had seen it the night of the murder. "Nothing seems disturbed." She turned to her immediate right to examine the alarm box mounted on the wall. "We should have this checked for prints. I know Kayla said the intruder wore gloves, but maybe we'll get lucky."

"So what are we thinking? Kayla gave out the code? Maybe to Tom or some other lover?"

Annalisa walked to the stairs and started up them. "Someone came in that night. Kayla would have no reason to disarm the alarm if she was the shooter."

"Unless she was set-dressing her frogman story."

"That's what the window was for. Whoever came in, he or she didn't want us to know they had the code." She reached the bedroom and stopped at the threshold. The bed had been stripped, leaving only the stained mattress. The bedside table on Leo's side still held the broken photo frame and the shattered glass. Annalisa moved until she stood approximately where the shooter would have been at the point they dropped the gun. She raised her arm as if to fire. "Call it ten feet to the bed?" she asked Nick.

"That's right."

"Pretty easy shot."

"Probably why they didn't miss."

"Yeah, that's my point," she said as she crossed to the far side of the bed and picked up the shattered picture frame. The photo appeared to have been from Leo and Kayla's wedding, judging from his suit and her white dress. Annalisa had to guess about the identity of the woman, though, because the bullet hole took off her head. "We had theorized the shooter missed initially, hitting the picture or the wall first and then taking out Leo. But Leo didn't move. His eyes weren't even open. A gunshot should have made him bolt right up in bed."

"You're thinking the killer shot Leo first and then the picture?"

She held it up for him. "What if it wasn't an accident? What if it was a statement?"

"But whoever it was, they didn't kill Kayla, even though they had the opportunity."

"Maybe the statement isn't against Kayla in particular. Maybe they didn't like the marriage."

"Well, then we ought to be talking to Maura Hammond. She used to live here. You think she knew the alarm code?"

Annalisa gave a wry smile as she regarded the picture in her hands. "Kayla Hammond redid this whole place from top to bottom. I'd bet you the first thing to get a makeover was the alarm code."

"Is that the first thing you did when I moved out?"

"Please. Our alarm was the creaky step outside the front door and Mrs. Nelson's hellcat that always sat on the fire escape. The one with only one eye?"

"I swear I once saw that cat with a cigarette. It was lit too." She laughed in spite of herself, and he grinned in reply. He wandered into the bathroom and then stuck his head back out. "What if Kayla was in here because she knew the shooter was coming? I might duck out if I knew my husband was about to be blown away. Just because I wanted him dead doesn't mean I'd like to watch it happen."

"Point taken." A noise from downstairs made her freeze. Nick's rigid posture echoed hers, telling her he'd heard it too. A door slammed. She heard male voices and hurried footsteps. Nick held a finger to his lips and they both crept out of the room and into the hall.

"Let's make this quick," one man was saying. "This place gives me the creeps."

Annalisa grabbed Nick's arm as she recognized the voice. "Leo's son," she mouthed to him. "Brian."

They listened as the footsteps crossed the downstairs of the house and stopped in the rear south corner. Annalisa shrugged at Nick and started down the stairs as quietly as she could. He fell into step behind her, and together they stalked the voices at the back of the home. "Shit, it doesn't work," Brian said.

"What do we do now, then?"

"Let me text my mom."

"Say hi from us," Annalisa said as she materialized in the doorway.

Brian yelped and dropped his cell phone. The other young man turned out to be Caleb, Brian's shaggy-haired roommate. Caleb put up his hands like a criminal while Brian scrambled on the floor for his phone. "God, you scared us," Brian said as he stood up, his skinny chest rising and falling with his rapid breathing.

"What are you doing?" Annalisa asked. She entered the room so Nick could move in behind her. She saw a wall safe had been exposed, presumably by removing the picture of a mermaid bulldog that now sat propped up on the floor beneath it.

Brian scratched the back of his head and looked around the room vaguely. "We, ah, we came to get some stuff."

"What stuff?"

"Nothing big. My mom has a few things she wanted . . . you know, for sentimental reasons."

Annalisa took another step closer to him. "Your mother moved out of here years ago. What did she want that she didn't take then?"

Brian seized the picture from the floor. "Uh, this. She . . . she loved this old thing."

"Uh-huh." Annalisa checked with Nick to see if he was buying even a word. He shook his head. Annalisa pointed behind Brian to the safe. "What's in there?"

"Nothing." His voice rose an octave. "I mean, I don't know. It was my dad's."

"His mother wanted us to get into it," Caleb supplied, and Brian glared at him in response. Caleb shrugged. "They can see what we're up to here, Bri. They're not exactly stupid."

"What's in there that your mother wants?" Annalisa asked.

"Not sure," Brian mumbled. "Treasury bonds, maybe some cash. She wanted me to take a look. But it doesn't matter since the combination she gave me doesn't work anyway." His phone rang and he answered it with a resigned sigh. "Hi, Mom. No, my birthday didn't work. Neither did Nicole's. I don't know their anniversary. Besides, the cops are here and . . . no, I don't know why. Mom, calm down, okay?" He wandered out of the room, his voice growing softer as he moved to the front of the house.

Nick started searching the desk, lifting up the blotter and opening the drawers. "What are you doing?" Annalisa asked him.

"Leo was old-school, pushing fifty. If I have to keep a list of my passwords written down, it figures he did too."

Caleb watched Nick's search for a moment and then turned his attention to Annalisa. "You figure out who killed Leo yet?"

"No," she told him flatly. "You have any ideas?"

He shrugged one shoulder. "Probably a long list. Leo was an asshole." He fixed her with a look. "But I'm guessing you already knew that." She didn't even twitch in response, but Caleb nodded like he understood. "Brian was only just figuring it out. He thought his dad was like, a superhero or something."

The Fantastic Four, Annalisa recalled. "How long have you known Brian?"

The shrug again. "About three years, I guess. I was working in a bike shop and he brought his Devinci in for repair. Turns out, we both like biking the trails around here so we started meeting up—you know, Raceway Woods and stuff. When he needed a place to stay last year, he moved in with me. It works."

"So you're roommates then?"

Caleb rolled his eyes. "Did Kayla tell you we're screwing each other? That's her thing, not ours. Brian has it bad for some coffee girl named Lila."

"Coffee girl?"

"Like, she works the counter at Starbucks? Bri keeps ordering these super-fancy froufrou drinks as an excuse to talk to her longer. He doesn't even like them."

"Found it!" Nick said with a triumphant grin. He held up a crumpled sticky note with a bunch of writing on it. Annalisa watched as he went to the safe and began trying the combinations. The first one didn't work. Neither did the second. Her attention wandered and she returned her gaze to Caleb, who was watching Nick's progress with wary eyes.

"You're concerned about what we're going to find in there," she observed.

He shifted uncomfortably and glanced in the direction Brian had gone. "Concerned for Bri, yeah."

"Why is that?"

He narrowed his eyes at her. "I think you know." When she didn't reply, he drew in a sharp breath. "That bike Brian brought to the shop, the Devinci? It sells for more than five thousand bucks. He said it was a gift from his dad. I thought wow, his dad must be in finance or some rich old doctor. Then later I found out he's a cop. So then I was figuring the money was from his mom's side, and Brian told me she's a housewife. The presents kept coming—Bulls tickets, a leather jacket, a 4D TV—stuff my family could never afford. Brian said his dad felt bad for leaving his mom, even after he had to give her some big payday in exchange for keeping this house."

"So you're wondering where Leo's money came from."

"Aren't you?" He looked to Nick at the safe.

"None of these work," Nick reported with dismay.

"Let me ask you something," Annalisa said to Caleb. "Do you know where Brian was the night his father got killed?"

The young man's expression hardened. "You're not thinking Brian did this."

"You said yourself he was figuring out his father was an asshole."

"Yeah, I meant like he's stopped accepting the gifts. Not like he'd murder him." He pushed off from where he was leaning on the bookcase and grabbed a picture from the desk behind her. "Leo might've been an asshole, but he was also his dad."

Annalisa looked at the photo, which showed a grinning Leo outside in the yard, striking a strongman's pose with little Brian and Nicole hanging on each arm. Leo mugged for the camera but his kids were beaming at him with enough love to warm the whole picture. She and Alex used to love to play with Pops this way, climbing him like a jungle gym while he roared with laughter. A painful lump sprang up in her throat and she carefully set the photograph back down on the desk. "So is that a no on Brian's alibi, then?" she asked, turning around when she could speak again.

Caleb appeared annoyed. "We ordered pizza around nine and played video games for a few hours after that. Probably went to bed around one."

"And you have separate bedrooms?"

"Jesus, we're not gay, okay?"

"I meant that you went to bed in separate rooms. You didn't see Brian after you retired at one?"

"No, but I would've heard him. The apartment's not that big."

Nick returned to his search of the desk, taking a seat in the rolling chair and turning over the Chicago PD mug that served as a pencil holder. Only lint, paper clips, pens, and pencils fell out.

Brian returned, his aura subdued, and he shuffled over to the wall safe. "Mom says to try his dog's name. The one he had when he was a kid." He raised his eyes to Annalisa's. "Can I?"

"Sure." She folded her arms. "Let's see it."

He put in the combination and it worked. Annalisa found herself holding her breath as he swung open the metal door. They all leaned forward for a look. "It's empty," Brian reported, running his palm over the inside to verify. "There's nothing here."

Annalisa thought of the tape on the front door that had been removed before they showed up. "Who else might have the combination?" she asked.

Brian and Caleb spoke as one: "Kayla."

"I think it's time we had another chat with her . . ." Annalisa turned to Nick to see if he agreed, but he'd disappeared completely behind the desk. "Nick?"

His head popped up from where he'd been searching the floor. He held up one arm to show off a piece of paper that he'd apparently discovered under the desk. "Who's Eddie?" he asked.

CHAPTER SEVENTEEN

....

ANNALISA REACHED KAYLA HAMMOND BY PHONE, BUT THE NEW WIDOW WASN'T KEEN TO TALK. "I'm real busy getting the funeral arrangements together," she said. "The chief of police wants to meet me tomorrow to discuss the ceremonies and I haven't even picked a casket yet."

"I understand it's a difficult time. But some new questions have cropped up in our investigation and it's important we get them answered quickly. Remember, the man who broke into your house and killed your husband . . . he's still out there."

"But I already told you everything I know. Plus, my lawyer said—"

"It's about Eddie," Annalisa said, cutting her off. Kayla went silent on the other end, and Annalisa bit her lip, wondering if she'd overplayed her hand. It was a big risk, confronting Kayla about Eddie when they didn't know who he was yet.

"Meet me at Bavette's in half an hour," Kayla said finally.

Annalisa hung up with Kayla and raised her eyebrows at Nick. "Seems like Eddie is the magic word," she said. "How do you feel about steak?"

"I feel passionately about steak, as you know. Why?"

"Because we're meeting Kayla at Bavette's."

Nick settled back into the seat of her car. "She may be a two-timing murderer, but at least she's got taste."

They drove to River North, passing a multitude of others to get to the restaurant Kayla had selected. Every city block in Chicago seemed to contain a Dunkin' Donuts, a Potbelly Sandwich Shop, and a steak house. Annalisa's budget typically only allowed for the first two. She parked and looked down in dismay at the road salt rimming her sturdy shoes. At least it was early on a Monday and the fancy dress crowd wasn't likely to be in just yet.

Inside, Bavette's had a speakeasy vibe, with dark wood, etched glass signs advertising cocktails, and buttery leather seats. Nick selected a curved booth and ran his hands over the round wooden table. "Forget those pictures they show you in Catholic school, the ones that show blond Jesus floating on a cloud? I'm sure this is what heaven looks like."

A waiter in a crisp white shirt and black vest dropped off their menus. Annalisa's chest tightened in pain when she saw the prices. "The crab is eighty-three dollars," she whispered to him in a horrified voice.

Nick perused the menu, unconcerned. "It's my treat."

"Oh yeah?" She arched an eyebrow. "You got a money safe at home too, Carelli?"

"No, I just know you'll order the salad." He glanced up at her. "You were always a cheap date."

"Great, so now I'm cheap," she said without rancor.

"No, I liked that about you from the first time we met. Some girls, they like to run up the tab—it's like a test to see how bad you want them."

"Let me guess," she said, leaning across the table in a suggestive fashion. "You wanted it real bad."

"Not you, though," he said as though she hadn't spoken. "You're never playing games or trying to be someone you're not."

She sank backward with a deep sigh. "The joke's on me, then, because it would be easier if I could." The waiter came to take their orders, and Annalisa selected the smoked salmon Caesar salad while Nick chose the French dip sandwich with fries.

Kayla arrived before the food did, dressed in body-hugging pink denim jeans, matching pink sweater, and enormous sunglasses that she removed as she slid into the booth with them. "I have twenty minutes," she said by way of introduction. "Ask your questions."

"Someone's been to your house recently," Annalisa said. "The tape was removed from the door."

She turned cornflower-blue eyes from one to the other. "And? Is that a question?"

"And we know it was you," Annalisa replied.

"It is my property. You have no right to keep me out of it. My lawyer said so."

"That's true," Annalisa allowed. "But most lawyers also tell their clients they should stay away from an active crime scene or they might end up incriminating themselves."

Kayla huffed and rearranged herself in her seat, fidgeting with her pink purse. "What does it matter? You already think I did it—which I didn't, by the way. I think the frogman must have known how ridiculous the whole thing would sound. That's why he left me alive . . . to set me up!"

"It's working pretty well," Nick agreed, and she shot him a withering glare.

"What was in the safe?" Annalisa asked her.

"What safe?"

"The one in Leo's office. The one you emptied out."

"I don't know what you're talking about." A wisp of platinum-blond hair had escaped her topknot, and she tucked it primly behind her ear. "Leo never gave me the combination to that safe, and I have no idea what he kept in there. Guns, maybe. Important papers."

Nick pulled out the note he'd found on the floor of the Hammond home and smoothed it in front of him on the table. Kayla's gaze followed every last wrinkle. "We found this on the floor," he said. "Where you dropped it."

"I did no such thing."

"Then your fingerprints won't be on it," he told her, and she turned a whiter shade of pale.

"Who's Eddie?" Annalisa asked her.

Kayla said nothing.

Nick nudged the note toward her. "It says, 'Make sure this gets to Eddie.' I'm guessing that applies to whatever you found in the safe. Money? Maybe drugs?"

"I don't know who Eddie is," Kayla said. She glanced up as the waiter arrived with the food. When he offered her a menu, she waved him away. "I'm not staying." She was already inching out of the booth. "I can't help you."

"Maybe we can help you," said Nick as he plucked a fry from his plate.

"Sure," she scoffed. "Just how are you going to do that?"

Nick chewed thoughtfully. "Well, whatever you found in that safe, Leo said it belongs to Eddie. Seems to me that Eddie might come looking for it, and the last guy to come looking for Leo, it didn't work out so well."

"I'm not worried," Kayla insisted through narrowed eyes, but her hands skimmed the table edge, searching for purchase. "Maybe Maura took what was in the safe. Or one of the kids. You should be talking to them."

"Or maybe we could ask Tom Osborne," Annalisa suggested casually.

Kayla tapped one gleaming nail on the table as she considered this. "Why would you care about Tom?"

"Because we found his hair in your bed." Annalisa fudged the truth, but Kayla wouldn't know that. Her pretty face did an entire gymnastics routine of emotions, from alarmed to confused to suspicious.

"That—that doesn't prove anything," she said with some hesitancy, as if she were testing her logic. "Leo could have brought them there when they fell off his clothes."

"They weren't head hairs," Nick said drily. "Unless you're suggesting Leo and Tom had an intimate relationship."

"No," she said, pulling a face.

"It happens," Nick told her.

"Leo and Tom were just friends."

"Some friends," Annalisa said, shaking her head as she picked at her salad. "Sleeping with your buddy's wife like that . . . oof."

"It would give him motive," Nick said to Annalisa as if it were just occurring to him. "Shoot Leo and get him out of the way. Then he could be with Kayla, no problems."

"What? No." Kayla's eyes turned anxious as she looked them over searchingly. "You think that? You think Tom killed Leo? It makes no sense. He had his own family to worry about, so why would he want me? And why the fuck would he get dressed up in a rubber suit?"

"You tell us," Annalisa suggested.

"He—he wouldn't do that. He wouldn't kill Leo." She seemed less sure. She slapped her oversized purse on the table and started rooting around in it. "I need my bergamot oil. Where's my bergamot oil?"

"If your story about the rubber suit is true," Annalisa began, and Kayla halted her search.

"Of course it's true! Why the hell would I make something like that up?"

"Then there's a killer out there who may worry you can identify him. You want to take that chance?"

Kayla sagged in her seat and pinched the bridge of her nose. "I don't know who he was. I told you he had on the full suit with the mask."

"What was in the safe?" Nick asked, leaning forward. "What was Leo mixed up in?"

"Like he would tell me," Kayla replied bitterly. She traced the strap of her bag with her finger. "He wasn't a bad cop, you know? My friend Lexi works as a waitress and a couple of years ago, she started getting creeped out by this customer named Joe. Joe always demanded to be seated in her section and he kept asking her out. One time he brought a bucket of soapy water and washed her car in the parking lot. I mean, who does that? The manager told the hostess to put Joe in a different section, and Joe went nuts. Lexi was afraid he'd follow her home or something. She called the cops, and you know what they did?" She folded her arms and looked at them accusingly. "Nothing. They told Joe to stay away from her, and that's it. Did he listen? No, he came back the next day and stood around outside, waiting for her. The cops said they couldn't do anything because he was outside just standing there on public property. So, Lexi called me and I called Leo. He went to visit Joe, and after that, Joe didn't come around the restaurant anymore."

"He beat him up?" Nick asked.

"No," Kayla said, her jaw hanging open in a horrified expression. "Leastways, he didn't say so. He said he found a gun in Joe's place and Joe was on parole for—get this—stalking some girl and attacking her. Which the other cops should have known if they bothered to check him out at all instead of just telling Lexi to calm down and say thank you for the clean car. Most cops don't give a shit about the average person. They're on the job just to hassle you. Leo was like the ones you see on TV—he got shit done."

"And maybe he done some shit too," Nick said.

Kayla's gaze flickered with anger, which turned to resignation. "Yeah, maybe," she said as she resumed searching in her purse. "He saw some bad stuff. I know he was bummed out about that guy they killed on accident. Some club owner? But that was an honest mistake."

"How do you know about that?" Annalisa asked.

Kayla's bag had nearly swallowed her whole head, and she poked it back out to answer. "Leo would have nightmares. He'd be crying in his sleep and say stuff like, 'It wasn't my fault' or 'I wasn't there.' Aha, here it is!" Triumphant, she removed a small vial, uncapped it, and started dabbing the contents at her wrists. "You want some?" she asked Annalisa.

"No, thanks."

Kayla shrugged. "Okay. No offense, but it seems like you could use it."

Annalisa could use a bottle of ibuprofen or at least one of the cocktails Bavette's had on the menu. "Tell us what was in the safe, Kayla," she said. "We can help you if you let us."

"As if. You still think I did it." Her full lips thinned with disapproval as she looked from one to the other. "Like I said: cops are on the job just to hassle you."

Annalisa took out her card and pushed it across the table to her. "If Eddie decides to come collecting, give us a call."

"Assuming it's not too late," Nick added.

Kayla hesitated a moment before grabbing up the card and stuffing it in her purse. "I don't know who this Eddie guy is, but I hope you find him. I hope he did it. Then we never have to talk to each other again." She slid out of the booth and stalked away, the heels of her boots *rat-a-tatting* her annoyance as she left.

Annalisa snatched a fry from Nick's plate. "Well?" she asked him.

"Whatever was in the safe, she took it."

"Down to the dust," Annalisa agreed. "But I almost believe her when she says she doesn't know who Eddie is. I think she came here hoping we'd tell her."

"What was the name of that guy . . . the one they shot at the club?"

"Cecil Barry." Not even close to an Eddie. "Hey, you know what's weird? Kayla said Leo had nightmares about the shooting, where he said he wasn't even there. But that's not true. Frankie Vaughn killed Barry, but Leo, Paulie, and Tom were all on the scene. All four of them were named in the lawsuit filed by Barry's widow."

"Maybe Leo wasn't in the room when it happened."

"Maybe." She watched with hungry eyes as Nick practically unhinged his jaw to take a huge bite of his juicy sandwich. "Or maybe Barry's shooting isn't what gave him nightmares."

"It's looking more and more like Leo was dirty," Nick observed around a mouthful of steak. "And it'd be pretty hard to be dirty and not have your partners know about it. Whatever action Leo had going on, ten to one the others had a piece of it too."

Annalisa pushed some lettuce around with her fork. "Great," she muttered. "Leo, Paulie, Frankie, and Tom—they all have pictures of themselves shaking hands with the mayor. If we go swinging for them, it'll be the shitstorm of all time. And you know what happens when it rains shit."

Nick looked resigned as he put down his sandwich. "Everyone gets the stink."

CHAPTER EIGHTEEN

FRANKIE STOPPED BY THE DEN WHERE MAGGIE HAD THE TV TUNED TO A *LAW & ORDER* RERUN, ONLY HALF WATCHING AS SHE CONCENTRATED ON HER KNITTING. She'd seen the series all the way through at least once already, but she never seemed to tire of it. On her lap, purple and white yarn was slowly turning into a baby blanket for their coming granddaughter, due in April. Pepper lay curled up on the couch next to her. "I'm heading out," he told her, his keys in hand. Pepper perked up her ears.

"Again? You just got home." Maggie frowned at him. "It's freezing rain out there. The streets are icy."

"You know cops don't punch a clock, Mags." He walked into the cozy room and leaned down to kiss her cheek. She turned her face away with a grunt and continued knitting. Pepper put her ears down flat in her own sign of disgust when she realized she wasn't coming.

"You made us a good life," she said. "Maybe it's time you stayed home to enjoy it for longer than five minutes."

"Hey, I'm young yet and there's plenty of time." He turned to the television and gestured at it with both hands. "Look at your boy Lennie Briscoe over there. He's got at least twenty years on me and he's still on the job."

"The bullets aren't real on TV, Frank."

"No shooting tonight. I promise." He leaned down again and this time she let him kiss her. He winced from his bones rubbing on each other as he righted himself but made sure she didn't see it on his face. Truth was, he should've gotten out years ago but there was always one more bill to pay—the house, the boat, college for the kids, Stacy's wedding, and now Maggie was talking about a vacation cottage in the UP. Maybe up there he could relax. Nothing but pine trees, cool blue water, and Maggie May in a bikini top and jean shorts, with a kerchief tied around her curls. The dream felt so close if only he could hold it together a little longer. Tom was coked up again, going off the rails with some crazy story about a killer in a diving suit, and now he was freaking out about Eddie. Frankie had to make him understand: they took care of Eddie a long time ago. Annalisa Vega was the problem now.

....

They met at Griddle 24, which was basically empty due to the drizzly winter night. Paulie ordered a boozy milkshake, slurping it through a straw like some sixteen-year-old kid on a first date. Tom had a plate of pancakes and he was shoveling them down as he talked a mile a minute. "Kayla knows about Eddie, which means Leo must have told her something. She's been on me for days about getting her a score or some money, and then all of a sudden, she only wants to know about Eddie. Why's she asking about him now, huh? What did Leo tell her?"

"Relax," Frankie said, looking around to see where their waitress had gone. She remained far away behind the counter, looking bored as she scrolled through her phone. "If Kayla's asking you, that means she doesn't know anything. Right?"

Paulie let go of the straw long enough to back him up. "Right. She's an airhead."

"No, I'm telling you, she's a problem," Tom insisted as he waved his fork in Frankie's direction. "She wants money and she knows his name. If she finds out what happened to him, she's going to come back to us asking for a payday, and I don't know about you, but I don't have it."

"If all she has is a name, we don't worry about it."

"Easy for you to say. It's my balls she's got in a vise."

"She's got nothing," Frankie said. "Tell her to piss off."

"He can't," said Paulie reasonably. "He was fucking her."

"What?" Frankie turned to Tom in horrified disgust, and Tom hung his head over his plate, looking sick. "Jeez, first Leo, now you? What's this girl got, a magic pussy?" Frankie flicked a straw wrapper at Tom and hit him square in the forehead. "You better hope Vega and Carelli don't find out. Next thing you know, they'll be liking you for the shooter."

"It wasn't me." Tom had turned so white Frankie worried he might vomit on the table. "I think it might be Eddie."

"Christ, this again—"

"He's out. I checked. He got released last year."

Frankie had a flash of himself dragging the unconscious man into the alley next to the precinct. He'd been going away on drug charges anyway—three strikes, you're out—so what did it really matter what the DA wrote on the bottom line?

"I'm telling you," Tom said, breathing unsteadily, "he's hunting us down one by one."

Frankie looked down at his hands and saw they were fists. "That's crap," he said, banging the table and startling Tom. "David Edwards is not some criminal mastermind. He was literally born a user, his mom taking crack like it was prenatal vitamins. It's all he's ever known and it's all he'll ever be. If he's out, then he's not going to be bothering with us. He's going to find the nearest corner candyman and get himself a fix."

"I—I don't know." Tom scrubbed his face with both hands. "I saw him. I saw something."

"You'll see pink elephants doing the cancan if you keep putting that junk up your nose."

Tom's nostrils flared. "I wasn't using that night. I swear."

"Look," Frankie said, softer now, his tone conciliatory. He had to rein Tom in, not send him galloping off on a drugged-up fantasy. "Forget the guy in the diving suit, okay? He's not real. Talk to Kayla. If anyone can find out what she knows, it's you. Maybe she'll say something about Leo, something that proves she killed him, and we can all sleep better at night." Kayla had a million reasons to make up a story about the diving man.

"You're forgetting one thing." Paulie picked the straw out of his milkshake and sucked the end. "What if she goes running to Vega?"

"Vega." Frankie reached into his jacket pocket and fingered the ChapStick he'd lifted from Vega's desk. "I've got a plan for her. She's not going to be giving us any trouble no more." One more sting for old times' sake. If this worked, maybe he'd hang up his shield and buy Maggie May the cottage she'd always wanted. Leo had said no one would get hurt, conveniently forgetting that Frankie had already taken a bullet to the shoulder from where Cecil Barry shot him coming through the door. It no longer mattered if they got away clean, as long as they got away.

CHAPTER NINETEEN

NIGHT SHIFT AT THE STATION SMELLED LIKE BURNED COFFEE AND FLOOR WAX. Stale heat pumped in through the vents and dried out every membrane in her body. Annalisa rolled her chair to the side to allow the janitorial staff to sweep under her feet, her eyes still glued to her screen. Across the desks, Nick rubbed the back of his neck and blinked rapidly at his monitor. "The Fantastic Four have busted more than two hundred guys named Ed, Edward, Teddy, or some variation of the name," he said.

"They've worked with two dozen more," she reported from her search.

"We don't even know if this particular Eddie is in the system."

"Or if he's connected with the case," she replied wearily.

He snapped off his monitor. "I'm going home," he said. "It's past nine and I need some sleep if we're going to chase our tails again tomorrow." He stood up and put on his overcoat, lingering nearby with an air of uncertainty. "You want to grab a bite or something?"

She flashed him the half-empty bag of trail mix she'd scored from the vending machine. "No, I'm good."

"Suit yourself," Nick said in a tone that suggested she always did. "See you tomorrow."

He wandered out into the rainy night, and Annalisa rolled her shoulders to loosen them as she settled in for another computer search. The annoying beep sounded, indicating no results found. Nothing in her databases showed anything on Vivian Catalano, the woman who had witnessed the white van outside Josie's house the night of the murder. Google was similarly no help. The woman may have married and changed her name or simply moved out of state and kept a low profile. If Annalisa could get the case file, there might be additional information in it on Vivian that would help track her down. But so far, her plea to Pops for help in getting the files had come to nothing.

Annalisa reluctantly powered down her computer and set out for her empty condo. The rain had picked up considerably, melting the snow into the streets so they ran like rivers. She practically floated home. Using some file folders over her head for cover, she made a dash for the front door. There she found a single white rose, wrapped in plastic and lying on her stoop. She grabbed it up and hurried inside with it, dripping in her living room as she assessed the flower. It had no note.

"What do you make of this?" she asked her plants at the front window, holding out the rose for their inspection. She had inherited the large potted greenery from her neighbor, Amy Yakamoto, and so far, she'd somehow kept them mostly alive. The fern swayed slightly but the hibiscus said nothing. Annalisa closed the blinds and put the rose on the end table next to the other plants. She had no secret admirers. She hadn't been on a date in nearly two years. There was only Nick, and while he'd made no secret of his admiration, he'd denied leaving the roses.

She sat on the sofa and fingered the velvety edge of the flower. Maybe Colin had sent them somehow. He had picked flowers for her back when they were kids. Her phone buzzed with a text, interrupting her reverie. The all-caps message came from a number she did not recognize and it read like someone shouting at her. *IF YOU WANT 411 ON BOCKS, MEET ME AT LINCOLN PARK ZOO, NORTH LOT, 30 MINUTES. DO NOT GET OUT OF THE CAR. DO NOT BRING ANYONE ELSE.*

Annalisa wrote back: *Who is this?*

There was no reply. A check of the number on the internet revealed no owner. She lost five minutes in her search, and now she had to move it if she wanted to make the meeting. She grabbed a water-resistant slicker this time and headed back out into the rain. It slashed at her car as she drove, water arcing out from under her tires on all sides. The streetlights turned to prisms and made it hard to see, but she could navigate her destination by motor memory alone.

She rolled up in front of Nick's place and took out her phone. His bedroom light was on, so he wasn't asleep yet. He'd accused her of running off on him, and well, now she needed backup. Screw the anonymous text and its orders to come by herself. For all she knew, it was Moe himself trying to set her up. She was about to put the call through when she saw his shadow appear, walking past the window. She felt a sharp pang at how instantly she knew him from shape alone, and the sudden tightness in her chest made her pause to catch her breath. The pause was just long enough for a second shadow to pass across the bedroom window. This one was slimmer, female, and unfamiliar.

Annalisa sat there idling, staring at the warm light in the window with the phone forgotten in her lap. *I've changed,* Nick had promised. Stupid her, she'd almost believed him. She wrenched the car into gear and took off for Lincoln Park. Whatever she found there, she'd handle it on her own.

The parking lot sat dark and deserted when she arrived; no other cars nearby. She circled once, rolling through the puddles, straining to see out the rain-splattered windows for any figure that might be hiding in the shadows. She pulled into a random space but left the engine on, the defogger running on roar to keep the windows as clear as possible. She checked her gun and waited.

The meeting time went by, then ten minutes more, her wipers swishing out the passing seconds. Annalisa twisted in her seat and tried not to think about the fact that the place was rumored to be haunted. The first Chicago cemetery had been located underneath the park. When the city was rebuilt, bodies had popped up out of the ground during construction. A sharp tap on her passenger-side window made her jump with a gasp. She saw a large dark figure in a raincoat outside but couldn't make out his face. He rapped again and shouted to her. "Dammit, Vega, let me in!"

She unclicked the locks with her left hand, the gun in her right. Rain and wind whooshed inside as the man heaved himself into the other seat. Water dripped from his coat and the brim of his old-fashioned black felt hat. He held a file folder box with a lid on it that barely fit on his lap, thanks to his considerable belly. He grunted when he saw her gun. "You gonna shoot me? Seems like it would make an awful mess of your car."

"You're Bob Dickey," she said, the terror in her chest easing as she recognized the face from her memory. Dickey used to play cards with Pops back in the day. Sometimes, she'd sat on Pop's lap for luck and he'd let her put the cards on the table for him.

"Who did you think I was?" he asked, annoyed. "You're the one who asked for this meeting."

"Right." She tucked the gun back in her holster and eyed the box on his lap. "Are those the files on the Blanchard case?"

"I made copies of everything I got." He cradled the box protectively. "I just want you to know. I'm doing this for George, not for you."

"Yeah? Did he tell you why he was asking?"

"Yeah. Bocks is a person of interest in the murder you're working—that cop, right? Leo Hammond." He crossed himself and shook his head. "What a fucking shame."

"Is that all Pops told you?"

"Ain't that enough? It's about time someone nailed Bocks to the wall. If it has to be you that collars him, then so be it."

"Bocks was bellied up to Pops's dining-room table the other day chowing down on my mother's food. He's dating Alex's wife, who's also the mother of two of Pops's grandkids."

His bushy eyebrows shot up under his hat. "No fooling? He didn't tell me that."

"Pops has a way of leaving out the important stuff," Annalisa said darkly. She reached for the box but Dickey held it back from her. "What?" she asked impatiently. "Are you going to help me out here or not?"

"I need your word that you leave me out of it. I got my pension to think about, and I don't need you to do me like you did George. I don't even want to be seen sitting in this car with you."

The wind picked up with a sudden gust, slamming a loose branch against her windshield. She barely had time to flinch before the wind rushed it away again. "Katie Duffy ended up just like Josie Blanchard in there," she said, gesturing at Dickey's box. "Someone came into her home and squeezed the life out of her. Pops covered it up. You think he shouldn't pay?"

"You think he hasn't?" Dickey shot back. "He took that weight all on himself."

"Now it crushed the lot of us," she said evenly. She yanked the box from him and took off the lid. "What's in here?"

He made a harrumphing noise. "Original case notes and witness statements, color copies of the photos. Everything I could find. I could get in deep shit if they find out it was me who smuggled them out to you."

"I suggest you run along, then." She picked up the copies of the photos and turned on the overhead light in the car so she could see them better. Dickey made no attempt to leave. He leaned over to try to examine the pictures with her, casting a shadow over the pages. "Do you mind?"

He drew back with a hard sniff. "There's like twenty cops who've looked at this stuff over the years. What are you going to see that they ain't seen?"

"It's not about the eyes. It's the perspective." She held up a photo of the murder weapon, which showed a length of wire perhaps twenty inches long and with a wooden handle on each end, painted a bright sky blue.

"That's the key, right there," Dickey said, tapping the paper in her hand. "Connect him to the weapon."

"DNA?"

He shook his head. "We tried that. Nada. I swear we ran down every single fiber, interviewed every neighbor, shook Bocks up and down until he rattled. We exhausted almost every angle on this thing and got nowhere."

"Almost every angle?"

He pursed his lips as if deciding whether to say more. "We pushed hard," he said, fisting one hand for emphasis. "And we got nothing. Maybe Moe Bocks committed the one perfect crime and he can spend the rest of his life having a good laugh at us . . . but I been thinking maybe . . . maybe the reason we didn't find anything on him is because he didn't do it."

CHAPTER TWENTY

....

Sassy bent over Carla's bed and tucked her daughter's wayward leg back under the blankets. Carla didn't stir. Asleep like this, her dark hair in waves around her face, she looked so much like her father it made Sassy's teeth hurt to look at her. She was perfection. Sassy had loved Alex since she wasn't much older than Carla was now, when he was a boy with a mop of curly hair daring her to climb the tallest tree at the park. She dreamed sometimes that they were still kids hiding in their boxy clubhouse, and she'd block the door to try to warn him about what was to come. *Don't go to Katie's house.* But he would laugh in the dream and say Katie made the best peanut butter and oatmeal cookies and they should go get some right now. Meanwhile, Annalisa banged on the door outside the clubhouse, demanding to be let in. Alex would try to push Sassy out of the way to let his sister inside and Sassy would scream, *No, no, no, she can't find you!*

Sassy left her daughter's room and bumped directly into Moe, who was standing in the darkened hall. She gasped in genuine fear. "What are you doing here?" She'd left him with a glass of wine downstairs.

"You were gone so long I wondered what was wrong. I thought you might need a hand."

"I'm fine." She put up her palms when he tried to reach for her. "Don't wake the girls."

She led him back downstairs and found her own abandoned wineglass, which he had thoughtfully refilled. "You seem tense," he said as he came up behind her and started massaging her neck. She raised her shoulders and moved from under his touch.

"It's a lot," she said. "The girls, work . . . I'm just tired."

"I see." He cocked his head and looked at her. "This isn't about my meeting with Annalisa, is it? Because she gave me no choice."

"No, I understand." He'd told her that his lawyer had instructed Annalisa to back off. He'd thought Sassy would be pleased. Instead, she felt nervous around him for the first time since they'd met. *You're going to hear some stories about me,* Moe had said on their first date. *Only half of them are true.*

You'll hear stories about me too, Sassy had admitted. *I'm afraid all of them are true.*

Moe reached out and took her hand with a gentle squeeze. "You can ask me anything, you know."

She bit her lip. "Why does it matter? If you're innocent, who cares what Annalisa does or who she talks to? Maybe she'll even find out the truth."

"For the cops, there is only one truth: I'm guilty. They've been harassing me for years, and I'm sick of it. I don't deserve it and neither do you."

She looked him over carefully. His face was open, his gaze clear and warm, but she felt like there was something he wasn't telling her, and it made her squirm. "I don't know . . ."

"Come with me." He tugged her hand and led her to the sofa, and she moved woodenly as if forcing herself along. He patted the cushions. "Let's sit." She sat on one end, far from him, and he slid in closer, his arm slung around her shoulders. "The police are wrong about me . . . but they're not entirely wrong."

She sat up and pulled away from him. "What?"

"I didn't kill Josie. I swear." He waited a beat. "But I was there that night."

"I don't—what are you saying?"

He sat back against the sofa with a deep sigh. "Have you ever been crazy in love?"

She folded her arms, hugging herself. "Part of me still loves Alex, even after what he did," she ventured cautiously. "I guess some people would call that crazy."

"I wouldn't." He gave her a sad smile and reached over to hold her chin in his hand. "I think it makes you lovely."

She didn't want him touching her just then. "You were saying about that night . . ."

"I loved Josie like a hurricane, like the force of it literally made me do insane stuff like smell her clothes and pull the hair from her brush so I could run it through my fingers. I wore the clothes I thought she liked and started sculpting my eyebrows. I bought the same shampoo she had and I told myself it was so she'd have it if she stayed over, but really I just wanted to smell her in the shower. You know, in the mornings, when I woke up—"

"Yes, I've got it," she broke in.

"I'd take a book from her bag and then claim she'd left it behind, just so I'd have an excuse to talk to her again. I bought her a three-hundred-dollar scarf."

"A scarf? That's a car payment."

"It was silk and the green in it set off her eyes," he said, reminiscing. "I asked for it back when she broke up with me and she said no, it was a gift. She kept the necklace I bought her too. She kept everything and left me nothing."

The mention of a scarf reminded her of Alex and what he'd done to Katie. She swallowed hard. "Maybe you shouldn't be telling me this. It's late, and—"

"No, I want you to hear it." He pulled her back down with him, almost forcefully. "After all this time, someone needs to hear the truth."

Sassy screwed her eyes shut, shaking her head. She'd screamed at Annalisa when Anna told her about Alex. Called her a liar. Anna had sobbed along with her. *It's the truth* . . .

"I started driving past her house. Sometimes I'd sit outside and watch it to see who went in and out. I knew she'd dumped me for some other guy and I had to find out who. If I drove by and saw the lights on, I'd start calling her. She had said she loved me not two weeks before. How do you love someone and then treat them like that?"

She could hear the anger in his voice even now. "Maybe she was scared," she whispered.

"Yeah? I was terrified. It was like she'd launched me into another dimension and nothing made sense. I wanted her to take it back, to make things right. The night she died I was in her neighborhood like always. She'd been out most nights, staying with other people—maybe with the guy she was screwing, I don't know. I watched the house until she came home alone, and it made me feel a little better. I went back to my apartment at my parents' house and I called her from there. I thought maybe now she was back by herself, she might want to talk to me again. But the phone rang and rang with no answer."

"She was dead."

"I didn't know it at the time. I didn't find out until a few days later along with everyone else." He ran his palm down her stiffened spine, trying to soothe her. "When I heard the news, I was devastated, but it was also like I woke up. I saw Josie was right. We were never meant to be together."

"If you talk to Annalisa and explain all this, maybe she'll understand." Annalisa had loved Colin Duffy enough to defy her parents and sneak out of the house at night. She stalked his social media even now. If anyone understood the pain of being denied the person you thought was meant for you, it was Annalisa.

"No," Moe said, his voice hardening. "All she will hear is that I was there. With everything else, it might be enough to arrest me. The cops have already half convicted me. You saw how Annalisa looked at me the other day."

Ever since the news broke about Alex, Sassy felt the neighbors watching her from behind their curtains when she took out the garbage. Lauren Guthrie across the street no longer let her boys play with Carla and Gigi. She'd made excuses the first few times Sassy had asked for a playdate—*we have swimming, we have karate, Timothy has a cold*—but eventually the truth came out. Gus, the husband, had said no more. *Their father strangled a woman to death. Who knows what else goes on over there?*

Sassy swallowed painfully and reached for her wineglass, gulping down a large swallow. She'd been so lonely when Moe asked her out. He knew about Alex but he didn't care. At the time, this lack of judgment felt like a balm to her scorched soul. Father Joseph at church promised God would forgive, but Sassy needed a human being, live and in the flesh. She'd told herself that Moe couldn't have done it or they would have arrested him. It wasn't like with Alex where the cops were in the dark for so many years. They just didn't have any evidence.

Moe tugged her against him and she went into his arms. If he pursued his restraining order against Annalisa, Sassy would have to choose. Maybe Annalisa was fine being alone. No man was ever right for her after Colin—she preferred the fairy tale to the real thing. Sassy had always admired her strength, but now she wondered if it was really weakness. If you weren't perfect enough for Annalisa, she cut you off. What was strong about that?

Moe flipped on the TV and Sassy tried to settle against him like normal, but she couldn't get away from her own thoughts, which remained sharp and painful. She shifted like she could physically distance herself from them. "You know, I think I need to get to bed," she said to Moe. "I have work in the morning."

He looked surprised. "You don't work Tuesdays."

She had a moment's pause that he knew her schedule. "Marcus is on vacation, so I picked up an extra shift."

"Okay," he said agreeably, turning the television off again. "We don't want you sleeping in the stacks." He kissed the top of her head and she saw him to the door. Once he was gone and she heard his car disappear, she let out the breath she was holding. She leaned against the door and put her hands over her face. She should feel reassured. Moe had come clean with her. But in her head she saw some faceless girl dead with a green scarf around her neck and all she heard was his voice saying, "I was there."

CHAPTER TWENTY-ONE

AFTER TWENTY-SEVEN YEARS ON THE STREETS, FRANKIE HAD LEARNED TO IMPROVISE. Pistol-whip some perp and there would be blood on your weapon, DNA that proved you did it. Shove his face into the floor and maybe he just fell down on his own. This time, the storm provided inspiration in the form of a downed tree limb that landed across Moe Bocks's street in Naperville. The houses were dark, set far in from the road, all the rich people tucked snug in their beds. Moe wasn't home yet. He was off banging his new conquest, which gave Frankie time to work. He dragged the limb in front of the iron gate at the base of the driveway to Bocks's place. Then he parked his car one block over, carefully hidden behind a tree line, and hoofed it back double time so he could be there waiting.

The rain had stopped and the temperatures dropped back down to the low thirties. He about froze his ass off crouched in the bushes across from Bocks's house for the better part of an hour. His knees locked up, and he wished he'd taken the naproxen Maggie May had offered him earlier that evening. *Too old for this shit,* he thought as he gritted his teeth to stop them from chattering in the cold. Finally, the Lexus appeared on the street, rolling slowly until it stopped short in front of the drive, its headlights illuminating the dead limb Frankie had placed in its path.

Moe got out of the car to move the branch, and Frankie struck with a quickness born of pure adrenaline, surging out of the dark. He pulled the ski mask down over his head with one hand and came up behind Moe with the bat in the other. The first blow knocked him to the ground, and he groaned as his face struck the pavement. Frankie added a second blow, then a third. Moe stopped moving.

Breathing hard, white puffs coming from his black mask, Frankie looked up and down the darkened street to affirm the lack of any witnesses. Then he took the lip balm from his pocket, tossed it down near the body, and went on his way.

CHAPTER TWENTY-TWO

AFTER THE POURING RAIN MELTED THE SNOWBANKS, THE OVERNIGHT DEEP FREEZE HAD TURNED THEM INTO SHEETS OF ICE. Annalisa took mincing steps across the skating pond that was the precinct parking lot. Inside, she saw Nick's computer was on but he wasn't at his desk. She took her seat and he materialized behind her a few moments later with a steaming hot coffee in a mug that read I LIKE BIG BUSTS AND I CANNOT LIE. "How much do you love me?" he asked as he set it in front of her.

She cupped her chilly hands around the mug and spun her chair around to regard him. He looked like he usually did after a bedroom conquest—satisfied and partially shaven. "In a hurry to get to work this morning?"

"Huh?"

She touched her jaw. "You missed a spot shaving."

He mirrored her gesture, frowning as his fingers found the stray stubble. "I didn't get much sleep last night."

"I'll bet," she said into the mug.

"I was thinking about the Eddie problem," he said as he took a seat on her desk, his ass literally on top of her file folder. She swatted him until he moved over. "I have a wild theory about who it could be. You want to hear it?"

"Sure," she said wearily. She hadn't slept so well herself. She'd been up past two studying the notes and photos that Bob Dickey had given her on the Blanchard murder. "Lay it on me."

"I was reading up on that wrongful death suit that Cecil Barry's widow brought against the Fantastic Four back in 2002. Turns out, Barry had a son, who was four at the time. His name is Theodore, but in a news story about the incident, his mother calls him Teddy."

"Teddy with a *T*. Doesn't fit."

"Yeah, but hear me out. Maybe Leo had the name wrong. We know from Kayla he was feeling guilty all these years about what happened, maybe because his buddy shot a guy who had a kid at home—one about the same age as Leo's son, Brian. So Leo starts socking away money to give to the boy to assuage his guilt."

"It's a stretch."

"Maybe you'll like this bit better. Theodore is all grown up now and he runs the Bass Lounge with his mom, Roxanne. The windfall she got from the settlement helped her take the place legit. They took out a big loan a few years back to buy the restaurant next door and expand into more daylight hours, only the restaurant isn't faring so well. They sure could use another injection of cash."

"Right, but by your own reasoning, they wouldn't know Leo has it to give."

"Maybe." He looked around and lowered his voice. "But Leo got that money from somewhere. If we're right and the Fantastic Four was really the Felonious Four, you know who would already have realized the truth."

"The people they were ripping off," she finished softly. She sipped the coffee and considered. "You know what Pops used to call that club back in the day."

"Sure, we all did. 'Debase Lounge'—whatever you wanted, whether it was a ten-dollar baggie of rock or an underage girl for sex, you could find it at the Lounge."

"And you say the widow took it legit?"

"I haven't done a complete audit, but yeah, after Barry got killed, Roxanne used the money to get out from under whoever he owed. The club started booking real musicians—Lupe Fiasco, Do or Die. It was hot there for a while."

"Not my scene, I guess." She set the mug aside.

"Well, maybe this is more your style. I did some digging on Theodore Barry and guess what popped up." He reached behind himself to pluck a printed news story from his desk, which he handed to her.

"He was on the high school swim team," she said as she scanned it. "State champions."

Nick raised his eyebrows at her. "Think he does any diving?"

....

Roxanne and Theodore Barry had the same listed address, an apartment above the Bass Lounge, and when they got no answer there, Annalisa and Nick tried the club itself. The doors were opaque and locked, heavy glass obscured by a velvet curtain, so Annalisa couldn't tell if anyone was inside to respond to their knocking. Eventually, a slim young man appeared on the other side, his tailored trousers, collared shirt, and glasses making him seem more like an accountant than a nightclub connoisseur. "I'm sorry, but the restaurant doesn't open until eleven," he informed them with a polite smile.

Annalisa showed off her shield. "We're not here to eat. Are you Theodore Barry?"

His expression closed off. "My lawyer's name is Sydney French. You can reach him at—"

"Whoa, whoa, whoa," Nick interjected, placing the flat of his palm on the door to keep it open. "Who said anything about a lawyer? You're not in any trouble. We just want to talk to you for a few minutes."

"What about?" He had not relaxed his defensive posture.

"About your dad," Annalisa said. "We're very sorry about what happened to him."

"Sure you are."

"Teddy?" A woman's voice floated from behind him. "Who's at the door? Oh," she said when Theodore widened the door to display Annalisa and Nick. "The police."

"Is it that obvious?" Annalisa asked with a wry smile as she gestured down at her off-the-rack suit from Macy's. Roxanne Barry dressed more the part of a nightclub owner, with a body-hugging dress in a zigzag pattern and knee-high fashion boots.

"No," Roxanne answered, her tone guarded. "I recognize you from TV."

Theodore plainly did not, because he turned a scrutinizing gaze to Annalisa, unable to place her. Annalisa nodded. "That's right. The Lovelorn Killer."

"No, you turned in your own father for murder." Roxanne paused. "He was a cop." Theodore's gaze turned speculative and Roxanne opened the door wider to admit them. "You're letting all the heat run out," she told them briskly. "Come inside and state your business."

Annalisa eyed the purple wall displaying signed photos that showed off various performers at the club over the years; Kayne West got prominent placement. "Your club has done well for itself," she said, and Roxanne narrowed her eyes.

"You make it sound like it runs on its own. This place is bathed in my blood, sweat, and tears. I'm the first one in and the last one out all day, every day. I got arthritis in both hands and I'm only forty-six years old." She put a hand on one hip. "But you didn't come here to hear about my busted joints."

"They were asking about Dad," Theodore told her.

"Really." She looked from Annalisa to Nick. "He's been dead for twenty years."

"We know," Annalisa said with feeling. "We're sorry. We were hoping to talk to you about what happened."

Roxanne considered for a moment and then gave an expansive shrug. "Whatever you like," she said breezily, pivoting toward the restaurant side of the building. "But it's going to be a quick conversation. I signed an NDA when they gave me the money. I don't even get to talk to my priest about Cecil's murder."

Annalisa, Nick, and Theodore trailed after her. In the dining room, she went to the bar area and resumed her work wrapping silverware in white napkins as if they weren't even there. Theodore went from table to table, straightening the black lacquered chairs, keeping wary eyes on Annalisa and Nick as he did so. Nick picked up a menu and perused it. "The pork ribs sound good," he told Annalisa.

"It's only nine a.m."

"Ribs don't punch a clock," he replied, and Annalisa thought she saw Roxanne smile.

"Best you ever tasted," she said without looking up from her work. "My mama's recipe."

"Tell us about Cecil," Annalisa suggested, and Roxanne's hands slowed in her folding and wrapping.

"What do you want to know, exactly?"

"Whatever you're allowed to tell us."

The woman slumped like a weight settled on her shoulders. "Someday," she said softly.

"I'm sorry?" Annalisa asked.

"I said 'someday,'" Roxanne answered as she straightened and resumed organizing the tableware. "That was Cecil. Always someday, never today. When he died, I had a half-done kitchen filled with stacked wood, cabinets with no doors on them, and a sheet of plastic for one wall. The basement had materials to put up a little play set for Teddy in the backyard. They'd been sitting there since I got pregnant. *Someday*, Cecil would tell me. *Soon*. He'd fix up the parts people could see—the stage shone like a black diamond—but meanwhile the computers we used behind the scenes kept freezing and crashing and the ceiling was falling down in the office. He always had a plan to get more money, get his act together, turn this into a showplace."

"You were young when you met him," Annalisa observed.

"Young and dumb enough not to see through the act. Cecil seemed like he was going places. Problem was, he never arrived." She grabbed a butter knife and pointed it at Annalisa. "They teach you in school that the world is round, but I know better now. It's got angles and if you're not looking straight, they'll slice your head clear off."

"Cecil liked to play the angles," Nick guessed, and Roxanne made a huffing noise that suggested Nick only knew the half of it. "Drugs?" He pressed her. "Guns?"

Theodore set a chair down with a bang. "What the hell do you care? He's dead. He called the cops because someone was robbing him, and you all shot him and let the robbers get away."

"Teddy, shush. I don't want you mixed up in this."

"He was my father! I never even knew him because some trigger-happy cop saw a big Black man and filled him full of holes—no warning, no questions asked. Never mind that he was on his own property. Never mind that he was the victim in the whole thing. They just executed him on the spot."

"Is that what happened?" Annalisa asked Roxanne.

"I told you I can't talk about it."

Annalisa tried a different approach. "One of the officers involved that night, Leo Hammond, was killed a few days ago."

"Oh yeah?" Roxanne's voice cracked at the end and she did not meet Annalisa's gaze. "How unfortunate."

"What happened to him?" Theodore wanted to know.

"He got shot Friday night," Nick answered. "Killed inside his home."

Theodore's face twisted into a rictus as his fingers curled around the back of a chair. "What do you know . . . maybe there is a certain justice in this life after all."

"You close your mouth!" Roxanne said with sudden vehemence. "That's why they're here, do you understand? They're trying to find out who killed him. I should've known they don't give a crap about Cecil. I want you both to leave—now."

"Wait," Theodore said, looking confused. "You think Mama killed him?"

"I told you to hush. They're leaving now."

"Or me?" He widened his eyes. "That's complete bullshit. We were here working all Friday night, up past two in the morning, and we've got a couple hundred witnesses to prove it."

"No one said you killed him," Annalisa said. "Actually, we're here because his wife said he remained haunted by this case. He had nightmares for years. He couldn't let it go, apparently."

"That's rich," Theodore scoffed with derision. "We're supposed to be moved by his compassion, is that it?"

"He should try my nightmares sometime," Roxanne said evenly.

Annalisa tried to imagine how it had gone down. "It was past closing that night," she said. "Saturday night, right? Peak earnings up for grabs."

"More than a hundred thousand," Roxanne agreed. "Sandra and I were counting it out when a bunch of guys in ski masks showed up. They took everything we had—the night's take plus what was in the safe. They held Cecil at gunpoint while I ferried the money to them. They didn't even know Sandra was there, because she hid under the desk when the shouting started. She's the one who called 911." She shook her head. "She never should've done that."

Annalisa was starting to get the picture. A woman called 911 and said they were being robbed. Then the cops showed up and shot the first man they encountered. "How long was it between when Sandra called and when the officers arrived?"

Roxanne shook her head. "I've already said more than I should've."

"Okay, then what is Sandra's full name and how can I talk to her?" Annalisa asked, pulling out her notebook. Sandra wouldn't be bound by any NDA clause.

"With a Ouija board," Roxanne told her. "Sandra's dead." She made a tutting noise as she rolled up a set of flatware inside the napkin. "Like I said, she should've known better."

Annalisa looked up from where she was writing *Sandra deceased* in her notebook. "Are you saying her death was related to what happened here that night?"

"I'm not saying nothing at all. Teddy, honey, can you show these kind officers to the door?"

"Yes, ma'am," he said.

"One last thing," Annalisa said, pointedly not following Theodore in the direction of the door. "Does the name Eddie mean anything to you?"

"Eddie who?" Roxanne asked, her face blank.

"That's what we're trying to determine."

Roxanne gave a disinterested shrug. "Try the phone book," she said, "under *E*."

Annalisa waited a beat but the woman didn't say anything further. Nick nudged her. "Let's go," he murmured.

As she turned to leave, Roxanne called her back, "Oh, Detective?" Annalisa turned to face her. Roxanne's gaze dropped to Annalisa's feet. "If you want to know . . . it's the shoes," the woman said in a dismissive tone. "They always give you cops away."

When they reached the door, Theodore practically flung it open for them. Annalisa prepared to thank him for his time anyway but as she opened her mouth, a squad car rolled up and stopped behind Nick's car on the street. She recognized the driver, a kid named Janek who looked barely old enough to shave.

"I thought you said we weren't in trouble," Theodore said darkly.

"Detective Vega?" Janek stepped forward in an awkward fashion. "I need you to come with me. Commander's orders."

"Come with you where?"

"Back to division. She wants you right away."

Her mind spun off in a million different directions: Alex might have been attacked in prison, Pops dead on the living room floor, or maybe someone found out that Dickey had slipped her the Blanchard files and squealed. "What's this about?" she said, struggling to sound calm. She hadn't moved from the doorway to the Bass Lounge. Neither had Nick or Theodore, who eavesdropped openly.

"I don't know the details. Commander wants to see you now is all I've got."

"Okay then," she said, steeling herself and moving for Nick's car. "Thanks for relaying the message. Carelli can drive me back to base."

"No," Janek said. He looked sheepish but he stepped in front of her to block her path. "He can't."

She noticed for the first time Janek's partner, a uniformed female cop new to the job. Annalisa had seen her around but didn't yet know her name. The woman sat shotgun in the patrol car, staring straight ahead like she wished she could be anywhere else. "What is this?" Annalisa demanded. When Janek said nothing, she raised her voice louder. "Come on, you must know something."

He worked his jaw back and forth, deciding. "Someone put Moe Bocks in the hospital last night," he said at last.

"Someone," she repeated, turning to Nick in a daze. His expression was stricken, blood drained completely from his face.

"Don't say anything," he urged her in a low voice.

"Let's go." Janek took her arm with one hand. With the other, he reached behind to open the squad car, and Annalisa realized with a start where she'd be riding: in the back.

CHAPTER TWENTY-THREE

JANEK DEPOSITED HER AT THE DOOR TO ZIMMER'S OFFICE, PRACTICALLY PERP-WALKING HER THROUGH THE STATION. People stopped what they were doing to turn and stare, a few of them muttering to one another with words she didn't catch but whose tone she understood. She opened the door, startling Zimmer, who looked at her with such a moment of true fright that Annalisa herself felt fear for the first time.

"You wanted to see me?" She asked the question of Zimmer, but her gaze rested on the unfamiliar man in the room, who stood up at her arrival. He wore a dark suit that offset his pale, drooping face.

"Detective Vega," he said in a gravelly voice, inclining his head slightly. He had the air of maître d' for a hotel that served only ghosts. "I'm Ralph DeNunzio from the investigation division in Naperville. I want to thank you for coming in so promptly."

"I wasn't aware I had a choice."

Zimmer frowned and gestured at the empty chair they had waiting for her. "Please sit."

Annalisa perched on the very edge. "What's this about?"

"I need to ask you where you were last night," DeNunzio said.

Annalisa licked her lips as she recalled her dark wet rendezvous with Bob Dickey. "I was home," she said, because for most of the night, this was the truth.

"All night?" DeNunzio asked. "You didn't go out for any reason?"

"I went for coffee," she hedged.

"What time was that?"

"Late. I don't remember exactly."

He flipped open his notebook and consulted it. "You have a receipt?"

"Not on me." Not anywhere, but he didn't need to know that yet. "Commander, what's going on here?"

Zimmer lined up the folders on her desk so that their corners matched. "Someone attacked Moe Bocks outside his home last night around midnight."

"Could that have been when you were out getting your coffee?" DeNunzio wanted to know.

"I'm not sure. But I am positive I didn't go near Moe Bocks." She looked from DeNunzio to Zimmer. "Why? Is he claiming I did it?"

"He has his suspicions, yes," DeNunzio answered mildly.

"Well, it wasn't me. I haven't seen Moe Bocks since he was here with his lawyer."

DeNunzio read from his notes. "Mr. Bocks has a security camera outside his home. It's some distance away from the end of the driveway where the attack took place, but it clearly shows someone under six feet tall dressed in black, dragging a downed tree branch in front of the drive to block the path. Around midnight, when Mr. Bocks arrived home, he exited his vehicle to remove the tree limb and then the same figure appears with a baseball bat. This person struck Mr. Bocks from behind and then hit him several more times while he lay on the ground. The attacker fled the scene on foot."

"I'm sorry for him," Annalisa said through gritted teeth. "But it wasn't me who did it."

DeNunzio withdrew a sealed plastic bag from the inside of his coat and showed it to her. "This was recovered from the site of the attack. Do you recognize it?"

Annalisa's blood froze in her body. It was mint-flavored ChapStick, her favorite. "I can't say for sure," she replied carefully, easing backward in her seat. *You're being set up,* she told herself. Her mind whirled. Bob Dickey could vouch for her, but maybe not. She'd seen him shortly after ten and they'd talked for around twenty minutes, which left her with just enough time to make it to Naperville and whack Moe Bocks. Moreover, if Dickey admitted to being with her in the car and handing over copies of the Blanchard file, he could end up in trouble himself, potentially losing his pension. She gripped the arms of the chair and held back a scream of frustration.

"Okay," DeNunzio said agreeably as he tucked away the lip balm. "We'll have it tested. You wouldn't mind giving us a sample of your DNA, right? Since you are positive it wasn't you."

"I do mind." She looked to Zimmer. "Maybe I should have a lawyer here."

"Oh, I don't think that's necessary," protested DeNunzio. "We're just having a friendly conversation and you've said it definitely wasn't you who attacked Mr. Bocks."

"No, I think a lawyer is a good idea at this juncture," Zimmer said, standing up. "Detective Vega will be in touch once she's retained counsel."

DeNunzio rose slowly to his feet. "If that's how you want to play it," he said, eyeing Annalisa. "But more than a lawyer . . . I think you should find that coffee receipt. Good day, Detective."

He shuffled out of the office and Zimmer closed the door behind him. "Thanks for letting me walk into an ambush," Annalisa said to her bitterly.

"Me? He showed up here out of nowhere demanding to talk to you."

"And you just let him in."

"I was hoping you had an alibi," Zimmer said darkly, retaking her usual seat behind the desk. Annalisa remained standing in protest.

"I don't need an alibi! I didn't touch Moe Bocks."

Zimmer sat forward with her head in her hands for a moment. "That story about going for coffee," she said when she sat up again, "was it true?"

"I did have coffee last night," Annalisa offered after a pause.

"Shit," said Zimmer, and Annalisa sucked in a breath because she'd never heard her boss curse like that.

"I didn't do it," Annalisa insisted. She'd have to find out who did. It was the only way out of this mess. If there weren't video of the attack, she might guess it was Moe himself. She had an image of Kayla's frogman appearing in the darkness with a baseball bat like some sort of deep-sea avenger, and a laugh escaped her at the absurdity of it all.

"Is this funny to you?" Zimmer asked.

"Not even a little," Annalisa replied, sober again. "I think someone is setting me up. Five'll get you ten that the lip balm comes back to me. I keep one in my desk drawer and anyone could've lifted it."

"If that's true, you really do need a lawyer. And maybe a priest."

"I need to find out who attacked Moe Bocks."

"Oh no. You're on administrative duties while this gets sorted out. You don't go near Bocks or this investigation. You understand me?"

"Desk duty? I'm being punished when I didn't do anything."

"You did something, all right." Zimmer looked her over shrewdly. "I just don't know what it is yet. At minimum, you were already antagonizing Bocks by poking around in the Blanchard investigation—that alone is enough to get you suspended. For now, you'll be doing paperwork and I'll assign someone else to work with Carelli on the Hammond investigation."

"But I—" Annalisa thought of the files she had at home and shut her mouth. Zimmer put her head down over her work again, flipping open a file folder.

"Dismissed," Zimmer said without looking up.

Annalisa sighed and moved slowly to the door. She opened it partway before turning around. "It wasn't me who attacked Bocks, and I think you know it. But someone sure didn't like me poking around in his case . . . or maybe in the Hammond case . . . and whoever that person is, you've just given them exactly what they wanted."

She shut the door behind her with more force than warranted, rattling the windows in Zimmer's office. Nick rushed up to her, his face ashen. "What happened?" he asked her.

"I don't want to talk about it." She pushed past him and all the others who had turned once more to stare. No way was she going to sit around filing papers while someone tried to frame her for attempted homicide. Trouble was, she didn't know what to do next without getting herself fired or arrested. She went out to the parking lot and sat in her car to think about the situation. She wished she could call up Pops and get his advice. Maybe she could use his lawyer—get some kind of Vega family discount. God knows they didn't have the money for another expensive trial. Tears burned unshed in her eyes and she tried to blink them away. Half the department would be thrilled she got strung up; the other half would figure she'd been dirty all along, just like her old man.

A sharp rap on her passenger window made her jump. Nick stood there with no coat on, and she reluctantly unclicked the locks to let him inside. "I said I didn't want to talk," she told him.

He rubbed his hands together briskly. "I told Zimmer you were with me."

She twisted to look at him in shock. "You what?"

He nodded as if trying to convince himself. "I said we were together last night, all night."

"Together doing what, exactly?" He gave her a meaningful look and she leaned back in her seat with a groan. "You told her we were screwing?"

"Well, I didn't use that term, but I think she got the general idea."

"Nick." She took a deep breath and put a hand on his leg. "I appreciate the support, but you don't need to lie for me. I'll figure something out."

"Look, I know you. You didn't take a bat to Moe Bocks's head. If this is a frame-up, we stop it dead right here, right now."

"Right. And when your latest conquest from last night shows up looking for another round? DeNunzio finds her and we're both actually screwed. Me for attempted murder and you for lying about it."

"What are you talking about?"

"The woman you had over last night."

He blinked in confusion for a moment, realization dawning on his face. "You mean my downstairs neighbor, Alana. Yeah, she stopped by for a few minutes because the heating vent was making some god-awful noise. Turns out my guitar pick fell in and was rattling around in there." He frowned at her. "How did you know about that?"

She felt her face grow warm. "I, uh, I stopped by your place and I saw her with you."

"So you were out last night," Nick said, crestfallen.

"Bob Dickey came through with copies of the Blanchard files," she said after a beat. "But I sink him if I admit he gave them to me, and I'm not even sure it would help. The timeline means I could still make it to Naperville to attack Moe."

"You should've brought me along for the meet."

"I tried! You were busy," she groused. "I was being thoughtful by not interrupting."

"You were being jealous," he returned with a smile.

She shoved him lightly and he jostled her in return. She bit her lip, growing serious. He'd put his whole life on the line for her—again. She grabbed his hand and gave it an impulsive squeeze. "Listen, thanks for backing me up with Zimmer."

He shrugged like it was no big deal. "Hey, I spent all those years lying to you. The least I could do was lie for you, right? We're still partners for the moment, anyway. If they're after you, they're going to have to go through me first."

Annalisa's cell phone buzzed and she dug it out to look at it. "It's Zimmer," she said. "Probably wondering why I'm not down in records yet." She took the call with a sigh. "Yes, Commander?"

"Where are you?" Zimmer demanded.

"Outside. I needed a smoke break."

Zimmer ignored the fact that Annalisa didn't smoke. "DeNunzio just phoned to say they've recovered a baseball bat they believe to be the weapon involved in the attack on Moe Bocks."

"Great," Annalisa said with relief. She hadn't handled a bat since she'd played center field in eighth-grade softball.

"Not great," Zimmer corrected her. "They recovered it from your house."

CHAPTER TWENTY-FOUR

LET ME LAY OUT YOUR PROBLEMS FOR YOU," DENUNZIO SAID TO ANNALISA AS THEY SAT IN THE WINDOWLESS GRAY BOX THAT PASSED FOR AN INTERROGATION ROOM IN NAPERVILLE. Manufactured heat blew down on them from vents in the ceiling, making her skin feel like shrink-wrap over her skull. She slumped in the uncomfortable plastic seat, picking at the label on the tiny bottle of water she'd long ago consumed. DeNunzio kept up his patter, conversational but relentless. "You and Mr. Bocks have a documented adversarial relationship. He's on record asking you to stay away from him. Then he gets whacked from behind by a baseball bat, and the ChapStick we found at the scene has your fingerprints on it. You're telling me you've never been to his house before, so how do you explain that?"

"I don't know. Maybe Bocks took the ChapStick from my desk when he was at the precinct."

"Now, why would he do that?"

"He's a freak. Why does he do anything?" She peeled more of the label and shifted in her chair, searching for a bearable position. Her rear end had gone flat from sitting so long.

"The only prints on the ChapStick are yours," DeNunzio said. "Not Mr. Bocks's. Then there's the matter of the baseball bat we found leaning up against the back stairs to your condo. We're still running tests on it, but I'm sure you know how sophisticated the forensic analysis is these days. Touch DNA, a single hair or speck of blood—that's all it's going to take to hang you. You sure you don't want to get out in front of this? Explain your side of the story?"

"I have explained. I went home. At some point, I went out for coffee, which I drank sitting in the lot of the Lincoln Park Zoo. Then I went home."

DeNunzio wrinkled his considerable forehead, creating creases upon creases. He went through his notes again as if puzzled. "The zoo is nowhere near your house. That makes it a funny place to drink your coffee."

"I'm a funny gal." She forced a smile. "Ask anyone."

"But no one saw you there," he said, no question in his tone because they'd been over her movements a dozen times already.

"It was after hours. No one was around."

"Right," he agreed. "Because who would be? It was dark and raining and all the animals were tucked in their beds. Nothing to see there. No reason to go." He said this like it proved she must be lying.

Annalisa rolled her neck around, desperate to loosen the tension that was seeping into her spine. She still hadn't called a lawyer. She didn't want to waste a hundred dollars an hour to have some guy in a suit tell her what she already knew. DeNunzio hadn't charged her with anything yet. He couldn't. A lawyer would tell her to keep her mouth shut and walk out of the interview, as was her right at this point. But then Annalisa wouldn't know what he knew. Wouldn't get the details of the frame. So, as much as DeNunzio wanted to keep her talking, she wanted to do the same. They'd gone over her statement a dozen times as he'd tried to ferret out even the smallest inconsistency, the tiniest lie. Annalisa countered with the simplest answers, all of them the truth.

"Let's go to the video again," he said, turning the laptop so she could see.

The camera from Moe Bocks's house was mounted to view the front door, not the driveway. Annalisa took a moment to note the irony that Bocks was wealthy enough to have the security system, but the big expensive house he'd bought with his money meant the driveway was long, and therefore, far from the camera at the door. As a result, the figure dragging the tree limb to block the drive was small and little more than a shadow.

"Now, Mr. Bocks wasn't home at this time. He was at your brother's house, where he's been taking over while your brother's doing time." He shook his head mournfully. "It ain't right. I agree with you there. Bocks skated free when everyone knew he'd strangled that poor girl to death. Your brother has girls, right? Young ones."

"You know he does."

He nodded. "You want to protect them. I'd do the same for my nieces. Can't imagine how I'd feel if I knew their mother was bringing a murderer home for dinner."

Annalisa glared at him as she ripped off the remainder of the water bottle label. She heard what he didn't say: Carla and Gigi had already spent every day with a murderer at the dinner table. "That's not me," she said, nodding at the grainy image on the laptop.

"Hard to say for sure," he agreed. "But you're tall for a girl. Five foot eight?"

"That's right."

He squinted at the laptop, measuring. "We're checking the neighborhood to see if there are other cameras. The attacker walked away on foot but I doubt they hoofed it all the way home. Not in this weather."

"Good," she said. "I hope you find something."

"We already got plenty. Like I said: there's the lip balm, your prints, the bat, the video . . . you've got lots of problems here, Ms. Vega."

"Okay," she said, flicking the label aside. She'd had enough. She sat forward and mirrored his folksy, hey-let's-get-to-the-bottom-of-this tone. "Let me lay out your problems for you," she said. "Mr. DeNunzio."

He made a sweeping gesture at the table between them. "Go ahead."

"There is nothing on that video that proves it's me. Sure, you can place my ChapStick at the scene of the attack, but you can't put me there. Similarly, you can't prove the bat you took from my yard belongs to me. You didn't find it inside my residence. You got it from the backyard, which is a shared space among the units and it's not fenced in. Anyone could have placed the bat there."

"Anyone including you."

"Why would I? I've been a cop for ten years. You think I would be stupid enough to bring the weapon back to my house and leave it out for everyone to see?"

He shrugged. "I've seen people make stupid mistakes a thousand times on this job. I bet you have too."

"Yeah, well, you have a bigger problem," she said as she retrieved her cell phone and put it on the table between them.

He looked down at it. "What's that?"

"It's a lot of things," she said. "Isn't it? It's a computer, a camera, a calculator, a phone, and a GPS—everything in one and it fits right in your pocket." She held it up to demonstrate. "My pops won't carry one. Says he doesn't need to pay a hundred bucks a month for government tracking. Me, I never go anywhere without it. I feel it's like a phantom limb if it's gone even for a minute."

DeNunzio frowned like he grasped where she was going with this narrative. She continued before he could say anything.

"So, while I can't give you a receipt for the coffee I had last night, I can give you a way to verify my whereabouts. You can subpoena the cell phone records and they will show you that everything I told you is true. I went out late and drove to the Lincoln Park Zoo, where I sat in the parking lot for about twenty minutes. Then I went home and remained there for the rest of the night. At no point did I go anywhere near Naperville or Moe Bocks."

"I'll, uh, I'll look into that."

"Great." She wrote down her cell phone number and passed it over to him. "I'm leaving now."

DeNunzio looked down at the number and then he turned to stop her as she reached the door. "Detective Vega?"

She waited in the doorway.

"If you didn't do this, someone sure went to a lot of trouble to make it look like you did."

"You're noticing that too?"

"Right. I guess I'm wondering why that is and who it might be."

She paused and then pointed to the little plaque on the outside of the door. "That must be why it says INVESTIGATION BUREAU on here. If you figure it out, give me a buzz on my handy little tracking device." She waved the cell phone at him and then stalked off, muttering to herself all the way. She headed for the exit but turned when she caught the glow of a soda machine at the end of the nearest dimly lit hall. Digging around in her pockets, she produced a loose dollar and went to fetch herself a rehydrating soda for the drive home.

The can landed with a *thunk* at the bottom of the chute, and she bent down to retrieve it. When she righted herself, she found Moe Bocks coming out of the men's restroom. He must be here for more interviewing, like her. He halted in shock when he saw her. "What are you doing here?" he demanded.

"You would know. You're the one going around telling people I attacked you." He did look like he'd been through a meat grinder. His face had road rash on one side, while the other sported a black eye. His left arm was in a sling and he had stitches in his chin.

"You thought I was dead. But you were wrong—I survived to tell everyone what you did."

"That makes you luckier than Josie Blanchard."

His mouth tightened, his bloodshot eye going wide. He took one step closer to her and lowered his voice to a growl. "Come near me again, and I'll kill you."

"You'll be wanting to skip Sunday dinners, then."

"I mean it."

She held his gaze. "So do I."

CHAPTER TWENTY-FIVE

TOM AGREED TO MEET KAYLA AT THE HOUSE. She'd protested at first—the place now gave her the creeps—but he didn't want any record of a hotel check-in this time and no way in hell was he going to invite her to his house, not even with Jane away at her book club meeting. She'd come back late and full of wine, and as long as he had his feet up in front of the TV by then, Jane wouldn't suspect a thing. He left his car a couple blocks over in a blind alley, which meant he had to navigate the slick pavement with his cane as he walked back, but it was worth it not to be seen parked in Leo's drive. Kayla was there. He saw her red Jaguar parked there with its identifying vanity plate, FABULUS. He stood outside and watched the lighted windows for a moment, thinking about what he had to do.

He sniffed hard. His blood already sang with a mixture of coke and adrenaline. Frankie had said they had to find out what Kayla knew, but Tom already had the answer: too much. They had tried going easy once before and look where it got them. Even Leo, who had resisted the idea so hard at first, eventually had to agree the solution worked. It was his screwup and yet somehow Tom had to clean it up. Whatever money Leo had stashed away, Tom deserved every red cent. He hobbled up the steps and Kayla opened the door before he could ring the bell, like she'd been watching for him the whole time.

"Oh, thank God," she said, yanking him inside so he almost went off balance. "I've been going crazy."

"Me too." He kissed her because she seemed to want it. Then he realized she was feeling around for his pockets. "Hey, hey, not yet."

She pouted. "You said you were going to bring the stuff."

"I did. But let's go enjoy it in style, huh? I know Leo keeps a bottle of Pappy Van Winkle around here somewhere for special occasions."

"Downstairs in the basement at the bar. But, I mean, can your leg handle it? The steps are kinda steep."

He dropped a kiss on her full pink lips. "For you, I can walk anywhere." He followed her down to the basement to the bar, where she poured them each a finger of bourbon. "Oh, come on, now," he said, nudging his glass back toward her when she tried to hand it off to him. "Leo's not here to care anymore." She rolled her eyes but added another shot to his drink.

They sat on the low-backed leather sofa and Tom admired the smooth feel of it under his palm. Leo could be a putz sometimes but he had great taste. The fuzzy yellow throw pillows on the ends were all Kayla, though. Tom raised his drink to clink with hers, and she smiled as she took a sip. "I feel so much better with you here. The whole thing with Leo has me completely wigged. And that cop, Vega. She doesn't believe me at all about the frogman."

He touched her cheek. It felt like a warm peach. "I believe you," he murmured as he stroked her with the backs of his fingers. She took his hand and brought it to her mouth for kissing.

"Is it party time now?"

"Sure," he said, feeling magnanimous. He pulled the baggie from his pants and she let out a squeal at the sight of it.

"You don't know how bad I need this," she confessed to him as she lined up the powder on the coffee table.

"I'm sure I do." He ran a hand down her spine while she did the hit, smiling as he imagined the zing hitting her veins. "I put a little something extra in it for you," he said in a conspiratorial tone.

"Oh man, I feel it!" She sat back with a giggle. "You're so bad," she said, her fingers finding his middle. There were pinwheels in her blue eyes. "I love how bad you are. I thought Leo was bad at first but he was just a mess."

"Leo was plenty bad," he assured her. He lined up another hit for her. "Try some more."

"Mmm, I don't mind if I do." She giggled again and leaned over to inhale. When she sat up, her pupils were so huge it looked like her retinas were trying to make a getaway. "Wow," she said, sniffing and lolling back against the cushion. "Aren't you going to do some?"

"In a minute."

She ran a hand up his thigh. "Maybe I was wrong about you. Maybe you're not that bad after all, Mr. Policeman."

"I think you're the bad one," he returned, rubbing noses with her. "I think you found Leo's money, and you're keeping it all for yourself rather than sharing with Tommy Boy here."

She wasn't so far gone that she missed what he was saying. She sat up abruptly and pulled away. "I don't know what you're talking about. I've got no money. That bitch cop had them freeze all of Leo's accounts. I can't access anything."

"I'm talking about the cash. The cash that tells you just how bad Leo really was. Hmm?" He toyed with the ends of her hair. "Tell me what you did with it."

"I don't have any cash." She grabbed her purse from the far end of the couch and tossed it in his lap. "Look for yourself."

"I don't think you have it on you," he said as he put aside the purse. "But you know where it is. Tell me and we can share it."

"Is this about Eddie?" She looked him over searchingly. "Why won't you tell me who he is? I know he must be some guy Leo owed money to. Is he a loan shark or something?"

He sighed with disappointment. "Leo owed more than money."

She shook her head. "I don't understand."

"C'mere, and I'll tell you a story," he said, slipping an arm around her. She snuggled into his shoulder, her breathing a little unsteady. He brushed the hair from her face. "Leo was indeed a bad boy, and he started young. He married Maura and popped out those two kids—don't get me wrong, he did love them—but Leo wasn't the faithful family type."

"I know it," she replied dreamily.

"I know you do," he answered, his voice tender. "But you're not the first lovely lady to catch Leo's eye. Back in the day, he was hung up on a waitress named Sandy. She worked at the Bass Lounge."

Kayla lurched forward in recognition. "I fucking love that place!"

"Yeah, it's great," Tom said drily as he gathered her back against him.

"If you like that sort of thing. But when Sandy worked there, the Bass Lounge did more than just drinks and music. Cecil Barry had a whole drug operation he ran out of the back office. Hanging around Sandy, Leo got wise to the situation pretty quick."

"Did Leo bust him?" She sounded drowsy now, her head heavy on his shoulder.

"No, he had a better idea. Cecil had a big score going down one Saturday night—close to a million bucks' worth of coke all in one deal. We could have set up a sting and gotten Cecil and the buyer both at once. Instead, Leo had a different plan. We'd wait for the exchange to happen, and then we'd hit the club ourselves. We'd get the take from the deal plus whatever the club took in from the regular business. What was Cecil going to do? Call the cops to report someone took his drug money?"

"Wait," she said, sounding hazy. "Isn't Cecil the dead guy? The one you killed by accident?"

"The first part went smooth like butter. We went in right after the buyer left, masks on and ready to rumble. We knew from what Sandy told Leo that there would be practically no one left in the club at that time—Cecil, his wife, and a couple of dumb wrestler types they used as bodyguards. Paulie held the muscle facedown on the dance floor while Leo, Frankie, and I hit up Cecil for the cash. He cussed us out, called us every name in the book, but he cooperated and handed it over with no troubles. It would've been all fine except we didn't count on Sandy. She was there too, and she called 911."

"Mmm . . ." Kayla was slumped against him completely now, totally out of it. He was telling the story only for himself.

"We had just left the club when we heard the call go out on the radio," he said to her as he eased her backward so she lay down. "Of course, we had to take it. So we ditched the masks and ran back in there. Only Cecil had taken the intermission to arm himself with a Glock 18. Frankie saw it coming so he fired first. Barry got off a couple rounds of his own and hit Frankie in the shoulder before Frankie took him down permanently. We found Sandy and the wife in the back, crying and hugging each other." He regarded Kayla's sleeping form and shook his head with regret. "That should've been the end of it. Let's hope this finally will be."

He took the shaggy yellow pillow from beneath her head and pressed it over her face. She didn't struggle at all for a long moment but then her brain's alarm system must have kicked in because she started fighting him. He put his knees on her legs and shoved the pillow more forcefully into her face, driving her deeper into the cushion. His hip started screaming at him, but he kept up the pressure. He had to be sure. After a few moments, she went limp and he exhaled as well. He sagged backward, spent.

A slapping sound behind him startled him upright, pillow clutched between his hands. The frogman stood at the base of the stairs, peering at him through the diving mask. In his hands, he had a gun. "Oh no," Tom said as terror seized him. "Don't." He tried to scramble off the couch but his bum leg wouldn't cooperate. "Please. I'll get you anything. What do you want—drugs? Money?"

The frogman said nothing. His flippers went ***slap, slap*** on the hard floor as he advanced on Tom. Tom tried to run but fell down between the couch and the coffee table. "Please don't . . . I'm begging you." The frogman's shadow fell over Tom and he cowered under the pillow he'd been so recently using to murder Kayla. He thought about Eddie. He thought about Leo and whether he would see him on the other side. Then the shooting started, bullets exploding at him like a party favor, and Tom didn't think anything anymore.

CHAPTER TWENTY-SIX

Annalisa returned to her darkened condo, which did not feel especially like home after learning that someone had been in her backyard, planting a baseball bat to implicate her in the attack on Moe Bocks. Moe's injuries were severe enough that she doubted he'd arranged the hit himself to be rid of her, which meant someone else wanted her out of the way. She shivered as she turned on the lights.

The buzzer at her front door sounded and she swore even her plants jumped. She left her coat on as she went to the intercom. "Who is it?"

"It's your ex-partner," Nick replied.

She opened the door to find Nick standing on her step with a large paper sack in one hand and a small purple-colored package in the other. "Ex-partner, thanks very much," she said as she let him inside.

"Hey, I had your bail money all lined up," he told her. "Emptied my couch cushions and everything."

She eyed him. "What's that?" she asked, arms still folded, gesturing at him with her chin.

He held up the sack. "Pho. I thought you might like dinner."

"No, the other thing."

"Oh, this? It was outside." He thrust it toward her but she did not accept it.

"No, it wasn't. I just got home and there was nothing outside when I came in." She'd hurried in from the cold, distracted and angry at being set up, but she would have seen something out there on the stoop. Wouldn't she?

"Okay, it wasn't there. It's a figment of our shared imagination." He was still holding it out in her direction, and she accepted it reluctantly. She discovered it was another flower, this one a bird-of-paradise wrapped in fine tissue paper. The amber crown stuck out from the split-leaf head and long pointed "beak." Someone had taken more care with this offering, as the stem had a plastic vial of water snapped around it to keep it fed as it awaited her arrival. As usual, there was no card attached. "Your admirer strikes again," he said.

She finally took her coat off. Nick did the same and helped himself to two large bowls in her kitchen, watching as she removed the vial and added the new flower to the vase with the white rose. "You really didn't see who brought it?" She touched her fingertip to the flower's nose.

"Maybe I brought it."

She put a hand on one hip. "Do you even know what it is?"

He paused to wrinkle his nose at it. "Sure. It's a flower."

"I rest my case." She got the spritzing bottle and began tending to her usual plants, checking them over for dead leaves as she gave them an evening bath. "It's a bird-of-paradise," she told him as she worked. "The orange, white, and blue flowers look like a crane, and it only grows in warm temperatures, which is how it gets its name. It's native to South Africa, but you can find it anywhere with a hot climate now."

Nick cast a dubious glance at the icy front windows. "Not sure Chicago qualifies. How'd you know all that? Did Mrs. Yakamoto teach you?"

"No, I knew before." Colin liked to photograph the wildlife wherever he traveled, and he'd been to South Africa twice. She'd read every piece he'd written, subscribing to travel magazines before she ever owned a passport. She put the misting bottle aside and took the stool next to Nick at the kitchen counter.

"Ah," Nick said as he shook up the sriracha bottle. "You know about the flowers from him."

"Him who?"

"The him. Colin. Don't try to deny it."

"Why should I?" She narrowed her eyes at him and shredded the mint into her soup. "He's a great writer and his articles are highly informative. He's been all over the world, you know."

"Oh, I know," he said, like he'd heard it all before. "He's practically Johnny Cash. He's been everywhere—everywhere but here with you."

Colin had left and she had stayed. After Katie died, they'd had no choice, and over the years, it was who they'd become: the one who left and the one who stayed. There was no way to meet in the middle. "His mother was murdered. Can you blame him?"

"Yeah, I can," Nick said flatly. "You gave him justice—this thing he supposedly wanted all these years—and this is how he repays you? He jets off to Kathmandu and stops taking your calls like it's somehow your fault?"

She opened her mouth to object, but then closed it and shook her head, which was beginning to take on a dull throb. "Truce, all right? Let's talk about something other than my sorry love life."

He waved the spoon at her, undeterred. "See? There you go. It's not love. If this guy really loved you, he would've stayed."

"Yeah, well, I guess you'd know all about that too." She gave him a pointed look and he glared back at her for a moment before softening with a grudging shrug.

"Okay, I guess I deserved that." He squirted another round of hot sauce into his soup, making it spicy enough that her own eyes watered just to look at his bowl.

"I don't know how you can eat that stuff. Doesn't it set your mouth on fire?"

"Not when you're already this hot," he told her around a mouthful of noodles. He nodded beyond her to the coffee table where she had the Blanchard files laid out. "Is that the stuff that Bob Dickey got for you?"

"Yes, but you might want to keep your distance. If Zimmer catches you sniffing around the case, you'll end up chained to a desk like me. No more promotions."

"I think we're alone now," he said, looking her over. "I'll risk it."

They both took their bowls to the couch to sit with the files. "There is one more bit of evidence that Moe's guilty," she said as she handed him a slightly grainy printout of an old photo of Josie. "See the necklace she's wearing? Moe bought it for her, and it was never recovered after the murder. Leo Hammond figured he took it with him as a trophy."

"But they didn't find the necklace on Moe," Nick replied.

"No, it's never been found."

Vivian Catalano's statement was out on the coffee table where she'd left it, which reminded her of the name and number she'd written in her notes. "Give me a sec," she said to Nick as she took out her phone and looked up the number she'd found for Lloyd Nelson, Vivian Catalano's landlord at the time she'd been a witness in the Blanchard case. "I finally got a possible line on that witness." Catalano had said she'd seen a van parked on the street, but now they knew Moe had been driving a Pontiac the night Josie was killed. If Catalano could put the Pontiac outside Josie's apartment, they would have Moe at the scene. Nick picked up a stack of photocopied papers and began flipping through them as Annalisa dialed Nelson's number.

"Who?" Nelson demanded when Annalisa reached him. He had the slightly shouty tone of an old man gone partly deaf.

She raised her voice and explained again about Vivian Catalano. "She was a tenant of yours in September 2002, the month that Josie Blanchard was murdered."

"I remember that poor girl. What a shame. Don't tell me you finally got the fella that did it?"

"That's what we're trying to do," Annalisa replied. "That's why I need to find Vivian Catalano."

"Trying?" he repeated, incredulous. "It's been twenty years. Josie's nothing but bones now, and meanwhile her killer jets around in his fancy cars. My wife tried to get me to buy a Lincoln from him a few years back, but I wasn't having it. I don't care how low the prices are, he's not getting a dime of my money."

"You're talking about Moe Bocks."

"For Pete's sake, who else would it be? We all expected him to be arrested right after they found Josie with the life squeezed out of her, and still here we are, waiting."

"Maybe Vivian Catalano can help," she said, trying to steer the conversation back to where she wanted it. "Do you remember her?"

"Dark-haired lady. Neat and quiet. She needed a place quick because her husband split on her."

"Do you remember his name?"

"I figured it was Catalano," he said with exaggerated slowness, like she was dim-witted. "Not my business anyway, as long as the rent clears."

"When did she move out?"

"Oh, it wasn't long after that ugliness with Miss Blanchard. I lost two tenants soon after that—both single gals living on that street and one block over. I guess you can't blame them. When the cops didn't arrest Moe Bocks, we maybe got to thinking it could be someone else that killed her. Someone random. My wife had me put dead bolts on all the apartment doors but that wasn't soon enough to stop the single ladies from moving on."

"I see. Did Vivian Catalano leave any forwarding information?"

"I can look at my records and get back to you. But I don't recall anything."

Annalisa paced with the phone, frustrated at coming up short. "Do you remember anything else about her? Where she was from? Any other family she mentioned?"

"I got the feeling she was from somewhere kind of rural, like being on her own in the big city was not something she was used to. She had this real pretty painting—like wheat fields under a blue sky? It was all golden and the artist made it look like they were waving in the wind. I remarked on it once and she said it reminded her of home."

Annalisa recalled Vivian's statement that she'd met Josie when she moved in. Josie had offered her help unboxing and hanging pictures. She wondered if the wheat fields had been among them. "Okay, thank you, Mr. Nelson. If you find anything else in your records, please let me know right away."

She hung up and Nick glanced her way. "No luck?"

"It's like this woman vanished into thin air."

"It's a long shot anyway. Even if she can put Moe Bocks's Pontiac on the street the night Josie died, it still doesn't prove he killed her."

"It's a lot closer than we are now," she said as she flopped onto the couch next to him.

"What's this?" he asked her, turning around a piece of paper so she could see it.

She squinted at it and then took it from him for a closer look. "It seems like an old telephone memo that got stuck to one of the neighbor's statements." They didn't use paper memos anymore; callers were transferred to the appropriate voicemail box where they left a message. This one was dated September 27, 2002, 9:08 p.m. The RE: field had a scrawl in it that read *Blanchard* and the caller was listed as Noreen Butler with a return phone number in the Chicago area. "I don't know who this is," she said of Noreen Butler. "She's not mentioned anywhere else that I've found."

"Can't hurt to try," Nick said as he dug out his phone and peered at the number.

"Can you imagine?" Annalisa asked as he dialed. "Hi, Ms. Butler, it's the Chicago PD returning your call . . . twenty years later." She waited, expectant, as Nick listened for an answer on the other end.

"Hello," he said at length. "I'm trying to reach Noreen Butler. Is she there? Oh, I see. Do you know where I might find her? Thank you." He hung up and gave Annalisa a shrug. "Wrong number. No one by the name of Noreen Butler lives there."

"Maybe she ran off with Vivian Catalano," Annalisa said as she picked up the pages that had color copies of the photographs from the original files. She quickly bypassed the ones that showed Josie Blanchard's body and settled on the close-up of the murder weapon: two sawed-off wooden dowels, painted bright blue, with a length of wire between them. Simple but deadly.

"It looks like chair legs to me," Nick said as he peered over her shoulder.

"Well, then the Bockses got rid of the chairs that matched it." She put the picture aside and took up the ones from the Bocks home at the time of the search. The garage had held a bunch of old wood, but none of it blue. She searched it again with her gaze, and this time, she stopped at the sight of a garden tool propped against the wall in the back. "Wait a second . . ." She reached for the magnifying glass and held it over the picture. "This rake is blue."

Nick leaned so far over he almost landed in her lap. "The color is a good match," he agreed. "But it's intact. Not sawed off. It didn't make the murder weapon."

Annalisa held the magnifying glass closer so that she could see the brand. "It's Garden Arts . . . see the *GA*?" She'd spent hours with one in her hands as Pops made her help clean the yard each fall and each spring.

"Yeah, so? Is it unusual?"

"No," she said, leaning back in defeat. "It's the most common brand around here." Her phone buzzed and she picked it up to check the caller. "Kayla Hammond," she said with surprise.

"Maybe we'll get lucky and she's calling to confess." Nick put his feet up; he wasn't betting on it.

"This is Vega," she said into the phone.

Kayla sounded hysterical on the other end. "He's dead! Someone tried to kill me and now he's dead. Do you believe me now?"

"Who's dead?" Annalisa traded a look with Nick, who sat up straight at her words.

"Tom. He's in the basement—where someone tried to kill me!"

Annalisa heard a car door slam and an engine start up. "Mrs. Hammond, wait a minute. Talk to me and I can help you. Where are you?"

"Freakin' out of here is where I am, where I should've been all along. Tell Eddie he can keep his money. I am *out*."

CHAPTER TWENTY-SEVEN

WHEN KAYLA SAID TOM WAS DEAD IN "THE" BASEMENT, ANNALISA AND NICK REASONED SHE WAS REFERRING TO THE BASEMENT OF HER HOME, SO THAT'S WHERE THEY STARTED THEIR SEARCH. Annalisa drove most of the way Code 3, blowing through traffic lights and careening around slow-moving traffic to reach the Hammonds' neighborhood, where she abruptly cut her speed and rolled up their street with no lights or siren. The area was quiet, with no neighbors about or any other signs of activity. "Basement light is on," Nick observed as Annalisa glided to a stop in front of the Hammond house. The bottom windows glowed with yellow light while the rest of the house sat in shadow. "Maybe we should call it in."

"Call what in? So far all we have is a light on." She got out of the car, taking care to close the door as quietly as possible. Nick followed suit and watched as she unholstered her weapon and started for the house.

"The front door is open," she whispered back to him. She nudged it with her foot, widening the space enough so she could slip inside. Nick, with a flashlight in hand, came in behind her and slanted the beam around the room. It appeared undisturbed. She pointed in the direction of the door to the basement and he nodded.

The door was shut and she held her breath as she cracked it open. No noise on the other side. Cautiously, she began her descent down the staircase. She hadn't gone more than three steps when she smelled the gunpowder. Nick froze behind her as it hit him too. She kept her back to the wall and her weapon at the ready as she descended the remainder of the stairs. The place appeared in order but she could smell blood now, coming from the couch. She braced herself for what she knew she would find: Tom, dead, with his mouth hanging open and his eyes wide with fright. Whatever had happened to him, he'd seen it coming.

Behind her, Nick checked the closets and the storage room. "Clear," he reported as he joined her by the sofa. They took in the line of coke sitting on the coffee table, the bullet holes in the couch, and a throw pillow with a smear of what looked like mucus and blood across one side.

Annalisa held it up. "Kayla wasn't kidding," she said. "Someone did try to kill her."

"Yeah, but who? Tom? It makes no sense. Why would he try to kill her? And then who killed him?"

"When I find her, I'll ask her."

"She could still be here. We should check the rest of the house."

"There are no cars outside. Kayla's long gone. So's whoever did this, I would wager." She gestured at Tom.

"I'm checking it anyway. Then I'm calling in."

Annalisa hummed a non-reply and went to the basement window that had been broken at the time of Leo's death. Someone had patched it with plastic, which appeared undisturbed. She checked the door at the rear of the house and found it unbolted. She opened it and checked the knob from the outside and found it did not turn. Someone could have left but not entered this way. She reached for the switches for the outdoor floodlights and turned them on, sending bright light across the raised wooden deck and shadows across the yard beyond.

The snow had melted, leaving behind dead grass and mud. She used her flashlight to study the ground, inch by inch, and by the edge of the deck, she found two large footprints, side by side and depressed a fair amount into the soft earth, as though someone had leapt from the deck. Maybe she was imagining things, but they looked faintly flipper-like. She came around the deck and used the two stairs to investigate the potential trail. The footprints went across the yard to the chain-link fence and disappeared, so the person had gone through the fence or over it. Annalisa gave it a shake and it held, meaning the only path was over the six-foot fence. She shined her light up and found a piece of something caught on one of the metal prongs. Sticking her toe in one opening, she hoisted herself up for a closer look: it was torn rubber, like from a diver's suit.

She hurried back inside to tell Nick of her findings, only to discover him standing, ashen-faced, holding a gym bag. "This was in the pantry," he said. "There's got to be a couple hundred thousand in here at least."

"Kayla said she was leaving Eddie the money," Annalisa replied as she peered in with a low whistle.

"Whoever did this also left it."

"Maybe they didn't know it was here. Just to add some intrigue, I found footprints in the yard and what looks like a torn patch of black neoprene on the back fence."

His eyebrows shot up. "Neoprene? Like a diving suit?"

"That's what it appears to me. We could be looking at the same shooter here."

Nick zipped up the bag and set it down so he could take out his phone. "I'm going straight to Zimmer with this—no radio."

She held up her hands. "If you're calling Zimmer, then I've got to disappear. She catches me here and I'm busted back down to patrol."

"No way." He fixed her with a hard look. "You can't leave me alone with this money. Who knows how much is here and where it came from? Maybe Kayla took half and ran. Maybe the shooter did. All I know is that I don't want anyone looking sideways at me if some of it turns up missing."

"Ha, you know everyone would just blame me," she said, but she stuck around because she owed him that much. She moved to the stairs and turned to assess the distance to the couch where Tom's body lay. The shooter either came down the stairs or had lain in wait in the storage room. If it was the same person who'd killed Leo, then they could have used the alarm code again, or perhaps the front door had been open as it was when she arrived with Nick. She tried to think of someone who would want Leo, Tom, and Kayla dead. The bag full of money seemed like a good place to start, but they still had no clue who Eddie was.

Annalisa checked out the inside of the storage closet, careful not to touch anything. She wasn't even sure what she was looking for—flippers? A diving mask? She found only boxes, fertilizer, some empty pots, and other gardening equipment, including a Garden Arts rake, this one with a green handle and a matching shovel. The ones her family owned had been a deep red, almost burgundy. She could smell the dead leaves and the wet dirt of her childhood memories, saw Pops with his work gloves on, doing the shoveling, yelling at her and Alex to stop clowning around and clean up. Alex had used his rake to joust with her, thrusting and parrying, until she fell backward into a leaf pile and lay there under the dizzy blue sky.

"Anna?" Nick poked his head in, jolting her from her reverie. "What are you doing?"

"Just—nothing."

"Zimmer said to wait outside. She's sending backup but warned us to put nothing out over the radio."

"A second dead cop inside of a week. Word's going to get out quick, no matter what we do." They climbed the stairs and left the way they'd come in, through the front door. "You know how fast the grapevine works."

"I've been thinking about that. Paul Monk and Frankie Vaughn were awful quick to show up here the night Leo got killed."

"Almost like they knew it was coming," she agreed.

They leaned against her car and she blew on her hands to warm them. Nick hunched deeper into his jacket. "That's a whole lot of green in there," he said. "More than I've seen at once, and more than I'm likely to see in a lifetime."

"Tempted, are you?"

He shook his head, bemused. "You don't encounter that stuff working assault cases or homicides. Maybe if you're like Leo Hammond or Tom Osborne, watching it go by under your nose every day makes you start to think you deserve it. I mean, who'd miss it, right? If you and I took off with that bag, no one would ever even know."

"And then one or both of us ends up like Tom in there." She considered. "Because that's the rub, right? We take that money, and sure, maybe Zimmer doesn't find out. Maybe we never get rousted by Internal Affairs. But you know who would know? Whoever had the money to begin with."

He didn't say anything for a long moment. "You ever take a free lunch?"

"What do you mean?"

"I mean maybe you're in uniform, and you have a tuna on rye or a BLT at the diner, and the owner waves you off when you try to pay. Says it's thanks for keeping the streets safe. Free lunch . . . or coffee. People try to give you that stuff all the time."

She shoved her hands in her pockets. "No."

"Why not?"

"Pops told me not to. When I joined up, he said it would be easy to start thinking you're entitled to more than your salary. You see the bad side of the city so much, when some nice citizen offers you a hot meal, you think it's only right they should thank you. What's a cup of coffee or a free beer here or there? But once you take it, you look the other way on the small stuff, and it becomes harder to see the big stuff." Start with a dollar, end up with a bag full of blood money and a dead man on the sofa.

Nick nodded. "The small evils soften you for the big ones." She gave him a look and he clarified, "That's what my training officer said when I started out. He said, 'The shield is to protect them, not you. The badge will get you anything you want, so that's why you can't want too much."

"The transfer and promotion, though. You want that." He'd earned it. Who was she to stand in his way?

He hesitated a beat and then gave a short nod. "I want saner hours. I want a family. For a while there, I thought . . . I thought maybe you wanted it too."

Nothing she wanted ever came true. The moment she looked at her future and said, *yes, I want that,* the whole thing went to hell. Like Nick had said: best not to want too much. The sirens started in the distance, growing closer. In a few seconds, Nick would be home free with plenty of cops to vouch for his honesty. She pushed off from the car and reached for her keys.

"Where are you going?" He caught her free hand.

"It's better for you if I'm not here," she said, pulling away. "Less complicated."

"You're ditching me again."

"I'm going home," she said. "Call me when you know something." She drove off in the opposite direction of the arriving squad cars, watching in her rearview mirror as Nick grew smaller in the distance. When she reached the first light, her car alone stood at the intersection. No one would care if she ran it, but she remained idling behind the crosswalk. She heard a crunching, metallic sound to her left, and looked over to see an older man in a huge puffy coat shoveling slush from in front of a closed bakery. He noticed her staring and righted himself to point at the light, which had turned green.

Annalisa saw only the shovel in his hands.

The shovel. Garden Arts sold it as a set with the rake. Moe had used the shovel's handle to fashion the murder weapon, leaving the rake behind. Annalisa muttered a curse and did a U-turn in front of the old man, who looked on in surprise. She sent a mental apology to Nick that she'd once again lied to him, but she was no longer going home.

CHAPTER TWENTY-EIGHT

Annalisa hit the button to call her parents' place, noting as she did so that the dash clock read almost one in the morning. Her mother's groggy voice filled the car as she came on the line. "Annalisa? It's so late to be calling. What's wrong?"

"Ma, I need you to do me a favor. You know the matching shovel and rake that Pops has? I need you to take a photo of them on your phone and send it to me right away. They both need to be in the same shot. If there's any serial number or other identifying marks, please take a close-up of that and send it too."

There was silence on the other end. Annalisa could picture her mother sitting up in bed, staring at the phone in confusion. "You want me to do what?"

Annalisa patiently repeated her request. "I'm sorry about the hour, but it's an emergency."

"A rake emergency?"

Annalisa winced. "Yes. Can you please just take the photo? I promise I'll explain later."

"I can't," her mother replied. "We don't have those tools anymore."

Annalisa, alone on the dark road, screeched to a halt. "What?"

"Your father can't tend the yard, not with his Parkinson's. He hasn't in years. You know we pay a service for that now. We gave all those tools away a long time ago."

"Gave them to whom?"

"Let me think . . . oh, it was Alex. Alex took all the garden things." She paused. "I guess he's got no use for them now either."

Annalisa had no time to ruminate on her lost brother. "Okay, Ma, thanks. Sorry to bother you." She hung up and dialed Sassy instead, driving onward, now that she had a new lead on the rake and shovel.

Sassy answered right away. "What is it?" Her voice had the same undercurrent of fear, the same bracing for disaster that Annalisa's mother had shown. Annalisa felt this was how they all lived now—in free fall, waiting for the bottom that never seemed to arrive.

"Sorry to wake you."

"No, I was up." She sighed. "I'm always up."

"I know the feeling." Annalisa checked her rearview mirror and found a pair of headlights. She kept an eye on them as she spoke to Sassy. Only now did it occur to her that Moe might be with her sister-in-law. "Listen, I need to know: Is Moe there?"

"No." Sassy's voice took on an edge. Annalisa heard her get out of bed and walk to the window. "Why? Are you outside stalking me again?"

"I didn't touch him, Sass. I know he says I attacked him but it wasn't me. I swear it."

Sassy didn't reply for a long moment. "I know," she admitted finally. "I told him that. We—we had a fight about it, actually. He's convinced it was you, but I told him you would never do that."

Annalisa let out a slow exhale. "Thanks for believing me."

"Yeah, well, you turned your own father and brother over to the law. I can't imagine you'd do different for Moe. Clubbing him over the head in the middle of the night doesn't solve anything—that's not justice, right?" Sassy didn't sound angry, just tired.

"Right," Annalisa said, gripping the wheel. "That's why I'm calling. I need your help with something important. Do you remember a shovel-and-rake set that Alex picked up from my parents? They are a matching set and have dark red handles."

"They're in the garage. Why?"

"Can you take a picture of them and send it to me?" She repeated the instructions she'd given her mother. Sassy didn't seem eager to cooperate.

"It's late and I'm not dressed. Can't this wait until morning?"

"No, I need them now. Please, Sass?" She would need proof that the pair came as a set when they eventually filed for a warrant. "It's urgent."

"Tell me why."

Annalisa opened her mouth but no sound came out. If she explained that she was still pursuing Moe, Sassy might refuse to send the pictures. But she couldn't lie, not to her best friend. "It's about the Josie Blanchard case."

"I see. You know, I told Moe that part too, how you wouldn't stop coming after him, and that if he did this thing, then you would prove it. It doesn't matter what the other cops did or didn't do on the case before. You're not like them."

"I didn't say it was about Moe."

"You didn't have to. He's the only suspect, right? He's all there's ever been."

"Maybe you should ask yourself why that is," Annalisa countered as she took a right turn into the Bockses' neighborhood.

"I don't have to ask. I looked up the news stories the same as you. It had to be Moe. They never looked for anyone else, because they couldn't. If it wasn't him, then he's reasonable doubt for everyone else . . . isn't that how it goes?"

"Sassy, there are a million guys out there you could be dating. Why this one? Why do you need him to be innocent?"

"Maybe he is. Did you think of that? And maybe ask yourself why you need him to be guilty. This isn't even your case, Anna! Why do you care so much? She's dead and she's never coming back, no matter what you do or how determined you are to set your career on fire. There's only us, the living people."

Annalisa said nothing for a long time. "Why do I get the feeling we're not talking about Josie Blanchard here?" she said finally. She checked the mirrors again and saw the headlights behind her had disappeared when she turned into the neighborhood.

"If I send you this picture, will you go talk to Alex?" Sassy asked her.

"Sassy—"

"Just talk to him. You haven't even done that much." When Annalisa didn't reply, Sassy pressed on. "If you won't do it for me and the girls, do it for Katie."

"Oh, that's rich. She's dead because of him."

"You think she'd be proud? You think she'd be pleased the way things turned out, with the family torn apart like this? Katie was always the first to forgive, to hug you and say it would all be okay."

Annalisa remembered those hugs. Katie always smelled like makeup and perfume, like adulthood. She'd squeeze you until her jewelry pressed into your skin but you didn't want her to let go. *There, there, baby,* she'd say in her Mae West voice, *it'll all come out in the wash.* Tears sprang up in Annalisa's eyes and she swiped them away as she pulled to a stop outside the Bocks home. "Please," she said, her voice rough. "Just send the pictures."

She clicked off and took a shuddering breath as she looked at the darkened house, partially visible beyond the winter-thinned trees. Only the floodlights at the front of the house were on; none inside the home, which made sense given the lateness of the hour. Her interest was in the separate garage, a large structure that might even have been a carriage house at one time. This was where the rake had been photographed twenty years ago. If she could glimpse it through a window to verify it was still there, she would have enough information to pass on to Zimmer to get a warrant. She took her flashlight and her pocketknife and put on a dark knit cap against the cold. They had ordered her to stay away from Bocks, but this was his mother's home, the place he'd been staying at the time of Josie's murder. Besides, she had no intention of disturbing the main house. All she wanted was a quick look in the garage.

The windows were dirty. She tried shining her light through first one and then the other, her face pressed right up against the cold glass. She saw two covered vehicles, cardboard boxes, and a push mower that looked like it had been around when Nixon was president. She tried the side door and found it locked. The garage entrances were both shut tight as well. However, the older windows were loose enough that she could slide her pocketknife in and unhitch the lock. Just a quick look, she promised herself. She crawled inside and nearly landed in a wheelbarrow. She dusted off her hands and then shined her flashlight around. One of the covered cars appeared to be a black Corvette. The other was a blue Chrysler with old-timey fins, and she knew Pops would be able to identify the make and model in an instant. Annalisa threaded her way past the vehicles to the back of the garage, where the tools were kept. A bunch of them hung on a pegboard. She found two rakes—neither with a blue handle—a hoe, garden spades, and a selection of watering cans. Maybe the family had gotten rid of the rake; it had been twenty years.

Her phone dinged and she about jumped out of her skin. Sassy's text. She'd sent the picture without comment and Annalisa saw her memory was correct: the rake and shovel had matching handles. She also saw that Alex had stored them under the long tool bench, presumably to keep them out from underfoot. The Bockses had a similar long table that sat under another drop cloth, which was then topped with cardboard boxes. Annalisa crossed to the table and bent down to lift the tarp. There it was: a blue rake nestled in among a pair of brooms. Her heart started pounding and she hurried to snap a few photos. She didn't even wait until she'd left the garage before she started texting Nick.

Here's the proof, she wrote. *The rake was part of a set. We need a warrant for the Bocks family home.*

She wriggled out of the window and checked the phone for a reply as she walked back through the trees toward her car. He had to still be up and working the latest crime scene at the Hammond house. Her message said it had been delivered but Nick hadn't seen it. Maybe she should call him.

"Stop right there."

She froze as Moe Bocks, his left arm still in a sling, emerged from behind a pine tree. His right hand held a gun. "Mr. Bocks," she said as she raised her hands to show she was unarmed. Her weapon remained in its holster. "Did you follow me here?" She had wondered about those headlights.

"Follow you? This is my house."

"It's your mother's house."

"The point is I'm allowed to be here." He took a step closer to her. "You're not."

"I'm sorry. I was just leaving." She tried to go but he advanced on her.

"I don't think so."

"You can't shoot me," she said, hoping she sounded reasonable.

"Can't I? You're on my property in the middle of the night. What were you doing here, hoping to take another whack at me? Trying to finish the job this time?"

"Mr. Bocks, I'm not the one who attacked you, so shooting me won't solve any of your problems."

"No jury would convict me."

"You don't know that. You never got in front of a jury, did you? You strangled Josie and got away with it."

"I didn't kill Josie." He ground out each word.

"I have the proof now. I've already sent it to my colleagues, so it doesn't matter what you do to me."

"That's a lie. I know it's true because there is no proof—because I didn't kill her. Also I know you're out here by your lonesome, skulking around in my backyard like a common thief. I've been watching you from the window. My mother brought me here to rest but I can't rest. There's a pin in my arm and a lump on the back of my head the size of a lemon so I can't even lie in bed at night without pain, thanks to you."

The gun wavered in his hand and she had a flash of true fear. She licked her lips. "Look, if you're not a killer, then you don't want to kill me. Put the gun down, okay? I'll leave and I promise I won't come back." She could send Nick and Zimmer for him, now that she had proof.

He gave a dark laugh. "I've heard that before. And yet here you are again!"

"I'm going." She edged toward her car, holding up her hands, showing him she only had her phone. "See? I'm leaving. You can't shoot me in the back."

"I'm not going to shoot you!" He snarled at her. "I'm going to have you arrested."

"Wait." He was putting the gun aside, going for his phone. This he could do and she'd be arrested, probably fired. The trees felt like they were closing in around her, panic rising, and she fought through it for one clear thought. Her body told her to run but she ignored it. Something else . . . "Wait, did you say I was in the backyard?"

Moe looked up, surprise on his face, and something hit her from behind. She felt her head split open, saw blinding white light and then nothing at all when she hit the ground.

CHAPTER TWENTY-NINE

SHE DID NOT WAKE UP DEAD. When Annalisa opened her eyes, she glimpsed a metal ceiling before slamming them shut again as pain lanced through her head like a knife to the skull. *Moving,* she thought as the nausea hit her. Her body swayed and she forced herself to look at her surroundings again. "Detective Vega," said an unfamiliar male voice. "Squeeze my hand if you can hear me."

She squeezed. ". . . 're am I?"

"You're in an ambulance and we're taking you to the hospital." The man shined a light in her eyes and she tried to shrink away from him.

"I'm . . . fine." She tried to sit up but a dizzying wave crashed over her and she sank down with a moan.

"Just sit tight. Take it easy. We'll have you there quick."

"What the hell were you thinking?" This voice was Zimmer's. Annalisa dragged her eyes open again to see her boss leaning over behind the EMT. "You could have been killed."

Moe Bocks, she remembered. *The rake.* She inhaled sharply and groped around to reach Zimmer's hand. "Did you get my texts? The rake is the proof. Moe killed Josie."

"You have more pressing problems," Zimmer told her. "Someone killed Moe."

"What?" She tried to sit up again but the EMT pushed her back down.

"Lie still. We're almost there."

"Residents reported gunfire. Responding officers arrived to find you unconscious and Moe shot twice in the back about fifty yards away, like he was running for the house when he got hit."

"Someone hit me from behind. I don't know who. Did you find the shooter?" Zimmer said nothing and the nausea in Annalisa's stomach coalesced into a ball of dread. "Commander?"

"The incident is under investigation," Zimmer said. "Two weapons were found at the scene—yours and a Walther P88 registered to Moe Bocks Senior."

"I know it well," Annalisa said through gritted teeth. "He was threatening to shoot me with it before I got clonked on the head."

"The weapon had been recently discharged." Zimmer paused again. "As was yours."

Annalisa gripped the side of the stretcher. "I didn't fire it. I didn't even unholster."

"Responding units found it on the ground near where you were lying."

Annalisa raised her hands in front of her face and regarded them like they were a separate entity. "I didn't shoot anyone. I didn't kill Bocks. I just went there to get the picture of the rake, the one I sent to Nick. Why would I do that if I went there to kill him?"

"I don't know," Zimmer said harshly. "Your actions recently have been mystifying. I don't know why you went there at all after you were given explicit orders to stay away from Bocks."

"But the rake—"

"No. I don't want to hear it. In fact, I don't think you should say anything further to me until you've spoken to a lawyer."

Annalisa closed her eyes and did not open them again until they reached the hospital. A brusque female doctor put her through a neurological exam without commenting on whether she'd passed. She got wheeled into radiation for an X-ray and then a brain scan to determine if she had any bleeding inside her skull. Every time she spoke or moved a pain went through her head so severe it made her teeth vibrate. When the scans came back revealing no fractures or internal damage, they finally allowed her to have a painkiller. Cotton candy filled up her head and she went to sleep right where she lay.

She awoke some indeterminate time later in a dimly lit hospital room. She tried to raise her head and groaned when the effort rewarded her with a throbbing across the back of her skull. "It lives," said a wry voice, and she blinked several times to clear her vision. The blurry image coalesced into the shape of Nick Carelli.

"Don't tell me you're here to arrest me," she rasped out with her dry mouth.

Nick went for the pitcher of water and poured her a cup. "Not me. You should look out for Zimmer, though. She asked me what the hell you were doing at the Bocks place, and when I didn't have an answer, she threatened to have me suspended on the spot."

She winced as she sat up to sip the water. "Sorry."

"No, you're not."

"I am. I didn't want you dragged into this. That's why I didn't tell you where I was going."

"You could have been killed."

"I just wanted a picture. You got it, right? You got the rake?"

He stood up, looming over her. "God, Vega, do you hear yourself? Bocks is dead, maybe shot with your gun. It doesn't matter about the rake."

"Someone's setting me up. Again."

"And they did a bang-up job this time."

She held out her hands. "Test me for powder residue. You'll see I didn't discharge my weapon."

He turned his head away. "Zimmer already had them do it while you were asleep. I don't know what the results say. No one's telling me anything."

"I'm sorry," she said with more feeling. She groped blindly for his hand because it hurt to move her head. He saw her grasping and shifted a fraction so she could reach him. When her hand closed over his, she held on tight. "You have to get Zimmer to do the test on the rake. The paint is going to match the garrote from Josie Blanchard's murder, and then we'll have the proof that Bocks killed her."

He shook his head like she was crazy. "No one's going to authorize that test now. Bocks is dead. It's over."

"The case can't be closed until we know. It's not over until someone calls Josie's mother in France and tells her that her daughter's killer has been identified."

He looked down at her. "Do you even speak French?"

"I'll learn."

A bark of laughter escaped him. "You never quit, do you?"

"I don't quit, but my hands are tied here," she said. "I can't push for the analysis from a hospital bed with Zimmer ready to slam the cuffs on me at any moment. But you could. You wanted to be my partner on this, remember? So get a warrant for the rake. Have the lab test the paint against the murder weapon and you'll see it matches."

"And if it doesn't?"

"It will." He pulled his hand free and his shoulders rose and fell with a great sigh. She smiled when she knew she had him. "Nick . . ."

"Hmm?" He was looking at the wall, not at her, probably contemplating the shitstorm that would fall on him if Zimmer found out.

"Be careful, okay? Keep it as quiet as possible."

"Oh, like you did?"

"Right," she agreed. "And look where it landed me."

The door to her room opened a few inches and her father's face appeared in the void. He moved forward inch by tortured inch, leaning heavily on a cane, apparently out of his wheelchair—and out of the house, which legally, he was not allowed to be. The shocking sight caused her to sit straight up in bed. "Pops, what are you doing here? Where's Ma?"

"She's outside."

Nick helped her father to the chair he'd been sitting in. "I'll let you two talk," he said. "Call me if you get out of here."

"They can't keep me," she replied.

Her father snorted. "That's my girl."

Nick closed the door behind him as he left and Annalisa regarded her father with a concerned gaze. "You shouldn't be here," she said in a low voice. "You're violating probation. If anyone notices you're out of the house, they could arrest you."

"Your commander calls and says you're in th-the hospital. Where else am I going to be? Then I hear there's a body and it's Moe Bocks. You were at the scene."

"I didn't kill him, Pops."

"S-s-someone did. Someone who wants it to look like you." His cheek twitched. When he spoke again, his voice cracked. "This isn't because of me, is it? Someone trying to get back at you . . ."

"No," she said. "I don't think so." Since he was here, she might as well ask him what he knew. "What can you tell me about Leo Hammond and the others in the Fantastic Four?"

"Hammond? Wh-what's he got to do with this?"

"Maybe nothing. Just tell me what you know."

He shrugged one thin shoulder, a jerky motion only partially controlled. "Big dicks, we used to call 'em. Headline cases. Lotta dope. Gang killings. Leo and his boys were on the front lines of the war. Down in the trenches, it always seemed like we were losing. You'd bust a punk for selling smack, and he'd be back on his corner ten weeks later. Or you'd find him OD'd somewhere, him or his latest girl, maybe with a kid crying in the background in a three-day-old diaper. W-wait long enough, and you'd be busting that kid too."

"You ever get a sense that those big dope raids weren't always kosher?"

His frown deepened. "What're you sayin'?"

"You know. They take eight kilos of coke but only six make it into evidence."

He shifted slowly, with effort, like his hip was hurting him. "That's—that's a serious charge."

"I'm not charging. Not yet. I just want to know if you heard anything."

He rubbed his chin. "You always had this vision of me as some TV cop, like I was out crusading the streets and every big case came to me. I wasn't. I was a beat cop most of my days, and proud to be one. I never cared about climbing the ladder."

She accepted this dig at her and her rank. "Leo and his partners did, but only so far. They didn't take any job that kept them off the streets."

"Maybe they liked the excitement."

"I don't think they like it so much now. Two of them are dead."

His eyebrows shot up. "Two?"

"Someone killed Tom Osborne tonight." Or was it yesterday? Her days blurred together like rain down a windowpane. "Also, Leo had a stash of money hidden away. I don't know exactly how much but it was at least a few hundred grand."

"Who has the money now?"

"Nick logged it. Why?"

He hesitated. "You hear stories sometimes. Half of them are exaggerated. People get nicknames like 'Slick Mick' for flirting with the ladies, or your boss, 'the Hammer.'"

"I know," Annalisa said. "She could drink anyone under the table."

"Yeah, well, a buddy of mine once called Paul Monk 'Felonious Monk.' I didn't think much about it at the time, but these names, they always come from somewhere. Maybe he didn't earn it busting felons."

"That's it? You don't know what he did to get the name?"

He eyed her. "Not my business," he said, a hint of petulance in his voice. "I'm no detective. Never was. But you be careful. I'm dead s-s-serious, Anna. If you've got dirty cops going back years, they're used to covering their tracks. They know all the tricks."

"You would know about that."

"So righteous. Look where you are. Somewhere, a judge is probably signing a warrant with your name on it."

"Don't compare you and me. We're not the same." She flung out the words to hurt him but they cut her just as deep. She'd spent years looking in the mirror and seeing his face, being happy with that reflection.

"Damn right we're not. I saved what I could. I saved our family. I took what happened and kept it inside where it hurt only me, you understand? Me and Alex. Then you come along, crack me open like an egg and spread the pain over everything and everyone." His head bobbed and he choked back a sob. "It was m-my sacrifice. Not yours."

"No, Pops." Annalisa's anger softened to pity. "It was Katie's."

With clumsy hands, he pulled out a handkerchief and wiped at his watering eyes. "Maybe you're right. I had my reasons and you had yours, okay? Leave it at that right now. But I mean it when I say watch your back. Wherever you've been digging, it's too close to where the bodies are buried. Two dead cops means you gotta be twice as careful of the others because they have nothing left to lose."

CHAPTER THIRTY

Frankie didn't kiss Maggie goodbye this time, partly because he didn't want to wake her when he slipped out past midnight, and partly because he wanted the universe to register the unusualness of his departure. He didn't kiss her, so he had to come back. It could not end like this. He took her Honda rather than his Land Rover. Paulie had a cousin in construction who gave them leads on empty buildings when they needed one, and tonight's meeting spot was in a rough side of town. *It's scheduled for demolition,* Paulie had said, and Frankie tried not to think about the symbolism of that as he turned into the dark alley behind the crumbling brick structure. He did not see Paulie's truck anywhere, so he located the plywood door, found it loose, and pried it open enough to slip inside.

The room was dim, with light from the street slanting in through the upper windows; the lower row had more plywood covering them. Rubble covered the floor—bits of Sheetrock, some loose bricks, paint peeled from the walls. Rust-colored water damage formed a stain across the ceiling. The counter at the back and the pass-through window to the room beyond it suggested it might have been a restaurant of some kind. Now it was a corpse, deader than any of the bangers that Frankie peeled off the city's pavement. He shoved his hands in his pockets and walked aimlessly, whistling past the graveyard. Spray-painted letters on the far wall said someone had been inside not too long ago. Frankie was studying the tag when he heard a footstep behind him, the sound of a boot hitting the grit that covered the floor. The door had not opened. The footfall came from nowhere. It was the kind of noise you heard before you got popped, and Frankie had a flash of terror and shame that he'd let someone get the drop on him.

He whirled and found Paulie standing there, where he must have been all along, maybe hiding in the kitchen. "What the hell?" he demanded. "You think this is funny?"

"You don't see me laughing, do you?"

Frankie saw then that Paulie had his piece out. "What're you doing?" He held out his hands—part protest, part peacemaker. "Put that away. You're not freaking out on me, are you?"

"Hell yes, I'm freaking. Aren't you? First Leo gets whacked, and now Tom. I don't know who's going to be next, but it sure as hell won't be me."

"Calm down. We'll figure it out."

"You've been saying that for a while now, and I got news for you, Frank—it ain't figured out. The only thing we've got is more shit. Today I heard Moe Bocks is dead too. Is that more of your 'handling it'? Because you're going after the wrong guy. No way Bocks is the one taking shots at us."

"What?" Frankie took a sharp breath. "Bocks is dead? How?"

Paulie narrowed his eyes. "Vega got him, at least that's the story. But that's how you drew it up in the first place."

"I had nothing to do with this."

"Sure," Paulie said, plainly not believing him. "Maybe you did and maybe you didn't. Maybe you had nothing to do with Leo and Tom either."

"Now you're talking shit," Frankie said. "You know that wasn't me."

"Do I?" Paulie waved the gun around in a way that made Frankie nervous. "Because only one of us solves things by whacking people, and it ain't me."

"Hey, you were in it the same as me with Sandra. Don't pretend you weren't." Paulie shook his head, turning away from him. Frankie moved so he was back in Paulie's line of sight. "Look, she gave us no choice. Even Leo knew that. We just have to figure this out. If someone's coming for us, it's obvious it was never Bocks. Who, then?" He paused to think. “Kayla was there. She was there both times.” He’d heard she was in the wind now.

Paulie made an incredulous face. “Kayla with the pink manicure and Gucci bag?”

“A manicure doesn’t stop her from shooting anyone. Carter told me they’re looking for her, that she’s a person of interest in Tom’s death. We already know Vega was looking at her for Leo’s murder.” He hoped to God it would be that easy.

Paulie’s expression turned speculative. “Is that all you know?”

“There’s more?”

“They found the money—Vega and her partner. Maybe it was Leo’s money, maybe Tom’s. I don’t know. All I heard is that they found a fuckload of cash in Leo’s house. If Kayla killed them, why wouldn’t she take the money?”

“Maybe she couldn’t find it. I don’t know.”

“Well, Vega has it now,” Paulie said meaningfully.

“We don’t need to worry about her. Whoever took care of her, they did it right this time.”

“I’m sick of you telling me what to worry about. I’m chewing antacids like they’re bubble gum and that was before Tom turned up dead.”

“Maybe . . . maybe they’re not related. Kayla shoots Leo and then Tom got mixed up in some side deal and it went bad. He was jumpy lately, you know, looking to score. You heard the way he was going on about Eddie.”

“Eddie.” Paulie whispered the name. He walked to the counter and leaned on it, testing its weight. “Leo went to see him, you know. After he finally got released to the adult transition center last year. He could’ve been out sooner only he’d never admit he’d done it. Leo sat outside the building until he got a look at Eddie. He said you wouldn’t recognize him now. Said he got old.”

Frankie grunted. “Him and the rest of us.”

“Leo said it probably cost half a million to keep Eddie locked up all these years, and he thought that was funny. Like Eddie got the same five hundred Gs as we did.”

“He didn’t talk to him or anything?”

“He said no,” Paulie replied. “Just looked. But I could tell from his face he didn't like what he saw. You say Leo was in it like the rest of us, but I'm telling you—he wasn't. He was sweet on Sandra."

"He was fucking her. That's not the same thing. And if he'd kept it in his pants, she never would have bothered us and we wouldn't have touched her. She's the one who forced our hand, and Leo is the reason why. Maybe Leo wasn't in the bathroom with her that night, but he sure as hell was responsible."

"That's what I'm trying to say. He did feel responsible. Maybe more than we knew."

Frankie looked at his hands. He couldn't see them clearly but he knew they'd taken on a leathery look in the past few years, brown age spots revealing themselves the way seaweed appeared when the tide rolled out. If he was lucky, he'd get three more decades. He didn't believe in the afterlife, which was why he grabbed everything he could in this one. Leo had made a show of the whole God routine. He'd gotten his kids baptized, sat in the pews in a clean suit on Sunday only to shed it hours later when he screwed some badge bunny in the back room of a bar. Leo might have gone to church but he'd worshipped elsewhere. Frankie had believed they were united in their lack of belief, that Leo understood there would be no higher reckoning than the law on earth, and on earth they were the law. But maybe Leo had age spots of his own. Maybe he'd glimpsed his mortality and seen ghosts waiting for him on the other side.

"You think he talked to Eddie." Frankie said the words quietly, like they were in church. "You think he told him the truth."

"Someone talked. That's all I know."

Frankie nodded faintly with grim understanding of what lay ahead. There was no higher power coming to save him, so he'd have to save himself.

CHAPTER THIRTY-ONE

ANNALISA DID NOT HAVE A FRACTURE OR WORRISOME BRAIN BLEED, BUT SHE DID SUFFER A NASTY LUMP AND A CONCUSSION. The hospital discharged her with a bottle of pills and orders to rest both physically and mentally. The concussion meant she should lie in a dim room, no television, no radio, nothing to engage her injured brain. Happy to comply, she turned her phone off, drew the blinds, and crawled beneath the covers for a medically aided sleep. She awoke again in the dark with a dry mouth but her head no longer felt like a piece of bruised fruit. She tried standing and found her legs would hold her at least long enough to get a carton of orange juice from the kitchen and return to her bed. She drank it while she consulted her phone to find out what she had missed over the past sixteen hours.

Two messages from her mother. One each from Vinnie and Tony. A missed call from Nick, but he did not leave a message. She had a voicemail from a number she did not immediately recognize. When she listened to it, she discovered it was from Lloyd Nelson, Vivian Catalano's old landlord. He had a lead on where she might be. The form she'd filled out for the rental unit listed her sister Bonnie Catalano in Michigan as an emergency contact, so perhaps Bonnie might know where to get in touch with Vivian. Nelson relayed the phone number with the caveat that he did not know if it was still good. Annalisa did not write it down. She didn't delete the message, but tracking down Vivian no longer seemed important. Moe Bocks was dead. Nick would come through with the paint analysis on the rake—she knew he would—and then Josie could finally rest in peace.

Annalisa switched over to Colin's social media photo stream, as she usually did when she was alone. The latest picture made her sit up straight and put aside the orange juice. It was a moody shot of Lake Michigan at dusk so that the water appeared glassy, almost green, and the skyline loomed black and jagged behind it. The cool blue sky held just a tinge of orange from the disappearing sun. She saw frost visible around the pylons in the water, which said the photo was current, or at least seasonal. Was Colin home? Her finger hesitated over the "like" button.

She slid out of bed and went to find the bird-of-paradise flower sitting awkwardly in its Mason jar of water. If Colin had given it to her, she had to know. She put it under the light and snapped a close-up photo, which she added to her own social media. She captioned it simply, "Paradise." Someone liked it immediately. Vinnie, she saw when she looked at the name. She tried not to be too disappointed as she abandoned the phone on the counter in favor of the fridge. She opened a carton of old sesame noodles and took a whiff. Smelled fine. As she fetched a fork, her phone beeped an alert. She stretched over to look at the notification. Colin had liked her photo. Seeing his name with a little red heart next to it made her go wobbly, like when he'd passed her notes in study hall. Did this acknowledgment mean he'd sent the flowers?

The phone buzzed, vibrating across the counter, and Annalisa shrank back like it might bite her. She didn't want to talk to anyone. It kept ringing, threatening to vibrate itself right to the floor, and she caught it with one hand at the last second. The caller ID said Zimmer. "Vega," she said, eyes shut, bracing for the worst.

Her boss showed surprising sympathy. "How are you feeling?" she asked.

"That depends on why you're calling."

"I've got to be honest with you . . ." Zimmer took a long breath. "It's not good news. The ballistics are a match. Your gun fired the bullets that killed Moe Bocks."

Annalisa sank onto the nearest stool and rested her head on her free hand. "I didn't do it."

"I believe you. Your hands came back clean. But the DA is saying that's insufficient proof."

"So I killed Bocks and then I knocked myself out with a blow to the back of the head? What sense does that make?"

"They're saying you pursued Bocks across the lawn and that you tripped on a tree root and hit your head after you shot at him."

"There was someone behind me, Commander. I saw it on Bocks's face right before everything went dark."

"Yes, well, he's not available to testify."

Annalisa changed tactics. "What about the rake? Did you get a warrant? Did Nick talk to you about the test on the paint?"

Zimmer let out a long-suffering sigh. "Vega, no judge is going to sign off on a warrant based on a photo of your parents' old garden tools." When Annalisa started to protest, Zimmer cut her off. "That's why I had the team impound the entire contents of the garage as evidence in Bocks's shooting. We're going to have his mother inventory it to be sure you didn't steal anything—including the rake."

A smile tugged at Vega's lips. "That's clever."

"They put me in charge for a reason." She hesitated. "But sometimes I have to make hard calls. I'm putting you on medical leave, effective immediately. You are not to come into the office nor work any active investigations. Do I make myself clear?"

"Commander, I'm fine."

"You're not hearing me. COPA has opened an investigation on you, Vega. Bocks's mother is on television screaming about the vigilante cop who killed her son. The chief wanted me to outright suspend you without pay, and this is the compromise."

"Doesn't anyone care who's setting me up?"

"You're the one best positioned to answer that. You're telling me you didn't see or hear anything last night?"

"I thought for a while someone was tailing me when I was driving to the Bocks house, but the car turned off when I hit the neighborhood. I didn't get a look at the driver but the car was a light-colored sedan."

"Maybe they realized where you were going. No need to keep close."

"Whoever it was, they sure wanted Bocks dead."

Zimmer made a chuffing noise. "By all accounts, that someone was you."

"No, I wanted him in prison." Now she'd be the lucky one to avoid it.

"Listen, you just lay low for a while, okay? If this is a frame-up, we'll beat it. Let me work the system. A bunch of big mansions like that in the Bockses' neighborhood, they've got to have cameras all over the damn place. If there was a second shooter somewhere, we'll find them."

Annalisa made a noise that might be construed as agreement without actually making any concessions. She hung up with Zimmer but kept the phone in an iron grip. Zimmer would do her best, of this Annalisa was sure, but she held no regard for "the system" and its willingness to help her. Pops had warned her how far dirty cops would go—they were already beyond the law—and she had a feeling one of them in particular wanted her out of the way. Frankie Vaughn had dropped by her desk right before her lip balm disappeared, and then it had mysteriously turned up at the scene of the first attack on Moe Bocks. In fact, it was Vaughn who put her onto Bocks in the first place. Meanwhile, two of Vaughn's partners were now dead and there was a bagful of money on the line.

Zimmer had ordered her to stay away from the precinct and not to work any open cases, but in this instance, Annalisa was the case. *If this is a frame-up,* Zimmer had said. *If.* Annalisa's whole life hung on that *if* and whether Zimmer could prove it. She wasn't about to sit around and wait. The car she'd glimpsed following her to the Bocks place was a sedan, either light blue or silver. She knew Vaughn typically drove a Land Rover but he might have access to other vehicles. It wouldn't hurt to take a spin past his house to see what else was parked outside.

She attacked the tangles in her hair with a brush until the pain convinced her to cram it under a beanie-style black hat. She wasn't planning on exiting her car, so fashion truly didn't matter. Rush hour was long past so the dark streets held only the usual traffic, allowing her to make good time. When she got to Frankie Vaughn's place she found the lights on, as expected for 8 p.m., with his Land Rover parked in the driveway next to the house. She was dismayed to see the other vehicle was a red Honda—no sign of a silver sedan. She pulled into an accessible parking spot on the street about half a block down to consider her next move. She didn't have access to the usual databases to determine if some other relative of Vaughn's might have driven a silver sedan. Also, there was the remaining Fantastic Four member to consider, Paul Monk. She had no idea what vehicles he owned or operated.

She was ready to go back home and crawl into bed when the front door opened and Vaughn stepped out. He walked with purpose to his car, not pausing to evaluate his surroundings, and backed out into the street, heading west. Annalisa restarted her engine and followed. Within a few minutes it was clear that Vaughn wasn't headed to his Central precinct. He passed two gas stations, a liquor store, and several convenience markets, so he wasn't out on a casual errand either. Annalisa tailed him as close as she dared, hanging back behind a half dozen cars. Vaughn had apparently paid for custom taillights; she could track him from a pretty good distance by the unusual swooping design of the orange-red signals.

As they idled at a stoplight on Halstead, Annalisa checked her own mirrors. She saw a silver, or maybe gray sedan several cars behind her. The glare from the headlights and streetlamps made it impossible to see the driver. She kept one eye on it as she followed Vaughn farther south, past Pilsen and into Bridgeport. The sedan kept pace with her. She eased off the gas, hoping to drop back enough to glimpse the driver, but the other car slowed when she did.

Vaughn turned right onto South Archer Ave. He was far from home at this point and out of his jurisdiction as well. Annalisa eyed the mirror and saw the sedan make the same turn behind her about twenty-five yards back. She had to make a quick decision: keep tailing Vaughn or figure out who was following her. Abruptly, she made a sharp left from the right lane and barreled down the side street, abandoning Vaughn. She kept going straight long enough to see a familiar set of headlights turn up in her rearview mirror. The sedan had taken the bait. She drove another block until she reached a public parking garage that had the first couple of floors reserved for nearby residents. She went up one floor and took an open space among a row of other cars. Quickly, she exited the car and crossed to the row on the other side, where she crouched next to a Nissan SUV. From this angle, she'd be able to see the driver of the sedan as he came up the ramp and turned the corner to follow her.

She heard the engine approaching at slow speed. The sedan's headlights hit her car and lit up her plate, and the driver stopped, not quite around the turn. The engine didn't cut out but she heard a door slam; the driver got out, probably looking for her. Adrenaline killed the pain in her head but she felt dizzy as she lurched to her feet "Freeze right there," she ordered. "Chicago PD." She had no gun. She had no authority either, but she was hoping he didn't know that.

The man put his hands in the air and she recognized his shape even before he spoke. "Nick Carelli," he said sardonically. "Also Chicago PD."

"Carelli," she said, her legs turning weak with relief as she relaxed her posture. He drove a nondescript, department-issue Chevy Malibu instead of his own red Infiniti coupe, so she had not recognized the vehicle. "Why the hell are you following me? Did Zimmer put you up to this?"

"I was following Frankie Vaughn," he replied. "That's why I borrowed a car. Imagine how surprised I was to see you on his tail too."

"Vaughn," she said, regret seeping in that she'd let him get away. "Why?"

"The last call Tom Osborne made before his death was to Vaughn. His phone was pinging off the tower near Hammond's place at the time, so he was already there. It's possible he told Vaughn he was there with Kayla."

"And then Vaughn showed up to kill him," Annalisa finished. "Why would he do that?"

"Don't know. That was the reason for the surveillance. Why were you following him?"

"I think he might be behind the setup."

Nick's expression remained neutral but he gave an almost imperceptible nod. "I'd had similar thoughts."

"Sorry about the interference." She winced. "Now we've both lost him."

"Not so fast. I've got a GPS tracker on his car." He consulted his phone and held it out for her to see. "He's stopped moving about three blocks from here. Want to check it out?"

She climbed in his passenger seat and Nick drove around the garage to the exit. Within five minutes, they'd located Vaughn's Land Rover

again; he had parked outside a small house on South Farrell Ave. The place was plain and boxy, with gray siding and a metal awning over the door, nothing like the fancy home Vaughn had. Vaughn stood on the cement steps, where he rang the bell. He had to ring it twice more before a white woman answered. She appeared to be late middle-age, dressed in jeans and a sweater, but the most interesting thing about her was the baseball bat she had in her hands. She held it like a grudge and she was yelling something at Vaughn.

"Who is that?" Annalisa asked Nick. They were too far away to hear what she said.

"I don't know yet." He was running the address through their system. "But she sure isn't happy to see him."

Vaughn took a step closer to the woman as they continued arguing. He seemed intent on getting past her. She blocked the door bodily and raised the bat.

"The house is rented," Nick reported. "The Focus parked in front is registered to Tamara Edwards, and she appears to be the tenant. At least, this is the address listed on her driver's license."

A man appeared in the doorway alongside Ms. Edwards. At the sight of him, Vaughn surged forward and dragged him onto the stoop. Ms. Edwards cracked Vaughn over the shoulder with the bat, and he took out his gun. The man stepped between the woman and Vaughn, his hands raised in surrender. "Uh, should we be intervening?" Annalisa asked.

"On whose side?"

Vaughn hauled the man down the steps and over to his Land Rover, where he put him up against the car and patted him down. Ms. Edwards continued to yell from the door but Vaughn ignored her. He still had his gun out as he confronted the man. "We have to find out who that guy is," Annalisa told Nick.

"I'm trying. He's not exactly wearing a name tag, you know." He did another search on his phone.

Vaughn had his gun right in the guy's face. "Are you seeing this?" Annalisa used her own phone to take a few pictures. "He acts like he's going to blow this guy away right here on the street."

The other man was a white male about sixty years old, mostly bald

and shivering now because he wore only a T-shirt and shorts and the temperature on the dash read twenty-one degrees. Vaughn's gun would be redundant soon; he was going to get the guy killed from hypothermia. The man held his arms around his chest and Annalisa could practically see his teeth chattering as he tried to talk to Vaughn. He appeared to be making elaborate denials, shaking his head as Vaughn yelled at him.

"Tamara Edwards has a brother named David," Nick said. "Released from Stateville last year. He's fifty-nine, balding, and six feet tall."

They both looked at the unidentified man, who fit this description to a T. "What was he in for?"

"Murder. He was convicted in 2003 of killing Sandra Romero. Sentenced to fifteen to life, paroled in May of last year. Before that, he'd run up a bunch of drug charges and one domestic assault in 1995."

"Did you say her name was Sandra?" Annalisa had a memory of writing the name in her notes on the nightclub robbery and Cecil Barry's death. Roxanne had told her she couldn't contact the other witness, a woman named Sandra, because Sandra was dead.

"There's more," Nick said, pulling her from her reverie. "Check out David Edwards's street name."

Annalisa leaned over so she could see the screen. "Eddie," she said.

CHAPTER THIRTY-TWO

....

VAUGHN SHOVED EDWARDS SO HARD THE HEAVY CAR JOSTLED. "I can't watch this anymore," Annalisa said as she moved to get out of the car, but Nick grabbed her arm.

"If we intervene now, we tip off Vaughn that we're tailing him."

"You, maybe. I'm not working, remember? Besides, I don't think he'll be surprised to see me."

She left Nick and jogged across the street to where Vaughn had Edwards by the throat with his left hand. The right one had a gun to the ex-con's temple. Vaughn appeared rage-blind and he did not notice her coming. "If you even drop a piece of litter, I'll have you back inside before it even hits the ground. You'll do the whole ticket this time. And if I catch you anywhere near me—"

"Vaughn," Annalisa called, and he dropped Edwards to face her.

"Vega." Her name was like ground glass in his mouth. She'd been right—he didn't look shocked to see her. "What the hell are you doing here? You following me?"

"I came to talk to David Edwards," she said, nodding at the shivering man. "You got a beef with him?"

"He's a scum-sucking murderer, so yeah, I got a beef with him." His left arm shot out to give Edwards a shove. "What'd you want to talk to Edwards about?"

"That's between him and me." She cocked her head. "Unless you want to tell me what you came to discuss with him."

Vaughn rolled his neck around and he chuckled without humor. “Maybe you can explain to him what you’re doing out here working. Last I heard, you got suspended after your suspect turned up with a bunch of bullets in his back.” Edwards shuddered and Vaughn clapped him on the shoulder. “You could be next, Eddie-boy.”

“You heard wrong.”

“Did I? Pretty sure it was all over the TV.” He reholstered his weapon. “Maybe I’ll have to call your commander and check.”

“You do that.”

Vaughn reached over and patted Edwards’s cheek. “You take care, Eddie. You were away a long time and the world has changed. It’s a dangerous place. I’ll be seeing you around.” Edwards turned his face away and said nothing. Vaughn adjusted his belt, coughed up a wad of saliva, and spat it at Annalisa’s feet. When she didn’t flinch, he laughed again. “I’ll see you around too,” he said, pointing at her.

They watched as he got in his Land Rover and drove away. Annalisa regarded Edwards with a worried gaze. “Are you okay?”

Edwards didn’t answer her.

“He can’t harass you like that. It’s illegal. I can show you how to make a complaint—”

“Just leave me alone,” he said with a burst of venom. He pushed past her and went back into the house. The woman, Tamara, stood in the doorway watching with a stony expression. She still had the bat.

“Why was Vaughn here?” Annalisa asked her. “What did he want with Eddie?”

“His name is David,” she said, enunciating each separate word.

Nick appeared out of the darkness next to Annalisa. “What happened? Did Vaughn say anything?”

Tamara Edwards took in the holster on Nick’s hip and the shield around his neck. “You cops are like cockroaches. Where there’s one, there’s many. Go crawl on back to your hole and leave us in peace, okay?” She shut the door with a firm click.

“I don’t get the feeling the Edwards family turns out for the police parade,” Annalisa said.

“What did Vaughn want?”

“No idea. Did you get anything more on Edwards?”

“He was a small-time dealer and a big-time user throughout the eighties, nineties, and so on. Pot and pills, mostly, but he sampled the whole buffet—speed, Molly, opiates. He did the usual revolving door of jail time and court-ordered rehab, but you know how that goes."

"Like the burger joint. In-N-Out."

"The afternoon of September 27, 2002, Edwards was found half naked and wandering his neighborhood, high as the Sears Tower. Patrol picked him up and brought him back to a holding cell at the Twelfth Division."

"Where Vaughn and the rest of them worked."

"That's right. But they were working the robbery at the Bass Lounge that occurred a few days earlier. Sandra Romero came in that night for a second round of questioning. It came out later that she knew Edwards from the club, where I gather he partied on occasion. He'd also worked for a while in a little corner market near her apartment, and he saw her there too—at least until he got fired a few weeks before all this happened. Anyway, details are sketchy, but I gather Edwards got kicked loose at about the same time Romero left after her interview. He followed her to a nearby alley and attacked her."

"Why would he do that?"

"The DA's case said he'd asked her out and she turned him down. Sometimes that's all it takes."

Annalisa looked at the house, where a curtain moved. They were still being watched. "Who made the collar?"

"Frankie Vaughn and Paul Monk."

"The last men standing," Annalisa replied. "Was there a trial?"

"Edwards pled guilty to second-degree murder, but the judge wasn't sympathetic. She gave him the max. The, uh, details of the attack are pretty gruesome. Sandra Romero suffered multiple blows to the head, cracked ribs, and she'd been choked across the neck with a foreign object, crushing her windpipe. She was found alive in the alley, barely breathing, but she died later at the hospital."

Annalisa's head injury throbbed at the words and she swallowed with difficulty as a wave of nausea went through her. "Sexual assault? Robbery?"

"He took her wallet, yeah. It had forty-three bucks in it." Nick hesitated. "No semen found on the victim. She had his DNA under her fingernails, though, and they also found her blood on his boots."

"Good God," Annalisa murmured. She was starting to understand why Vaughn had roughed the guy up. "But if this guy is Eddie, why would Leo feel bad for him? Why would this case be eating him twenty years later?"

Nick looked up at the house. "There's only one person alive who might be able to answer that, and he doesn't want to talk."

"He's on parole for murder," Annalisa replied as she started for the front door. "He doesn't get a choice." She rapped assertively on the door and waited. No one answered. She banged harder and called out to the people inside, "You can talk to me here or I can take you both downtown. Your choice." This wasn't strictly true; Nick would need to get a warrant to force them, and the late hour and flimsy pretext made this unlikely.

The door cracked open and Tamara reappeared with a cigarette in her hand. "You don't have cause to be harassing us."

"Your brother is in violation of his parole," Annalisa said.

The woman's mouth curved into a bitter smile. "That's a lie. Of course, you cops lie like you breathe—it doesn't even take thought."

"He's living with you, yes? The terms clearly state he cannot live anywhere that has a weapon present."

"What're you talking about? I don't have no guns here."

"You have a baseball bat. I saw it. In fact, I saw you use it to assault a police officer."

Tamara groaned and flung open the door. "David," she hollered to the back of the house. "You got company—again."

Annalisa and Nick walked past her and into the front room where a television played on mute. David shuffled out, now fully dressed in jeans and a faded Bears sweatshirt. He kept his gaze down and his hands visible. At almost six feet, he was a large man, but it was hard to square his cowering under Vaughn's tirade as the same individual who had brutally attacked Sandra Romero. "You can't bust me," he said, but he didn't sound sure. "I'm clean and you can ask my P.O. about that. I got a job at the gas station and I pee in the cup every week."

"Pure harassment," Tamara hissed from the hallway. Annalisa ignored her.

"What did Detective Vaughn want to talk to you about?" she asked Edwards.

Surprise flickered over his features. "He wanted me to stay away from him. I told him the truth—if I never saw his face again, it would be fine by me. I ain't bothered him or any of his buddies."

Tamara came and put an arm around her brother. "If David's not at work, he's either visiting our aunt Trudy, helping her around her place, or he's here with me. You've got no cause to be messing him around like this."

"Do you own a wet suit?" Annalisa asked, looking around. She saw a few family photos and a needlepoint of two cardinals.

"A what?" David asked, his face wrinkling in confusion.

"A diving suit. Rubber that keeps you warm in the water."

"Where am I going to use something like that? On my Bahamas getaway?"

"What about you?" Nick chimed in, asking Tamara.

"Oh yeah," she replied with sarcasm. "I've got a dozen in different colors. But I keep them down at the marina on my yacht."

"Then you won't mind if I look around," Nick said.

She threw up her arms in surrender. "I'm sure I can't stop you."

As Nick moved to check out the house, Annalisa watched Edwards. He appeared pale and nervous, his eyes downcast. "You and Detective Vaughn go way back," she said to him. "He knew you from before."

"He and the others, they busted me a couple of times for selling pills." He looked at her quickly. "But I don't touch that stuff anymore, hand to God." He raised one palm for emphasis, but she'd heard this plea too many times to place much stock in it.

"They also arrested you for murder."

His lips thinned. "I know what it says in the file."

"You pled guilty," she reminded him.

He shook his head. "The lawyer said I had no choice. He said if we went to a jury, the DA would go for murder one and then I'd never get out. I'd never done more than thirty days before, and they were talking about locking me up for life."

"He didn't do it," Tamara said acidly. "Not that you care."

"Is that true, David?" He walked away and lowered himself to the sofa, where he put his head in his hands. Annalisa crossed the room to crouch in front of him. He would not look at her. "Tell me what happened," she said softly.

His shoulders hitched. He was crying, she realized. He didn't answer her, but Tamara had plenty to say. She moved until she could look down on Annalisa. "He was sick back then from the pills. The night that girl got killed, David blacked out. He doesn't remember anything beyond bits and pieces. They picked him up outside and took him to holding, and he thought he was going to sleep it off like always. Next thing he knew, he was in an alley and it was dark outside."

"Is that where you met Sandra?"

"He doesn't remember her. He said he never saw her that night."

"But you knew her," Annalisa pressed. "You'd seen her before."

He pulled his hands away from his face and she saw his cheeks were wet. "She came into the store where I worked sometimes, her and her kids. She had one who was walking and a baby on her back. Both of them had pink cheeks and blond curls, like you see in church paintings of baby angels. I used to make faces at them so's they'd laugh. Kept them happy while their mom picked out what she needed."

"What about their mom?" Annalisa asked. "You liked her? Maybe wanted to ask her out."

"No, ma'am. She was a nice-looking young lady, but she had those kids and I didn't want to be anyone's daddy. How could I?"

Nick returned to the room. "The place seems clean," he said.

"Thank you for the seal, Mr. *Good Housekeeping*," Tamara replied sarcastically. She folded her arms and looked at her brother. "Tell them about the broom. Go on, tell them."

Edwards scowled at her. "It don't matter now."

"Whoever attacked that lady," Tamara said steadily, "they choked her with something across the neck. Something wooden. The exam found splinters in her and the autopsy doc said he thought it might be from a broom handle. But no one ever found a broom in the alley. Didn't find it in David's place either. Seems it up and disappeared."

"The cops said I must've hidden it somewhere," David said as he wiped his face with his hands. "But I never would've hurt Sandra like that. I know I don't remember what happened, but I'm sure whatever I did, it wasn't that."

“You had her blood on your shoes,” Nick said. “You were at the scene.”

“I don’t remember,” he replied mournfully. “I’ve tried a million times. When I got out, I went back to that alley and looked around. I took a bunch of flowers and I put them down for her. I don’t even know the exact spot because I don’t remember it. I stood for a while and I said sorry to Sandra—not for hurting her because I didn’t do that—but I must’ve been there, and if I was there, then I could’ve seen who did it.”

Nick’s phone rang and he excused himself to the hall. Annalisa rose from her crouch and touched her fingers to her temple. Rising like that from a squat made her dizzy again. David looked at her with concern. “You all right? You want some water or something?”

“Water would be great, thank you.”

He looked to Tamara, who folded her arms across her chest in a “no way” gesture, so he sighed and pushed himself up to do it. “Why are you here asking questions, anyway?” Tamara demanded when her brother had gone. “What’s done is done. That girl’s cold in the grave, but David’s got some life left if you’ll just let him be. Then maybe I can finally have one too.”

“What do you mean?”

“I spent the past twenty years writing letters for him, driving up to the prison to see him every week, making sure he’s got supplies, making sure he’s eating. Our parents are gone. Trudy’s got arthritis. Who else was going to see to David? I worked two jobs. I spent my money, I spent my time, all on David. The guy I was engaged to when David got arrested, he backed out when he saw what was happening. I don’t blame him. Who’d sign up for this? But David, he had no choice, and so neither did I.”

David returned with a glass of water and a paper napkin. “Here you go,” he said, handing it to Annalisa.

“Thank you.” She took two sips before Nick poked his head back in and signaled for her to join him. She excused herself and joined him in the hall. “What is it?”

“I’ve got to go. I can drop you back at your car if we leave now.”

“Why? What’s happened?”

“DNA came back on the neoprene patch you found at the Hammond house.”

"The killer's in the system," she said with relief.

"Not quite. It's a partial match to Leo Hammond's DNA—a close male relative."

"How close?"

"Fifty percent." Nick looked glum but resolute. "It's Leo's son. I have to go arrest Brian Hammond."

CHAPTER THIRTY-THREE

ANNALISA LAY AROUND HER APARTMENT, LANGUISHING FOR TWO DAYS AND MARINATING IN A GROWING STACK OF DELIVERY CONTAINERS AND EMPTY SODA CANS. When the news about the rake arrived, it came by text at 7:56 at night. Her commander didn't even want to talk to her. She'd probably put off even writing until the very end of her shift. *Paint on the rake not a match to the garrote from the Blanchard case,* Zimmer wrote.

Annalisa sat up on her couch and stared at the glowing screen in disbelief for a full minute before she could make herself reply. *Are you 100% sure?*

Dyes are completely different. One has iodine, the other not. No match. Zimmer appeared to be writing a lengthy follow-up comment, but when the next text appeared, it was just one word: *Sorry.*

Annalisa sagged into the couch cushions and stared at the ceiling. She'd bet the house and lost. Maybe literally, since she couldn't pay her mortgage if she didn't have a job. She'd been so sure the rake would match. Positive down to the marrow in her bones. She'd been right so many times before, even when it would be easier to be wrong, even when she could have looked the other way. She'd shredded her whole damn life and now she felt the blade up against her neck. Ma and Pops had raised her in the church and it had seemed easy back then: only ten simple rules to follow. The church made martyrs into saints, but Annalisa noticed they were just as dead in all their glory. Maybe this was the lesson she'd missed. No one on earth ever got what they deserved.

Annalisa hoisted herself off the sofa like a stiff old woman. She wasn't going to church, but she did need to make a confession, which meant venturing into the outside world for the first time in days. She drove to Sassy's house and sat parked outside for a few moments. Sassy's bedroom light was on, the rest of the house dark. Annalisa looked again at her phone and the text she had sent Sassy days ago: ***I didn't kill him. I swear it.*** Sassy had seen the text but not replied. Annalisa got out into the frigid air and went to the door. Her anxious breaths curled like smoke in the yellow light of the streetlamp. She sucked in one hard breath and held it, frosty air stinging her lungs as she screwed up the courage to knock on the door.

Sassy opened a minute later with a wine bottle in hand. Her robe sagged open, revealing a ratty old Hootie & the Blowfish T-shirt that Annalisa knew Alex had bought for her on one of their first dates. She didn't say anything at the sight of Annalisa on her porch, just leaned against the doorjamb and took a swig right from the bottle.

"I'm sorry about Moe," Annalisa said finally.

Sassy snorted. "No, you're not."

"I didn't shoot him."

"It doesn't matter. He's dead. You won." Sassy shook her head vaguely, her gaze fixed past Annalisa to the street beyond.

"Not exactly." Annalisa drew a steadying breath. "The paint on the rake didn't match."

"What?" Alert now, Sassy pushed off from the doorframe and pinned Annalisa with a hard stare. "So you were wrong."

"Yes." Annalisa closed her eyes and forced the word out.

"Moe didn't do it. He didn't kill anyone."

"We don't know that. But the missing shovel wasn't used to create the murder weapon."

"And now he's dead," Sassy said, her voice rising, "For nothing?"

"I don't know who killed him or why. Zimmer is investigating, but it's not my—"

"You were there!"

"Someone else was there behind me," Annalisa said urgently, moving to block her when Sassy tried to turn away. "Someone who knocked me out and took my gun. I'm being set up, Sass."

"Maybe," Sassy cut her off sharply, "maybe it's not always about you, Anna. You had your reasons for going over there in the middle of the night, I'm sure. You always do. But this time Moe ended up dead, and if someone else followed you to him, that's still on you. You didn't have a warrant. It wasn't part of the job. It was personal." She hissed the last word like it was an insult.

"I was trying to protect you. You and the girls."

"Congratulations, then. You did it." She shut the door and Annalisa heard the dead bolt slide into place with a chilling finality. She stood there on the cold porch for a long time, thinking about the day she'd helped Alex and Sassy move into the place. Alex had carried Sassy over the threshold. Sassy had given Annalisa a spare key. She fished it out now and looked at it dangling on her key chain, the metal glinting at her in the soft light.

She got in her car and drove around aimlessly for a while, not eager to go back to the shrinking walls of her condo. Home looked like prison when you had no choice but to be there. When her phone rang, she hit the answer button eagerly, hoping it was Sassy. It wasn't.

"Detective Vega? This is Maura Hammond."

The first Mrs. Hammond, Annalisa recollected. She pinched the bridge of her nose, suddenly tired despite the fact that she'd slept sixteen of the previous twenty-four hours. "What can I do for you, Mrs. Hammond?"

"I need to talk to you. About Brian. He didn't kill Leo or Tom Osborne."

"I'm afraid that's not my case anymore."

"Yes, I know. But your partner doesn't seem to be listening to us. Brian would never kill his father. Someone is setting him up."

The words hit home for Annalisa. "Where are you?"

"We're at the house. My house."

"I'll be there in twenty minutes."

Annalisa found not just Maura and Brian at the house but also Leo's daughter, Nicole; her husband, Luke; and Brian's roommate, Caleb. Brian's eyes were rimmed with red, like he hadn't slept in days. Or like he'd been crying. "We've been putting our heads together," Maura explained as she ushered Annalisa into the living room. “Trying to help Brian.”

Annalisa regarded the young man with interest. “You haven’t been charged?”

He shook his head. “Not yet, but your partner said it was coming soon. They took DNA from me. They searched our place and took a bunch of stuff from there too.”

“Stuff like what?” Annalisa asked as she removed her coat.

“My shoes. Some clothes. They say they already have a DNA match from one of the crime scenes, but that’s crazy. I didn’t kill anyone. I’ve never even shoplifted.”

The piece of wet suit found at the Osborne murder had come back as a 50 percent match to Leo. “What about a diving suit?” she asked him. “Did they take one of those?”

“No, because I don’t have one.”

Annalisa looked to Caleb. He lived in the house too. He raised his palms in defensive fashion. “Me neither. I don’t even like swimming.”

“Do any of you have a wet suit?” Annalisa asked them.

Maura shook her head. Nicole looked pained, crossing her legs first one way and then the other. “Luke has one,” she muttered finally.

Her husband stiffened at her side. “It’s in storage in the basement. I haven’t touched it in years. You know that.”

“But you do have one,” she said in a small voice.

“Great! Drag me into this. I came here to help and you’re feeding me to the cops like some suspect.” He looked at Annalisa. “I’ve got nothing to hide. I didn’t shoot anyone. I can get you that diving suit and you can do whatever you want with it.”

“That would be helpful, thank you.”

“Luke, I’m sorry. I can come wi—” Nicole reached for her husband’s arm as he got up to go but he shook her off.

“I’ll be back soon,” he said before departing through the front door with a violent slam.

“I didn’t know about Luke’s suit,” Brian said the moment he was gone. “I didn’t touch it.”

“What were you doing the night of February fourth?” Annalisa asked.

Brian blew out a frustrated breath and ran his hands through his spiky hair. "I already went through this a hundred times. I was home alone, okay? Caleb had work. So I watched the Bulls game on TV and then played video games the rest of the night. I didn't go out anywhere, and no one came to see me. I didn't realize I'd be needing an alibi."

Maura rubbed his shoulder in comforting fashion. "Of course you didn't, honey."

"You had work that night," Annalisa said to Caleb. "What time did you get home?"

"We closed up at ten, but I stayed to finish fixing a bike. Missed the bus. I didn't get home until close to midnight. But Brian was there playing *Call of Duty* when I got in." Caleb turned earnest blue eyes to hers. "It seemed like he'd been there awhile. You know, dead beers on the coffee table, pizza crusts just sitting there."

Beer cans and pizza crusts could not testify at Brian's trial, should it come to that. "Did you make any calls that night?" asked Annalisa.

Brian looked sheepish. "My phone was dead. It's a couple years old, and the battery runs down real fast. I got caught up in my game and I didn't charge it until I went to bed."

"Which was when?

Brian and Caleb exchanged a look. "Maybe one? One-thirty?"

Annalisa shook her head. There was nothing she could do here. "Look, I'd like to help you, but—"

"Detective," Maura said, rising from her seat next to her son, "maybe you could join me in the kitchen for some coffee."

"I've really got to get going."

"Please. Just for a minute."

Annalisa followed the older woman to a galley-style kitchen with an eat-in nook at one end. She smiled when she saw the old-fashioned coffeemaker. Ma and Pops had a similar one when she was growing up, and its glubs and growls had formed the soundtrack to her morning routine. Maura Hammond's unit was silent, the coffee long brewed. She pulled down a pink mug and poured a cup for Annalisa. "You take milk or sugar?"

"This is fine." Annalisa had no intention of drinking it.

"The reason I asked you here is because you got that guy, the Lovelorn Killer. All those cops after him for years, even the FBI, but it was you who solved the case."

"I was lucky," Annalisa said, although it felt strange to use that term to describe a case where she'd almost died.

"You got him." Maura jabbed at Annalisa with a stubborn finger. "You. I could tell you were a good cop when you first came here. I've got experience, you know, telling the good from the bad."

"Which one was Leo?"

Maura grunted and poured herself a coffee. "If you're asking, then you already know. I told you what he did to me. What he got the rest of them to do to me when I finally said enough. On the job, though, Leo was tough. He didn't take crap from nobody."

"Maybe he took other things," Annalisa suggested lightly, thinking of the pile of cash.

Maura turned her head sharply, her expression shrewd. "If Leo took a slice, that's because he thought he was owed. He and his buddies, they were on the front lines, you know? There's a war out there. The city's overrun with gang lords and drug dealers—all of them armed to the teeth—and the mayor says, 'Go stop them, but make sure you follow the rules.' Well, that's fine except the other side don't play by any rules. If you try to play fair with a banger, he'll shoot you between the eyes before you have the chance to say, 'You have the right to remain silent.'"

"So Leo made his own rules."

Maura gave a short nod and stared into her coffee cup. "Are you married, Detective? Got any kids?"

"Divorced, no kids."

Maura grimaced. "It's a hard thing, isn't it? Knowing when to stay and when to go. Leo didn't always treat me right, but then I wasn't always sweet to him either. He was a good dad. He must've spent three weeks working with Brian on their little car to enter into the Cub Scout race. When Nicole was three, she got strep. Not the kind where you drink the pink antibiotic for two weeks and then you're fine. She ran such a high fever she had a seizure and stopped breathing. They said the bacteria went to her heart. We weren't sure if she was going to live or die. I prayed harder than I ever had in my life, but Leo, he went out and got a tattoo. It was a little heart that said 'Nicki' on it, and he showed it to her while she lay sleeping in her hospital bed. He said he wanted to make her permanent somehow. Make sure she knew she was supposed to stay. I don't know. But it worked—she woke up the next day."

"How much does Brian know about Leo's approach to his work?"

"What do you mean?"

"Like where the big piles of cash came from."

Twin stains of pink appeared on the woman's cheeks. "Brian's not mixed up in that."

"But he knew." Maybe as a kid, Brian hadn't been aware of where the money train originated, but as an adult, he had to look back on the expensive trips, cars, sports tickets, and wonder how the math played out.

"You don't understand." Maura set the cup down hard. "Brian and Nicole, they're the reasons I finally left. They weren't babies anymore. They saw how their dad treated me. When Leo took up with Kayla, they started hating us both. Him for running around and me for taking it. If Brian were going to shoot anyone, it would've been Kayla three years ago, and he would've had to get in line behind me to do it. Now?" She shrugged, ***c'est la vie***. "Maybe I was wrong to stick it out as long as I did. In my defense, all my options were equally shit. Leo had the money."

"Yeah, but you knew where it came from," Annalisa said. "You had leverage."

"Hey, I earned every cent I got out of him. I cooked, cleaned, and raised his kids so he didn't have to worry about any of it. In return, he laid every third-rate floozy from here to Sheboygan. I could ignore the signs. The stray earring in the car. Lipstick on his shirt. For a detective, he sure did a shit job covering his tracks. But then one day we're at the breakfast table with the kids, and he goes, 'Pass me the milk, will you, Sandy?' We all froze. The kids were little back then but they knew my name sure as shit ain't Sandy. Leo knew he'd fucked up right away. He tried to laugh it off and say there was a new secretary at work named Sandy who kind of looked like me, and he just got mixed up. But when he didn't come home that night, I called the station. I talked to Tom and asked if there was a new girl there named Sandy. He said no."

"Did you confront Leo?"

She looked pissed off. "The thing is, he didn't say her name when we were in bed. He said it over breakfast. The party girls, you can ignore, but this was serious. If I called Leo on it and he denied it, what would

I get? Smacked upside the head, probably. I could've tried to find her, this Sandy. I could get proof he was fooling around and file for divorce. Then I would've been on my own with two kids under five, living in some crappy apartment, working a retail job all day just to pay someone else to look after my kids."

"So you decided to stay."

"I decided to wait and see. It felt like I was holding my breath for weeks. Like it was one of those sliding doors moments, you know? He goes or I go and life turns out different . . ." She bit her lip. "But Leo didn't slip up again. In fact, he started showing up for dinner more often. He said we should plan a trip, just the two of us, and we went to Las Vegas for a long weekend while my mom took the kids. We went at it like a second honeymoon, and I won two hundred and fifty dollars playing blackjack." She gave a wobbly smile.

"And Sandy?"

"He never said her name again." Annalisa could feel her relief even now that the threat had passed.

"When was this?" Annalisa asked. "Do you remember?"

"I'll never forget. It was right after the Fourth of July in 2002. We'd just had a big family barbecue with my sister and brother and Leo's cousins. I got the pictures back—remember when you used to have to get them developed at the drugstore? I'd picked them up the afternoon before and looked through them with the kids. Everyone was smiling and having a good time. Then Leo goes and says 'Sandy' and I started wondering if we'd ever be together, all of us, like that again."

"Detective Vega?" Brian called her name from the doorway, where he lingered uncertainly. Maura frowned and turned away, like she was embarrassed at what he might have overheard. "We thought of something that might help." He stepped into the kitchen, followed by Caleb. "Tell her what you told me."

Caleb took a breath. "I texted Brian when I was leaving work because I was going to pick up a sub on the way home and I'd get him one too if he was hungry."

"Brian's cell was dead," Annalisa said.

"I used an app," Caleb said. "It goes through the computer and the gaming console as well as the phone."

"I saw it while I was playing and I told him I already ate. But this could prove I was home, right?"

"I don't know," Annalisa said truthfully. Cell phones pinged the nearby towers and could be used to trace a person's position, but she had no idea if an app could serve the same purpose. "What time was this?"

"Maybe a little after eleven?" Caleb said. "I can check my phone." He consulted it for a moment and then turned the screen around to show Annalisa. "It was 11:17. See? Brian answered me right away. How could he have done that if he were off somewhere shooting someone? He didn't have his cell working."

"It's thin," said Annalisa. "But it might help if the timing can be verified through the game."

Caleb looked dismayed that his text didn't appear to be a magic bullet. Brian chewed his thumbnail, his eyes still frantic. "I didn't kill anyone," he muttered. "I didn't."

"Mom?" Nicole materialized from the other room, clutching her cell phone between her hands like a talisman. Her face was ashen. "Luke just called from the house. He can't find the wet suit. I guess it's missing."

CHAPTER THIRTY-FOUR

You believed your own press, Annalisa told herself as she drove. All the news articles after her capture of the Lovelorn Killer had praised her tenacity, quick wits, and valor. The stories that followed depicted her as a tragic figure. Pity Annalisa. She'd had to choose between family and duty, but the citizens of Chicago could rest easy because she picked the right one. Didn't she? After everything, this was what she had left: *she was right.*

She remembered the soul-crushing moment she'd discovered Alex murdered Katie Duffy. Not the horror of the revelation or the dread of what she had to do with the knowledge. Those weighed on her, a lead blanket in her bed at night when she tried to sleep and forget. But that moment of clarity was so strong it felt like a vision. She wasn't especially religious. God didn't talk to her. Yet somehow time and space arranged themselves to create that moment, a few precious seconds in which every element fell into place to allow her, and only her, to see the truth. She'd felt that same tingling certainty when she noticed the blue rake in the photos from the Bocks house. Moe had killed Josie Blanchard, and she, Annalisa, had found the proof. Now that the lab results came back with no match, she felt duped. Tricked somehow. Her shroud of righteousness went up in smoke around her.

So it was with a new tentativeness that Annalisa circled her latest intuition. She had no proof of anything yet and Zimmer probably wouldn't even take her call if she tried her. Besides, it was Nick's case now. If anyone, she should call him. His last text had arrived a couple of hours ago: *I heard about the rake. Sorry.* It was the sorry that rankled her. What the hell was he apologizing for? If it didn't match, it didn't match. Evidence didn't lie and it didn't have feelings, so the sorry was for her. *Sorry you screwed up.*

She drove with no particular destination in mind but somehow found herself in front of the Bass Lounge. If she was right, the answer would be here. She had no badge or gun, but she didn't expect trouble. She didn't plan to make any arrests. The perpetrators had fled the scene twenty years ago; she was so far behind that she was chasing their ghosts. She had to knock to enter the club, which had closed an hour ago. A slim young woman with an angled Afro and golden eye shadow cracked the door. "We're closed now," she said, polite but firm. Her perplexed gaze took in Annalisa's jeans, boots, and beanie hat. No doubt she failed to match the usual hip clientele.

"I'm Detective Annalisa Vega, and I need to speak to Roxanne Barry."

The girl's eyes turned suspicious. "I don't see any badge."

"I'm off duty," Annalisa hedged. "Please? I'm not here to hassle her. I swear."

"Let me check." She left Annalisa standing in the cold for several long minutes, and when the door opened again, Roxanne Barry stood on the other side.

"I had a feeling I'd be seeing you again," she said as she admitted Annalisa.

"Oh yeah?"

"All the times the cops have been here, they never sent a woman before." She did not sound admiring, but at least she had agreed to talk.

"I'd like you to walk me through the night of the robbery. The night Cecil was killed."

Roxanne's eye twitched. "I told you that's history now. Over and done." She walked away in the direction of the bar, her heels clicking on the empty dance floor. Annalisa followed.

"It's not over," she called out, her voice echoing through the large hall. Roxanne froze but did not turn around. "I think maybe you know that."

"I don't know nothing." She turned and Annalisa saw she was scared. "I got the settlement and I signed the papers saying I wouldn't talk about it. I have a good life, and you have no right to come in here and ask me to throw it away."

"I would never do that."

"Oh no? I think you know. You're a woman, but you're a cop. Cops are all on the same side."

"Not this time."

Roxanne turned her head away, chin raised, defiant. She said nothing. Annalisa tried a different angle. "The other woman who was here the night of the robbery, the waitress named Sandra Romero," she said. "Did she go by Sandy?"

Roxanne regarded her, wary. "Sometimes."

Annalisa nodded. "And did she have a relationship with a cop named Leo Hammond?"

Roxanne shut down again, her lips thinning as her jaw tightened. "I don't know what she did on her own time," she said eventually. "Sandra was pretty. Lots of guys liked her."

"Yeah, but she liked Leo back. Didn't she." It wasn't a question and Roxanne didn't take it like one. She shook her head and walked away. Annalisa went to the bar and ran her hand over the smooth wood. "When you mentioned Sandra died, you didn't tell me she was murdered."

Tight shrug. "Not my business."

"You must have been terrified. Both the night of the robbery and then when you heard about Sandra. Cecil was dead and you were on your own with Theodore. He couldn't have been more than four at the time. You were all he had left. Your life, your choices—the only things standing between your boy and the good life."

"I did give him a good life," Roxanne said fiercely. "I did."

"I believe you. But I think maybe Sandra made a different choice." She walked around the far side of the bar toward a black door marked EMPLOYEES ONLY. "You and Sandra were in the back when the robbery happened. That's what you said. Was it back here?" She opened the door without asking and found a large windowless office. There was a long shiny black table with a few slim chairs around it, a big mahogany desk, a white leather sofa, and framed posters of music artists on the wall. Roxanne had trailed her to the doorway but she went no farther. "Is the safe in here?"

"Yes, behind the signed Prince poster." A nervous smile shivered across her lips. "That was Cecil's idea to put it there, because he liked to say 'Prince is money.'"

"You and Sandra were loading it up when the robbers hit. But it didn't just have the weekend take. Cecil had done some kind of deal that night." She couldn't prove this part. Probably never would.

"I told you I'm not saying anything." Roxanne folded her arms across her chest. "Cecil's been dead twenty years now. Whatever he done or didn't do, it doesn't matter to me anymore. Nor should it bother the Chicago PD. They got statutes of limitations on these things, or haven't you heard?"

"You went to help him when you heard the robbers." Annalisa looked past her, trying to imagine it. "Or maybe they came in here after the contents of the safe. That makes the most sense, right? But you said Sandra was hiding . . ." Annalisa made a slow circle of the room. The table provided no protection. The sofa had only about six inches of clearance under it; even petite Sandra could not have fit there. "She must have been under the desk."

Annalisa wedged herself underneath and imagined Sandra lying there, trying not to breathe. The desk had short legs that provided her with a sliver of a view. She saw the carpet and Roxanne's signature purple suede boots. *The shoes,* Roxanne had said to her. *They always give you cops away.* Shit. Annalisa sat up so fast she hit her head. Pain shot through her like a lightning bolt and she moaned softly as she crawled out from under the desk.

Roxanne looked concerned as Annalisa struggled to her feet. "Are you all right?"

"Four robbers hit your club that night," she said, gritting her teeth against the wave of nausea. "Right?"

"Four, yes, all wearing masks."

"And then four cops responded to the 911 call."

Roxanne sighed and perched on the edge of the desk. "Yeah, and one of them shot Cecil as soon as he came through the front door. Serve and protect, my ass."

"Cecil fired first. That's what the inquest found."

"He didn't know Sandra called 911. He thought it was the robbers come back."

Because that's how quick they got here, Annalisa thought. Leo and his pals had been here all along. When the 911 call came through, they had to take it. "They had time to ditch their masks and jackets, but they couldn't change their shoes. Sandra saw them from her hiding spot. Maybe she even recognized Leo's shoes in particular when she had a moment to think about it. She figured out the cops and the robbers were one and the same, and somehow, they knew she knew."

Roxanne started shaking her head, denying it. "You better go now. You're talking nonsense and I don't want any part of it."

"You figured it out too," Annalisa realized. "Maybe that night. Maybe when Sandra got killed. It was the same cops on the case, right? Funny how that works."

"Ha ha, yeah, funny." Roxanne started steering her toward the door. "You've got to go. I told you I don't know anything that can help you."

"They killed Sandra to shut her up. One or more of them. You don't want to help me get them for it?"

"Help you? God no. Listen, I got one piece of advice for you and it's the same thing my mother said to me when I was small: you can't fix no one but yourself. Sandra's death is a tragedy, but I am not going to throw myself on her funeral fire, you get me? If you're right, then whoever came for her, they could come for me." She eyed Annalisa. "Or you."

"But they murdered her. They probably meant to kill Cecil too."

"Yes, and I survived." Her chin stuck out. "That's all that matters to me anymore."

"Sandra must've had family. Parents, siblings? Someone who would want to know the truth about how she died."

"Sandra was alone in this world, as far as I knew, except for Jasmine and Edgar. She clearly wasn't thinking about them when she opened her fat mouth about that night. What did she think would happen?"

"Jasmine and Edgar?"

"Her kids. Both little blond things, cute in a china doll kind of way. There wasn't any father around, so I guess the state took them after

Sandra died. Maybe they found a relative somewhere, I don't know. I made sure nothing like that happened to my boy. Can you imagine? Your mama's killed and you get sent off to live with strangers. The girl was only four, and Eddie . . . he was just a baby."

CHAPTER THIRTY-FIVE

ANNALISA BLEW THROUGH THE DOORS OF THE CLUB WITH HER PHONE ALREADY IN HAND. Her head still ached but underneath the pain she hummed with adrenaline. She cursed when she got Nick's voicemail. "Carelli, call me the second you get this. I'm leaving the Bass Lounge, and I think I've finally got this whole mess figured out. We've been looking at the wrong Eddie." She clicked off but before she could pocket her phone, a male voice shouted from behind her and someone grabbed her arm to spin her around.

"Hey!" Her phone got knocked from her hand and slid across the slippery pavement into the dirty remnant of a snowbank. All six feet, four inches of Theodore Barry stared down at her, his face full of fury. The streetlamp made the whites of his eyes glow against his dark skin.

"What the hell are you doing?" she asked him as she yanked her arm free.

"What are you? My mother's in there crying—just like the last time you came around here. What do you want? What can we give you so that you'll go away and leave us alone?" He fisted one hand, but she didn't think he meant to harm her. "My dad calls 911 because he's being robbed, and you people show up and shoot him. The robbers get away. Now you come around here, hassling my mother over some dead cop? Making her feel ashamed and scared inside her own club? You got a hell of a nerve, lady."

"Did you ask her why she was crying?"

"She said none of your business. But it is. She's my mother."

"You should go in there and thank her."

He drew up short and looked at her with lingering suspicion. "What for?"

"For protecting you all these years. That woman has kept a heavy burden all to herself." Roxanne had remained silent about the stolen drug money and the cops who likely stole it. It must have terrified her when Sandra turned up dead; Roxanne was the last living witness to the robbery, and she would have worried they would come for her next. So she let Sandra's murder go unpunished—what could she have proved, anyway—and accepted the "accidental" homicide of her husband. In return, she got the money from the settlement and young Theodore got to keep a sainted memory of his fallen father.

"What do you know about it?" Theodore asked, still belligerent, but he sounded less sure.

Annalisa touched his arm. "Go be with your mom. Tell her she won't have to worry much longer. Lock your doors and don't open them for anyone until you hear back from me."

He still didn't move. "Who we got to be afraid of?"

"Right now? Anyone with a badge."

Theodore hesitated a moment as he decided this was true. Then he reached down into the snow and returned her phone. "Looks okay," he told her as he handed it back. A grudging beat of silence. "Sorry."

She started edging away from him, eager to get on her way. "I'll be in touch," she called over her shoulder. "Call me if there's trouble." He shook his head, bemused, but he did as she asked and returned inside the club.

Annalisa wiped her phone on her pants to dry it off and consulted it for any response from Nick. Given the hour, he was probably sleeping. She dialed him again as she strode into the alley next to the club where she had parked her car. It rang twice before she felt the gun at her back.

"I'll take that," said a gruff voice. He plucked the phone from her hand.

She didn't have to turn around to know who he was. "Frankie."

He replied with a low chuckle. "I told them you were going to be a problem. I said it from the start. I said, that girl don't know when to mind her business. The others didn't want to believe me, and now look, here you are. Hands on the hood right there." He jabbed her hard with the gun in the direction of her car. She complied as he started patting her down.

"I'm not carrying," she said as he manhandled her. "You know I'm on leave. You know it because you arranged for it to happen, didn't you? You set me up."

"Never know what kind of heat you might have on you. Don't know many cops who own only one gun." Satisfied he'd come up empty in his search, he eased back from her. She scanned the darkened alley for anything she could use as a weapon—a board, a loose brick. All she saw was fast-food wrappers and dirty snow. "Let's go," he ordered, poking her with the gun again.

She turned in time to see him turn off her phone and put it in his jacket pocket. "Where are we going?"

"Somewhere quiet. Start walking." He pushed her in the direction of the other end of the alley.

She dragged her feet, stalling as much as possible, still looking for something to defend herself. If he got her into his car, she was probably dead. "I know you pulled the robbery," she said to distract him. "You and Hammond, Monk, and Osborne. Did Hammond tip you off to the deal going down that night? Maybe Sandra said something about it. The score was too big to resist."

"Shut up." He shoved her and she stumbled into the wall. Her hands scraped against the brick but her knee knocked on something hard. A loose bike tire. She gulped and bent over like she might be sick. Frankie kicked at her and cursed her out. "Keep moving."

She seized the tire and whirled around, aiming for his head. She caught his shoulder and he yelled in surprise as he got knocked to the ground. The gun fell from his hand and skittered sideways down the alley. She saw it disappear into the shadows as she raised the wheel to strike Frankie again. He rolled away and her blow barely glanced his side. The tire didn't have enough weight to do real damage, but it was all she had. She raised it again and her vision blurred as her arms went over her head. The concussion made her unsteady. She struck blindly in his direction. He was crawling away from her; she heard him grunting and the sound of his body scraping the pavement. She followed the sound, smacking at it with the tire. She made contact with his lower body but he just kept going. She screamed and hit him as hard as she could. The sounds stopped. She sucked in ragged breaths, trying not to pass out, and her vision cleared.

She looked down, expecting to see Frankie lying there, but the alley was empty.

"Looks like we're doing it the hard way," he said, breathing forcefully behind her. It was the last thing she heard for a long time.

....

She woke up when the car stopped. Consciousness returned gradually, like her brain was fighting through a receding tide, and she moaned softly as the pain returned. She cracked her eyes open and found it was dark. Frankie had handcuffed her and put her in the backseat of his Rover. She lay on top of a blanket that smelled like a dog. Wherever they had stopped, it was dark and quiet. She could no longer hear street noise.

He opened the back door and hauled her out onto her feet, which skidded briefly on the unpaved road. "This way," he ordered.

She recognized the location now. The swampy air, the train tracks, and the huge old cement grain elevators rising out of the ground like an industrial sphinx—they were down by the Port of Chicago. Frankie poked her again with the gun and she wondered if he planned to drown her in the icy lake. Surely there would be cameras. The grain elevators were ancient relics by now but the port still did business. At least some of the towering structures were used for storage. "What's the endgame here, Frankie?" she asked as they walked. "You think killing me will solve your problems?"

"Hey, my problems are your problems now. You should've played it straight. Stuck to Leo's murder."

"I did."

"You fuckin' didn't!" he roared at her, and the noise made her head ring. "Kayla blew Leo away for the insurance money. Then she did Tommy too."

"Kayla didn't kill anyone."

"Shut up. It doesn't matter now. It ain't your case anymore, sweetheart."

He grabbed her shoulder to slow her down as they approached a line of broken windows at the base of the enormous silos. "Here," he said as he located the one covered with a tarp. He took out a knife and slit it open from one side. "Get in there."

"And if I say no?"

"Then I shoot you out here and stuff you through the window myself."

She played the only card available to her and stalled for more time by cooperating. Inside the grain elevator was pitch dark. It smelled like rust and wet cement. Frankie turned on a pocket flashlight and shined it around until he located a decaying metal staircase. "Over there," he said. "Start climbing."

"People will look for me," she said as she started up the stairs. "I'm not like Sandra with no one but little kids to care about her."

"Yeah, you got lots of friends right now."

They climbed one story, then two. "Where are we going?" He did not answer her, just jabbed her with the gun to keep her moving. "You aren't even a little curious who killed your friends? Because it wasn't Kayla."

"I told you I don't give a fuck. Keep climbing."

"You can't fix it by killing me. I've already told my partner—"

"Oh, save it. I heard you on the phone back there. He didn't answer you. He probably thinks the same as everyone, that you're a whacked-out nutjob. But don't you worry. No one's going to find you here, because no one's been inside this place in at least twenty years. I'll make sure little Nicky stays busy looking elsewhere."

She stopped moving as his words struck a new chord of fear. "What do you mean?"

"Nicky's not like you. He plays by the rules. He believes the evidence in front of him, and I've got a big shiny clue right here." At her confusion, he took out her cell phone from his pocket and waved it in front of her. "Thanks to your little stunt in the alley, your blood's already there. Imagine if your phone turned up in Theodore Barry's car, with his prints on it. It wouldn't look good for him." He shook his head sadly, imagining it. "Wouldn't look good at all."

"That's how you did it before," she said. "You got David Edwards to take the fall for Sandra Romero's murder."

"We're done chatting. Let's go."

He forced her up two more flights to a landing area. It contained several large bins about the size of dumpsters, each with a tight lid on top that appeared to open via a crankshaft. Frankie shined the light in her eyes and nodded at the closest bin. "Open it."

"I don't think—"

"Then I shoot you," he said as he trained the gun at her head. She started turning the crank. It took all her might to get it to budge and her vision started swimming with the effort. She worried she might faint again. At last, the lid opened fully and she sagged against the container, spent. Frankie motioned at the bin with his gun. "Now, get in."

Her limbs became heavy with dread as she eyed what was to become her metal coffin. "I can't. It's too high." She gave a halfhearted jump to illustrate that she couldn't reach the edge of the container.

Frankie located a crate and kicked it over to her. "Use this."

Annalisa swallowed her fear and climbed over the rim. Every part of her was shaky now. Would anyone ever find her? Her mother would live out her days not knowing what had happened to her only daughter. Nick would look, she was sure of it, but eventually he'd have to give up. Take the promotion and move on. "Please don't do this," she whispered painfully as she hovered on the edge, one leg in and one leg out. "You have a family, right? A wife and kids? What would they think to see you right now?"

"This is on you," he said, so cold she knew he believed it. "You made me do this. Now, get in."

Annalisa hung on with her hands and dropped down into the dark metal storage bin. She could barely make out the mouth of the chute above that had been used to drop the grain into the containers for storage. Frankie's face appeared in shadow as he leaned over the edge to peer down at her. "You're just going to leave me to starve like this? Shut the lid and trap me here alone?"

"No," he said. "I've got a heart." She saw the glint of his gun as he brought it over the rim and aimed at her. "I'm going to shoot you first."

The gunshot echoed in the cavernous building. She cried out at the noise and covered her head. Several seconds went by and she remained clenched, crouching in the corner of the bin to make a smaller target of herself. Her ears rang. She could taste blood in her mouth. But beyond that, she realized, was silence. She staggered to her feet in wonderment that she was alive. She did not see any sign of Frankie.

She groped at the steel walls in the dark, looking for purchase, glancing overhead every few seconds to see if Frankie had returned. The face that appeared was so shocking it knocked her back against the wall. A round head with no hair, just black rubber. The oval-shaped diving mask. He stared down at her with his head cocked in curiosity, like he was an alien encountering humans for the first time.

"Eddie," she breathed.

He drew back, startled. Disappeared from view.

"Eddie, please. I need your help. I have to get out of here. Please help me."

His head appeared once more. She couldn't see his eyes or any distinct features, only his silhouette. Relief flooded her veins like a shot of heroin. He was still here. She was saved. She leaned against the wall to steady herself and called up to him. "There's a crate by the side of the bin. If you throw it down here, I might be able to climb out."

She heard him moving. Closed her eyes and relaxed. Her eyes flew open again in alarm when the grinding noise of the crank turning began reverberating through the metal walls of the bin. "No, no," she called desperately. "Don't!"

The two sides of the lid came across the top of the bin and met in the middle with a *thunk* as all traces of light vanished above her. She heard his footsteps walking away. After that, only quiet.

bolt once more but froze when she heard a distant sound outside. She pressed her ear to the wall and listened again. A male voice. Maybe Eddie had come back. She redoubled her efforts with the bolt, banging it frantically, blood roaring in her ears, and this time, she did yell. "Help! Please help me!"

She sobbed in relief when she heard the crank start to turn. He'd come back for her. When the lid parted, a bright flashlight shone down on her and she winced from the pain of it, shielding her face with her hands. "Annalisa?"

Nick's voice. Not Eddie's. "Nick." The word came out like a desperate plea. "Get me out of here."

"Hang on. Okay? Just hang on." She heard other footsteps, other voices. He hadn't come alone. Nick dropped in first one crate and then a second. "Can you climb out now? I can come down and—"

"No, I've got it." She mounted the crates and tried to lift herself out of the bin, but her arms gave out with the effort. Nick caught her before she fell back down.

"Easy there. I've got you."

She panted, still terrified as she scrambled over the edge and into his arms. He grabbed her tight and she held on for dear life. His hands were gentle as they traveled over her body, assessing and comforting at the same time.

"Are you okay? Are you hurt?"

He tried to pull back to look at her but she clung to him. His flashlight sat on the rim of her prison, illuminating all the scratches she'd put on the inside wall. It looked like a tiger had tried to claw its way out. She smelled her own sweat, her own fear, and she hid her face in Nick's jacket as she took one long, steadying breath.

"I'm okay." She eased back cautiously, testing whether she really meant it. She noticed Detective Kurt Reyes standing fifteen feet away, but he wasn't watching them. He was examining something on the ground. Frankie Vaughn, Annalisa remembered. "Is he dead?" she asked Nick, and he answered with a short nod. She rubbed her hands together, suddenly cold as the sweat dried off her. She'd left her jacket in the storage bin.

"Here, take this." Nick removed his own coat and put it around her shoulders. "We need to get you to the hospital."

CHAPTER THIRTY-SIX

Annalisa tried jumping but she couldn't reach the lid. She felt dizzy from the exertion and, she realized with alarm, the thinning levels of oxygen. The metal bin was airtight, or at least nearly so, which made sense when she considered it had been designed to protect the grain from bugs and mold. She would not survive even a day in the container. Yelling for help seemed not only fruitless but also foolish, given that she would use up her oxygen twice as fast that way. She scuffled around in the dark for anything she could use to help her situation. Her hands encountered dirty corners filled with leaves, small animal bones, and a rusted metal bolt about the size of her finger.

She tested the bolt against the metal wall of the bin. It didn't dent it, but the noise carried through the wall in a tinny sort of echo. Maybe the bolt could make a big enough sound to be heard on the outside. She began banging the bolt on the bin as hard as she could. *Help me, help me. Please.* She wanted to shout the words with all the breath in her lungs, but she gritted her teeth and held them in because no one would hear her. Sweat broke out over her brow, and she paused to shed her jacket before resuming her clanging. The repetitive banging sounded like a jackhammer inside the bin, and her wounded head throbbed with each smack of the bolt against the wall. She kept it up so long her shoulder started to ache.

She paused to wipe the sweat from her face, her energy flagging as she felt the air growing thinner. She raised her arm again to try the

Her head ached and her ankle throbbed from her fight with Vaughn in the alley. "I'm fine. How did you even know I was here?"

"You weren't answering your phone. I went by your place and you weren't home. Then I went by Vaughn's place and he wasn't there either. I thought, what are the odds of that? The last time I saw you, you were following him. So I checked the tracker on his car and found he'd parked down here by the port at two in the morning. I couldn't think of a good reason why he'd be doing that, and with you missing, I grabbed some guys to check it out."

"I'm grateful you did." She got up slowly and limped over to look at Vaughn's body. Frankie lay faceup, his eyes open in surprise, his jaw slack. There wasn't a mark on him from this angle. Nothing to say he wasn't coming back.

"Shot from behind," Reyes said, glancing at Annalisa. "You see it happen?"

"Sort of. He was getting ready to shoot me when someone else took him out." She looked to Nick. "It was the guy in the diving suit."

"Diving suit?" said Reyes, his face crinkling in confusion.

"He's the one who locked me in. Eddie."

"You said on the phone we had the wrong Eddie," Nick replied to Annalisa, ignoring Reyes for the moment. "What do you mean by that?"

"Sandra Romero had a son named Edgar that she called Eddie." She paused. "And I think maybe Leo Hammond was the father."

Nick let out a low whistle. "That would explain the note Leo left with the money."

"And the DNA from the wet suit. It wasn't Brian's. Leo had a second son." She started walking gingerly for the staircase, babying her hurt ankle. "Come on, we don't have a lot of time if we're going to stop him."

"Vega . . ." Nick followed, but his tone wasn't pleased. "You need medical attention. We can put out the word on Eddie Romero. Have someone else pick him up."

"That might be too late," she said as she continued down the stairs as fast as she could. "Eddie knows I know. I know who he is. He has one more person to kill and he wasn't going to let me stop him. That's why he locked me in the storage bin."

"One more person . . . who?"

She stopped to turn and look up at him. "Paul Monk." The last of the Fantastic Four.

"Why does he want to kill Monk?"

"Because he's one of the four of them who pulled the robbery at the Bass Lounge, the only one still alive. Sandra Romero figured out it was them. Maybe she threatened to tell. Maybe she just wanted a cut. Either way, Hammond, Monk, Vaughn, and Osborne decided they had to get rid of her."

". . . and then they pinned it on David Edwards," Nick finished as he put the final piece together.

"Right. But time is running out for Eddie to complete his revenge plan. We've got to get to Monk's place—fast."

Nick didn't argue further, nor did he force her off on the arriving medical personnel. He handed her his phone as he drove. "See if you can get a line on what happened to Edgar Romero," he told her. "I'll have backup meet us at Monk's."

"No lights or sirens. No one approaches the house. If Eddie's sitting in a car outside waiting to make his move, I don't want to spook him. I also don't want some hothead taking him out before we have a chance to talk to him."

He looked sideways at her. "This guy nearly killed you too, remember."

"I know, but there's been enough killing already—more than twenty years' worth. It's time for it to stop." She performed all the usual searches on Edgar "Eddie" Romero's name and did not come back with an obvious match. "Romero doesn't seem to have an Illinois driver's license. He hasn't been arrested here."

"Yet," Nick said with steadfast determination as he shifted gears. His red coupe tore through the empty city streets, dodging the occasional slow-moving car.

"Eddie was a baby when Sandra got killed. Maybe he was adopted and changed his name. Roxanne said there was a girl too. Eddie's older sister. If we find her, she might know where he is."

"You said we'd find him at Monk's."

"I'm afraid he may have been there and gone." What would Eddie do once he'd completed his mission? He might kill himself. He might try to fade back into society the way that Leo Hammond and the others had done. Handing out justice to others but avoiding it himself.

The car fishtailed slightly as Nick turned a hard corner. "This is the street," he said as he slowed to a crawl. "And that's his bungalow right there."

Annalisa observed a light on at the front of the house, but the shades were drawn, so she could not see inside. Monk's F-150 sat parked in the drive. The street was otherwise dark and quiet, with no sign of anything amiss. The few nearby cars did not have anyone sitting in them. Nick stopped his car across the street from Monk's house and squinted at it. "What do you think?" he asked. "It looks intact."

"Eddie didn't have to break into the Hammond house, because he had the code."

"You think he's got a way into Monk's place too?"

The M.O. so far was inconsistent. Two of the men shot were killed inside the Hammond home, but Frank had been gunned down out in the open. "I think we should check the back."

"Just a sec." Nick reached over her lap and unlocked the glove box. He handed her a Smith & Wesson .38 revolver. "Take this."

"Aw, this is the nicest present you've ever given me," she said as she turned it over in her hands to check it was loaded.

He frowned. "Hey, I bought you a diamond engagement ring."

She smiled and reached for the door. "I said what I said." They exited the car quietly and jogged across the street to the house. Nick motioned that he would go around the left side, and Annalisa took the right. On the way, she encountered a side entrance, and the slice of light coming from it indicated it was partially open. She checked more closely and saw the lock had been forced. Eddie was here.

Her heart rate picked up and she readied her gun as she went inside. She found herself in the kitchen, which smelled like Monk had fried steak for dinner. The dishes still lingered in the sink. She paused to listen but heard no sound. Cautiously, she crept to the threshold and peered into the next room, which was the dining area. It sat in shadow but light spilled from the front room beyond. Annalisa halted as she heard a floorboard creak. The noise came from the room at the front of the house and she moved closer to it. She held her breath as she came around the corner, and then loosed it in surprise at what she saw.

Paul Monk sat in a recliner by the window, holding his police-issued weapon. He had it trained, center mass, on a man in a diving suit, who held a gun of his own. The diver had his weapon pointed at Monk's head and Annalisa knew he could shoot. Either or both of them could be dead in a second.

"Police," she said. "Put the guns down."

"Fuck off," Monk replied without looking at her. "I am the police, and he broke in here. I can blow his head off and the mayor will throw me a parade."

"Not if I kill you first." The frogman's gun wavered with the intensity of his anger.

"Go ahead," Paul goaded him. "Try it."

"Shut up!" Annalisa glared at him and took a step toward the diver. She kept her tone soft. "It's over now, Eddie," she said. "We'll take it from here."

The young man let out a sob, but he did not turn his head to look at her. He also didn't lower the gun. "No, I have to. I have to kill him."

Annalisa took another step, this one sideways so that she was almost in front of Eddie. "You don't have to kill him. I know everything now. I know what happened to your mom."

Nick arrived on the scene behind them and he immediately drew his own gun. She motioned for him to stand down. He ignored her and kept the gun pointed at the diver. "Drop it, son. We've got the place surrounded now."

"No . . ." Another anguished sob tore out of the young man, and his mask began to fog. "He has to pay for what he did."

Annalisa gave a small gasp of surprise as she finally recognized the voice and the shape of the man in front of her. *Of course,* she realized. *He's been here all along.* Slowly, she reached for his gloved hand, the one holding his gun. "He will pay," she said. "I promise you. Caleb." At the sound of his name, he started crying in earnest as her hand closed over his, and he let her take the gun.

Nick moved in immediately to cuff him. Then he pulled off Caleb's mask and began to read him his rights as Caleb wept softly. Paul Monk got up at last and stalked over to them with his gun still in hand. "Who the fuck are you?" he asked Caleb. He looked at Annalisa. "I thought it was Eddie."

Caleb found his anger again. "I am Eddie, you piece-of-shit coward murderer." He spat at Monk's face and Nick hauled him backward.

"I've never seen this guy before in my life," Monk said with a flinty smile, waving his gun in Caleb's direction. "But I will enjoy watching him fry."

"About that," Annalisa said. "Carelli?"

Backup had arrived and Nick was handing off Caleb to them. He looked back and Annalisa gestured at Monk. "Hmm? Oh. Wait, Givens . . . give me your cuffs, okay?" The uniformed officer handed over his cuffs without question, and Nick brought them to Annalisa.

"Please put your gun down and turn around," Annalisa told Monk.

He looked at her like she was crazy. "What the hell is this?"

Nick still had his gun at the ready. "Do as the detective told you," he said to Monk.

"The fuck I will. That asshole broke into my house. I didn't do anything wrong, and you know it."

"You're being arrested on suspicion of murder," Annalisa informed him coolly. She reached over and took the gun as he blinked in shock. Nick took custody of the weapon.

"I didn't murder him! He's walking out of here. You're one crazy bitch, you know that? Maybe even crazier than that asshole in the wet suit."

He tried to walk away but Annalisa grabbed his right arm and twisted it behind his back. "That asshole is Eddie Romero," she said as he struggled. "Son of Sandra Romero."

Monk froze at the name. "What—what did you say?"

"I said you're under arrest," she repeated harshly as she snapped the cuffs on him. "For murder."

CHAPTER THIRTY-SEVEN

THIS TIME, ANNALISA WAS NEITHER THE HERO NOR THE VILLAIN. In fact, if you believed the news reports, she wasn't there at all. She remained on medical leave with no legal authority so Nick got credit for the arrests of both Caleb Ingram and Paul Monk. Her last contact with Caleb was leaning down to talk to him through a squad car window, where he'd apologized for nearly killing her at the grain elevator. "I would've come back for you. I swear. I wasn't going to leave you there locked up like that."

She might well have run out of air before he'd returned. "You should have come to us," she said. "When you learned the truth about what they'd done."

"You guys had twenty years to figure it out," he said, his head lolling back on the seat. The emotion left his eyes. "Four robbers, four cops. Money never recovered. If I figured out they were dirty that quick, someone else could've done it. No one bothered to try."

Annalisa had no answer for this. "If it matters, Leo Hammond did have regrets." She didn't mention the pile of cash, because it was in evidence now, and Caleb would probably never see a dime. "About you and your mother. He couldn't sleep, had nightmares that woke him screaming at night. He did remember you."

"Yeah?" His blue eyes fixed beyond her with a slight squint, as if searching for something he couldn't quite see. "I don't remember him.

Not from back then. My sister did, a little. She told me my dad had red hair and his name was Leo like a lion. Later, when I looked him up, I found out he had kids. I followed them a couple of times but didn't have the guts to talk to them. When Brian showed up in the bike store, I couldn't believe it was him, that he'd just walk through the door and talk to me. At first, I worried he'd figured it out, but no, it was random. He didn't know me. We became friends and I got to see what I missed. I got to see Leo be a dad to his real kids. But I don't remember what happened before my mother got killed. I don't remember him." He didn't say anything more and Annalisa stood and watched helplessly as the squad car took him away. She'd stopped a murderer but she felt no victory.

Back at her condo, she recuperated like a hibernating bear—lights off in her bedroom cave, no noise from the TV or contact with the outside world. She swallowed as many painkillers as she dared, enough to block out all negative sensation so that she didn't have to feel anything. Only on the third day, when she showered and saw the bruises decorating her body, did she admit how close she'd come. She put on soft pajamas and went to the windows to water her plants. They sat drooping under a sunless sky. The dark clouds tumbled over one another but the storm didn't break. She felt its restlessness in the wind that battered her outside walls.

When the buzzer sounded, she opened the door to admit Nick. His dark hair was windswept, his warm smile a contrast to the gust of cold air that accompanied him into the house. He held a shopping bag in his hands. "I brought you some food. Soup from the deli you like. A few wrapped sandwiches."

"Ugh, thanks. But all I've done is eat. Eat and sleep." She flopped on her couch in dramatic fashion, and the motion didn't hurt as much as it had at first. Time really did heal.

Nick noticed. "You must be feeling better."

"Well, my injuries are fading at least." She gestured at the other end of the sofa. "Sit down. Tell me what's going on with the case."

Nick took off his coat and helped himself to one of the sandwiches he'd brought. "The DA says there's not enough evidence to charge Paul Monk in either the robbery of the Bass Lounge or Sandra Romero's death. Roxanne Barry won't testify, and David Edwards was already convicted for Sandra's murder, so the burden of proof is unusually high."

"So he just gets away with it?"

"Not quite. His arrest generated some headlines and one of his informants called in to say that Monk paid him a grand to finger a particular dealer for some murder. When the dealer got arrested, the informant got drugs and another five thousand."

"And what did Monk get?"

"He didn't know for sure, but he says there were two suitcases full of dope involved in the deal, and only one got logged into evidence. Monk is suspended pending further investigation."

Annalisa shook her head. "Feels weak. He should pay for Cecil Barry's death. He should pay for Sandra."

"Well, we'll keep digging, but it's been twenty years, and Caleb Ingram unfortunately took care of three other witnesses. Paul Monk knows he's the last man standing, and he knows enough to keep his mouth shut." He took a large bite of his Italian sub and chewed with such relish that she held out her hand.

"Okay, I give. What else have you got over there?"

He grinned and pulled a second sub out of the bag. "Turkey BLT," he said.

"Has Zimmer said anything about me coming back?" she asked, trying to sound casual as she unwrapped the sandwich.

"No. But she hasn't packed up your desk or taken your picture down."

"Great."

"And," he added around a mouthful of food, "remember Central just lost four detectives. They're going to need bodies."

"Somehow I don't think they'd welcome mine."

He put down his sandwich and regarded her seriously. "You do have friends out there, Vega. Don't forget that." When she didn't reply, he grinned and leaned into his bag once more. "Speaking of, I have a little something for you."

He handed her a brown shoebox with a pink bow stuck to the lid. She put it on her lap to open it and found the .38 he'd lent her at Monk's place. "This is yours."

"It's yours now. I have the paperwork to make it legal."

"I thought you said Zimmer hadn't counted me out yet."

"She hasn't. I just thought you might need a backup." He was smiling, pleased with himself.

"Thanks," she said, glancing down at the gun. "I appreciate it. But we both know you're my real backup." She looked at him to answer his smile and found his expression had turned guilty. "What?" she said when he didn't say anything.

He gave her a pained look. "My, ah, my promotion came through. I transfer over to Area Four in two weeks."

"What?" She blinked from the shock of it, but of course this made sense. He'd just made two high-profile busts. "Con-congratulations," she managed to get out as she shifted the box with the gun off her lap. "I'm happy for you."

"Hey, no one will hassle you anymore about our relationship, right? No more whistling 'Here Comes the Bride' and all that crap."

"Right," she said, too brightly. "And none of your pistachio shells all over my car."

"Well, if you'd only let me do all the driving . . ."

It was stupid to feel crushed. She'd divorced him, protested his return, and shot him down every time he'd tried to renew their relationship. She just never believed he'd actually walk away. After an awkward pause, he gestured at her sandwich. "I guess you really weren't that hungry."

"Guess not."

He nodded to himself. "I should go and let you get some rest."

She didn't argue as he gathered his belongings, simply trailed him to the door with her gaze on the ground. "Thanks for coming by," she said around the lump in her throat, not quite looking at him. "Thanks for telling me in person about the transfer."

He touched her cheek with his fingers and held them there until she met his eyes. "Of course."

"I guess you get the last ditch," she said, trying for humor as she held his palm to her face. "And the big exit. I need you to teach me when to leave."

He smiled sadly as he pulled away. "You don't need me, Vega. You never have."

She stood in the open doorway watching until his taillights disappeared in the distance. With a shiver, she shut the door and returned to the disarray in her living room. Her boots stood where she'd shed them three days earlier, a crust of road salt and mud around them. Dirty dishes sat stacked on the end table by the lamp. The coffee table still held the files from the Blanchard murder. She curled on the sofa in front of them, almost defensively, like they were judging her. Pops had once warned her about the special hell of the unsolved cold case. *You're usually the only guy assigned to it. The only one left to care. You always feel like if you just talked to one more person, you'd have the answer.*

She started clearing the papers away with short, angry movements. Returning them to the box. Moe was dead. Leo Hammond, the cop on Josie's case, was dead too. She'd run out of people to talk to and frankly the energy to care. The noise of the door buzzer made her stop with surprise. Nick, she guessed. Maybe he forgot something. Maybe he'd changed his mind.

She went eagerly to greet him, flinging open the door without first checking to see who was on the other side. "Oh," she said when she saw she'd been wrong about her visitor. "Um, hi."

"Hi." He offered a crooked smile and she felt fifteen again.

There was only one man on earth who could do that to her. It was Colin.

CHAPTER THIRTY-EIGHT

....

COLIN DRESSED SLEEK AND SOPHISTICATED LIKE THE WORLD TRAVELER THAT HE WAS, IN DARK-WASH JEANS, BOOTS, AND CUT-WAIST BLACK JACKET THAT LOOKED MADE FOR HIM. "Can I come in?" he asked when she did not move.

"Oh. Of course." She stood aside, awkward in her pajamas and messy topknot.

He paused on the threshold to hand her a small bouquet of daffodils. "I heard you were convalescing."

"They're beautiful, thanks. I'll just put them with the others. Please make yourself at home." She set the flowers in a water glass and checked her appearance in the reflection of the microwave. "I saw you were in town," she called as she tugged the tie from her hair and ran her fingers through the messy waves. "But I didn't expect to see you." She gave up on fixing herself and returned to the living room, where Colin stood in front of her array of plants by the window. She lingered shyly at a distance. "I didn't think you'd want to see me." She left off *ever again* but it was there in the silence that stretched between them.

"I could say the same about you," he countered. "You didn't call. You didn't write."

She spread her hands in a helpless gesture. "What could I have said?"

Colin nodded a little to himself and turned to admire the ficus tree near his elbow. "You've kept them all alive for more than a year," he said, touching a green leaf. "I'm impressed. They look good, even. I'm not home enough to keep anything other than a cactus." He lived in Texas now when he wasn't traveling. Chicago had not been his home for years. After what happened, Annalisa figured it never would be again. Still, it made her heart beat faster to see him. They'd made so many plans and promises together, imagining a future for themselves that they never managed to create in reality; maybe that was why they always felt unfinished.

"Do you want anything?" she asked him. "Coffee or soda? I have a bottle of wine around here somewhere."

"No, thanks." He moved on with cataloging her apartment, shifting his attention to the bookshelves. He read the spines with interest and picked up her white ceramic rabbit for inspection. Its ears faced the window per Sassy's instructions to bring good luck. He put it down in the wrong direction but she didn't correct him. The lucky rabbit hadn't been all that lucky for her so far. "Your family photo is gone," he observed, turning to her. "The one with all of us when we were kids."

She hadn't been able to bear looking at it. "I still have it," she said. The end table had a drawer, and she opened it to remove the picture, which she gave to him. "You can keep it if you want."

He smiled faintly at her words. "I'm trying," he murmured as he studied their youthful faces. He looked up at her. "I saw Alex today."

"You—what?"

"I went to tell him that I will testify at his sentencing. I'll be asking the judge for leniency."

"But why? After what he did . . ." She still had a hard time with the words. "He murdered your mother."

"I know. I know everything now, thanks to you. How your dad and my mom cheated with each other and then my mom got pregnant. She didn't live long enough to find out whose baby it was, but maybe it doesn't matter. Two families were coming apart at the seams, and Alex went over to our house that night to try to stop it. I understand that part. It's the rest where I struggle to understand."

"Me too." She took a tentative step closer to him. If Colin could forgive Alex, maybe there was hope he would forgive her too. "I'm so sorry, Colin."

He smiled at her sadly. "Mona Lisa, it was never your fault." He reached over and stroked the hair back from her face and she tried to smile for him the way she used to do. His hand fell away. "Alex can't explain why he did it. I'm not sure he understands himself, but I do believe him when he says he's sorry. He never wanted this to happen."

"So that's it? You forgive him?"

"I want to," he said. "I'm trying. I think, more than anything, I'm testifying for my mother. She wouldn't have wanted this either, not any of it. She loved you and your brothers. She would be horrified to see you estranged from your family. She'd hate for Alex to miss raising his kids."

"She'd hate to be dead," Annalisa pointed out.

Colin dropped his chin to his chest, conceding her point. "Yes," he whispered finally. "She got cheated. She missed so much. I just want it to be over now, for the suffering to end. Alex can't bring her back and he should pay a price. I think, having to see his girls from inside a prison, he is. But maybe if there's a chance for him to get unstuck from this whole mess, then maybe there's a chance for all of us. Maybe then it won't hurt to look at all these pictures."

He handed it back to her and she glanced at it. "It just feels like lies," she murmured. "These happy people weren't ever real." Within five years of that photo, Pops would be cheating on Ma with Katie, betraying Katie's husband also in the process—a man who had been his police partner and best friend. When did it start?

"They were as real as the bad times," he insisted. "It wasn't all lies. I refuse to believe that. Because that would mean we never loved each other, and I know that's not true."

A small sob escaped her and Colin enfolded her in his arms, their shared history trapped between them by the old photo. "You make it sound so easy," she said into his shoulder.

"It's not. It's the hardest thing in the world. But I've known you your whole life, you've never backed down from hard things."

She sniffled as she drew back to look at him. "How long are you staying?"

"Just through the sentencing."

"Oh," she said, disappointed.

He hesitated and laced their fingers together. "I know what it costs you to stay here. I know because it's not a price I'm willing to pay. I have a three-week scheduled jaunt through Thailand and Vietnam." Once, he'd offered her the chance to go away with him. She'd said no then, but she wasn't sure she would have the strength to say it again if he renewed the offer.

He said nothing. She took a deep breath and rocked on her feet. "Then I guess I'll see you at the sentencing," she said.

He looked her over searchingly. "Will you testify?"

"To which part?" She regarded the photo in her hand—a time bomb of memories.

He kissed her forehead. "To all of it."

....

Once Colin left, she was alone again with the silence and the files on Josie Blanchard. As she resumed clearing them away, she thought about what Toby Flanders had said about his infatuation with Josie: it was like a fever. He'd made decisions with a broken, diseased brain only to feel foolish and ashamed when the fever broke. She wondered if it was like that for Pops and Katie, whether the baby had been the cold water they needed to wake up. But by then it was too late.

A CD case slid out of the sheaf of papers in her hand and landed on the floor. She retrieved it and found it labeled JOSIE BLANCHARD NEWS FOOTAGE. That the footage existed on CD showed how cold the case had gone. Everything was digital now. Cops kept copies of news reports because sometimes the murderer would hang around the crime scene to watch the investigation; she knew of one case where a reporter actually interviewed the killer on camera. CONCERNED NEIGHBOR, read the chyron at the bottom, while the man on-screen broke down and cried about the missing woman. Out of idle curiosity, Annalisa dug out her laptop and connected it to a CD player so she could view the footage. Maybe the elusive Vivian Catalano would appear on-screen.

Instead, she found multiple interviews with Moe. He appeared weepy and desperate, but most of all she noticed how young he looked, with a full head of dark hair. Guilty or innocent, this case had dogged him for almost half his life. The couple who lived downstairs from Josie were also interviewed about how unsafe they felt with a murderer on the loose. A beefy, mustached man from down the block said he hoped the killer would come back because he'd be waiting for him.

WGN had sent a reporter to the university where Josie worked. They filmed her desk with its empty chair and the pink sweater hanging on the back. In an interview, Toby Flanders stood outside his building near a tree with blazing red leaves—already dead but beautiful as they fell—where he waxed on about Josie's lost promise, as though she too had been most beautiful right before she died. "Her excitement was contagious, and she was passionate about making medicine better for the patients. Not just about research but its real-life impact. When she was working with people in our Medication Management program, that's when Josie glowed. She'd make the rounds and the patients just loved her. She remembered not only their diseases but also their kids' names, their pets' names, and where they grew up."

The shot switched to the reporter doing a stand-up shot from the parking lot of the school. A white van behind her had a caduceus on it and the seal of the University of Chicago. PUTTING PATIENTS FIRST, read the text on the side, and Annalisa realized this was probably the van Josie used to make her rounds. Wait. A white van. That's what she'd been looking for. She scrambled to freeze the image and then she dug back through the box to find Vivian Catalano's statement about the vehicle she'd seen driving away the night of Josie's murder.

A white van driving away in a hurry, Vivian said. It had writing on the side. And maybe some sort of bird, like an eagle.

Leo Hammond and Tom Osborne had thought the bird might be from the flag-and-eagle design Moe Bocks, Sr. used to sell his cars. But no such truck ever turned up with the logo on it. Annalisa looked at her computer screen again, squinting at the wings at the top of the caduceus. At night, from a distance, you might think it was an eagle.

CHAPTER THIRTY-NINE

THE NEXT DAY DAWNED SUNNY AND COLD. Annalisa bundled up for her trip to the University of Chicago campus in Hyde Park, both against the temperature and her trepidation. She and Colin had planned on attending the school together back when they'd been dating as teenagers, but then his mother was murdered, he moved away, and her previously stellar grades faltered in the wake of all the tragedy. Her application had been rejected. Colin went to Princeton instead. She'd always chalked that lost future up to Katie's murderer. He'd not just taken her life but altered so many others in the process. Now that killer had a face, one once familiar and dear to her, but she still couldn't forgive.

Absent her badge and gun, she had no authority to set foot on campus, this place that had told her she wasn't good enough for them. She knew she was hardly alone; UChicago was a top-ten school that rejected thousands of applicants each year, and she'd done fine at the University of Illinois. But here the looming Gothic-style towers made her feel as though she were an unworthy peasant approaching a wizard in his magic castle. The bare trees added to the stark, enchanted feel. Annalisa encountered only a handful of students hurrying from one building to another, their eyes on their phones, not seeming to notice her.

She located the biological sciences building and the nearby parking lot that had appeared on the news footage following Josie Blanchard's murder. There was no white van, but she didn't expect to find it twenty years later. Instead there was a blue van that had similar markings rendered in white, including the university's seal and the caduceus. She snapped a quick photo with her phone before going into the building in search of Toby Flanders. The directory at the front door indicated he was on the third floor. When she hiked up the stairs, she discovered the entrance was locked and she would need to scan her ID for entry. She was stuck loitering until a young woman in a lab coat emerged. Annalisa grabbed the door before it closed and smiled in what she hoped was a reassuring, confident manner. "Thanks."

The woman looked confused for a moment but Annalisa pushed past her before she had any chance to object. Locating Toby Flanders proved surprisingly easy. He sat behind his desk in his office working, with no secretary present to run interference. "Detective," he said, looking up when she knocked on the open door. "Did I forget we had a meeting?"

"No, I was just in the area and I wanted to ask you a couple of follow-up questions." Her eye was drawn to the large painting behind him, which showed an expanse of blue sky over a red farmhouse and golden wheat fields. The image felt familiar somehow but she couldn't place it.

"I really don't see how I can be of any further help to you." He did not invite her to sit. "Moe Bocks is dead, right? I would think that the case rests with him."

"Someone sure wants us to think that," she agreed, taking a chair in front of his desk anyway. She looked again at the painting, trying to place it. "I have some questions about the vehicle your lab was using to make the community visits like the ones Josie was performing. It was a van?"

He appeared perplexed. "Yes, it was a Dodge, I believe."

"Who was the owner of the van?"

"The university."

"And who had access to it?"

"Anyone in the lab, I guess. Also people in Stephen Roper's lab. We shared the van across different projects. He moved to UCLA about ten years ago."

"I see," she said, taking notes now. "So there were multiple sets of keys?"

"I had a set and so did Roper."

"And where did you keep them?"

"On my desk in that bowl right there."

She glanced at the blue ceramic bowl that indeed held a key fob, presumably to the current van. "Were there any sort of records kept about who was driving the van and when?"

"No," he said slowly. "We usually had only a couple of students who needed it at any given time."

"What about you?" she asked, keeping her tone neutral. "Did you ever drive the van?"

"I'm sure I did at times. Why?"

"Did you ever drive it to Josie Blanchard's place?"

A frown appeared on his face. She could see him thinking, trying to get ahead of her in the conversation. He was a smart man, maybe even brilliant, so it had to be frustrating for him not to know the right answers to give her. "I can't think of a reason why I would have," he said carefully, and she recognized this was not a denial.

"But you might have driven the van there?"

"Sometimes I accompanied Josie on her rounds. It's possible I might have had reason to pick her up at her apartment to do so, in which case I would have taken the van."

"So, you did drive it there."

"I said it was possible," he said, irritated now. "Why all these questions about the van? What does this have to do with anything?"

"Maybe nothing. If I wanted to find that van now, where would I look?" She knew of cases where forensics had been able to lift hairs, fibers, or DNA years later from vehicles that had changed owners in the meantime.

"I have no earthly idea," he said in a tone that suggested she was an idiot even to ask him. "As I said, the university held the title."

She looked at the painting again, which was still niggling at her. "That's a beautiful painting," she said, gesturing at it with her pen. "It looks familiar to me somehow." She wondered if it was a reproduction of the original, and maybe she had seen it in a book somewhere. Perhaps Colin had photographed it in his travels.

He turned with surprise to glance at it. "Really? My mother-in-law did it. She was a painter, like my wife. I guess artistic flair runs in their family."

"It's gorgeous. Was it ever on exhibit anywhere?"

He laughed gently. "No, Vivian was talented, to be sure, but she never really made a name for herself outside of her community in Taos."

Annalisa sat forward in her seat. "I'm sorry, did you say her name is Vivian?"

"Yes. Vivian Catalano."

The painting described by Vivian Catalano's landlord, Annalisa realized. That's what had pinged her memory. ***Wheat fields that seemed to move across the canvas.*** She stared at the painting so long that Flanders cleared his throat to get her attention.

"If that's all your questions, I really need to get back to work."

"Where can I find her?" Annalisa demanded as she leapt to her feet, her gaze still on the painting. "Where can I find Vivian Catalano?"

"At the cemetery," said Flanders, and she looked to him in shock. He had a gleam in his eye, now that he'd regained the upper hand. "She died of cancer in 2001."

CHAPTER FORTY

ANNALISA WENT BACK TO HER CONDO AND SPENT THE ENTIRE DAY GOING THROUGH THE BLANCHARD FILE WITH NEW EYES. She called the number the landlord gave her, the one for Bonnie, Vivian's supposed sister. It turned out to be a pizza place. Vivian had existed, or at least someone calling herself so had given a signed statement to Leo Hammond on September 22, 2002, the day after Josie was found murdered. But Leo wasn't around anymore to identify her or help track her down. Annalisa was beginning to fear she might get away with it.

Twilight cast purple shadows over her walls before she got up from the couch. She headed to the kitchen for some water, but the buzzer at her front door made her turn around. It was Nick, and he held a bottle of champagne in his hands. "I have good news. Thought you might want to celebrate."

"I got my job back," she blurted, and his face fell.

"No. I mean, not yet. I haven't heard anything."

She pulled him in out of the cold. "Okay then, tell me what the news is."

"We got him," he said, eyes shining, his cheeks pink from a mix of winter air and excitement. He paused from unwrapping the foil at the top of the bottle. "Well, not quite yet, but we have evidence that the Fantastic Four were up to their necks in Sandra's murder. Definitely enough to make Paul Monk nervous."

"Spill," she ordered him as she got down two glasses.

"Do you still have that old memo from the Blanchard file? The one stuck to the back of the report?"

"Sure." He poured the bubbly while she dug up the copy of the paper with the memo stuck to it. "Here it is," she said, sliding it over the counter to him.

"Look at the date. September 27, 2002."

She hadn't realized the significance before. "The night Sandra died."

"That's right. I'm thinking that's why no one ever called Noreen Butler back about her tip. Leo Hammond was too busy framing David Edwards for Sandra's murder that night."

"Yeah, but you can't prove that."

"Not so fast. You see that brown stain at the top? We thought it was coffee and that's what stuck the memo to the paper."

"It's not?"

"When I saw the date matched, I had the lab boys test the original for evidence. That stain is blood. Sandra's blood."

Her heart soared for a moment before shattering like it was shot from the sky. "It doesn't prove anything," she told him with dismay. "Leo was at the scene in the alley where Sandra was found. He could have gotten blood on him then."

"Sandra wasn't found until after eleven o'clock. This call came in at 9:08."

"Maybe," she said. "It's pretty thin."

"Well, then perhaps you'll like this better." He took out a folded piece of paper from his pocket and handed it to her. It was a copy of an old requisition form from the 12th precinct, dated September 28, 2002. The men's bathroom on the ground floor needed a new plunger because the old one was missing.

"The wooden splinters they found in Sandra," Annalisa whispered.

"And look who signed the form."

Her gaze dropped to the signature at the bottom. Paul Monk. She imagined him scrawling his name and handing it over, this tiny mistake, never dreaming it would someday come back to bite him in the ass. "This is good work," she told Nick. "I'm impressed."

"Never would've seen the memo if you hadn't talked your way into the Blanchard files. This was a team effort, partner." He raised his glass to toast with her.

She gave him a grudging clink but didn't take a sip.

"What's wrong?" he asked her. "Oh crap, is it your meds? I should've known not to bring you alcohol . . ."

"No, no, it's not that." She hadn't even taken the painkillers today. "I think I've finally figured out who murdered Josie Blanchard but I have no way to prove it." She filled him in on what she'd learned and her hunch about the mysterious Vivian Catalano. "Even if I can get the landlord to ID her, it won't prove anything."

Nick sipped his drink as he considered. "Well, there's only one angle you haven't tried yet." He tapped the piece of paper between them, the copy of the old memo from Noreen Butler. *Suspicious person near the trash,* it read. The date was a week after Josie's body had been discovered, which did not seem promising.

"You called the number," she reminded him. "No Noreen."

"So we run her down, dead or alive."

She looked sideways at him. "We? Aren't you transferring elsewhere any second now?"

"I'm not gone yet." He cracked his knuckles. "Let me have your laptop and we can use my log-in to get into the system."

They moved to her sofa, and she gave him her computer so he could search the official databases that she currently did not have access to, thanks to her suspension. She pressed up against him, shoulder to shoulder, as he ran Noreen Butler through the registry of licensed Illinois drivers. For once, it was easy and her name popped right up along with a picture. She was seventy-two years old with a listed address in Englewood. No available phone number.

Nick looked to Annalisa. "Want to take a ride?"

"Race you to the car."

Nick drove, and they rolled up to Noreen Butler's bungalow just before eight o'clock. At the door, Annalisa heard a television playing loudly on the other side. It went silent as she rang the bell. A few moments later, a woman's voice called through the door. "Who is it?"

Annalisa nodded to Nick, who displayed his ID. "Chicago police detectives, ma'am."

"I didn't call the police," she replied sharply. She did not open the door.

"We're following up on a call you made about twenty years ago," Annalisa said in a raised voice, straining to be heard through the wooden door. "About Josie Blanchard's murder."

She heard a bolt slide loose and the door opened to reveal an African American woman with glasses on. She peered at them like a disapproving librarian. "For land's sake, it sure took you long enough. Come on in."

She insisted on serving them some of the tea she was drinking, along with homemade cherry-chocolate cookies. "I've been making these for my grandbabies since they were little. They're all grown now, but they still come around here for the cookies."

"I'm sure they do," Annalisa replied. She nibbled one and it did taste delicious in her mouth. She just couldn't force any food into her stomach at that moment.

Noreen lowered herself into her well-worn recliner with a heavy sigh. "Okay, now that we're all comfortable, suppose you explain why you're coming around all these years later to ask me about that phone call?"

"Do you remember making it?" Nick asked, and she scowled at him.

"Of course I do. Just because there's snow on the roof doesn't mean there's not fire in the chimney," she said, pointing at her gray hair. "I called a couple hours after I saw her skulking around that dumpster."

Her, Annalisa thought, seizing on the word. "Which dumpster?"

"The one in the alley next to my building—the place I was living back then."

"In Logan Square."

"That's right. I moved here in 2004 and been here ever since. Back then, I had my daughter and two grandsons living with me. Alisha was working and going to school at night, so I looked after the boys. Kevin, the baby, he was fussy. So I was walking him around near the windows, singing nonsense and bouncing him like you do, and that's when I saw her. She parked her BMW and got out all stealthy-like. She had a hoodie up and she looked around like she was afraid someone was watching." Noreen shrugged. "So I did."

"What did you see?"

"She took a trash bag from her trunk and put it in the dumpster. Then she drove away."

"Did you get the license?" Annalisa asked eagerly.

"I did back then. But when y'all didn't come around asking about it, I figured it wasn't important and I threw it away."

"What about the woman?" Nick wanted to know. "Could you describe her?"

"White lady, on the taller side. Not skinny, not fat. I didn't get a good look at her face and I don't know how old she was. Middle-aged, I guess, but it would be just that, a guess."

Annalisa sank into the couch cushions as she felt this lead also slipping away. Noreen Butler wouldn't be a useful witness at this point. Of course, it was Leo Hammond's fault for not following up at the time, when Noreen's memory was fresh and she'd had the license plate. Hammond had been too consumed with the robbery at the Bass Lounge and Sandra's murder to work Josie Blanchard's case properly. A crooked cop messed up even the straight cases.

"So you saw this woman put the trash bag in the dumpster and drive away," Annalisa said. "And she was suspicious enough that you decided to call the tip line about Josie Blanchard?"

"Well, not right away." She sipped her tea. "I didn't call until I went down to the dumpster and saw for myself what she had put there in the trash."

CHAPTER FORTY-ONE

YOU WENT DOWN TO LOOK IN THE DUMPSTER TO SEE WHAT THE WOMAN PUT THERE?" Annalisa asked.

Noreen nodded and set aside her teacup, exchanging it for a cookie. "My daughter came home when her class got finished, and I told her what I'd seen. We both were curious what this woman could've been stashing in there. I recognized all my neighbors by then, and I know I'd never seen her before. White lady in a BMW? I'd think she'd have her own trash receptacles—no need to come to our alley to ditch her stuff. So, I went down to have a look-see for myself what she left behind. It was a weird mix of stuff. Garden-type gloves, a spool of thin wire, dried-out old paintbrushes, half a can of blue paint, and little blue wooden stool that had one leg missing. I didn't think too much about it until my daughter reminded me that the woman who got strangled a few blocks over was murdered with some sort of wire." She shrugged. "That's when I called."

Noreen Butler had succinctly described all the ingredients to Josie Blanchard's murder. Nick looked at Annalisa, his expression pained, and she knew he felt the agony of the lost evidence. Still, she had to try. "I don't suppose you kept any of what you found in the bag," she said to Mrs. Butler.

"I did for a while. But when the police didn't call me back and I saw on the news they wanted that young car salesman for the poor girl's murder,

I got rid of it. I figured it was just trash." She leaned forward with interest. "You're saying I was right? That woman was up to no good?"

"You did the right thing by calling," Annalisa assured her. "I'm sorry no one followed up."

The woman sighed with regret. "The stool was no good with only two legs. The paintbrushes were all hard and useless. I kept the wire for a while but never found a use for it so I chucked it around the time I moved to this place. The blue paint . . . well, I used the rest of that when I painted the little chairs I picked up to go with my grandkids' art table. I got them from a garage sale and they were kind of a pinkish white, chipped in places but still sturdy. I sanded 'em down and repainted them blue, which my babies liked better anyhow."

"Wait," Annalisa said, extending a hand toward her. "You used the paint?"

"Was I not supposed to?" Her brown eyes turned worried. "I figured it was fine since she threw it away . . ."

"It's fine. It's more than fine. Please, I need to know . . . do you still have those chairs?" She held her breath awaiting the answer.

"Why yes, now that you mention it, I guess I do. I put them in the basement years ago when the boys outgrew them. They're both over six foot tall now, God bless 'em. It's hard to think they were ever small enough to sit at that little table. It's like a miracle."

Nick grinned. Annalisa laughed and wanted to hug the woman. "Mrs. Butler, yes, it is."

....

Two days later, when the lab reports came back on the chairs, Nick allowed Annalisa to tag along as he paid a visit to the Flanders household. They brought a pair of black-and-whites with them but told the units to stay put until they called for them. It was the dinner hour and the grand old Flanders house glowed with warmth, yellow light spilling out from the giant windows. *Think of what I almost lost,* Toby Flanders had said, marveling over his near affair with Josie Blanchard. Annalisa took in the stonework and the carefully tended evergreen landscaping, the kind of stalwart home that had stood for a century and surely would never fall. It was the people inside who bore the cracks.

Nick carried the large paper sack containing their evidence. Annalisa rang the sonorous bell.

Toby Flanders answered. "Look here, this is bordering on harassment," he said when he discovered her on his stoop. "I'm going to have to contact my lawyer."

"I think you should," Annalisa said, pushing past him into the house.

Nick followed her. "Is your wife at home, Mr. Flanders?"

"My wife? Why?"

Tabitha Flanders appeared in the foyer behind him. "Toby, who is it? Oh." She halted when she saw Annalisa and gave a faint frown. "The police again? We're in the middle of dinner."

"It's about the murder of Josie Blanchard."

"I told you I had nothing to do with that," Toby sputtered.

"No, but your wife did. Right, Tabitha?" Annalisa turned her attention to the wife. "Or should we call you Vivian?"

"That's preposterous," Tabitha said. "I never even met that girl."

"Oh, yes you did. When your husband became obsessed with her, you staked out the enemy. You moved into the apartment across the street from her using your mother's name. You even befriended Josie and asked her to come help hang your pictures—with picture wire you later used to strangle her."

Toby moved to his wife's side. "That's impossible."

"You weren't the only one standing on that precipice," Annalisa informed him. "Imagining how things might turn out. Your whole life could have gone a different way if you'd kept on pursuing Josie. Maybe you'd have won her over. Maybe you would've made such a fool of yourself that she had to press charges. Most women don't, you know. They go away quietly, forsaking their degrees or their careers or whatever dreams they had. But Josie wasn't quiet, was she? She had spunk. She had confidence. The same qualities that drew in everyone around her, they meant she wouldn't back down. Well, neither would your wife, and both outcomes seemed bad to her. If you won Josie's heart or if she ruined your career over your harassment, Tabitha lost either way."

"Nonsense," Tabitha said, clinging to her husband's arm. "Toby, make them leave, please. This is so upsetting."

"Yes," Toby agreed, patting her hand. "Unless you have some sort of warrant—"

"We do," Nick replied as he took it out from his breast pocket.

Toby looked it over. "This says you're looking for a black jogging suit with a white stripe down the sleeve. What the hell has this got to do with Josie's murder?"

"I'm getting to that," Annalisa said.

"No, unless you can explain to me what right you have to be here, I'm asking you to leave and not return until I can have my lawyer present." He marched to the door and opened it, allowing the cold to rush inside.

Annalisa and Nick did not move. From his vantage point, Toby glimpsed the squad cars waiting outside, and for the first time, his face turned troubled. "She tried to frame you," Annalisa told him.

He froze. His eyes squeezed shut and he shook his head. "No."

"She knew you had no alibi that night. So, when the cops asked her for a statement, she gave one that implicated you." She looked to Tabitha. "You didn't want to be too obvious, so you told them you'd seen a white van with an eagle on it, trusting they would put the pieces together when they inevitably questioned Toby. But they zeroed in on Moe Bocks instead."

Tabitha's mouth twitched. "I don't know what you're talking about."

"Did you really want him to go away for it?" Annalisa asked. "I'm guessing no, since you ditched the materials to make the murder weapon in a dumpster rather than planting them in your husband's car or office. Maybe you just wanted him to sweat a little, to suffer like he'd made you suffer."

"Enough!" Toby clung to the open door, his face twisted in agony. "No, I don't believe you."

"I don't believe it either," Tabitha said coolly. "You have no proof."

"We have a sworn statement from your old landlord identifying you as the Vivian Catalano who rented the apartment across from Josie Blanchard," Nick told her.

"So? My husband and I were separated. I needed a place of my own. Somewhere private to work things out."

"To plot and murder the woman you thought was breaking up your marriage," Annalisa corrected her. "The police were never clear why, if it was a stranger who killed her, Josie would let him in the door. No forced entry. It didn't make sense. Even Moe, she would probably not have let inside at that point in their relationship. We theorized maybe he'd somehow climbed onto the front balcony and entered through an open window, but you didn't, did you? You just needed to ring the bell. Josie wasn't afraid of you. Maybe she turned her back to get you a drink. She let herself be vulnerable because she didn't see the threat."

"This is a fairy tale, and not a very good one," Tabitha said briskly. "Toby, close the door, for Pete's sake. We're not heating the entire city." Toby moved woodenly to comply with her request but he did not re-join her. She moved to him instead, and he let her take his arm. "Look around all you want," she said to Annalisa. "I have nothing to hide."

Annalisa didn't budge. "I must have made you nervous when I showed up here looking into Josie's murder. It had been quiet all these years. Leo Hammond was certain Moe Bocks had done it."

"So were you," Tabitha reminded her tartly.

"Yes." Annalisa pursed her lips. "I was wrong. But the fact that I was asking questions again was already a bad thing for you. You thought you'd had this buried. Now it might come back to life again. You started following me, trying to figure out where I was going and who I was talking to. That's how you ended up at the Bocks estate the same time as me, and that's why you took the opportunity to kill him. With Moe dead, I'd be satisfied and the whole thing would blow over again."

"I did no such thing."

"You're on the neighbor's camera cutting through the backyard," Nick told her. "You're wearing a black tracksuit with a white stripe on the sleeve. We've also got your BMW on a separate camera two blocks away."

Toby turned away fractionally. "I'm calling that lawyer now."

"You can't prove it," Tabitha insisted, her voice rising. "You can't prove any of it."

Annalisa nodded at Nick, who leaned down to withdraw the child-size chair from the bag they'd brought with them. "We've been trying for years to match the paint on the garrote used to murder Josie Blanchard. You got rid of it, along with the stool, the wire, and everything else.

But someone fished the paint out of the garbage and used it to spruce up her grandchildren's chairs. I'm sure your artist's eye recognizes this particular shade of blue."

Tabitha paled. Toby looked at her as if seeing her for the first time. "There are hundreds of blues. Many of them look similar," she said, her voice brittle. "Ask anyone who's ever tried to do a spare bedroom."

Nick took out his handcuffs. "Science says the human eye can see around a million different colors," he said as he turned her around. "The trouble for you, Mrs. Flanders, is that the mass spectrometer sees a million more. It measures the exact weight of all the different particles in the paint, and it tells us that this one here is a perfect match to the blue on the garrote that strangled Josie."

"Toby! Toby, help me," she said as Nick snapped the cuffs on her wrists. "Call Jason Thorpe. He'll know what to do."

Toby watched in silent horror as Nick read Tabitha her rights and prepared to hand her off to one of the units outside. Annalisa looked at Tabitha's diamond stud earrings, the roped silver around her neck, and the jewels in her rings, imagining them stripped from her the way Josie's necklace had been torn from her throat. "Wait," she said, catching Nick's arm as he tried to pass her. "There's one other thing I think you should check." She told him her theory and he nodded, heading for the stairs.

"You still have no hard proof of anything," Toby said in a hollow voice. "We'll get the best attorneys in the state."

"I think you're going to need them."

A few minutes later, Nick came down with a wooden box in his hands. Toby looked askance. "That's part of Tabitha's jewelry collection. You can't take that."

Silently, Nick opened the lid and pulled out a gold chain with a bejeweled elephant pendant hanging from it, complete with emerald eyes. This was Josie's missing necklace, the one Moe had bought for her. The color drained from Toby's face as he looked at it with horror. "I'm guessing you recognize where this came from," Annalisa said. "Your wife snapped it off of Josie Blanchard the night she strangled her." To Nick, she said, "Bag it."

Toby stepped in front of Annalisa as she moved to go. "I don't understand. If it's true what you say . . . if my wife did these horrible things and tried to frame me for it . . . why would she come back to me?"

"Because," Annalisa told him simply, "she'd won."

He opened his mouth but no sound came out. His giant brain had broken under the weight of the cognitive dissonance. He stood on the threshold of his lavish home that had been tastefully decorated by his artistic wife, every piece selected for style and image and enhancement of an aura that said *I made it.*

Look at everything I might have lost, Toby had said to her. But it had been lost to him a long time ago, maybe even the first time he looked at Josie Blanchard with lust in his eyes.

Only now did he finally see.

CHAPTER FORTY-TWO

Annalisa stood in the precinct bullpen, watching the closed door to Zimmer's office. Nick was in there trying to plead her case. Annalisa remained on the outside, with nowhere to stand that wasn't in the way. She lingered near her desk but not at it. The last time she'd sat there, she'd only busted one cop for murder. Since then, she'd been instrumental in charging four more, although Paul Monk was the lone survivor. She could feel everyone trying not to stare at her. It would be easier if they'd just give in and gape. One of the old guys, Sergeant Givens, bumped her from behind when he tried to squeeze past on his way to the filing cabinets and she jumped a country mile. "Sorry," he muttered.

She smoothed her hair and tried to look natural. "No problem," she said, relieved her voice didn't come out shaky.

Givens didn't immediately move on, just shuffled his feet and looked at the floor. "Hey, listen, I want to tell you good job with the Hammond case. Figuring out all that shit about him and the rest of them—Osborne, Vaughn, and Monk."

"Yeah?"

"Yeah." He hesitated again and looked her right in the eyes. "Between you and me, I might've let the kid finish the job. Monk is lucky it was you working the case."

"I doubt he sees it that way. But thanks." Across the room, Zimmer's door opened and the commander stuck her head out. She signaled to Annalisa. "I've got to go."

"Good luck in there."

Inside the office, Nick's usually moussed-to-perfection hair appeared haggard. His tie was askew. She knew he'd been putting in long hours, trying to put all their active cases to bed before he left for his new post at Area Four. He didn't need to take precious time out to argue for her reinstatement, so she was touched he'd bothered at all. Zimmer's impassive expression gave nothing away as she ordered Annalisa to take the seat next to Nick.

"So." Zimmer folded her hands in front of her. "Thanks to your partner's detailed accounting of all your efforts to bring justice in the Hammond murder and the Josie Blanchard case, I'm now aware of even more instances of blatant insubordination, legal violations, questionable judgments, and dangerous pursuits. I have half a mind to suspend the both of you now."

"Commander," Nick objected, and Zimmer held up a hand.

"I'm not finished." She looked right at Annalisa. "You could have died."

Annalisa waited for Zimmer to continue speaking, so when she left the flat statement hanging there like an accusation, Annalisa shifted in her seat like she could physically ease the weight of it. "Yes, ma'am. I'm aware." Her bruises hadn't faded entirely and staring at a lighted screen for too long still gave her a headache.

"Are you? Because that's the common thread I'm seeing in your actions—a disregard for your own safety. I can't put an officer on the streets who knowingly puts her life at risk."

"Risk comes with the job."

"That doesn't mean you have to seek it out at every opportunity. What are you trying to prove? And who are you trying to prove it to?" When Annalisa didn't answer, Zimmer continued. "Because Carelli here is ready to pin the medal of valor on you. Me? I think you're one of the smartest, toughest cops on the beat. You've convinced us. Who else is there?"

"My father," Annalisa began, but Zimmer stopped her with a quick shake of her head.

"He was a coward," she said in a clipped voice. "He didn't fix anything by shielding your brother all those years. He just put it all on you, which makes him a lousy father as well as a lousy cop. He's the one who dishonored the badge, not you. It's his shame, not yours."

Annalisa's gaze slid to the door and the bullpen beyond. "Not everyone believes that."

"What do you believe?" Zimmer asked as she leaned across the desk. "That's what matters." Annalisa said nothing, and Zimmer relented, relaxing back into her chair. "Look," she said with a sigh, "I need more people like you, Vega. Hell, I'd take a dozen of you tomorrow if I could put in my order. But I can't be worrying every second that you're doing something stupid out there because you've convinced yourself it's you or no one else. Now, you've been through some hard stuff lately, with more stress than most of us encounter our whole careers. It's understandable you might slip up a little here and there. If you're willing to attend counseling sessions, I'd like to welcome you back to the force."

Annalisa had been bracing to be fired. Her head jerked up when she heard Zimmer's offer. "I have to see a shrink?"

"I do," Zimmer replied. "I think it should be mandatory for all of us." She eyed Nick, and he avoided her gaze, taking a sudden interest in his fingernails.

Annalisa had in fact considered seeking help the year before after her encounter with the Lovelorn Killer. There were nights she'd lain awake in her bed and felt like the only person left on earth. But the press had followed her everywhere at that point, even to the dry cleaner's. She could only imagine the headlines if they'd caught her going into a psychiatrist's office. But after what happened with Pops and Alex on top of that, and then the personal and professional fallout that followed, Annalisa strongly suspected an objective outside observer would look at her life and say: quit. They would say she was too cracked up to do the job or that the job was too cracked up for her to survive it. Either way, the badge was all she had at that point. She didn't want it taken away.

She cleared her throat and drummed her fingers on the edge of the chair. "What if . . . what if they say I should stop?"

"Then I think you should listen," Zimmer said gravely.

Annalisa thought about it some more before nodding. "Okay," she said finally. "I'll try."

"Good." Zimmer signed the forms in front of her and then reached into a drawer to retrieve Annalisa's badge and gun. Annalisa extended her hands for them, but Zimmer held them back for a few moments longer. "These are tools and symbols, Vega. They don't define you. You define them."

"Yes, ma'am."

She accepted the gun and the badge and returned them to their usual places on her person while Nick looked on, his expression hard to read. "Dismissed," Zimmer said, her head bent over her work again.

Outside the office, Annalisa gave a grateful look to Nick. "Thank you," she said with feeling as she enveloped him in an impulsive hug.

"Whoa." His arms were more tentative as they closed around her. "Visible signs of affection while on duty. I believe you said this was forbidden."

"You're leaving, remember?" She pulled away with a sniff.

"Yeah, right." He halted as something over her shoulder caught his eye.

"What is it?" She turned to see Brian Hammond slouching awkwardly near her desk, chewing his thumbnail.

"You want me to talk to him?" Nick asked.

"No, I'll handle it. You get coffee or a steak or something . . . you've earned it."

Annalisa crossed the room and Brian startled at the sight of her. "Hey," she said gently as she approached. "It's good to see you. How are you doing?"

He jerked his neck to one side, like he'd tried to nod but couldn't. "I'm okay. I just—I needed to come and ask you. What's going to happen to Caleb?"

Annalisa bit her lip. "Come on," she said. "Let me buy you a Danish." She took him across the street to the coffee shop frequented by all the cops. It was snowing again, just a few flurries, but the contrast of the cold air and the warm, aromatic shop steamed up the big front windows. Annalisa and Brian took a booth to themselves, one on each side, with cups of hot coffee and a selection of pastries on a paper plate between them. Brian didn't touch them but Annalisa devoured a maple pecan sticky bun.

"Caleb killed at least three people," she told him. "He's going to be facing murder charges, probably in the first degree as it pertains to your father."

"But he stopped Tom Osborne from killing Kayla. And Frankie Vaughn would've killed you if Caleb didn't shoot him first. That has to count for something, right?"

Annalisa put her bun down in surprise. "How do you know all this?" He was correct that the cops had located Kayla Hammond and her account supported this version of events, as much of it as she could remember. But none of this information was public yet.

"I went to see him," Brian said, picking at the rim of his paper cup with one thumb.

"In jail?"

"Yeah. We lived together for two years. He's my best friend. That doesn't all go away, right?"

"He knew who you were and sought you out so he could better stalk your family. He killed your father."

"It wasn't like that," Brian insisted. "Not—not always." He attacked the paper cup some more. "You know why he picked that diving suit?"

"Sure. Leave behind no skin, no hair, no fibers. If we matched his DNA to your dad's, we'd figure it out." In fact, that's how it had happened.

Brian shook his head. "It was just part of it. He got the idea when he saw that picture—the one of me, Nicole, and our mom and dad when we all went scuba diving in Hawaii. Caleb, he should've been there too, you know? My dad just left him." He looked at her with haunted eyes. "Is it true, what he says? My dad and the others murdered Caleb's mom and pinned it on someone else?"

"The details aren't clear yet."

"Don't bullshit me!" His voice was raw with emotion and loud enough the other cops around them took notice. Annalisa motioned for them to stand down. Brian wiped his face with one hand. "Sorry," he muttered. "I'm having a hard time with this. I need . . . I need to know the truth."

"I understand." She handed him a paper napkin, which he balled into his fist. "But unless Paul Monk confesses to everything, we may never have the whole truth."

"But Caleb is right. They robbed the club and then killed his mom to keep her quiet about it."

"I think that's right, yes." She chose her next words carefully. "It doesn't mean Caleb was right to do what he did."

Brian slumped in the booth, shaking his head. "My sister wants him to fry for what he did, for killing Dad like that. She says he could've just gone to the press or Internal Affairs or something. She's especially pissed that he didn't come forward when I got arrested."

"It's understandable to be angry about that. Look, Brian, your father and his partners were mixed up in some pretty heavy stuff. They deserved to be held accountable. But not by Caleb and not like that."

"By the system, right?" he said bitterly, turning his face to the foggy window. He used his sleeve to wipe a patch and stared outside toward the precinct. "They were the system."

Annalisa said nothing for a long moment. "What do you think should happen to Caleb?" she asked eventually. "If it were up to you, I mean. What's a fair outcome?"

He sat up, looking surprised at the question. He considered at length. "I guess there's nothing fair for Caleb anymore. Nothing since his mother was left to die in an alley. But I don't care what Nicole or my mother have to say about it—I'm going to support him at the trial. I'm going to keep visiting him, no matter what happens."

"He was your friend," Annalisa agreed softly.

Brian turned his face to the window again, his eyes searching. "He's my brother."

CHAPTER FORTY-THREE

SHE RECOGNIZED ALEX THE MOMENT THE DOOR BUZZED OPEN AND THE GUARD USHERED HIM INSIDE THE VISITING AREA. It would have been easier if she didn't, if he'd resembled some stranger, but his face was as familiar to her as her own. All four Vega kids had inherited Pops's prominent forehead, Roman nose, and lopsided smile; they all got Ma's thick dark hair and tawny skin. Alex's curls were gone, though, his hair cropped close to the bone and his flesh had winnowed away with it. He was pale and down at least twenty pounds since she'd seen him last. But still, she knew him.

"I didn't believe it," he said as he took the seat on the other side of the visitor's table. "I didn't believe it when they said you were here."

"It's been a while."

He stretched his hands out toward her but she kept hers in her lap. She couldn't look at his hands without imagining them around Katie Duffy's neck. "Ma told me you got hurt," he said, sounding concerned. "That you were in the hospital."

"It wasn't that bad. You know how Ma gets about that stuff. I'm fine now."

"Yeah? That's good." He nodded to himself and sniffed hard. "I've been practicing so many times what to say to you, and now that you're here, I don't even know how to say it. Like, what words are going to help anything now? But I am sorry."

"I know," she said hollowly. How could he not be, given where he'd ended up?

"Sassy told me she's been leaning on you to testify for me at sentencing. I want you to know that's her idea. Her and the lawyer. I never asked them to talk to you. In fact, I said to leave you alone. You don't need to worry about it, okay? It's all on me. Whatever they decide to give me, it'll be less than I deserve."

She looked at him then and he nodded to show he meant it.

"I blamed everyone else at first. I blamed Katie. I blamed Pops. I blamed the booze that got me there at her house that night. But it wasn't the booze, Anna. It was me who went there. I just wanted to talk to her, to . . . to convince her to leave Pops alone, but when she started yelling at me, telling me to shut up and get out, something just snapped. I put my hands around her neck to make her stop and suddenly I started squeezing. I just wanted her to stop. I don't know what happened after that. I think I blacked out. But I'm the one who did it and I am so sorry. I'm so ashamed. I want to say this isn't who I am, but it is who I am. I wish I could take it back. If I could trade my life for hers, I'd do it in a heartbeat. You have to know that."

Annalisa looked away. She didn't know anything for sure anymore. If Alex could strangle the life out of someone, it seemed like anyone could. A hot tear escaped her eye and ran down the side of her face. She swiped it away with an angry gesture. "You took so much," she whispered. "You don't even know."

"I'm sorry," he said, pleading with her. "I know I ruined everything. For you, for Sassy and the girls, for Ma and Pops . . ."

"They may lose the house! That was our home."

He winced, drawing back from her. "I know. Like I said, you owe me nothing. Testify for their side at the hearing if you want. I don't blame you."

She shook her head. "You don't get it. Their side is my side. Or it was. Now, thanks to you, I can't sit anywhere and be comfortable. Pops still blames me. He covered up for you and I came along and ruined it all."

"I don't blame you."

She chuffed. "Sure you don't."

"I don't. I did at first, but not now. Not for a long time. You were right to turn me in, Anna. You made the hard call when Pops wouldn't. When I wouldn't. I know what it cost you. I know it hasn't been easy with the family, with work. I know you lost Colin . . ."

"I lost you!" She was crying now because he still didn't see. "You were my closest brother, my friend. We did everything together growing up and then suddenly after what happened with Katie, you were gone. You didn't talk to me. You didn't sit with me. I get why now. I mean, I understand why you couldn't hold my hand at the funeral or comfort me when they shipped my orphaned boyfriend off to live with relatives. I thought it was the alcohol that kept you away but now I know the truth."

"I'm sorry," he repeated, his face anguished.

"Then you got better," she continued like he hadn't spoken. "It was like a miracle. You dried up and became my brother again. We could laugh, watch football, even talk about old times without you having to hit the bottle afterward. You married Sassy and had two great kids. I envied you so much for that." She swallowed hard, bracing herself for the next part. "And then you made me have to wreck it. I don't just miss Colin and being home for Sunday dinners. I miss you, Alex, and I feel like I can't say that to anyone and have them understand. That's your fault, you hear me? Yours. Not mine."

"I know." He grabbed her hands, clutching her. She didn't pull away. "It was me. I'm sorry. I'm so sorry this all fell on you. Tell me how to fix it. Tell me what I can do to make it up to you. Anything."

She looked at him through her tears because this was the hard truth that had kept her away for so long. "You can't." There was no going back. She had to find her way forward without the man she'd considered the love of her life, without the admiration of her colleagues, and without her favorite brother. She squeezed Alex's hands and then released him. He looked at her with wet eyes, awash in quiet devastation. "Tell your lawyer I'll testify if he wants me to," she told him.

His gaze turned searching as he studied her face. "What will you say?"

"The truth. But this time, I'll make sure to tell all of it."

....

Annalisa drove around thinking for a couple of hours before stopping at a corner store to buy a six-pack of Pabst, which had been her and Nick's choice back when they were scraping and saving for a future that never came. They'd blown the money on a divorce lawyer instead. Standing in the checkout, she spotted a bucket of flowers that included a dozen yellow roses, just barely past peak. She plucked them out on impulse, the stems dripping on the dirty tile floor at her feet. They'd had yellow roses at the wedding too. Her choice. She'd chosen everything and Nick went along with her decisions, including the one to get married in the first place.

She drove to Nick's building and parked outside. The lights were on in his unit, indicating he was home. She looked at the beer and the flowers on the seat next to her and thought about how many different ways the conversation could go. She wasn't entirely sure which outcome she favored. But, like she'd said to Alex, she wanted to tell the whole truth this time. With a deep, fortifying breath, she grabbed her presents and mounted the steps to the door. "It's me," she said when he answered the buzzer. The door unclicked and he met her at the threshold to his apartment with a welcoming smile.

"You have good timing. I was just making dinner."

"Hope it pairs with Pabst," she said, holding out the beer.

"Is there anything that doesn't? Come on in."

She entered and smelled sautéing onions and garlic from the kitchen. "Smells great," she said. "Like Ma's kitchen."

"Ha, I wish." Nick turned the heat down under the pan and returned to take her coat. He stopped when he saw the roses. "What's with the flowers?"

"Oh." She looked down at them. "Well, I figured since you'd been sending me flowers, I should return the favor." She met his eyes and dared him to deny it.

"Jeez, it took you long enough," he said. He reached over and took the roses from her.

"I was slow," she agreed. "The evidence was right there in front of me too. They always seemed to show up when you were around. But I told myself you'd denied it. Only when I replayed those conversations in my head, I realized you never actually said no, it wasn't you. In fact, you said the opposite and I just didn't believe you. You answered my questions with questions or you changed the subject. Classic avoidance. *No* is just two little letters—easy to say when you don't have to lie about it."

"I promised never to lie to you again," he said as he moved to put the flowers in water.

"Yeah, but you didn't exactly tell me the truth." She shed her coat and laid it across the back of the sofa.

"I would have." He hesitated with a vase in his hands. "But you wanted them to be from him."

The blank look on Colin's face when he'd seen the flowers at her house had been her first clue. "He came to see me the other day," she admitted as she took a seat on a stool at the kitchen peninsula.

"Oh yeah?" Nick fluffed out the flowers, not looking at her.

"He's going to testify for Alex." She paused. "So am I."

Nick did look to her then, and his brown eyes were kind. "You're more than he deserves."

"Maybe. Maybe not. But I'm the only sister he's got." She sneaked an olive out of the container near his elbow.

"Well?" Nick turned the vase to her, showing off his handiwork. "How do they look? As fresh and springy as our wedding day?"

Her jaw fell open. "I didn't think you even remembered."

"I remember more than you think," he said in a low voice, reaching for her hand. She let him take it. "For example, I remember there was that dog who crashed the reception in the backyard."

She giggled. "Mrs. Danforth's cocker spaniel, Daisy. I think she ate half the mini quiches off the table before anyone noticed her. Ma chased her off with a broom. Maybe that should have been a sign."

"Of what?"

"What do you mean 'of what'? That we had no business getting married. We barely knew each other."

"We know each other now." He let her hand go and she missed the warmth immediately. He returned to stirring the contents of the pan. "I'm still fuzzy on some details, though. How do you feel about capers?"

"Capers are good," she said, taking another olive. "Can I help?"

"No, you just relax. After all the major busts you got me, I think I owe you one."

"Well, then maybe you can help me in return."

He turned with a frown, concerned again. "What is it? What's wrong?"

"I have a problem at work. My boss was kind enough to give me my job back, but I don't have a partner." It was a big ask—huge, even—suggesting he might want to pass up a transfer and a shot at promotion. Her cheeks turned hot at her audacity.

"I see." Nick drew closer to her. "What happened to the old one?"

She gave a studied shrug, avoiding his gaze. "Long gone. I can't blame him. I'm not the easiest person to work with."

"Well, I don't know about that. You do have some good qualities. You're smart, driven, honest, loyal—"

"You make me sound like a golden retriever," she said, making a face. "Plus, you forgot stubborn, opinionated, impulsive, and prone to running off on my own."

He grinned. "Now you do sound like a dog."

She swallowed. Of all the truths she had to tell, this was the hardest one. "You were wrong, you know. I do need you." Her voice barely rose above a whisper. "I just don't know how to say it."

Nick's smile stretched to fill his whole face. "I think," he said, "you finally did."

ACKNOWLEDGMENTS

Seven books in, I am more grateful than ever for the team that brings the story to life. I am indebted as always to the great folks at St. Martin's Minotaur, especially my discerning editor, Daniela Rapp, who saves me from myself. This book is stronger for her input. Cassidy Graham is nimble and helpful and somehow creates order from chaos. If you heard of this book and found it somewhere, that's probably due to the hard work of Kayla Janas, Mac Nicholas, and Danielle Prielipp. They are creative and amazing!

Thanks also to my terrific agent, Jill Marsal, for her invaluable counsel and support.

My deepest gratitude to #TeamBump, for your feedback and encouragement. You help keep me sane in what is sometimes a crazy business. Thank you, Katie Bradley, Stacie Brooks, Rayshell Reddick Daniels, Jason Grenier, Shannon Howl, Suzanne Magnuson, Robbie McGraw, Michelle Kiefer, Rebecca LeBlanc, Jill Svihovec, Dawn Volkart, Amanda Wilde, and Paula Woolman.

In what was a tougher-than-average year, I am especially grateful for my two humans in residence: my husband, Garrett, and our daughter, Eleanor. We've been together 24/7 and still like each other. Love you both to the moon and stars and back.